Freeman Wills

W.G. Wills

Dramatist and painter

Freeman Wills

W.G. Wills
Dramatist and painter

ISBN/EAN: 9783337304362

Printed in Europe, USA, Canada, Australia, Japan

Cover: Foto ©Raphael Reischuk / pixelio.de

More available books at **www.hansebooks.com**

W. G. WILLS

DRAMATIST AND PAINTER

BY

FREEMAN WILLS

LONGMANS, GREEN, AND CO.
39 PATERNOSTER ROW, LONDON
NEW YORK AND BOMBAY
1898

CONTENTS

i

W. G. WILLS,

DRAMATIST AND PAINTER.

CHAPTER I

A NINETEENTH CENTURY OLIVER GOLDSMITH

THE poetry of the stage-play is as far from the
highest poetry as the drama of the poet from
the requirements of the stage. But, measured
with those who have devoted poetical gifts to
practical stage-work, the author of ' Olivia ' and
' Charles I.' may fairly be considered the poetic
dramatist of the Victorian era. Even in the height
of his fame, however, W. G. Wills was personally
so little known, and was so free from self-advertise-
ment, that his biographer is under a disadvantage,
for his subject is but a name. He had many
claims to rank high among his literary contempo-
raries. He restored poetry to the stage at a time
when the poetic drama was supposed to be dead.
He successfully took up the thread of history plays
when managers were saying that Shakespeare
spelled ruin. His dramas were literature to the
cultured, while they were human nature to the
crowd, thus acquiring among all classes a wide-
spread popularity. Some of them, like the two I

B

have mentioned, have taken their place as classics, and his name as a dramatic writer is interwoven with those of the best actors and actresses of his day. But with all his claims the man himself, so whimsical, so warm-hearted, so generous and unworldly, remained unknown save to his intimate friends. In a monotonous day, when all men are fashioned alike, he was unlike everyone. He had the eccentricity of genius without its affectations. An inward industry of thought made the man appear indolent, and his versatility seem desultory. The work which he did was often careless, but for this very reason the flashes of graceful fancy and genius which illumined it came upon one as surprises. He was abstracted and inconsequent, and while as a result he appeared sometimes to be wanting in tact, he had the tenderest and most indulgent regard for the feelings and foibles of others, not without a quiet eye for the study of their character, and a strange insight into its subtilties.

The great Bohemian of his day, indeed the only survival of his kind among prominent men of letters, he met the highest or the lowest on a footing of good-natured equality. A quiet dignity checked the tendency to familiarity on the part of any, of whatever degree, who might presume on his simplicity of manner and total absence of affectation, but he often lived surrounded by friends few men would have cared to have, and treated them with all the consideration which others would have bestowed on their most desirable acquaintances. He would not have hurt the feel-

ings of the man he caught with his hand in his
pocket ; and while for many years of his life he was
making large sums of money, he was so surrounded
by parasites and harpies that he was always poor,
and sometimes penniless. The best description
given of him was, that he was an ' Oliver Goldsmith
born a century too late.'

Perhaps the kinship of genius and nature to the
author of ' The Vicar of Wakefield ' was the secret
of the extraordinary success with which he evolved
from the story a play which Goldsmith himself
might have written.

How there came to be a man with gifts so
varied and unusual in combination, who could
write plays that touched the heart like ' Olivia '
and ' Charles I.,' and at the same time paint such
graceful portraits of the Court beauties of his day
that the Queen summoned him to Osborne ; who
could be indifferent to the social distinction of his
fame and live in almost squalid surroundings,
a strange mixture of the most pronounced
Bohemianism and refinement of art and literary
taste, may be understood by those who will follow
me in dipping into his early life and its mixed
surroundings.

It almost goes without saying that he was an
Irishman. His father, James Wills, belonged to a
wealthy county family, settled for three hundred
years in Ireland, a scion of which was the General
Wills who, with General Carpenter, defeated the
Pretender. James Wills's mother belonged to a
very old family in the West of Ireland, of which
Lord Oranmore and Browne represents the elder

branch. He and his brother entered Trinity College, Dublin, as fellow commoners, about the year 1810. They were left jointly, as children of a second marriage, an estate called Annalea, and were as idle as well-to-do young men in those early times usually were. James Wills gained the Oratory Medal of the College Historical Society, his competitor being Charles Wolfe, author of the famous lines on the burial of Sir John Moore. After graduating, he went to the Temple to eat his dinners for the Bar. His law studies, however, were interrupted by a misfortune befalling his brother Thomas who, in ignorance of the nature of a document he was signing, made himself liable for another man's debts. Rather than submit to a fraud, Thomas Wills refused to pay, and went to prison, but when it was evident that his mind was becoming affected, the young law student persuaded him to yield, and with disastrous consequences to himself later on, took the steps necessary to enable his brother to raise money on their joint property. After this he did not return to England, but lived a desultory life between Bray and Dublin, amusing himself by contributing verses to the periodicals, and he became known in Irish literary society as 'Wills the poet.'

After remaining a bachelor up to the age of thirty, he fell in love with and married a granddaughter of Mrs. Bushe of Kilmurry, mother of a Chief Justice, and sister of one of Ireland's most gallant soldiers, General Sir John Doyle, who raised the 87th Regiment, and at Aboukir gave it its famous motto, 'Faugh a ballagh,' signifying

' Clear the way.' It may be of interest to state that another of Sir John's nieces married Sir Edward Bulwer Lytton, and was the mother of the late Lord Lytton.

Mr. Wills's marriage brought him into association with the most brilliant society in Ireland ; and it was with his mother's relatives, the Bushes and Plunkets, that my brother spent the formative years of his life, and he was indebted for much of his success to the literary and scholarly habits of life and thought which they inherited from Chief Justice Bushe. In most cases talent seems to die with its possessor, or lies fallow in succeeding generations, but it was not so in this instance, for he handed down to his family many of the peculiar qualities of his own mind. Charles Kendal Bushe was the son of a Kilkenny gentleman who ran through his estates and was obliged at last to sell the family residence, Kilmurry. He entered the University of Dublin at thirteen, gained a scholarship, and after a distinguished career worked his way to the Bar. His reputation as a speaker preceded him from the famous Historical Society, the cradle of Irish oratory. He soon rose to eminence, and was elected a member of the Irish Parliament. He was one of the little band of incorruptible patriots who to the last night and the last vote fought against the Union. Ireland never had a more polished orator, and his eloquence was entirely free from the exuberance and exaggeration which are deemed the faults of Irish oratory. His power of narrative was unmatched at the Bar, and when the fire lighted behind his grey-blue eyes, he wielded a forcible and classic invective which few cared to encounter. In private life he was one of the gentlest, most genial and just of men. When he became Solicitor-General he bought back the family place, and there was a picture at Kilmurry which he prized for its particular bearing on that circumstance—it was the return of his sword to one who had honourably won back his fortune and position in the State.

W. G. Wills's mother was present when, on his appointment to the Chief Justiceship, he came from taking his seat on the Bench to Ely Place, and knelt in his robes to receive his mother's blessing.

That he should take holy orders had been made the condition of Mr. Wills's entering the estate of holy matrimony, and it was intended that the Chief Justice should get a living for him; but, immediately after his ordination, a Government came into power from which it was impossible to ask this favour.

For some years the young couple lived in Dublin, but in 1827 they moved to Blackwell Lodge, to be near Kilmurry and Kilfane—the latter the residence of Sir John Power. Here Mr. Wills spent his time in writing for 'Blackwood' and other periodicals, and by way of light recreation devoted himself to metaphysics and the higher mathematics. The country round was then much disturbed by the Whiteboys, but he made himself respected by a combination of courage and justice in the management, which he had undertaken, of his landlord's property. No man could have been more unsuited to agricultural pursuits, but his diary is full of entries as to the

sale of cows and pigs, mingled with suggestions
for poems and magazine articles, grave moral reflec-
tions, and records of his mathematical studies. The
constant intercourse with Kilmurry and Kilfane
had a stimulating intellectual influence, and there
are notes as to the Chief Justice having pulled him
up in his classical quotations which show there was
a grindstone on which to whet his wits. Nowhere
in Ireland in those days was there a more brilliant
society than in the neighbourhood of Kilmurry.
Floods, Langrishes, Saurins, Bushes, and Powers
made it the Attica of Ireland. It was a backwater
in which the eighteenth century with all its sparkle
seemed to have lingered. The two latter families,
the Bushes and Powers, between whose houses a
broad gravel walk led from door to door, lived in such
close intercourse that they were almost like one
Henry Grattan was a frequent visitor at Kilfane, the
mistress of which united the blood of the Grattans
and Bushes; and many notable people were to
be met with under that hospitable roof. It was in
this happiest time of his life, when his means were
yet competent and his social surroundings the
cultured society I have described, that his third
child (his elder children, Elizabeth and Thomas,
were born in Dublin) arrived on the scene, and
there occurs in his diary the very earliest notice
of the future dramatist, recording his birth on
January 28, 1828.

The following year an unforeseen change occurred in the circumstances of the family. Like
the Vicar of Wakefield, from having lived in
comparative affluence Mr. Wills was suddenly left

without means, his fortune being run away with, not by a knave, but by a madman. His brother, who ought to have been kept under restraint, sold the joint estate of Annalea for a large sum—it was said thirty thousand pounds—and sailed for America. This event for years afterwards, so long as there was the dimmest hope of his being heard of again, was naturally uppermost in the minds of the family, and W. G. Wills, from the main incident in his home life, and seeing the manly spirit in which it was borne, was able feelingly to realise the situation when he put those touching words into Dr. Primrose's lips, breaking to his family the sudden stroke of fortune which had left them penniless :—

'And now my good wife, my beloved children —Olivia, come thou nearest—I've news to tell you which cannot be long secret. I've always thought that the holy hour of night, just before even-prayer, was the best time to tell and hear sorrow. Now that the happy day is over, I must tell you of a great misfortune, and let there be no murmuring, no complaints, I entreat. We have long enjoyed independence, and I hoped to leave my children provided for at my death. But Heaven has decreed that I must end my days honest but poor, and like the ravens my children must depend upon the goodness of the Great Father of all. I've learned this evening that the merchant with whom I lodged all my money has stolen it and fled. I am a ruined man and cannot even call yon roof-tree my home. God gave and God has taken away. Let us submit ourselves.'

CHAPTER II

STIRVILLE

THE earliest days of the dramatist were spent in a literary atmosphere. Nothing was ever heard of our Uncle Thomas and the thirty thousand pounds, but the discovery of some of his effects in the shops of dealers in Liverpool led to the belief that he was murdered by his valet. Mr. Wills, who moved with his wife and family to Dublin, was therefore thrown entirely upon the resources of a fertile pen, which produced with equal facility reviews, stories, poems, and dramatic compositions.

On the understanding that everything he contributed should be accepted, he became a regular writer for the 'Dublin University Magazine,' and for a short time took Mr. Isaac Butt's place as its editor. He also contributed to 'Blackwood's Magazine,' the 'Edinburgh Literary Gazette,' and various other periodicals.

Among his greatest friends were Sir Samuel Ferguson, one of the most delightful and racy of Irish writers, and Dr. Anster, the translator of 'Faust'; and the boy, destined to be the successful dramatiser of Goethe's poem, was the playmate of its famous translator's children, and almost an inmate of his house in Dublin, and his mind was early peopled with the characters of the legend.

In the Irish capital there was then a large and brilliant literary society, for the grace of the days when Dublin was a national centre had not yet departed. London was a long way off in the age of sailing vessels and stage coaches, and the Channel passage was one of the strongest arguments for the repeal of the Union. It was a physical obstacle to the depletion of the Irish capital, which accordingly continued to have its own sparkling society and social distinction.

The bed-rock of childhood has no little to do with the turn of our minds in after-life, and Willie Wills before he went to school at Lucan under Dr. Dee, as he did at the age of twelve, had not only lived among the cleverest and wittiest of Irish *littérateurs*, but had enjoyed the advantage of being a great deal in the society of his mother's family. One of the Chief Justice's daughters had married a son, who afterwards succeeded to the title, of the great Chancellor, Lord Plunket, and there was a warm boyish friendship between Willie Wills and his young cousin, the future Archbishop of Dublin. Another of the Chief Justice's daughters was married to Judge Fox, and their clever son, Loftus Bushe Fox, was also his intimate friend from boyhood.

At school he got a good grounding in the classics, and evinced great natural talent for drawing. He also took kindly to music, and showed a taste for it which broke out in a desultory way as he grew up, in fiddlings and flutings. Like many other things, he took up musical instruments as if only to satisfy the desire to overcome the preliminary difficulties, for he hardly ever pursued anything with a view to a practical end. When he was about fourteen his father's pen began to have a difficulty in keeping pace with the growing expenses of his family, and his sensitive pride made him a man whom it was difficult for friends to assist. His half-brother, Mr. William Wills, who had inherited the estates in Roscommon, having married a co-heiress of Lord Mount Sandford, moved to Castlerea House, and offered him the use of Willsgrove, a large house built by his grandfather. It was, however, disproportioned to the means of a struggling man of letters, and he did not accept the offer; but he had some sentimental regrets afterwards, when it was converted at the time of the Irish famine into a temporary workhouse. It suited Mr. Wills's position better to take a curacy, which was a sole charge and a complete sinecure, in a remote corner of the county of Kilkenny. The seclusion of this place was adapted to a literary work of some importance which he had undertaken for a firm of Scotch publishers, they supplying the books of reference. My brother was taken from his school at Lucan, and the family moved down a hundred miles south to the parish of Polroan, of which the glebe was called Suirville. The house where the boy lived a lonely youth was a tall haunted-looking building which rocked to the storms that raced down the long reaches of the river Suir. The river was wide; small ships passed our house and a collier was once wrecked in front of our windows. The equinox was dreaded at Suirville, for the house was old and in an exposed position. But when the river was at rest, with the fishermen's ' cots,' two and two, drifting down the tide and drawing their salmon nets between them, while the wooded hills of Curraghmore, the Marquis of Waterford's place, lay on the other side, backed by the blue Comeraghs, the view was worth fighting for with the giants of the equinox. Adjoining the glebe was the old churchyard, and the parish church was a roofless, ivy-covered ruin. It was so old that probably the last service performed in it was the mass of the Roman Catholic Church. An elder-tree that must have watched over the dead of many generations grew in the middle of the chancel.

The peasantry living around us were a most lovable race. As for the boys, I will not say the serpent had not found his way even there, for I am afraid he had; but taking them all in all, there could be no simpler or kinder peasants, and their priests were as kind-hearted and lovable as themselves. Willie Wills, a sturdy, well-set lad, was now sent with his elder brother Tom, who had hitherto been educated at home, to Waterford Grammar School of which the Rev. Dr. Price was headmaster. The only tradition of his schooldays was a fight with Mulcahy senior, in which he behaved creditably and got a black eye.

His first poetic attempt dates from his schooldays. It was a little poem addressed to a star, and sung to a simple tune which was probably also his own composition, for while the first part was high and cheerful, the second was on a lower and minor key, and very despondent. The lad must have been

about nineteen when he and his brother Tom
entered the University of Dublin together. In the
meantime three younger children, preceding the
last and seventh, had died, thus reducing the
family to four. After his entrance to the university, he began to show a strong turn for painting
and an unconquerable objection to reading for his
examinations. The unsettled and Bohemian pro-
pensities of his paternal grandmother's family were
stirring in the veins of the youth. One of his
grand-uncles was a captain in the Irish Brigade,
another held a like rank in the German Legion,
while in the preceding generation, Field-Marshal
Count Valentine Browne, served in the Austrian
service, and was killed at the battle of Prague.
The boy would have been a soldier of fortune himself if he had lived in the preceding century.
He was already beginning to be a wanderer,
and would walk long distances, with his box of
paints slung over his shoulder, to the houses of
friends, where his paints and brushes were his
passport, and in a very crude style of art he practised on his entertainers by painting their portraits.
More ambitious compositions he also attempted,
preparing his own canvases and grinding his own
colours. They were uniformly morbid in character.
Among the subjects were 'One more Unfortunate,'
'The Sands o' Dee,' and one suggested by the
sudden death of a Kilkenny lady, remarkable for
her charms, as she was dressing for a ball. These
scarcely cheerful subjects expressed the tendency
of his mind. Even his 'Ophelia,' with all its
beauty and painted with the degree of skill he

acquired later on, was a morbid subject, for not
many would care to have a mad woman staring at
them from their walls. However, this is going a
long way ahead. For the present his art was in
the crudest stage, and it was severely discoun-
tenanced at home. It was a struggle few parents
so circumstanced would have faced, to put all
their sons through the University, and they were
naturally disappointed that the cleverest of them
was not making more of the chances they gave him
with so much difficulty. He scrambled somehow
through his examinations, but read for them very
little, and once was 'cautioned.' His mind was
taken up with these outbreaks of colour and stirrings
of the poetic spirit. On his lonely walking expe-
ditions he had a way of composing verses in his
memory, without committing them to paper, and
his poetry, like his pictures, was of a morbid
character; generally some foreboding or description of the sensations of death, which had always
a painful fascination for his mind.

His only college success was the Vice-Chancellor's prize for English verse. The prize was 20*l.*,
which set him up in brushes and colours. The
subject was ' Poland,' and it was the kind of poem
to gladden the heart of a Don. While, however,
on the subject of early poetry, it is only fair to say
that he was not poetic or morbid from ill-health.
On the contrary, he was a respectable athlete, and
his running jump, which he practised with the
active young peasants about, was over twenty feet.
This may appear incredible to those who knew him
later, in his sedentary days, but it is nevertheless

a fact. He was an excellent swimmer also, and I
remember seeing him at Suirville, after he had
been across the river and back with a strong tide
running, go out again to rescue a lad who was
being carried away by the current, and bring him
safely to shore. The action was not unattended
with risk, for the lad was struggling desperately.

Our home life was very much self-contained.
Willie Wills was the best of brothers, but he could
tell delightfully horrible stories which froze the
blood of his little listener and were generally told in
the uncanny moonlight. He would try boisterously
to laugh away the impression, but that was not so
easy. But his boisterous laugh at the end of his
horrible tales was characteristic of the mingling of
buoyant good humour with the gloomy and morbid
elements of his nature. Though solitary as a youth,
he was also sociable and good-humoured, and sometimes a trifle combative. In the twilight at home,
a very pleasant time was that round the tea-table,
when Mr. Wills would discourse by the hour, and
the two collegians would daringly engage him in
arguments in which Mrs. Wills used to step in as
a moderator, for she disliked the strife of tongues.

The household rule, which I think conduced
very much to my brother's freedom from ill-nature,
was that persons should never be made a subject
of discussion. Indeed, we had not many neighbours to discuss, even if personalities had not
been forbidden, for Suirville was completely iso-
lated from the rest of the world, and a visitor
was the greatest rarity. But the evenings were by
no means dull, for besides the intellectual excite-

ment of such discussions, they were spent in
family readings, and Willie Wills was sometimes,
very unwillingly, pressed into the service as reader.
All Scott's novels were thus read out, and our
mother used to translate such French works as
'Sully's Memoirs'—which were an inexhaustible
delight—Molière's plays, 'Gil Blas,' and other
books from which she left out the passages we
should have liked to hear. No pains were ex-
pended upon housekeeping, cut off as we were
from the civilised world, and my brother learned at
Suirville the perfect carelessness about the conven-
tionalities of life which made him always averse to
their trammels. Desultory, unsettled habits, and
art and literary aspirations, although alike congenial to such a household, were not traits which
were welcomed by his parents. They had hoped
the talents he evidently possessed might lead to a
successful career in one of the three learned professions; but all efforts to direct them into such
channels, were vain and fruitless. I can recall the
Rev. James Wills in a grey shooting jacket—for he
dressed clerically only on Sundays—delivering a
tirade against portrait-painting as a pursuit unfit
for a gentleman. His family pride was excessive,
but my brother always stoutly stood up for the
nobility of art in all its branches. It was not necessary then to press the question of his future career
to a decision, but while his parents destined him
for the Bar, he destined himself for art and literature. Painting, drawing, flute-playing, writing
poetry, were his only occupations, apart from the
study of the masterpieces of the last century, in

which he delved and sunk himself, allowing his college studies to lie neglected to the last moment before the examination.

His father could hardly complain of his son's following so closely in his own footsteps, for the desultoriness of disposition was hereditary. In a passage in the Blackwell diary of which I have spoken, he accuses himself of the same want of application, although the stress of necessity forced him later on, as it did his son, to devote himself to persevering work. The preaching of a plodding professional career was therefore contradicted by his own life devoted to poetry, painting, science, dramatic writing, metaphysics, criticism and miscellaneous literature. The stories he told of his early life tended to unsettle his children. He used to absorb us in accounts of literary society in London, meetings at a famous publisher's, breakfasts with Rogers, adventures when reading in the Temple. Sometimes he would give divinity a turn, and write essays which took even learned professors out of their depth. This versatility descended to his son, and had a good deal to do with unfitting him for the staid routine of a profession.

Free then from the prosaic aspirations which a more commonplace round of home life might have bred for the Bar or Bench, Willie Wills made for himself in his long rambles a lonely world of his own; in short, he was a dreamer. He would climb to the top of Tory Hill, or clamber up the square keep of Grannagh Castle, and seat himself in one of the empty sockets of those half-ruined windows that look out upon the Suir. Often, too, in an old

C

churchyard he would sit and dream among the tombstones; but, with a Hamlet-like melancholy, he shared also with the Danish prince a turn for whimsical freaks, of which the following may be given as examples.

Our only neighbour was a worthy clergyman who lived a mile higher up the river at Clonmore. One evening, at the hour of dinner, my brother, dressed up as an old beggar-woman, seated himself on the doorstep. A plate of fish and potatoes was sent out to the old crone, who seemed bent double with age and rheumatism ; but an observant eye was kept on the plate. Having finished the repast, the beggar-woman was seen hobbling off with it, and the clergyman, who was long and thin, promptly gave chase. The ungrateful mendicant, however, developed an unexpected speed, and led her pursuer a long chase through the fields, clearing hedges and ditches, till at last the bareheaded clergyman had to give up, in disgust, all hopes of recovering his china, and to the end never knew it was Willie Wills who, disguised, had slipped away undetected to the shelter of Suirville.

A similar freak was nearly attended by unpleasant consequences. He alarmed some prim ladies, whose frigidness he wished to disconcert, by appearing on the road and impersonating a madwoman. Two constables who were on patrol duty were sent in pursuit, but he escaped by wading and swimming the stream. On another occasion, in Dublin, he induced two college friends to go out with him as ballad singers, and the trio returned home loaded with coppers. Even when he was much older,

similar aberrations from his usually grave temperament appeared in a modified form.   His school-
boyish freaks were amusing as illustrations of his
simple inconsequent character even when without
much wit in themselves.   He would take up
whimsical ideas, such as to sail out in a boat on
the sea in a pitch dark night, or row to the Goodwins to bring back a bottle of the golden sands, in
which great ships with their cargoes lie engulphed,
as he would describe with all his command of
imagery.   Combined with all this, he was morbid
and abstracted; and sometimes as he lay awake
at night his thoughts troubled him and he would
jump out of bed in a state of nervous excitement. At
this time, too, he received religious impressions.
We had little intercourse with the other side of the
river, and for ladies the want of any boats except
the little fishing cots made it only possible to cross
when some larger boat could be borrowed from a
vessel anchored in the stream.   A state visit was
then sometimes paid by Mrs. Wills to Curraghmore;
but Willie Wills was often at Portlaw with Dr.
Martin, who was medical attendant to the Water-
fords.   The doctor lent him good books which
turned his mind to religion.   His friend and
cousin, the late Archbishop of Dublin, whose grave
and beautiful character influenced every one
brought into contact with him, may have helped
in producing those impressions, for the time at all
events.   He was fond of repeating some lines of
the archbishop's in those days, and I do not know
if they have ever appeared in print :—

                                    c 2

'Tis sad when life is o'er
  To hope for no to-morrow--
To fall asleep to wake no more—
  Alas, those words of sorrow !
To wake no more !

But who hath power to save
  Our soul from that dark prison ?
What conqueror hath burst the grave ?
  Hath ever sleeper risen
To sleep no more ?

Yes, trembler, cease to weep !
  Thou shalt not be forsaken :
Jesus has slept as thou must sleep
  He woke as thou shalt waken,
To sleep no more.

CHAPTER III

ENVIRONMENT

A CHANGE in his father's fortunes brought the young artist and dramatist into a neighbourhood which afforded more social intercourse and greater opportunities of development.

Dr. O'Brien, Bishop of Ossory, an old college friend of my father, promoted him, on the death of the old vicar, to the sinecure living of Polroan, and this proved a step to further promotion which followed shortly after. Polroan was not indeed a rich living, but the farmers and peasantry about us overflowed with kindness. Many were the presents of oaten cakes, butter and eggs, sent from time to time to the vicarage. Although without exception Roman Catholics, they could not have been more free with their offerings to their own parish priest. If not spiritually, Mr. and Mrs. Wills were able to be of much service to their parishioners, one in legal matters and the other with medicine and advice; and gratitude was a great virtue among those poor people. When the glebe-land became ours it was thought advisable to turn it into tillage, and this was done by the farmers and labourers, who came with horses and ploughs and worked without payment. They had a dinner outside on the lawn when the work was done, at which many of the labourers tasted meat for the first time in their lives. The harvest was reaped in the same way and the hay cut down and saved. We never paid for a horse or cart. They were always supplied freely. If we wanted to drive to Waterford, a shopkeeper in Moncoin lent his horse and outside car, and we had only to say we wanted them. When the vicar of Polroan was promoted to the rectory of Kilmacow and the time came for moving, the people brought a long string of carts and packed up, and carried away all the furniture and belongings of the family, a distance of nine miles, to the new glebe-house.

Intercourse, the friendliest though free from familiarity, with the primitive warmhearted people of that back-country place, had an influence which might be traced both in my brother's character, and in his strong sympathies, as shown in his novels, with the peasantry of Ireland.

Our new home was very different in its surroundings. A brother of the Earl of Mayo had held the living for forty years, and everything about the glebe, that is when we went there first, was in spick and span order. There was a delightful garden, evidently belonging to an older rectory house; for the yew trees were of a great age, and there was an ironbound arbutus tree which was rooted, it was said, in the time of the Plantagenets. One recognises in a poem called 'Pride,' the impression this garden, with its wealth of old-fashioned flowers, left on my brother's mind. In addition to the advantages of pasture land and garden, and a well-appointed farmyard, there was

a little colony of neighbours, many of whom became fast friends—the Flemings of Greenville, the
Rennies of Dunkitt, and the Elliots of Rathkurby;
and the village furnished the church with a tiny
congregation at the one service held on Sundays
(when it was fine). Willie Wills attended church
and, listening impartially to his father's discourses,
found our large square pew a comfortable place for
his own meditations.

There was, about a mile away, a Quaker
family (not a part of the congregation or of 'the
neighbourhood') named Humphreys, the great
millers of the place. We grew very fond of their
puritan manners and simple goodness, and they
were more cultured than many country gentry,
though pretending to no social standing. The
river formed at Upper Kilmacow where they lived
a small lake to turn their great mill-wheel; and
their pretty house, called Hermitage, among its
perfumed gardens, stood on the slope above.
Henry Humphreys and Willie Wills became in-
separable companions. The young miller had a
sanctum in the mill, and the subdued hum of the
house of wheels made a drowsy accompaniment
to the poetry he loved to chant. He knew by
heart most of the modern poets, and would drone
them for hours if he could only find listeners. He
afterwards left the Society of Friends and migrated
to London, where he got on the staff of the 'Morning Post' and ultimately became its foreign editor.
At this time there was a literary society in Waterford
chiefly consisting of members of the Quaker colony;
and Humphreys induced his friend to read papers

before this learned body, and take part in its
' philosophical discussions.' Some of the subjects
were ' Ghosts,' ' Mesmerism,' ' Spiritualism '—they
were generally of that sensational kind—and my
brother acquired some practice in speaking, and
made the hair of the literary society bristle by
his ghost stories, invented on the spot and well
authenticated by their narrator. The power which
he then acquired of speaking in public deserted
him when he became immersed in literary life.
On one occasion, when he was called upon to
respond to the toast of the Drama at a Mansion
House banquet, he felt so much out of his element
that he could never again be drawn into making
a speech. However, the literary society had a
stimulating effect on his intellect in those days.
' Do the roses still bloom by the calm Bendemeer? '
Does its literary society still lend sweetness and
light to the *Urbs intacta* by the silver Suir?

Except so far as he was drawn out of himself
by our friends the Humphreys, my brother led an
absent-minded life and did not join in our country
recreations. He was inwardly absorbed and nearly
as abstracted as Mr. J. M. Barrie's Professor
Goodwillie. In this he took after his father, of
whose abstraction I remember many amusing
instances. To mention one, it was his habit, watch
in hand, to act as time-keeper while an egg was
being boiled for Mrs. Wills. He stood by the fire
one morning, watching mechanically, until habit
told him the time was about up. Then first he
became aware that the hands had disappeared from
the white dial, then that it had grown oval, then

that it was an egg, then that his gold watch was at full boil in the saucepan. So like were father and son in this respect, that my brother has been known to go out into the street with a lighted candle in his hand as if he were about to do a public penance. When you spoke to him sometimes, if he were deep in thought, he would raise his eyebrows and survey you with a puzzled expression, as if his body were waiting for his spirit to come back from a great distance ; and when you recalled him from the depths of his abstraction he looked at you with a slight cast in his eyes, which he had not at other times, as if one eye had been recalled to earth while the other was still keeping in view a distant object of contemplation. He completed his University career but never took his degree. In later years, when he became famous as a dramatist, there was some idea of conferring one upon him, *honoris causâ*, but his friends would hardly have known the genial Bohemian, who painted a portrait of himself with a pipe in his mouth, if the degree of LL.D. had been appended to his name.

It was in those days he planned a poem on a Moorish subject which was to be a *magnum opus* in several cantos, and he composed and bore in his memory hundreds of lines which he used to repeat in a voice of suppressed intensity. No fragments of this long poem remain, and other projects made him abandon it. His father's dramatic sketches, 'The Last Days of Nero,' 'Domitian,' &c., gave his mind dramatic inclinations, and a cousin named Freeman Crofts, a young barrister of Cloheen House, near Mallow, who was violently stagestruck, and

on his visits to us used to act Hamlet and Macbeth
in our drawing-room, encouraged the embryonic
tendency. Among his first literary attempts were
short poems, which he sent to the editors of magazines with the usual result—they were returned
as ' unsuitable.' In the bitterness of his heart the
following boyish lines were written :—

'Not suitable ! Not suitable.' Yes, always that reply—
A flattering hope that reaps at last a discontented sigh.
I toiled for life and bread ; my hod of toilful bricks I brought
To help to build that stately pile, the edifice of thought.
But I was gently pushed aside, those words I hear them now,
'Not suitable ! not suitable ! ' still answered with a bow.
'Tis tedious to go spinning on the weary thought cocoon—
To ply the shuttle of the mind to failure's dismal tune.
How many sleepless scribblers starved upon that answer mild,
That phrase which sounds a funeral knell to every mind-born
     child !
The stillborn thought, the feeble voice that's stifled ere 'tis heard
By that sweet phrase ' Unsuitable '—I sicken at the word.
I wonder will my coffin suit this weak, decaying frame ;
I wonder if a sculptured stone will give me so much fame.
I think I hear in fancy now the gownèd sexton cry,
'Not suitable ! not suitable ! Here, sir, he must not lie.'
'Not suitable ! not suitable ! ' 'tis ringing in my ears,
It seems to be the chorus song of all my future years.
Through life that hateful burden rings, through every hope
     and plan,
And follows, like a haunting voice, the disappointed man.

A wide gap was caused in our home circle by
the death of my sister Elizabeth, the eldest of the
family. She had a great deal of influence over my
brother, and used to make him brush and smarten
himself up, and would try to draw him out into
society. There was not indeed much scope in our
neighbourhood for this social polishing, but she got
him asked on visits to our relatives the de la Poers

of Gurteen, whose hospitable country house was always full of pleasant society. Count Edmund de la Poer was then a boy, but his father was the *beau idéal* of a kind-hearted, dare-devil, Tipperary gentleman. The stories of his mad freaks recall those told of the Marquess of Waterford of that day, his kinsman in blood and character. Many a wild riding or fishing excursion long after midnight issued from the gates of Gurteen, night there being frequently turned into day. When driving a light dogcart he would scorn to have the low gates on the Avenue opened, but would whip his horse at them and drive over.

Both Elizabeth and Willie Wills were favourites at Gurteen; but Elizabeth's death, which occurred at the Ansters' House in Dublin, was the end of those enjoyable visits, and removed an influence which might have considerably chastened my brother's Bohemianism.

In writing about his early life, it seems natural to speak of him by the familiar home-name; but I must explain that the child's name became the man's, and that owing to the peculiar charm of his character—the sympathy and tenderness which made him immediately friend to both young and old—he got to the last to be known, spoken of and spoken to, as 'Willie Wills.'

CHAPTER IV

DUBLIN LIFE

EARLY attempts in verse were followed by the more ambitious project of writing a novel. His method of writing was from the beginning fragmentary. Odds and ends were written on loose sheets of paper in a very small, artistic-looking hand, difficult to read. They were at all angles to each other, and he put these *disjecta membra* together afterwards in a fair copy.

A curate was the hero of his story, in writing which his mind was on his old home. I well remember the concluding sentence, which dwelt in my child's recollection. He repeated it over many times, and it came to have that kind of extraordinary effect produced by some jingle of words which it is impossible to analyse : 'When the curate shall have been presented with sod and twig of the incumbency *in perpetuo*, and love and Mary shall be forgotten things.' The name of the novel was ' Old Times,' and it was dedicated to his friend Humphreys. I believe there was some association in those concluding words with the ceremony of induction in the roofless church at Suirville, when a sod of turf was cut in the chancel and a twig broken from the elder tree and presented to Mr. Wills by the rural dean.

It was in order to illustrate this book that he taught himself the arts of wood and copper engraving. Dickens's later novels were at that time appearing in monthly parts, and my brother arranged with a printer in Waterford to produce his story in the same manner. The parts were bound in green covers, on which the massacre of the innocents with crowquills by heartless Roman soldiers, and Justice blindfolded with his manuscript in her scales, and a villainous-looking man at her side holding down the balance, symbolised the too probable fate of his book at the hands of the ruthless critics. This novel, which came out irregularly, in parts intended to be monthly, was, however, well reviewed. The 'Athenæum' said, 'The tale opens sweetly and poetically. That the author can write is proved from the first number'; and the 'Spectator' observed that it gave indications of power and some freshness.

In its first piecemeal production it could not be said to have been published, but he paid a visit to London and left numbers of it in Fleet Street coffee houses, which in his imagination still held the position they did in Johnson's days, and were the general resort of the literary world. To taste the pleasures of authorship he watched the faces of those who dipped into his story. One can enter into the feelings of an author who has broken the village bounds, and sees London reading his book, and, in the customers of the coffee houses, the fancied Steeles and Addisons of the hour; he knows the exact passages they are reading, the pet phrases and quaint thoughts actually passing from the page into their minds.

The book was afterwards published in a collected form by Piper, Stephenson, & Spence, of Paternoster Row, and McGee of Dublin, and subsequently, in one volume, by Saunders & Ottley (1857). Though the story was somewhat rambling the style was fresh, and the characters firmly drawn, and it left an impression long after it was read, which is a good test of merit.

My brother now began to forsake home and to live in Dublin, and studied in the Life School of the Royal Hibernian Academy; but art was then at the lowest ebb in Ireland for the obvious reason that there was no market for pictures. The oil paintings exhibited in Abbey Street were wall disfigurements, and though a meritorious school of water-colour painters still existed, Irish talent had for the most part migrated to England No good thing could come out of the Hibernian Academy, and it was a pity the young artist did not spend the years he gave to art studies in Dublin to studying in London or Paris. Want of means was of course the chief difficulty. In Dublin he was at home and was able to earn the little he needed. Sir Joscelyn Coghill and Loftus Fox, relatives of his, had started a periodical named the 'Metropolitan Magazine,' and to it he contributed a serial story called 'Life's Foreshadowings.' He was the only paid contributor, and received ten pounds a month. The story was afterwards republished in three-volume form by Hurst & Blackett; and although they paid him nothing for it, it served as an introduction to his other books. He drew in his novels from his own experiences, and his characters were people he had met. Indeed, his fondness for studying character and analysing the idiosyncrasies of his friends often gave them great annoyance. He searched out their most sensitive feelings without any idea of hurting them, but impelled by his art temperament and a genuine wish to advise and assist them. This habit sometimes detracted from his great popularity; and the worst of it was that if the victim showed irritation he would assume an air of cool and offended dignity, having been sincerely desirous as a counsellor and friend of doing a thankless office of kindness.

In addition to writing for the 'Metropolitan Magazine' he occasionally got a commission to paint a portrait, but he received very small sums for his pictures. He made copies of a picture of Chief Justice Bushe in his scarlet and ermine for different members of the family, for each of which he received five pounds. All through life, however, he managed to eke out money enough for his needs by his varied talents—but his needs were very modest. He was by nature extremely abstemious, and perfectly careless what he ate or drank, or wherewithal he was clothed. He was just as happy roughing it in his own bare and untidy rooms as when living as a guest on the fatness of the land. One of his copies of Cregan's portrait of 'the Chief' enabled him to pay a fortnight's visit to Paris, to which he made his five pounds stretch, crossing in a collier, dining at the cheapest restaurants or having no dinner at all, and sleeping in what would

in London be called a 'Doss House,' where the
lodgers slept upon shelves, like the berths in a
ship, one above the other. For the rest, he fared
sumptuously every day on imagination. The ut-
most luxury he allowed himself was to sit at a
table in one of the boulevards sipping a small
portion of absinthe and conjuring up visions. None
could take keener delight than he in the sights and
associations of Paris. He revelled in the Morgue ;
he felt the centuries crowd upon him in Notre
Dame ; he steeped his senses in the glamour of
worship at the Madeleine, and without a penny in
his pocket, and minus a waistcoat, he landed on
the quay in Dublin. But his imagination had
enabled him to derive far more enjoyment from his
cheap trip than all the magic of money could have
procured. Paris teemed for him with visions—
the scarecrow *jacquerie*, the mob storming the
Bastille or dancing the frenzied *carmagnole*, the
tumbrils loaded with their victims, and the red
harvesting of the Reign of Terror. What were
the inconveniences of a plank bed or a scanty
dinner to a mind fed on such illusions ? It was
indeed one of the drawbacks to the pleasure of
living with my brother that, owing to the mastery
of his imagination, he could not see unpleasant-
nesses in his surroundings, which, to the common
eye, were painfully obvious. He rivalled Don
Quixote himself in the way he invested his
environment with romance and beauty.

For those interested in him as a dramatist and
who have seen his plays at the Lyceum, to linger a
little about his early days hardly needs an apology.

Various influences of men and books were at work in those idyllic days in the formation of his literary taste, and first among them I would put German poetry. He had long been a student of Goethe, but it was not till some years later, when his study of the greater poet had ripened his powers, that he was to come under the stimulating influence of Heine. The effect was immediate, and it was lasting. I once possessed a small vellum-bound copy of the poet, dog-eared and mutilated by the rudest usage, but with its margins covered with minute annotations in my brother's *pattes de mouche* handwriting. He had, indeed, a morbid affinity for that mixture in Heine of sentiment and sarcasm, of mocking bitterness and vain longings and regrets. The Brontë's novels, too—most of all ' Wuthering Heights ' and ' Jane Eyre '—left their imprint upon him, and were formative influences. This class of reading led him to the choice of depressing themes, from which, later in life, he had great difficulty in freeing himself. Everything he produced was conceived more or less in a minor key. Happily for him his friend Humphreys was a fund of literature of a healthier kind—his society was that of a library not of a man. He widened my brother's literary tastes and put books in his way.

Another of the friends who influenced his mind, in those Dublin days, was Charles Pelham Mulvany, a man of extraordinary promise and little performance. He was a brilliant scholar, wrote clever verses and parodies, talked Hegel, was a free lance in the front rank of the University thought of his time, the best hearted of beings, but one of the

D

most eccentric and impulsive. He left the reputation of a man who could have done anything he had chosen if he had only been ballasted with a little dulness and common-sense to keep that cork-like cleverness of his from turning over. He had a mad look, and was very careless about his person and dress. His eyes, which gazed intently, were somewhat bleary, and his lips pursed out as he said odd, original things in a high monotone, or intoned eloquent bits from Professor Ruskin or John Henry Newman. His coarse shock of hair stood up in intellectual revolt, and the hand that held his pipe showed a superiority to soap and water. A rusty graduate's gown hung about his shoulders, while a battered trencher cap, stuck on the back of his head in dissipated fashion, crowned the edifice. He had extraordinary versatility. He could go into the divinity school, where, amongst budding curates, his Bohemian presence might almost be deemed a profanation, and carry off the prizes held out to encourage pious merit; while in the law school he snatched the bait of learning from voracious law students. When I last met him he had joined the medical school, and was, as usual, carrying everything before him. It was his unhappy fate to get into the Church, for which, though deeply Ritualistic, no man could have been more wholly unfitted. The Bishop who suddenly laid hands on him must indeed have been unmindful of the Apostolic admonition. As might have been expected, he ended his days, under a cloud, out in the backwoods of Canada.

Mulvaney was chosen to be my mentor when I

entered the University, and for a couple of terms
we had rooms together in Trinity College. In this
way he became acquainted with our family and
was invited to Kilmacow Rectory, and he and my
brother soon struck up a friendship. In Dublin
they constantly met at Dr. Anster's house. The
Collegian introduced his friend to a set in the
University a good deal his juniors, and at their
convivial meetings his geniality and talents made
him very popular.

It was from his own family, however, that my
brother's natural genius derived most of its culture.
The pleasant houses of relatives, among whom he
was a favourite, were always open to him. Mr.
Arthur Bushe, a Master in one of the courts, lived
in Fitzwilliam Square ; a stone's throw off, Mr.
John Plunket, afterwards Lord Plunket, son of the
Chancellor, in Upper Fitzwilliam Street ; Mrs. Fox,
with whom lived the Chief's widow, had her house
in Fitzwilliam Place. Other branches of the
family were scattered about town, forming a
numerous clan, remarkable for culture and hereditary talent. In their houses my brother spent
much of his time. There were also in those days
many friends of his father's who made him warmly
welcome. This pleasant society held him in Dublin
for fully a dozen years, after he had left the University, years which were the seed-time of his
literary career.

His earliest dramatic composition was written
for the Plunket children, and performed in their
hay-loft ; one of the actors being Charlie Hunter, a
nephew of the late Archbishop Magee. The family

D 2

talent he possessed might have shone as brightly
on the stage as it did on the archiepiscopal bench
in his grandfather and uncle. Indeed, the performances in the hay-loft were worthy of a better
theatre, and my brother's reputation was well
established in the schoolroom and over the stables
before he wrote the little extravaganza ' Luralie '
for performance in the drawing-room in Fitzwilliam Street. In this, Mr. David Plunket, now
Lord Rathmore, who was a very promising actor
and would have made a great name on the stage,
played the gallant hero. The little play was
written at Bellevue, a house belonging to the
Power family, opposite Waterford, and overlooking
the windings of the river Suir, out of which the
river king and his daughter were evoked by their
author. The songs in ' Luralie ' were set to
popular dance music, and it had the unprecedented
run of two nights at the Plunkets' house, and was
then transferred to that of Mr. Power, a Poor Law
Commissioner, who lived in Fitzwilliam Square.
This gem of dramatic authorship was published
in a collection of drawing-room plays, of which the
remainder were written by the Honourable Mrs.
Greene, fourth daughter of Lord Plunket. She
was the authoress of many clever and touching
books for boys, and to the end of his days one of
my brother's best friends.

He and I were then living together, and on one
of those play-nights, as we returned home, screams
and cries of ' Fire ' attracted our attention, and we
saw a woman in Salem Place rush in her night-
dress out of a house in the upper windows of which

the glare of flames was visible. The South Circular Road was deserted at that time of night, not even a solitary policeman being in sight, and we learned that an old lady was sleeping in the room which was in a blaze. My brother had a notion that by crawling upstairs on his hands and knees the smoke would be less stifling, and he actually succeeded in this way in reaching the old lady, whose candle had set fire to her bed curtains, and carried her safely downstairs into the open street. He also managed to get at a small table, which was said to contain a large sum of money, and to fling it out of the window. The whole woodwork of the room had by this time caught fire, and my brother bid me fill buckets of water in the kitchen and hand them up to him, while he, having wrapped round his head a wet cloth to save himself from being scorched, with great courage attacked the flames, until the fire was practically extinguished. It was only then that a douche of water which we received in our faces on the stairs made us aware that a fire-engine had arrived. The Dublin newspapers next day gave a very brisk account of the fire, the rescue, and of the extinction of the flames by an amateur fireman who had refused to give his name.

And, yet all through his life, and then even more than in later years, my brother had the reputation of a dreamer, and of a man incapable of action or energy. This estimate of him was shared by the very relatives whose admiration for his ability was perhaps less marked than their genuine affection for him individually. They could forgive

the unconventio.. .lities of his ways and the
Bohemianism which was all the more marked in
those exclusive Dublin circles. They overlooked
these things for the charm of his conversation,
quaint, original, sympathetic, attractive to all the
women he knew, and to children simply irre-
sistible. He loved, like another Rip van Winkle, to
collect round him, on the smooth gravel walks of
Fitzwilliam Square, his little audience of children,
some sitting on his knees, some perched on the
rail of the iron-backed bench, all crowding round
him, fascinated by those stories, whose sudden
unexpected endings had always a touch of drama
which never failed to tell. So he would hold them,
poised between mirth and terror, their elders even
caught into the gathering, and kept within the
group by the grotesque humour of the improvised tales. Sometimes the little listeners would
go home silent and awed, and the mothers, domestic
rather than literary, would beg of him the next day
to make his stories for the future less upsetting to
their nerves. All his life he loved children, and
knew them and understood them—his simplicity,
akin to theirs, and his tenderness and gentleness
making them at once his friends.

He had an unfortunate but deserved reputation
for breaking engagements, sometimes more from
disinclination than forgetfulness. He would go
out of his way to oblige his friends, correct their
manuscripts, and lend them his brains; but the
distaste of doing what he had bound himself to do
grew upon him as the time of fulfilment drew
near. He would do on impulse what he disliked

doing on compulsion. This applied to money matters also. He was generosity itself when he had money to lend or give away, provided it was to a person who had no earthly claim upon him. Among his Bohemian friends one might apply to him the words of his own song in 'The Man o' Airlie,'

> A mint o' kindness was his hand,
> His heart a mine o' pity.

An amusing story, that illustrates his caution in paying and his carelessness in giving money, may be told here, although it belongs properly to his London life.

He came into the Garrick one evening, having just received a large cheque for a play, and a friend, who had lent him 5*l*., naturally thought the time propitious to ask for repayment. My brother assured him that pressing demands of all kinds (which very likely existed) made it impossible to pay him just then. Probably he had made the same excuse often before, and the words had become a mere common form for him. His friend was rather crestfallen ; but, knowing his man, and that he would completely forget all about his excuses in half an hour, tried another plan. He came in later in the evening, when the cheque had been cashed, and this time, saying nothing about a debt, asked boldly for a loan of five pounds. 'To be sure, my dear fellow,' said my brother, taking out a handful of sovereigns, 'take whatever you like.' To lend or give away, which, in his case, were practically the same, was delightful to

him; but to pay had not the same relish, and was
only fulfilling an irksome obligation. I would not
imply that he did not pay his debts, but he put off
doing so. How freely he lent and gave away
money there are sheaves of cheques to prove. He
was not a man to borrow, even when he had need,
for he had a sturdy independence, and his lending
was often but a delicate way of giving.

One of his old friends of those early Dublin
days told me that he was once walking up Regent
Street with my brother when they were stopped by
a gentleman who soon showed by his manner that
he had a grievance to air. 'You were to have
dined with me last Thursday,' he said to Willie.
'You fixed the day yourself, and I arranged my
party that the guests might be friends you would
like to meet. You never turned up, and you never
even wrote my wife a line of apology. It was
really too bad.' My brother's concern was great
and very genuine, and he showed it in his face and
in his manner. The other was pacified, and they
were parting good friends, so much so that he
said he would once more try to have him at dinner,
and once more let him fix his own day. That day
was fixed, and they parted. 'Willie,' said my
brother to the friend with whom he was walking,
'I suppose you know who he is; for I have quite
forgotten his name.' I tell this story of my
brother, not, I hope, at the expense of his sincerity, but to show how oddly sensitive he was of
hurting the man's feelings, and at the same time
how blindly he trusted to the chapter of accidents.
He shrunk from telling the acquaintance whom he

had treated so badly that he really could not remember his identity, and allowed himself to rely on the chance of its being known to the friend, W. L. Woodroffe, with whom he happened to be walking at the time. Everyone who knew him well will have had some such story to tell of him. On one occasion, when his cousin, the late Archbishop of Dublin, went to dine with him, and arrived at his studio at the appointed hour, the host had gone out for the evening, and was having his solitary chop at Gatti's. Indeed, if invited by him to dine at his club, his friends knew that it was wise to prepare for eventualities by an early dinner. The cordiality of his invitations could only be equalled by his consternation and blank astonishment at finding he had forgotten all about them. He would ask one to wait for him for five minutes in the street, and not return for the rest of the day. While he would break the most solemn engagements, if he had made a promise to do something utterly unfair and detrimental to himself, and were urged to retract it, he would say doggedly, 'I have promised,' and nothing on earth would induce him to protect himself from the consequences of his want of business capacity. His eccentricities, however, never made him less welcome among his friends. On the contrary, with the unbounded sincerity of his apologies, they gave a zest to his character for which he was all the better liked. He was indeed hail-fellow with sets and in circles completely out of touch with one another, and as popular with the muscular school in the University—through his cousins Percy and

Artie Bushe, men of renown in the D.U.B.C.—as in its literary and intellectual coteries. He was such a good fellow that he was liked by opposites, and in all companies made equally welcome; but the one thing that it was most difficult to get him to face was any public function, especially one in which a member of his family was concerned.

Towards his younger relations he assumed a protecting and advising tone, not in the least offensive, but arising from real distrust of their abilities—most of all in regard to public speaking.

I can remember an instance of such anxiety of mind on the occasion of his last visit to the University of Dublin. It was the opening night of the College Historical Society, and it fell to my lot, as what is called auditor, to deliver the annual address. The Viceroy, the kind-hearted and popular Lord Carlisle, presided. A blue riband, a fuzz of white hair, a stately presence, a sonorous speech, with well-rounded periods and a peroration ending with *Floreat Academia*, are all that I remember now. Willie Wills was seated on the platform beside his father, who was decorated with his Oratory medal won in earlier days, when he, too, had been an office bearer in the Society. Willie always called me 'my man,' and my task that evening filled him with distrust and alarm. After all, however, had passed off well, and the public speeches were over, we adjourned to the customary supper, and this amiable concern for a member of his family was again called into play. Chief Justice Whiteside made a witty speech, as he always did on such occasions, and alluded, in a humorous and bantering way, to his friend of early days, Dr. Wills. This brought the old country clergyman to his legs, to his son's consternation, and on the spur of the moment he made a reply which outshone the legal luminary, and successfully turned the laugh against him. The speech raised the old medallist to high popularity among the students present, who said, with the genial irreverence of youth, that he was a 'fine old cock.' Shortly after, having already taken out his Doctor's degree, Dr. Wills was appointed Donnelan Lecturer in the University of Dublin ; but, of all his life of lost talents, that night, when he revisited the scene of his youthful success, and gave the young fellows a taste of the extempore speaking of fifty years before, was, I think, the most gratifying triumph.

My brother had now considerably passed the rubicon of thirty, and was becoming conscious of the fugaciousness of the years. There was a suspicion of autumn in the falling of his hair, the loss of which caused him much distress. He adopted an expedient to hide it, which made Punch, when he had risen to fame, customarily allude to him as 'Willie Wiggs.' He used to say 'we grow old in our sleep,' when, on getting up in the morning, he saw in the looking-glass the lines which came in the night. He began to feel how little he had accomplished—one novel stillborn, and one published in an amateur Magazine of Irish circulation. Indeed, it would then have seemed a very rash prophecy to say that a man who had apparently wasted half his life, and had been given time to show his capabilities, would in a few more years have won a high literary position in England, and be known to fame throughout the United Kingdom. It was, I believe, in some degree owing to the influence of his friend Humphreys, who was already planning a new career in London, that he at last made up his mind to seek his literary fortunes in the English capital, and leave behind, as he used to call them, his 'daisy-picking days.'

CHAPTER V.

HE GOES TO LONDON AND BECOMES A BOHEMIAN.

My brother's first journey to London was by sea, and in a sailing vessel. This slow, roundabout method of travel had the advantage over the express, which whisks the traveller from capital to capital, that there was time fully to feel the sensations proper to entering the realms of history. As he entered the Thames and saw the Tower in the early dawn, silent and with its shipping clustered by it, the crowd of memories it awakened made him burst into tears. After experiencing them so keenly himself, he always enjoyed receiving the reflex of such sensations from others. I well remember an instance, many years after, when I travelled with him to London for the first time. Owing to the famous Abergele accident on the road, the train was delayed many hours, and we arrived at Euston at daybreak instead of in time for dinner. Even at that untimely hour he carried me off—tired out and hungry as I was—to Fleet Street, and then in a cab to the Tower, that he might see the effect upon me of a first introduction to Temple Bar and the historic fortress. His own first visit

to London was in 1855, and I do not know where
he put up then, but when he came to stay in 1862
he simply crossed the road from Euston Station and
took root, like a seed blown by the wind, on the
spot on which he had fallen. Afterwards, when
Humphreys, who had severed his connection with
the Mill and the Quakers, arrived in London, the
two friends took chambers in Clifford's Inn, close
by Temple Bar.

Six years' residence in Clifford's Inn formed a
distinct phase in my brother's life—the period of
literary activity. From the quiet shades by the
mill-pond at Hermitage, where they watched of
summer days the brown trout move like shadows
in the water, or the wood-pigeons flutter in and out
of the woods of Greenville, they were now transported to the fever of Fleet Street, entirely dependent on their own exertions. Humphreys had
the better chance of the two, for he was one of
those men whose general information seems to
ordinary mortals omniscience; and omniscience,
coupled with a high speed in shorthand, marks
out a man for a Parliamentary reporter. On the
other hand, as his prospect of a living, Willie
Wills had only the vague uncertainties of literature,
and the little poem 'Not Suitable,' quoted in the last
chapter, shows how disappointing he had already
found them to be. The two men lived as chums,
in the garrets of No. 1, and must have felt the music
there is in the distant noise of London streets, even
in the endless rolling by of the wheeled traffic, to
those who hear it for the first time. That continuous
roll is full of vague possibilities, and gives a pleasant

sort of new-world sensation. The hardships and privations are part of a romance; and of these my brother had, at the commencement, his full share. He was writing 'Notice to Quit,' but was often without money, and, save for Humphreys, without friends. Scarcely conscious, in his abstraction, of the privations he was enduring with manly cheerfulness, there yet were times when it was forced upon him that he was hungry and had no money to buy food. He used to tell how one morning, after having gone to bed over-night supperless, he got up breakfastless. The void within made him restless, and day was but dawning as he sallied forth and walked down Fleet Street. As he passed along in the growing light he and a policeman at the same moment saw a bright half-crown gleaming on the pavement. Both made a dash for it, but the hungry man was the quicker, and secured the prize; and so he got his breakfast. The first friend he made in London was Joseph Knight. That was in the year of his arrival for good, 1862. Shortly after they became acquainted, Mr. Knight went to call upon him at Clifford's Inn, and had an intuition that his friend was hungry. He asked him to come and have dinner with him at Carr's restaurant, close by, and the great readiness with which he consented to dine showed Mr. Knight that he had made a shrewd guess. They had a good dinner together, and under its influence the mortified and crestfallen expression passed away, and he became his own hearty self. At the time there was nothing on either side which implied one man wanted a dinner, or that the other saw he did;

but, three or four years after, Willie Wills said, to a
mutual friend, ' There's the man who gave me a
dinner when I hadn't one.' And when he became
better off, and the lean kine of the years had given
place to the lustier ones, he insisted on showing
his gratitude for that dinner at Carr's by doing a
pastel portrait of his friend's eldest daughter. In
those early days Knight and he were a good deal
together, and read their poetry to each other. He
was an excellent literary adviser, a better judge of
other people's work than of his own, and he used
to say to his friend, ' Put in something grim—give
the grim suggestion,' and Mr. Knight owns that he
learned from Wills the value of the deeper note in
his work.

His early struggles and privations, added to the
natural tenderness of his heart, made him very
compassionate to broken-down men of letters.
Whenever he himself had money in his pocket he
was always ready to share it with the literary
wrecks that drift about so hopelessly in the neighbourhood of Fleet Street. One of those whom he
thus assisted was a man named Pyecroft. On a
cold winter night, returning to his rooms, he found
Pyecroft coiled up outside his door asleep. He
brought him in and improvised a bed for him on
chairs, and in the morning shared his breakfast
with him. Pyecroft showed an appreciation of his
hospitality by staying on for many months, becoming a fixture in the chambers. Some days after he
was thus installed, a friend visited Willie Wills
and found him muffled up in his great coat,
smoking a pipe on the stairs outside his own door.

He was naturally a chilly mortal, and used to say
his epitaph would be

> Here lies Willie Wills,
> Who was very subject to chills;

and it was then bitterly cold weather. 'Why don't
you go indoors?' asked his friend. 'Well,' he
said, 'Pyecroft has the greatest objection to the
smell of tobacco, and I would not like to offend
him, as he is my guest.' Those whom he treated
with such gentle consideration, and whose feelings
he would not have hurt for the world, were often
utterly selfish and careless of his, and robbed him
right and left without compunction.

At this time novel writing was his sole occupation, and he had entirely laid aside the brush.
'Notice to Quit,' on which he was engaged, was a
gloomy story, suggested by one told of a distant
relation who went to a doctor to be medically
examined for an insurance on his life. The
medico, after applying a stethoscope to his heart,
and listening attentively for a while, looked up
calmly and said, 'I hear your death-knell ringing,
sir.' The novel is a psychological study of a man
thus brutally warned. He dies at the moment of
a dramatic success. There is a loud call for the
author, and he comes forward and bows, and for a
moment the audience are astonished at his bow
amounting to a prostration on the front of the
box, but a bright stream of crimson tells them
that he has obeyed a higher call. It is a grim
story, and some of it was written at our home in
Ireland. The author studied a book on heart

E

disease, and expatiated on the symptoms until we all fancied our hearts were affected.

The publishers, again, were Hurst and Blackett —and they paid him, in royalties, fifty-two pounds ten shillings. The same firm published 'The Wife's Evidence,' written at Clifford's Inn in 1863. It was republished in a cheaper edition in 1876, by Ward, Lock and Co. The idea of the book was to illustrate the injustice of a wife being compelled to testify against her husband in bankruptcy, while in a criminal case she is incompetent to give evidence. The principal incident is that of a son taking the guilt of his mother, while the wife, who witnesses the crime and whose evidence, in spite of himself, would save her husband's life, has her lips sealed by the law. The germ of this novel was a story his father, Dr. Wills, used to tell of a Mr. McLaughlin, with whom he was acquainted. He was hanged for a murder really committed by his mother. The incident of his asking her to stand where he could see her in the crowd on the morning of his execution was part of Dr. Wills's story, but there was no question of a wife's evidence for or against McLaughlin. As to plot, this novel with a purpose, in point of construction was the best of his works. It had a considerable degree of success in this country, and in America both it and 'Notice to Quit,' which critics have spoken of as the strongest books of their time, have become standard works of fiction. 'The Wife's Evidence' was dramatised by the author for Mrs. Vezin, the play being called 'A Mute Witness.' The murderer in this was the father of the hero. I doubt, however, if it was ever produced. The position he gained by those two novels gave him an introduction to 'Temple Bar Magazine,' then edited by Miss Braddon, and published by Mr. John Maxwell; and he wrote for it a serial called 'David Chantry.' It is the story of a man who lives down the disgrace of a fraud committed by his father, and not only supports his mother and sister by his literary efforts, but repays by monthly instalments the fortune of the heroine. My brother was accused of inability to deal with figures, for, at the rate stated, the repayment would have taken a hundred years; but this involved the assumption that the instalments were never to increase. The novel is interesting, as forecasting the author's own life of devotion to his mother, the purpose of which was probably present to his mind at this time. The accusation was made against him that he had copied Thackeray's style; but, as it was undoubtedly the natural style in which he always wrote, this was an undesigned compliment. 'David Chantry' was republished by Ward, Lock and Co., in 1877.

It was while he was living at Clifford's Inn, in 1863, an incident occurred illustrative, like that in connection with an opposite element in Dublin, of his combination of modesty and courage. He was strolling, one Sunday, with Mr. Thomas Hewitt, a barrister (from whom I have taken the facts) towards London Bridge, and on getting to Old Swan Wharf, they saw an excited crowd on the bridge and edge of the wharf, and learned that a blind youth had fallen from a barge moored above and was being carried out by the strong current of the ebbing tide. No one had made any attempt to save him, but in a moment, Willie Wills sprang on a barge, and leaping into the river in his coat and boots, was strongly swimming in the current, urged by hundreds of directing fingers and voices to the spot where the lad had sunk for the second time. A shout announced his reappearance above the surface, and the swimmer redoubled his efforts to reach him before he sank for the last time. The lad's struggles or some bend in the current carried him out still further, and it appeared that the attempts to rescue him must fail, although only a few yards now separated them. The drowning lad was evidently going down, and only an arm appeared above the water when, by a fortunate dip, a man on a passing barge hooked him up. Willie Wills had a desperate struggle to reach the bank, but succeeded, after great exertion and peril, and took refuge in a tavern from the crowd of his admirers, afterwards escaping by a side door, and steadily and characteristically refusing his name and address. In a few weeks' time a parchment certificate, which hangs before me on the wall, came from the Royal Humane Society. Mr. Hewitt says that it caused much amusing amazement and speculation on his part as to the witnesses who could have recognised him and given the informa- ation; and he never guessed the obvious solution of the riddle, that it was Mr. Hewitt himself. In faded ink it records the admiration of the Society for his intrepid and humane exertions. The parchment is dated October 21, and the act to which it refers took place on August 16. His friend Mr. Woodroffe has told me that intimately as he knew my brother, and over a period of more than thirty years, he never heard him allude to this adventure, and his first knowledge of the existence of the parchment was when it was found by some friends in a drawer full of dusty papers in a corner of his studio in Fulham Road.

The success of 'The Wife's Evidence' was signalised by the unwonted chime of gold in its author's pocket, for Hurst and Blackett paid him one hundred and twenty pounds down for the book. This stroke of good luck enabled him to join the Arundel Club, which was then one of the meeting-places of the rising talent of the day. Among its frequenters were Mr. Clement Scott, the Hon. Lewis Wingfield, Edward Blanchard, Joseph Knight, Denis Deane, painter and writer, Swinburne, W. S. Gilbert, John Oxenford, and many prominent actors, including Irving, Bancroft, and Toole. An influential member of the club, James Anderson Rose, became one of the young author's warmest friends, and often invited him to his place at Wandsworth, where he had a splendid collection of engravings, afterwards lent to the Arundel. Many were the pleasant evenings spent under his roof with men who have since made their names famous in art or letters; but with regard to my brother the kind master of the house soon adopted the rule of never waiting for him, as his remarkable talent for forgetting the most sacred engagements was speedily recognised.

Anderson Rose was a solicitor, much respected in his profession, with proclivities towards both art and

letters. To his feckless friend he was a tower of
strength and counsel, and his admiration and affection for him were unbounded. My brother's novels
and some grim Rabelaisian poems circulated in the
club had established his literary reputation among
the members, and socially he was a great light and
very popular. There was a strong contrast between
the sombre and morbid character of his writings
and the cheerful boyishness of himself; for among
his friends there could not be a more genial companion. The six o'clock dinners at the Arundel,
which enabled actors and critics to get to the
theatres, were the most sociable and delightful club
dinners in London. The club after dinner suffered
eclipse until midnight, when the actors and jour-
nalists had finished their work at the playhouses
and newspaper offices and returned to keep up the
entertainment till daylight was well advanced.

By degrees my brother grew such a part of
the establishment that he subsequently, in 1867,
moved from Clifford's Inn, where his friend Humphreys had taken to himself a wife, and small voices
invaded the literary sanctity, and had rooms in
the Arundel, very high up and over-looking the
river. He continued a constant frequenter of the
club until 1871, and used often to bring in his
cousin, Mr. David Plunket, on his entering Parliament in 1870. After the success of 'Charles I.'
he joined the Garrick, of which Mr. Plunket also
became a member, and they were thus a good
deal in each other's society.

The dramatic quality of his novels had been
commended by the Press; and this, along with

early suggestions and his life among actors at the
Arundel Club, induced him to try his hand upon a
play. He wrote 'St. Cyr,' afterwards called
'Ninon,' in the year 1864 or 1865 ; and his friend
Knight, who formed a high estimate of its merits,
took it in charge. It was by him offered to
Benjamin Webster, and others, but in those days
no manager believed in poetic drama. Knight
read it to Kate Terry (Mrs. Lewis), who was greatly
impressed by its merits. She was then about
retiring, but said that she would play it if she ever
returned to the stage. However, for a number of
years after that it remained on the shelf.

Another pleasant literary opening was afforded
to my brother by the introduction his father gave
him to Dr. Westland Marston, a poet and dramatist, best remembered by his play 'The Patrician's
Daughter.' On the rare occasions of a visit to
London, Dr. Wills, who had formed a friendship
with Marston when he was a student in the
Temple, was a welcome visitor at his house in
Regent's Park Road, a great meeting-place of clever
people. The Irish *littérateur* was a brilliant talker,
and recklessly flung about original ideas and clever
sayings, and his host had to take him aside and
warn him confidentially that they would be picked
up and appropriated by his other guests, who, he
assured him, always took care to keep their good
things to themselves, but had no scruples in
annexing those of other people.

Dr. Wills met there, among lesser lights, Baily,
the author of 'Festus,' Douglas Jerrold, and Heraud,
the writer of a mighty epic, called 'The Flood,'

besides dramas, of which one named 'Gorbudoc,'
is reminiscent of Shakespeare's 'Lear,' and
another, 'The Descent into Hell,' of Dante's
'Inferno.' At one of these symposia, Heraud,
a little man with long hair, who was regarded
as somewhat of an infliction, asked Douglas
Jerrold: 'Have you seen my "Descent into
Hell"?' 'I wish to God I had' replied Jerrold.

Dr. Marston took a liking to his old friend's
son, and invited him to his Sunday evening and
Monday morning levées of artists, actors, and men
of letters. Among the men of a later generation
he became acquainted with at these gatherings
were Dante Rossetti; Parnell, who wrote under
the signature 'Q'; 'Earthly Paradise' Morris;
Horne, author of 'Orion'; Hepworth Dixon;
Ford Madox Brown; Herman Vezin; the company, besides, including sundry of the leading
spirits of the Arundel already known to him, such
as Swinburne and Joseph Knight. In this literary
coterie Willie Wills has been described as slovenly
in his dress, with a pipe sticking out of one pocket
and a roll of manuscript from the other, and,
generally speaking, with a smudge of charcoal or
daub of colour, like an American Indian's war paint,
across his face; but wearing, nevertheless, the un-
mistakable air of a gentleman.

His host had a charming and amiable daughter,
and between Nellie Marston and my brother there
grew up a little romance, which led, however,
to nothing, and she afterwards married Arthur
O'Shaughnessy, the poet; but their union was
short, as he only lived a year after their mar-

riage. Her brother, Philip Marston, the blind poet, has also passed away, and not one of the family round which that bright circle gathered now remains.

After the pleasant symposia at Regent's Park Road, in the small hours of the morning, my brother often walked home with Herman Vezin, and thus struck up an intimacy and friendship which led to the first production of a play of his on the stage.

It is curious that this admirable actor should have been the discoverer of two such dramatists as Albery and my brother. Albery began life with disadvantages of social position, which made his subsequent success the more creditable. Vezin nursed his dramatic genius for some years and ultimately procured for him his first opening. 'Dr. Davy' was the joint production of Albery, Vezin, and my brother; but it was chiefly the work of the last-named, though produced under Albery's name. Gratitude is the exception in this world, and the man who laid both the rising dramatists under so much obligation drew, in this respect, a contrast. My brother used always to point to him and say: 'There is the man who first opened the door of fame to me.' The opportunity occurred in this way: Vezin, when in Germany, had seen Carl Von Holtei's play 'Lorbeerbaum und Bettelstab' (Laurel-tree and Beggar's-staff) and he asked my brother to adapt it. The adaptation was called 'A Man and his Shadow'; it was played without success in the provinces, and in Edinburgh had the bad fortune to be sandwiched between Charles Kean's visit and the Italian Opera. The adaptor

afterwards found in it the germ of ' The Man o'Airlie.' This, however, is anticipating; it was something to have made a beginning. On novel writing
he still depended for his livelihood, and his next
book was 'The Three Watches' (Hurst and Blackett),
and for this, also, as for ' The Wife's Evidence,' he
received 120*l.* down. It is dedicated to Arthur
Bushe, Master of the Queen's Bench, Ireland, and
the preface is dated from Clifford's Inn. His hero,
a rude and simple sea-faring man, is intensely real :
Will Blair, the unstable, and Mosie with his dog-
like fidelity, the clergyman of St. Bees, and the old
stoker, step out of the canvas living beings. This
novel he wrote in the form of a serial for ' Tinsley's
Magazine,' and it was followed by the ' Love that
Kills,' which was an analysis of the strongest
passion in our nature, in its most sinister form,
inflamed by jealousy and partaking of insanity from
physical injury. It drew striking pictures of the
relations between landlord and tenant in Ireland,
the Irish Famine, and the Rebellion of 1848; and
it showed a warm glow of sympathy with the Irish
peasantry, which no one would have suspected
in a man apparently so wholly out of touch with
politics. The book bore on its title page a motto
applicable less to the contents than to the author's
state of mind, when, having written his last novel,
he was about taking up his brush again :

> For I am weary
> Of dropping buckets into empty wells
> And growing old in drawing nothing up.

An incident happened in connection with this
novel which threw him into the greatest distress

of mind. One of the reviewers spoke of 'naughty Mr. Wills' borrowing whole pages from his own novel, 'Old Times' and using them in the serial novel running in 'Tinsley's Magazine.' As already explained, 'Old Times' had not really been published at this time, and he not unfairly regarded it in the light of old material which might be worked up again. For a man with such fertility of mind it was curious how he would sometimes, to save the trouble of inventing, thus repeat himself. But he fancied, when Mr. Tinsley sent for him, that he might be accused of having done something dishonourable; and as he went to see him in company with Herman Vezin, muttered again and again, as if the character he might have claimed for himself was a lost possession—*sans peur et sans reproche!* In half an hour he came out from his interview with the publisher greatly relieved. Mr. Tinsley instantly accepted his explanations, and his face no longer wore the expression of anxious misery.

For a very short time after leaving Clifford's Inn he came to live with me in Great Percy Street, and he also revisited Dublin, and spent some pleasant months with his old friends and relations. He and Mr. David Plunket were then thrown together more than in the old days before William Conyngham Plunket, his cotemporary and early friend, was made a bishop, after which they seldom met. Willie Wills used at this time to have many pleasant walks and much genial intercourse with his cousin, and he delighted in the humorous reminiscences they recalled together, adding touches of his own which heightened the joke, and he was never more full of spirits or in more complete enjoyment of life. This preceded their intercourse in London, and must have been in the early part of 1868.

Before quitting the subject of his novels, I may notice the distinction he always drew between novels and plays. The simile he used was derived from his other art of painting.

'The novel,' he used to say, 'is a large canvas, on which you have plenty of room for atmosphere, foreground, middle distance, and vague horizons; you can give yourself wide scope in the development of your characters and their surroundings. But in a play you have room for nothing that does not advance the action; every sentence must have a purpose, and the relative values of all your materials must be most carefully preserved to make perfect the stage perspective.'

A great change was now coming over his life. It was from his home in Ireland it came, and transformed the idle literary man about town, making his hundred or two hundred a year by writing stories for the magazines, into an industrious worker earning a considerable income. The change would never have come from within himself. Failing something to keep him up to it he would not, merely for the sake of making money, have devoted himself to work as he did for the next few years, until hard work was less necessary, and he became able to earn money with greater ease.

In the five or six years of purely literary life he only occasionally visited his home. He did, however, pay at least one visit to Attanagh during the life of his father, who was promoted to this living in 1860. Great was his mother's joy and pride when her wandering son came back, bearing with him his sheaves of literary distinction. Attanagh is near Castle Durrow, in the Queen's County. It was at one time an episcopal residence, and the house is a long, low building, with a range of rooms, in our time disused, and, it is unnecessary to say, haunted. It boasted a Deer Park, but without deer, and what was dignified as a lake containing several islands on which the swans nested. There was also a well-stocked fish-pond, and a trout stream bordering the place. By the banks there was a pleasant walk shaded by ancient beech trees, called the Twelve Patriarchs. A great ecclesiastical community of rooks held convocation in the tops of the old trees which met over the avenue, and stood round the little churchyard like solemn elders. In vacation times, Mr. David Plunket, an ex-University fast bowler, came to us and trained some of the village youths, who, on one occasion, defeated the redoubtable eleven of Ballyragget. In this place, and in the ancient garden, with its sun-dial and trim yew hedges, Dr. Wills's last days were placidly spent. His death occurred in the year 1868. Had he used his talents as counters in the game for advancement in the world he might have won a distinguished position; but he was a philosopher, and, like his son, devoid of personal scheming and contrivance, which are so indispensable to success. He was buried under the shadow of the little church of

Attanagh ; and after the funeral my brother carried off his mother to Dublin, and there took a house for her. He engaged the house entirely on his own responsibility, undertaking to meet all expenses, although hitherto he had earned only enough for his own small personal outlay; and, leaving her there, he went back to London to make an income for her. From that hour he supported her in comfort, for the twenty years of her widowhood, and the cheque never failed to come in good time to meet every expense of her little household.

CHAPTER VI.

TAKES A STUDIO.

Mrs. Wills used to say that Heaven blessed the chivalry of the son she loved so well. Certainly, from the time he took 35, Wellington Road, and left her there to go to earn money for her in London, he did succeed as he had never succeeded before. He gave up novel writing and returned to painting. Leaving his rooms in the Arundel, he took No. 15, The Avenue, Fulham Road, a studio that had large doors opening out on mews at the back, which suggested that it might once have been a coachhouse. The front door, however, opened on a long corridor common to the artists, who had studios at each side of it.

His chances of success as an oil-painter would have been slight, but he took up pastels with great success. He now developed an extraordinary power, through the medium of pastels or coloured chalks, so easy to work in, of making portraits, and catching the dainty evanescent charms of expression in refined faces. Of children he could catch infantile meanings and traits with a wonderful subtilty, and at the same time simplicity. He thoroughly understood them, and, as before noticed, had a great power of winning their confidence.

There is among his pastels a delightful little

picture--which is a whole chapter in baby psychology—of an infant, in a white cap, sitting on
the ground surveying a huge pumpkin, which con-
fronts it with menacing rotundity, and has been
endowed by the artist with the hint of a smug and
contemptuous personality. Contending emotions of
curiosity, anger, and fear, strive for the mastery in
the baby face, and are expressed by every finger on
its little baby hands, and every toe of its bare feet.
The fingers and toes express perplexity and alarm
no less than the face ; and I doubt if there was ever
a better study of an infantile mood, or one that
showed more knowledge of babydom.

The wizard power of holding children spell-bound
and drawing out the play of expression greatly
helped him as an artist. He told them stories and
transferred to his mill-board the artless grace that
he had freed from all restraint of self-consciousness.
As a portrait painter of children in this particular
medium, he has had few equals ; and if, some time or
other, a gallery of his pastels were brought together,
they would illustrate a rare genius, one that in a few
years—five or six—came and went.

His success in this line of art was very quickly
gained. He began by asking five guineas, but was
soon able to charge twenty for a small picture
finished in three or four sittings.

Some friendly sitters advertised his pictures
by sending them to the exhibitions, and showing
them in their drawing-rooms. Soon people began
to flock to his studio. He understood women as
he did children, in all their moods and meanings ;
and he brought out beautiful expressions, and then

translated them with an easy, careless touch of the chalk and a rub of the finger. The secret of his success was a gentle-born mind interpreting gentle-born faces.

Among his best were Lady Granville, Lord Garmoyle, and the Marchioness of Bute. It was phenomenal the suddenness with which he developed this new art, and the success which he reached within a couple of years. In practising at the Academy Life School he had used pastels in drawing from the figure, and perhaps this suggested chalks as a medium in which he might exercise his talent of firm drawing and dainty colouring, without being impeded by the tyranny of technique. He had always loved the softness of Greuze's paintings, and pastel drawing lent itself to soft outlines. The limpid eye, the poetry of the Cupid's bow lip, the fine spirit of the nostril and the delicate poise of the eyebrow, the graceful balance of the head and turn of the neck, the tint of sea-shell ears, the comb-confined shower of hair, idealised portraits of hands at ease, the whole daintily framed in gold, began to fill a place of honour in many drawing-rooms. The struggling literary man had already blossomed into the successful artist. If he had lived up to his success he might then have become one of the fashionable painters of the day in this particular line of minor art, and in a while might have charged a hundred guineas for a baby gem. That he had some idea of the necessity of this was shown by the institution of a page in livery. But he got no further, and the little attempt at smartness quickly

F

faded away. The crowning point of his career as an artist in pastels was when the Queen's Secretary wrote requesting him to attend at Osborne to do portraits of Her Majesty's grandchildren. The Queen had no more loyal and loving subject, but his Bohemian instincts were averse to going; what other men would have deemed the greatest honour of their lives he looked at simply from the point of view of his untrammelled way of life which would be cabined and confined at Court; and it seemed to him the simplest way out of it to write a polite note to the effect 'that he regretted a prior engagement would prevent his having the pleasure of attending.' Captain Campbell, whom he had met in Dublin, as aide-de-camp to the Lord Lieutenant, coming into his studio found the summons to Osborne on the floor; but he was unable to explain the etiquette with respect to royal invitations to the artist, who had gone out for the afternoon, having pleasantly thrown the subject off his mind. The next day a telegram came from Osborne to the following effect :—' The Queen commands Mr. Wills to attend at Osborne immediately.' Startled by this message, and enlightened by his friends as to the solecism he had committed, he started off at once and stayed for a month at Osborne painting the royal children.

As might well be supposed, his life at Osborne was rather uncongenial, and his natural freedom and ease were curbed. When he was doing a portrait of a royal baby, on all fours, and good-humouredly said, 'Look up, little one,' the lady-in-waiting reproved his familiarity, and told him he

must address the infant as ' Princess,' or ' Your
Royal Highness.' One of the children of the Duke
of Edinburgh he christened ' The Imperial Baby,'
which amused the Queen so much that she often
asked how Mr. Wills was getting on with the
' Imperial Baby ' ? Although the altitude of the
Palace seemed to him a little difficult to breathe in
freely, he was greatly charmed with the kindness
of Her Majesty, who treated him with none of the
distance and hauteur of which he was conscious in
the manner of the Court functionaries. The pastel
portraits, which he did, hang at Osborne ; and, of
course, royal patronage gave a great stimulus to
sitters, and shortly afterwards he went to Dublin
and reaped a large harvest there also. When he
returned to London he found a crowd of commissions awaiting him at his studio.

But oil-painting was his ambition, if pastels
were his livelihood. Sometimes he persuaded his
sitters to allow him to do full or half-length portraits of them in oils, and some of these appeared
in the Academy or the Grosvenor, one of the best
being a portrait of Lady Wenlock, which, though
badly hung, was admitted to have fine qualities of
colour, and to be painted in a firm, broad, and well
restrained style. He did a full-length portrait of
Princess Louise, which was not, however, by any
means a success ; but Her Royal Highness took
lessons from him in pastels, and showed much
kindness to the young artist.

From a very early period ' Ophelias' began to
appear. Always a great student of Shakespeare—
every page of Bell's twenty-volume edition, on my

shelves now, was familiar to him—the distraught
beauty of Ophelia haunted his imagination. I can
remember four Ophelias all more or less alike, and
with a reminiscence of one sweet face—a young
relative who died in early life, and of whom Willie
Wills was very fond. 'Here's Rosemary, that's
for remembrance. Prithee, love, remember,' is the
legend of the picture. The finished edition of
'Ophelia and Laertes' is in Mr. Irving's possession,
and hangs in the vestibule at the Lyceum. He
never could recover the face that he had painted in
the early study for the picture, and at last adopted
the strange expedient of cutting it out and in-
serting it in the larger canvas. The picture, in
style and colouring, reminds of Watts; but although
overloaded with colour it is to be doubted if anyone who was a mere painter, however admirable,
could have painted its equal, for it is a dramatist's
realisation of a dramatic conception. The sweet
madness in the eyes contrasts with the sad
intensity of manly grief with which Laertes con-
templates his distraught sister; the wild-flowers
and herbs she has gathered drop from one listless
hand, while the other proffers the sprig of rosemary.
The pose of the figure is wonderfully graceful, and
expresses dazed and hapless waywardness. If not
as a work of high art, yet as a dramatist's poetic
realisation of Shakespeare's sweetest creation the
picture will always be extremely interesting. The
painter had generally a great objection to going to
see his pictures in the exhibitions, and got others
to tell him how they looked; but when this
one was hung in the Academy he stood near it

shyly courting the public verdict—just as he had watched the readers of his first novel in the Fleet Street coffee-houses—and, himself personally unknown, saw two painters in passing pause beneath the picture, and remark that in conception it was more than the work of a mere artist.

It is curious that only four or five paintings should remain of a life which was so much devoted to art. So far as I know, he never sold an oil-painting, though an enthusiastic American in Paris offered him a large sum for his 'Ophelia and Laertes.'

His only other paintings that I can remember were ' The Mediæval Bell Ringers,' exhibited in the Grosvenor Gallery ; a large picture, A wood-nymph music-bound by a baby satyr's pipes ; A Scottish mother rescuing her infant from the eagle's eyrie ; A young girl, in meditation over a letter she has dropped, in unpoetic surroundings ; A sea-nymph in an iridescent shell receiving the visit of a goggle-eyed gurnet. Another, an unfinished picture, re-calls an amusing and characteristic story. Danton, André Chénier, with other victims of the Revolu-tion, are being dragged on a tumbril to the place of execution, surrounded by the surging Paris mob.

My brother, fond of contrasts, had painted the poet with his weak, sensitive face leaning on the strong-jawed, determined-looking Danton, both shadowed by the doom to which they were being hurried. He had worked at the picture all the week, bringing out the character in the faces of his Danton and Chénier, and leaving the rabble in mere out-line till he should find the kind of model that answered to his idea. On Saturday afternoon he

went off to spend a delightful two days of rest with
his friend Rose. On Monday he returned to work,
letting himself into his studio. There he found
an ungainly-looking man, quite at home by the
fireside, and, in fact, seated in the one comfortable
chair of the place—the sitter's chair, which my
brother used to call the throne. This rough-
looking customer, marvellously ill-featured, was
obviously in possession. My brother, wholly un-
suspicious, accosted him cheerily, 'Well, my
friend, what can I do for you?' 'I am the
Queen's Taxes,' said the man, retaining surly possession of the throne. Willie had left this debt
unpaid through sheer carelessness. He was well
in funds at the time, and, as he told his friend
Woodroffe, had received 'several papers with
" whereas,"' and had triumphantly used them for
lighting his pipe. He now took his cheque-book from
his pocket—he always carried it in the pocket of
the long ulster which he wore summer and winter—
and proceeded to write a draft for the amount.
But the 'Queen's Taxes' gruffly announced that
he was not going to be done like that. My brother,
I need not say, would have been incapable of such
a deception—*he* was not going to take a cheque, *he*
wanted cash down—quids. Then Willie begged
him to go to the bank and get the cash. But the
'Queen's Taxes,' with a knowing look, declined to
abandon his distress. A friend at this juncture
chanced to come in, and volunteered to go to St.
James's Square and bring back the money. When
he returned, a surprise awaited him. On the daïs,
in an inconceivably unpicturesque attitude, he saw

the ill-favoured bailiff posed and motionless, and
standing in front of his easel, the great canvas
upon it, my brother looking intently up, with that
stand in one eye which was a peculiarity of his
when he was painting, and contemplating his sitter
with undisguised approval. Indeed, the ' Queen's
Taxes ' was not more delighted to gain his entry
into the studio, than my brother to receive and
keep him there. Here, at last, he found the very
face he was looking for. The great picture, laid
aside for so long, might now be proceeded with.
Moreover, the bailiff proved a lie to physiognomy.
He was a most intelligent, companionable fellow,
eager, indeed, in the pursuit of his profession (and
his public), but rich in anecdote which delighted
my brother. The appreciation was reciprocal;
moreover, his vanity was flattered by being asked
to sit. And whenever he had a vacant two hours
he would come to the studio, mount the daïs, take
his pose, as an execrating mob, and was heard to
say that ' Mr. Wills paid better than the Queen's
Government.' I don't know what his salary was,
but feel quite sure this was true.

In this studio, large and lofty, all the arts in
which my brother dreamed away his life were
represented—his clay modellings, his camera and
chemicals, picture frames without pictures, and
pictures without frames, pieces of ancient tapestry,
bric-à-brac, painting materials, manuscripts, and
books. But the genial master seemed contented,
unconscious of the confusion by which he lived
surrounded. He was so lovable and whimsical in
all his acts and ways that those who came to see

him delighted to make him a study, for he lived in an ideal world to which the outer only lent suggestion. Out walking with a friend he might find fault with the ungainliness of a cloud, and say that it would debar any artist's picture from admission to the Academy, but the domestic disorder to which he was so accustomed he was happily, or unhappily, incapable of seeing. For the unfortunate, or even the unworthy, he had unfailing toleration. His imagination invested them with interesting and prepossessing qualities which no one else could discover. He had no eyes but for the good in those he pitied, and, like divine charity, believed, hoped, endured. His gentleness and good nature suffered him to be infested by loafers, to shield whom he would often, in his excess of generosity, sacrifice his real friends. One instance only is recorded of his ridding himself of a studio parasite. This individual, like Pyecroft at Clifford's Inn, had become a squatter in the studio, but took an opportunity, after some months of hospitality, of stealing a considerable sum of money. With great ruth and unwillingness to deprive even such an unworthy *protégé* of the shelter of his roof, my brother invited the thief to an expensive restaurant, and stood a sumptuous repast; and having raised the culprit's spirits to a high state of buoyancy dropped two sovereigns into the hand that had stolen his money, and regretfully said good-bye.

Even animals seemed to be aware of the gentleness and pity that reigned in this temple of art. My brother had a theory that cats in London were of one sex, and that there were no toms. There

came, however, a visitor to the studio that upset
this cherished belief. The magnificent proportions
of the creature, the fair round face, the ample
whiskers and dignified bearing put beyond doubt
that a genuine tom-cat had sought the asylum.
This rare animal became a special favourite; my
brother was fond of it, and it was fond of him. It
would jump on his knee and sit there and purr,
and often when his pipe had gone out he would
abstain from bending forward to light it, lest he
should awaken tom. But this illusion was to pass
away, for about a month after his arrival tom
became a mother. This indiscretion on tom's part
was the origin of the studio kitten.

Among the happiest memories cherished by my
brother of those days were the visits paid to the
Avenue, Fulham Road, by Princess Louise, who,
an adept in the art herself, took interest in his
pastels, an interest which was strengthened by the
Marquis of Lorne's appreciation of the artist as a
literary man and a rising dramatist. There was
great excitement among the loafers at the studio
when the Princess was expected, and for once they
were bundled out; but if my brother had been
receiving his royal guest in a palace, instead of a
scene of such desolation and disorder, he could
not have been more self-possessed or have met the
Princess with more genial *bonhommie*. Her Royal
Highness, who liked the unconventional artist, was
much amused at the general *ménage*, and, with
the greatest good nature, allowed my brother
affably to introduce the sitter, who happened to
occupy the daïs. He was quite unconscious in

doing so without permission of any breach of etiquette, and Her Royal Highness, who recognised, under his artistic Bohemianism, the culture and manners of a gentleman, by her gracious demeanour allowed no hint to escape that he had committed a solecism.

The scene of confusion the studio presented was at all events large, and its ingredients artistic, and pardoned by one who always, like Princess Louise, sympathised with art. There were others, however, to be reckoned with who had even less knowledge of Court etiquette than the artist himself. The studio kitten was one of these. It would spring on the Princess's train, and, much to her amusement, dart after the trailing garment; while a monkey, whose habit it was to let itself down on visitors from the gas bracket as from a trapeze, screamed with fury at the sight of a lady's dress.

It will easily be understood that sitters of less exalted rank did not make the same allowance, and were infinitely less tolerant, and gradually they diminished in number, until at last driven away altogether; but by the time the last of them had disappeared he had begun, in the third phase of his life, to make an income in the new character of a poetic dramatist. Where relays of smart people had been idealised on his millboard, scenes of drama sprang into existence, and imagination created worlds out of chaos.

Long, however, after the sitters had ceased to come, Willie Wills believed that painting the oil pictures which he never sold was the one plank he could trust to for a living. He spent money on

models, and, the better to study French art, he
took a studio in the Impasse Hélène, Rue de
Clichy, in the artists' quarter up by the heights
of Montmartre. If any one suggested that these
were useless expenses—the studio in Paris, especially, as he seldom went there—he would show
that he felt deeply hurt, and with gentle dignity
would remind the remonstrant that he had a
mother to support. Of course he could not quite
ignore the fact that his dramatic work did contri-
bute to his income ; but he always remained to
himself the artist, as in truth he had been for a
while, but not in the form of art he loved. It was
truly said that he would freely have given all his
dramatic laurels for one success as a painter, and
that he fretted out his heart at his life-long
failure.

His friend, Karl Ambruster, director of the
orchestra at the Court Theatre, often invited him
to feasts of delightful chamber-music, to which
gathered all the most appreciative. At one of
these parties, a lady who had been greatly excited
at the prospect of meeting the author of ' Charles I.'
gushed out with a little speech on the honour of
meeting the first dramatist of the age. He replied,
with a courtly bow, which acknowledged the compliment and duly recognised her personal charms :
' Madam, I am a poor painter, who writes plays
for bread.'

It would have been difficult to have had a more
delightful guide in a picture gallery than this poor
painter, who wrote plays for bread. He had a rare
poetic insight which showed you much in meaning

and effects that the commonplace eye had missed.
I have spent hours with him in the National
Gallery and South Kensington Museum, the Louvre
and Versailles, and seen through his eyes more than
I ever saw before in pictures. Yet with all his
knowledge of the ways of art and his capability of
revealing them to others and making poetry of
painting, it was curious how he escaped being a
successful artist in oils. The hindrance to success
was more than imperfect acquaintance with art
processes or inability to produce effects at the first
intention without labouring them with colour. Nor
was it merely want of facility in finding Nature's
equivalents, or slovenliness in detail. There was
some other limitation to his powers. His mind
teemed with fancies, but they did not fertilise into
many conceptions on canvas. His art was barren;
like a man who can be in love with only one
woman, he seemed to be capable of having only one
picture on his brain. Poor mad Ophelia haunted
him always.

CHAPTER VII.

It is impossible to be strictly chronological in writing the life of one whose occupations were so scattered. As it was in his literary period he put forth his first dramatic effort, his second falls within the few busy years spoken of in the last chapter, while he was a fashionable portrait painter in pastels. The inspiration of 'The Man o' Airlie' was drawn from an early poem of his own, which, for that reason, he wished should never see the light; the subject of it was the Burns Centenary. The idea of the last scene is taken from this, but he also borrowed a dramatic germ from his adaptation of the German play 'Lorbeerbaum und Bettelstab.'

The drama was written for Herman Vezin, and he had in its construction the advantage of the actor's advice and criticism. An agreement was drawn up, for he always, with unsophisticated seriousness, played at being businesslike even when the agreements were to his own disadvantage; and although he liked to have something 'in writing' he invariably lost the paper. Only one single agreement out of all his numerous plays was to be found among his papers at his death. On the occasion of the last visit he paid his friend, Vezin told him the outline of a plot,

which moved him so much that he exclaimed, in
his impulsive way, ' I'll write a play on it. Write
down an agreement on half a sheet of paper '—
the half sheet implying that the terms would
be nominal. The agreement in the case of ' The
Man o' Airlie ' was that he should share the
profits up to a hundred pounds ; but, as he had
received fifteen pounds for ' The Man and his
Shadow,' which had been a failure, he consented
that this should be included as a part of the consideration. Ultimately, as there were no profits,
but, on the contrary, Vezin lost by the play, he
received nothing. A very small scrap of paper
would have been enough for this agreement. As to
his indebtedness to 'Lorbeerbaum und Bettelstab,'
Tom Taylor, who had read the German play, said,
in the ' Times,' 'The author of " The Man o'
Airlie " is fully entitled to the honours of original
authorship.'

Much of this play was dictated to Vezin, and
so slowly did the author move in the unaccustomed
medium in which he afterwards wrote so rapidly,
that the amanuensis has said he sometimes felt impatient enough to jump out of the window. His
stage knowledge frequently obviated the need of
scene changes, and, if a passage was not well
written, he insisted on the author re-writing it.
In the last fine scene of the play, my brother
brought the crazy poet to the foot of his own
statue, and he was indignant when Vezin, unappre-
ciatively, asked him what he was going to do with
the statue : ' Can't you see the depth of tragedy
and the satire of the old beggar poet sitting under

the statue raised in his honour?' he exclaimed
angrily. Vezin pointed out the necessity of not
leaving this to the imagination, and my brother
then struck out the scene of the unveiling of the
statue by the wealthy peer who had treated the
poet as a poor dependent, but grew eloquent over
his memory, and claimed the credit of having discovered his genius—as, in the early poem I have
mentioned, ' Prim fashion lisped its parrot praise
with condescension latent.' The play was produced in July 1867, at the old Princess's Theatre,
with Mr. Vezin in the character of James Harebell.
It was his greatest performance, and one never
to be forgotten by those who witnessed it. But
the business of the piece was discouraging to him
as manager. He was playing in ' The Man o'
Airlie ' to an average of thirty pounds a night.
The weather was oppressively sultry, and the
theatres were doing hardly any business. Of course,
they were not confessing to this, but keeping up
the usual game of bluff, while instead of 200*l.* or
250*l.* houses, their receipts were as low in some
cases as ten or twelve pounds. In reality, therefore, although he did not know it then, Vezin was
doing extraordinarily well ; and if he had not been
disheartened, might have made a great hit with the
piece later on, when the weather cooled and town
filled again. Strange to say, the play has never
had a fair hearing in London. To describe the
effect which it produced I cannot do better than
transcribe the words of a famous critic, George
Henry Lewes, who thus wrote in the ' Spectator,'
July 27, 1867 :

'Mr. Herman Vezin, lessee of the Princess's Theatre, has made a very audacious experiment. He has ventured, in an era of burlesque, melodrama, and great triumphs of carpentering, to bring out on the stage a genuine and modern English tragedy, " The Man o' Airlie," by Mr. W. G. Wills, author of the remarkable novel reviewed some years ago in our columns, called, " Wife's Evidence." We do not know that " The Man o' Airlie " will succeed—indeed,we shall give, by-and-by, some reasons for suspecting that it will not; but of this we are certain, that Mr. Wills has produced a very original, and, in many respects, a very noble work, a prose poem of a high and simple kind, rather than an ordinary drama. He has ventured, in defiance of all traditions, to place upon the stage a play entirely tragic, in which there is no plot, in which the action does not turn upon love, in which there is no first-class female part, in which there is no room either for the comic or the farcical, and in which the main interest is of a kind the mass of playgoers necessarily cannot appreciate, yet which produces on the majority of them a most overpowering effect. The writer had strolled on the second night of the performance into the pit, knowing nothing of the piece or its author— rather expecting a kind of Highland melodrama, and he can bear unbiassed testimony to the depth of feeling several times displayed. Women, evidently of the lower middle classes, who scarcely understood the bad Scotch in which the dialogue is carried on, were sobbing unrestrainedly; and if the stout Scotch tradesman who stood next me

was not crying, he ought to consult an oculist
about the state of his eyes. The value of this
emotion as a test of the value of the piece is in-
creased by the fact that it is due exclusively to
sympathy with mental pain of a rare and spiritual
kind—the agony of a ruined and maddened poet :
agony no doubt in part that of a bereaved husband,
and therefore common to mankind, but in part,
also, of a blasted literary and poetic ambition,
which might under other treatment seem ridiculous. To make shop-girls care—care to pain—
because an ignorant simpleton in a plaid cannot
get his " sangs " published, seemed to us a triumph
of art.

'Vezin used Aberdeen Scotch, the most difficult
of all for Englishmen to follow. " Oh, hang it ! "
said a man near me, " that's a fine beggar, what's
he saying ? " And then, and all through the piece,
extempore translations were offered in audible tones
in four or five parts of the pit.

'The second act is deficient in action, though
it might read well. In the third, however, the
action quickens. Harebell has accepted the situation as private secretary, his wife has died of the
close city air, and the poet, frenzied by her loss,
saddened and bewildered by the blasting of his
hopes of literary fame, wearied with incessant
copying of documents, gradually loses his reason,
wakes for a moment to refuse to betray the man
who has plundered him, and finally fancies he
sees his dead wife, and walks over the stage with
his arm in that of her invisible spirit, his face
expressing a bewildered fondness, his left hand

G

patting the air where her head should have been.
In the strange affectation of insanity, Mr. Vezin
did the scene well; there was no applause, except
from one fool of a *claqueur*, who, we hope, will read
this opinion of his judgment; but over the house,
dropping as it were from gallery to pit, descended
a dead strained silence, a silence such as we never
but once recall in a theatre, succeeded, as Harebell
vanished, by a roar of recall. Every side of an
emotion of extraordinary complexity—insanity produced by grief, but shot as it were with literary
vanity and regret, and tempered by natural sweetness, courtesy and simplicity of nature—had, we
are satisfied, been caught by the least trained
portion of the audience.

'In the recognition and death of Harebell, no
words can fairly express the dramatic power of the
scene. It carries away the audience, overwhelms
the somewhat artificial dialogue, conceals as in a
mist the woodenness of the actors, who, Mr. Vezin
excepted, seem not to have a conception of the
situation they are depicting, and while the audience
quiver with emotion, are intent upon attitudes of
the most Philistine staginess. The blasted life
of a poet culminates in a situation which makes
his failure and his grand success, the fulfilment
and the futility of his hopes, his misery and his
pride, his triumph and his utter fall, patent to
men who, in all probability, never read a line of
poetry in their lives. To make such a destiny so
manifest, to show an artist utterly beaten down
by a fate as remorseless as ever Æschylus imagined, yet, in the moment of utter prostration, by

the innate power of his art, beating that fate down,
rioting in the rapture of a victory which leaves
him an idiot beggar, is an effort for which, in an
English playwright, we were not prepared. There
is nothing whatever to break the unity of the plot.
The hope and the failure and the triumph of
a poet furnish the beginning and the end of a
tragedy of which a great poet might be proud.'

The secret of the effect was that the author
wrote straight from his heart to the heart of the
audience. The nature of his poet was in many
respects his own. Harebell did not mean in his
song 'The Man o' Airlie' to stand for himself,
though the neighbours saw the unconscious portrait; nor did Mr. Wills, though friends suggested
lines from it for the stone above his grave.

> Oh, there abune yon heather hill
>   Where foot-fa' comes but rarely,
> There is a house they point at still
>   Where dwelt the Man o' Airlie.
> He wore a coat of hodden-grey,
>   His hand was hard wi' labour;
> But still he had a hamely way
>   O' stannin' by his neighbour!
>
>   Oh! up and down, and roun' and roun',
>   And o'er the hale world fairly,
>   Ye might hae searched, but never foun'
>   Anither Man o' Airlie.
>
> His burly laugh made folks rejoice;
>   His words the neighbours guided,
> But little bairnies loved his voice,
>   And in his smile confided.
> The word to-day that left his lip,
>   Became a deed to-morrow;
> Hoot, mon! the friendship o' his grip
>   Would lift the heart of sorrow.
>
>   Oh! up and down, &c.

G 2

He was nae loud, he was nae proud,
    He lacked in learnin' sairly,
And yet ye'd pick him frae a crowd
    The honest Man o' Airlie.
His wealth, it was nae in the land,
    It was nae in the city ;
A mint o' kindness was his hand,
    His heart a mine o' pity.
        Oh ! up and down, &c.

He's dead and gone, this Prince o' Fife—
    Hushed is his burly laughter ;
But oh ! the music o' his life
    That lives wi' us lang after.
His memory lives —the man may die—
    That lingers bright and looin'
Just like a star lost frae the sky
    Whose ray outlives its ruin.
        Oh ! up and down, &c.

My brother did a sketch in oils of the unveiling of the poet's statue, which was that modelled by Durham, the sculptor, representing Harebell in highland costume, carrying in his hand his cap or bonnet. While the author was painting this sketch, which Vezin wanted for the front of the house, some ladies came to Clifford's Inn to see it. Mrs. Humphreys, who was in *déshabille*, hastily concealed herself, at my brother's suggestion, in a cupboard. There she was kept for more than an hour, the absent-minded painter having entirely forgotten her, and, to her anguish, pressing his visitors to stay on, each time they spoke of going. When at last the coast was clear, he was horrified to hear a feeble voice issuing from the cupboard, and, on unlocking the door, found poor Mrs. Humphreys in her contracted position, cramped, and nearly suffocated.

CHAPTER VIII.

THOUGH 'The Man o' Airlie' from the financial point of view was but a *succès d'estime*, yet even that success encouraged my brother to write two other plays, suggested and produced by Mr. Herman Vezin. The first of them was 'Hinko; or, the Headsman's Daughter,' produced at the Queen's Theatre, and founded on Ludwig Storchs' historical novel, adapted for the German stage by Madame Pfeiffer; but the dialogue, characterisation, and *dénouement* of the piece were entirely original. Even unfriendly critics acknowledged the literary merit of the drama, and the sonorous force of the blank verse, which contained many noble lines that lingered in the memory. The play, however, was gloomy, and the theatre so cold that people were obliged to wear shawls and greatcoats in the stalls, and though the company, which included Mrs. Billington and Mr. Rignold, believed in the piece, it did not stand the ignoble test of merit—of having money in it. My brother had, however, proved his metal enough to be accepted as a *collaborateur* by a dramatist of Dr. Westland Marston's standing, and they produced between them a play called 'Broken Spells.' This would have better suited the taste of the Boulevards than of a healthy English audience. Mr. Herman Vezin was again the hero, and Miss Ada Cavendish was the heroine, and the play was produced at the Court Theatre; but the luck was again disastrous.

Collaboration with Marston, however, and the credit of having written something, at all events, grim and original, even though unsuccessful as a drama, brought the new playwright's name to the front, and formed the prelude to two successes in the same year, but one rising high above the other.

It was about this time that a clever youth began to frequent the studio, and sometimes to act as my brother's amanuensis. I have a mirror which often reflected the anxious, absent-minded face and disordered attire of the dramatist on which this apprentice in the art, as he afterwards became, has left his name scribbled with a diamond, where his kind friend's image will never again be seen. 'A. C. Calmour, 1871,' is the inscription, and fixes a date; but I do not think it was until a year or two later that he became installed as my brother's secretary, and took down and copied his plays in a handwriting which, though more legible, was remarkably like his own.

My brother, indeed, needed some friend near him, for in his studio life he became quite imbedded in his occupations, and forgot time and food, and even toilet. He would jump out of bed intent on some of the alterations he was always making in his pictures—it might be to paint out Joan of Arc's golden hair and give her instead raven locks, or to

change Ophelia's blue dress for a white one, or to put
rosemary instead of rue into her hands, and then
he would entirely forget how incomplete had been
his toilet.   Presently, if not awakened to the
consciousness of it by his friend, he might walk
out into the street in his painting coat of many
colours.

A man so absent-minded and good-natured was
the natural prey to beggars and borrowers, and to
those who, without either formality or good intention, helped themselves to his money.   Sometimes,
indeed, they hardly left him a sixpence.   He must
have made very large sums in the days of his pastel
painting, but occasionally he had not money to pay
his studio rent, and had to stand siege against his
landlord.   All through his life his mother was his
first consideration, and his filial love took care that
she should never want; and, as it happened, the
landlord of her house in Dublin, Dr. Simpson, was
the kindest of friends, and gave directions to his
agent never to trouble 'the dear old lady' if the
rent should ever be in arrears.   The tobacco-jar
on his chimney-piece in which he artfully concealed his loose change, the hiding-place being
known to all those loafers of the studio, is certainly
not a myth; and he has told me confidentially that
it was strange, if he left loose sovereigns in his
pockets when changing his dress, he never could
find them again when he went to look for them.
I think he had a glimmering sub-consciousness
of how it happened.   In a queer poem of his,
called 'John o' Dreams,' a name he used to apply
to himself, the following lines confess to an

insight his kind heart would never outwardly
admit :—

> Oft was he cheated, yet at least he knew it ;
> As one deceived he listened to a lie.
> He winced at work, but was the man to do it—
> He dreamed whole evenings 'neath a lonely sky.

Of the extent, however, to which he was robbed
he was certainly never aware.   He was annoyed if
the suspicions of others were reduced to words, and
disliked to inflict humiliation even if he found any
one out, and he would try to prevent others from
hurting the feelings of the thief.   At the South
Kensington Museum he picked up a strange ragged
literary man named Russell, whose antecedents
were a mystery, and whose accomplishments were
almost universal.   One evening his old friend, Mr.
W. L. Woodroffe, called about seven o'clock and
found him engaged to dine with Lord Cairns at
Cromwell House.   His habit on such occasions was
to send to a small haberdasher's round the corner,
and buy a shirt.   The shirts were made with
buttons in front, and he had a preference for studs.
His method of adaptation on such occasions was
to stab with a penknife both folds of the shirt, and
so, with an ingenuity on which he prided himself,
to improvise button-holes.   Mr. Woodroffe, on that
day, had in his shirt three curious old studs, made
of carved turquoises and diamonds, all connected
together with very fine gold chain ; they must have
been a hundred years old, and were rather valuable.
He offered to lend them for the occasion, and left
them behind.   Three days afterwards he called
round and asked for them, and my brother told him

that Russell had stolen the shirt—that was quite a
matter of course—but that he had also pawned the
studs; he begged Mr. Woodroffe, however, as a
personal favour to himself, to say nothing to
Russell on the subject, as he had spoken to him
very seriously about it, and Russell had faithfully
promised him that such a thing would never occur
again. It did not suggest itself to him that the
nett result of the whole transaction was the loss to
his friend of his valuable studs. He objected even
to ask Russell for the pawn-ticket; he said that
after the conversation he had with him, it would
hurt his feelings to reopen the subject.

Among those who made common property of
that studio was a disciple of the pre-Raphaelite
school, a sharp-featured, rather picturesque artist,
who had been secretary to a celebrated painter.
This man, having lost his employment, carried his
painting materials to my brother's studio, and from
that time he always had an easel set up in the
place of honour, so that visitors, again and again,
eager to say something gratifying, would compliment the owner of the studio on the pictures
mounted upon it, my poor brother's own work all
the time turned to the wall, as if in disgrace. In
the latter days, this man became a bird of ill-
omen at the studio; but, until its gentle and
unselfish master was gone, never took his shadow
from the door.

At this time, however, life was bright and
vigorous, and my brother had troops of friends to
draw him out of his studio in the evenings. These
were often pleasantly spent at Dr. Marston's house,

where, notwithstanding the breaking off of the little romance with Nellie Marston, and the other 'Broken Spells' with her father, he was still welcomed, or at Rose's, or at Lewis Wingfield's. The convivial party used to break up in the small hours, and walk home in the moonlight across London on their several ways. It might be Vezin with Dante Rossetti walking in front, Wills with Sandys bringing up the rear. Sandys, the clever draughts-man, takes it into his head that his friend Wills, as being entitled to the honours of a dramatist, should walk in front of Vezin, a mere actor. Wills adopts the idea, and striding forward, with mild dignity, keeps in front of Vezin. Presently, however, having maintained this order of going long enough to pro-tect the rights of dramatic authorship, they roll back together in a hansom, Vezin and he, the rest of the way to the studio, lulled to sleep by the motion. The playfully assumed dignity is forgotten by the time they arrive at the Avenue, Fulham Road ; but it was characteristic that, when a little convivial, a lingering boyishness appeared. It was about 1871 that Vezin introduced him to Mr. Bateman, the lessee of the Lyceum Theatre, whose clever daughter (later Mrs. Crowe), was then the star actress. Mr. Bateman read my brother's 'Ninon,' and was so favourably impressed with the talent it indicated that he gave him a commission to write a play for his daughter, and my brother became a frequent guest at those pleasant little supper parties which, after the performances, the genial manager used to give. It did credit to Mr. Bateman's astuteness that he should not only thus

have given a comparatively untried writer such a
commission, but have entered into a five years'
agreement with him at a salary of three hundred a
year to be the dramatist of the Lyceum. The
manager was to have the refusal of any play he
wrote during that period, and to pay, in addition
to salary, a hundred pounds for a five years' lease of
every play accepted. The first under this agreement was the adaptation of the ' Medea ' which
Legouvé had dramatised for Rachel. She did not
play the part, but Ristori, in an Italian version,
created the *rôle* of the barbarous enchantress. It
required some audacity to attempt adapting the
Greek masterpiece. The critical audience would
be difficult to satisfy. The adaptor, however,
like his prototype Goldsmith, was gifted with a
versatility which triumphed in tasks the most
remote from one another. A distinguished but
unsympathetic critic has said of his 'Medea,'
in a book on English dramatists of to-day : ' Mr.
Wills has narrowly escaped producing a great
play, and a lasting addition to English literature.
" Medea in Corinth " deals with a genuinely tragic
theme, and, so far as construction goes, deals with
it in a really able fashion. Mr. Wills has freely
and skilfully remoulded the matter afforded him
by Euripides, and has ably fitted the action to the
requirements and conditions of the modern stage.'

Whether the play had a narrow escape of being
great, or realised greatness, must be judged by those
who read it hereafter in print. It was, at all
events, undoubtedly successful, and successful in a
field and under conditions which made the success

the more remarkable. On the modern stage it is
not easy to find anyone to realise one's conception
of Jason, the leader of the Argonauts:

> A stranger? Nay, some journeying God!
> Vast-chested, glad-eyed, beautiful!

Miss Bateman played, with much intensity, the
barbarian enchantress, and her sister, with taste
and feeling, Glaucea. The play opened the door
to a succession of poetic dramas from the same
pen, and created an expectation on the part of the
public and the critics of higher achievements still.

CHAPTER IX.

WRITES 'CHARLES I.'

IT was the good fortune of the rising dramatist of the Lyceum that, after the success achieved in his play by Miss Bateman, a new actor joined the theatre who gave him his great opportunity.

Mr. Irving had proved his tragic power in ' The Bells,' and it was a happy inspiration, due to his personal qualifications to represent the king, which suggested, as a subject, ' Charles I.' Mr. Bateman was diffident of the success of such plays as ' Charles I.' and ' Hamlet.' Blank verse was still regarded as hazardous, and Mr. Irving's successes had previously been won in melodrama. Many a battle was fought at the Lyceum supper parties, but the actor, with great tenacity of purpose, urged a repetition of the experiment which had been so successful in the case of ' Medea.' The play was written at express speed—partly at the Studio, and partly at 37, Sydney Street—and it was produced on September 28, 1872. By this drama the author established himself as an original dramatist of great power, and Mr. Irving, who had previously been spoken of as a ' promising young artist,' was at once raised to the first rank of his profession.

As was said in the preface, written by a distinguished critic, to the first published edition of the

play, the fortunate conjunction of the dramatist
and the actor resembled that of Shakespeare and
Burbage. 'The actor and the dramatist were
complementary to each other: the dramatist needed
the actor, and the actor needed the dramatist.'
Mr. Bateman used often to say that there had been
no such poetical dramatist since the Bard of Avon
himself. In this play, Mr. Wills certainly gave proof
of power, equalled by none of the poetic dramatists
that intervened, and if he did not in subsequent
work always reach this high level, it must be
remembered that it was difficult to get him to
apply his powers to dramatic work, and he often
wrote against the grain. Consequently, though he
wrote many plays, his true talents were sampled
by but a few. The wealth of his imagination
was only partly brought to the surface. One
of his intimates remarks that, in private intercourse, 'he was a man full of bright and sweet
imaginings, and he would reveal perfect glimpses
of a fairyland of a mind full of tender thoughts
and delicate fancy.'

But he was impatient of much of the dramatic
work he was commissioned to do, and when this
was the case, he did it badly, selling his name and
not his talents. It was when writing for worthy
interpreters that his genius awakened; and only
by the plays written for them, ought he to be
judged hereafter.

His painting was a hindrance. The curious
perversity of his nature asserted itself again and
again to his detriment. When there was a pressure
of urgent dramatic work, he has been known more

than once to jump out of bed and seize his palette
and brushes ; and to keep him at work with his
pen, he would have to be watched and goaded on.
The critics were provoked by the falling off shown
so markedly in some of his plays, and when he did
rise to the height of his powers they not all of them
forgave him, or did him full justice. ' Charles I.,'
however, stands as an evidence of what he was
capable of doing, and worthily takes its place in the
catena of the great history-plays of England. A
few words from Miss Ellen Terry, in a letter found
after his death among some treasured papers, written
when the end was not very far off, must have come
like a ray of light in the gathering gloom. The
artist who interpreted was not perhaps wrong in the
fame that will belong to the artist who wrote :

4th March, 1891 : 22, Barkston Gardens.

I'm just returned from our last rehearsal of ' Charles I.'—and
coming along in my carriage, have been reading the last act,
and I can't help writing to thank you and bless you for having
written those *five last pages*. Never, *never* has anything more
beautiful been written in English —I know no other language.

They are perfection—and I—often as I've acted with Henry
Irving in the play, *am all melted* at reading it again. An immortality for you for this alone. God bless you.

Yours, with intense appreciation,

E. T.

How strange it is now to turn up some of the
criticisms of the time, and to find more than one
writer asserting that the first scene had absolutely
no significance or *raison d'être*, and another, that
the last can have had no object but to bring the
characters in the play on the stage, and if so

(hectoringly), 'so much the worse for the drama. We wonder what manner of man he could have been who wrote those words of the 'last five pages ' of which Miss Terry says ' an immortality for you for this alone.'

Indeed, we might ask, what manner of man was he who said that the first act had not a fibre of interest, did not begin the story, and was wearisome to the audience and dispiriting to the actors ? Who would venture to say so now ? No one had a better eye for the perspective of a play than the author of ' Charles I.' The bodings, the pulse of the time, the vain attempt to satisfy the insatiable, the domestic scenes—all this was necessary to the interest and sentiment of the whole. It has been truly said it is the sentiment which the first act suggests that links together the not very closely connected play. This foreground was therefore essential. In a historical play, which, however unhistorical in parts, deals with persons who live in our mind's eye, the intricacy of plot is not needful. It needs only to be like life, not like a play.; the clockwork of melodrama would be entirely out of place. Indeed, if plot were essential, where would Shakespeare be ? It is the sentiment binding the parts together which supplies its place and is the one thing absolutely needful.

Whether we, who know the play so well, do not for that reason feel differently with regard to the first act from those to whom it was still on the verge of the unknown, one cannot say ; but for us, in that garden scene bounded by the Thames at Hampton Court, the delightful picture of the King's

home life is charged with the pathos of the trouble
and tragedy to come.

When we visit Hampton Court everything
in that first act haunts us, despite the Cockney
crowd. Our eyes grow ghostly, and we see the
Court gossip, Lady Eleanor, finding the King's
gentle traces in the games, the Zittern, the book
for children :

> Read with quaint utterance and rueful brow,
> And with such awful liftings of the finger,
> As hold a babe betwixt a laugh and shudder.

We hear her describe the King, notwithstanding
the bogies in London streets, and the world gone
mad :

> Calm as the moon
> Seen through a panic of storm-driven clouds,
> In perfect peace among his wistful stars.

A very typical cavalier grows out of the past in
the person of Huntly, and in vain the gossip of the
Court tries to extract his news; for, that some
strange events are afoot, it needs not her fortune-
telling powers to perceive—the hurrying to and
fro, the hasty coming of the King, followed by the
Queen 'as ruffled as a bird 'scaped from the
fowler,' and Moray with his holiday smiles. And
then, out of the thin air of those quaint gardens
comes the Queen, with the prettiness of her French
accent, with her foibles, and her faithfulness ; and
we seem to see, again, her loyal concealment of her
chagrin when she hears of the dismissal of her
French retinue; her wifely anger with Lady
Eleanor for questioning the King's good pleasure.

H

There rises before us the boding vision of the fortune-telling dame :

> Methought in England was a mighty fairing,
> A fair such as there never was or shall be
> Under the Sun.   The Nation gathered busily
> To buy and sell.   And in the midst of them
> Methought there was a spacious sable-booth,
> All hung with fair black crape.   And as I looked
> And marvelled what it meant, lo ! at the opening
> A sad and courtly figure stood alone,
> In deepest mourning : torn and soiled his cloak
> His eyes exceeding sorrowful, yea, till tears
> Came to the eyes of all ; and as I gazed
> Methought I knew the face.
>
> THE QUEEN (eagerly) : It was——
> LADY ELEANOR : The King's.

And the Queen's pretty pathetic turn, when she has questioned and heard he was alone :

> I don't believe it !
> If thou did'st see aright, I, his true wife,
> Was at his side.

And her reproof of Lady Eleanor's 'spying upon Providence,' come back to us, as she fades again into the haunted air, searching for her lord.   His is the ghost that now comes on the scene, and grows to most vivid life, with a frantic shouting and outburst of applause, as if arising from all sides of us, that seems phonographed from the first great night when Hampton Court was mimicked on the stage of a theatre, and the perfect illusion of Charles I. appeared carrying Prince Jamie on his shoulder and leading the Princess Elizabeth by the hand.   There, as it was said, was the somewhat gaunt figure, the lank face, the sharply cut features, the long hair parted in the middle, with which everyone is familiar; a picture of Vandyck's seemed to have started living from its frame.

And the gardens grow empty, but of this great pathetic memory of the King making holiday with his children, reciting to them the ballad of 'King Lear,' with Elizabeth sitting on his knee, and little Jamie, another sad chapter of history in miniature, beside him:

> King Lear once ruled the land
>   With princely power and peace;
> And had all things with heart's content,
>   That might his joys increase.

Then, again, the Queen becomes illumined to the mind's eye, fretfully attempting to draw the King from this delightful abandonment to his children, till at last he puts them aside to calm her complaints of neglect, and being kept in suspense at Whitehall:

> Dear heart! now all is over and at rest.

And when she refuses, with plaintive petulance, to be so easily comforted, he points with those words that seem to linger about the gardens as their perpetual consecration:

> Nay, look around. There is no riot here;
> A wondrous peace walks through the leafy chasms
> Of Hampton groves. Nature and we alike,
> Keep peaceful holiday.

The Queen, still hovering round, in fretful lapwing mood, interrupting the sad old ballad, strives to draw Charles back to the cares of State from which this peaceful hour is snatched, and we hear his gentle remonstrance:

> To-day we rest .
> The wind is fair, and we will float to Richmond,
> Returning with the tide. Moray will join us,
> And, if we may prevail, thou and thy dame.

But this suggests her personal grievance :

> *A la bonne heure !* when Catherine comes back
> To curl my hair, and when Matilde returns
> To make my toilette. When Picot's here
> And Julie : to attend upon the Queen.

And then, with what tender seriousness he bids his little sweethearts go and see the barge, which must now be in sight, while he turns to smooth away her discontent :

> Come hither, little wife, and bring thy grievance,
> Or if thine heart be full, still vent thy anger,
> A word will presently explain it all.

Her jealous attack is directed against Moray, the King's favourite :

> You do not like my French, *bien !* they are gone ;
> I do not like your Scotch, let Moray go.

And when the King replies, it is the old jealousy which troubled her with his dear Buckingham, and wishes all were as loyal and true as Moray :

> I'll tell thee when thy Moray will be loyal,
> And I can tell thee when he'll prove a traitor :
> When thou dost flourish, and the sun is shining,
> Then Moray's loyalty, worn like a feather,
> Insults the very air with flaunting challenge ;
> But should rebellion thrive, and danger-clouds
> Rise in the sky, then Moray will be false.

Charles, half playfully, half seriously, asks, is the Queen wholly faithful ? That babbling tongue of hers has given him his first defeat. It let slip the plan of banishing the five members ; one hint, and

like a flock of piping curlews they had been up and
flown. From Lady Eleanor to Catherine, and so
it ran through all the servants to the town. No
more French monkeys here, or prating parrots.

QUEEN : Ah ! Charles, I fear thou wilt not trust me more.
KING : In faith, with no more secrets.
Mary, a secret in a woman's breast
Is like a thistle on a windy day,
Which wafts off many couriers of down,
Till all the flower in hints is filched away.

And then, returns to us that scene with loyal
Huntly, in which he stoutly remonstrates with his
royal master, and tells him the result of his unwise
attempt—a triumph to the Commons :

The malcontents
Are now the laurelled heroes of the hour ;
The party cry, that the captain of all mischiefs,
That fiend that rides the air before a mob,
Is ' breach of privilege.'

The demands of Parliament know no limit,
and the King sees in them a menace to the
throne :

I see them, like the Netherlandish sea,
Rise grey and sullen, level with the sea-moles
Stealing the soil by their insidious wash
Eating through iron clamps, till through new fissures,
They enter with a silent fatal leakage
To flood the land, yea, sweep away the throne.

The Commons keep back supplies to force the
King to barter away more of his prerogatives :

Within Blay Harbour rode our merchant ships,
The French, in times of peace, seize on our goods ;
Methinks this thing doth touch the English honour.
    The King, the guardian of the English honour,
Would raise a fleet to fright encroaching neighbours,
Would levy taxes to maintain an army,

If only to protect our trade and homesteads,
And never to forget our nation's history,
Where is no record of unpunished insult!
Under such challenge and just cause of war,
Methinks the humblest ploughman in my realm
Would clench his fist and clap me down his groat
For King, for country, for our cherished homes.

Lord Huntly has come to propose a secret meeting with Cromwell, and the indecision of the King's character and proneness to indirect methods in affairs of State give faithfulness to the portraiture :

We must be crafty for an honest end ;
The path seems crooked while we toil along it.
But, left in distance, all the petty curves
Melt from the vision ; it looks straight and fair.
Then let old Justice Time assoilzie us :
Time is the tardy advocate of Kings.

But the Charles of the stage, as drawn for us by Mr. Wills's pen, was too upright and honourable to succeed in Machiavelian arts. His turnings are as those of the hunted creature, which excite our compassion, not our contempt. We are made to feel sorry for him, and we love him the better for his weaknesses. The belief, which he, alone, maintains in the treacherous Moray, shows how little craft he possesses. He is a simple, honest English gentleman, trying to be very cunning, and pathetically failing. When Huntly blurts, in the face of the smooth and plausible traitor, that the Commons supplicate his dismissal, though we wish the King's eyes were opened like ours, our sympathies rally to him like loyal subjects when he here puts down his foot and refuses to sacrifice his friend as in an unhappy hour he sacrificed his good angel Strafford.

I would be called the King of Liberty!
I say, strike every chain from off my people ;
Let Liberty, like crystal sunlight, enter
And fill each home—illume each road and highway,
Till the King's bodyguard, when he rides forth,
On either side be Love and Loyalty.
But for these Commons—well, some silken fetters,
Or, on my life, they'll manacle their King.

Moray's plausible professions pass before us, and then the garden of Hampton Court resolves itself into the well-known and popular picture of 'The Happy Days of Charles I.,'[1] and, as the royal party embark in the state barge, the air grows eloquent with that concluding speech :

After long care and moil, I thirst for peace,
Yea, as the Psalmist longed for wings to escape,
Yea, for dove's wings to fly and be at rest.
So now the gentle sail shall be our wing,
The air we rise upon shall be sweet music :
Breathe music softly till the wave shall seem
To move in silent glamour, and the banks
Be rimmed with rainbow, and the great sky cope
Seem like the haven we are sailing for.

The second act is the meeting of the King and Cromwell ; the third, the battle in which Charles is betrayed ; the fourth, the parting.

The controversy over the second passed the bounds of criticism, and became almost a political question. It was said that, though the author's pity and reverence were all along enlisted on the side of the martyr King (we were brought up with those feelings at home, and the ' Eikon Basilike ' was a book much revered) yet Cromwell, as my brother originally wrote the part, was a strong

[1] The title of Goodall's picture, from which the scene was copied.

though sinister character. 'The wretched exigencies of the drama would not allow him to adopt
this treatment, and notwithstanding stormy alter-
cations between the author and private friends, he
sought his inspiration for the character of Cromwell
in unworthy pamphlets of the period.' This may
be so ; there may have been more Cromwell—
hardly a stronger, in the first rough draft.   But
the play was not written for Belmore ; and it was
necessary to give all the honours to the great
actor.   It is all very well to speak of the 'wretched
exigencies of the drama,' but those who write
dramas without attending to those wretched exigencies write bad dramas ; the best drama is that
which fulfils them best.

The writer's design throughout is to garner all
sympathy round the central figure of the King.   It
would have been bad art to divide it.   At all
events, the play being admitted to be one of the
greatest of the century, it would need that it
should be re-written to prove that the division
would have resulted in a greater.   My brother was
of opinion that the one niche in the play was
for Charles and his Queen, and that Cromwell's
should be, in contrast, the strong repulsive face on
the gargoyle.   Although he admitted the charge
that Cromwell had a price was baseless, he did not
acknowledge that the making use of it changed
what Lessing called 'the typical significance of a
historical personage.'

The scene in which Charles is placed so
splendidly in the right, and in which, after his
insolent and exorbitant demands, the parliamentary

champion exposes himself as the 'mouthing patriot
with an itching palm,' and gives the King an opportunity for such crushing denunciation, entirely
fulfils what was said to be the intention of the
author. The play was to be typical of the meeting of opposing forces of the Monarchy and the
rising Democratic spirit. It was to be 'the clash
of two mighty storm-clouds.' All this it is. Certainly, in the theatre, night after night, before
the endless succession of audiences, it called forth
cheers and counter-cheers, following the speeches
of the King and the Democratic leader. And when
the King at last finds the chink in his opponent's
armour, and gives him such mortal thrusts, there
passed a chill and tingling of the flesh over the
audience such as probably no scene ever caused
the like of upon the stage before.

The third act throbs with the excitement of
battle. The contused air is stunned by the boom
of cannon. The Queen, in an agony of suspense
for the King, is persuaded to rest in her tent, and
overhears a subdued conversation between Moray
and an emissary from Cromwell, and taxes the
favourite with treachery. The King, in hot haste,
enters with Huntly and followers. It is the critical
moment of the battle. He cannot listen to the
Queen, but breathes again at the sight of Moray,
whom he has been seeking over the field in vain.

In front they are holding their own against
Fairfax, but Cromwell, with his Ironsides, is stealing round his native fens to attack them in the
rear, which the Scotch army must cover or the day
is lost. To the desperate demand of the King

for the help he promised, Moray returns halting
replies :

KING : Why dost thou tarry ? Moray, dost thou sleep
When brave men die ?
MORAY : My liege - oh ! let these tears speak for me now,
I know not what to say.
KING : Say nothing, man, or let thy speech be brief ;
It is an hour when words should be like blows.
MORAY : Lord Lothian and Lord Leven both intend
To make good terms.
KING : Would'st drive me mad ? Good terms !
Lord Lothian ! Haste ! The troops you promised me !
MORAY : I would, my liege, I knew the words would soothe
you.
KING : Thou soothest me as little as a dream
Of water soothes the swollen tongue of fever.
I tell thee, man, I dare not credit now
All the cold comfort written in thine eyes.
MORAY : I must explain. A few words will suffice.
KING : Dost know the price of every idle word ?
A precious, precious life ? Thy slow excuse
Is echoed yonder by a true man's groan.
The troops you promised me !
MORAY : The Scotch are faithful ! If your Majesty
Would let me tell them you embrace the Covenant.
KING : I only know our covenant of honour.
The troops you promised !
MORAY : Nay, your Majesty !
KING : The troops you promised !
MORAY : 'Tis impossible !
KING : Sorer than Marston Moor or fatal Naseby
Is this last blow.

The hideous treason of his cherished friend seems
still incredible. The Queen entreats him to fly.

Peace, Mary. I am here for life or death !
I grow here by a hundred bleeding roots,
My friends, who shed their blood for me to-day—
How can I tear myself from such dear soil ?

The feverish power of the scene in which the

King wrings from the heart of Moray a late repentance reaches its height in this appeal :

> I'll not believe thee false. Give me thy hand.
> Thou art young to die. Thy company I ask not—
> It is mine hour not thine to win or lose.
> Fulfil thy pledge, and if I live through it,
> As heaven doth hear me in this piteous hour,
> Choose from my hand the gift that tempts thee most—
> Of title, wealth or honour—thou shalt have it,
> And in the annals of my hapless reign
> I'll set this faithful action, jewel-bright—
> How Moray kept his promise to the King,
> And saved the throne of England.

But it is too late ; the road has been left un-
guarded, and Cromwell enters with Ireton and his
soldiers. That the King has been betrayed by his
friend is disclosed by Cromwell's bidding Moray
remove his locust army—the gold will follow ; and
before delivering up his sword, Charles thus addresses the traitor :

> I saw a picture once, by a great Master,
> It was an old man's head.
> Narrow and evil was its wrinkled front—
> Eyes close and cunning : a dull vulpine smile.
> 'Twas called a Judas. Wide that painter erred ;
> Judas had eyes like thine, of candid blue,
> His skin was smooth, his hair of youthful gold ;
> Upon his brow shone the white stamp of truth,
> And lips, like thine, did give the traitor kiss.
> The King, my father, loved thine—at his death
> He gave me solemn charge to cherish thee,
> And I have kept it to my injury.
> It is a score of years since then, my lord—
> Hast waited all this time to pay me thus ?

Nothing more pathetic than the last act has ever
been penned. The Queen pleads with Cromwell,
who is disquieted by visions and troubled by the

influence of his beloved daughter Elizabeth. There
is a mixture of crafty policy with conscience
qualms in his offer of the King's life, on condition
that the young Prince of Wales should give himself up. The mother refuses to make herself a
decoy to bring both her son and husband into
Cromwell's power. The parting scene which follows is charged with exquisite pathos and beauty.
What tears have flowed over the Queen's charge
to her children :

> Look at him, all brave and smiling,
> Give him one sweet long kiss, and say good-bye !

In Charles's last farewell of gallant Huntly, he
asks him if he remembers the coronation morning,

> When from the balconies in smiling clusters
> Bent down to greet me England's chivalry,
> And all along a bright cleft sea of welcome?
> Upon that morn I had no sprightlier cheer,
> Trust me, no sweeter speed, no surer hope,
> Than I shall carry forth with me to-day.

The cheery talk with his children, all unconscious of the tragedy, and begging him to go back
with them to Hampton Court ; the veiled farewell,
sending them to the window to see the bonny
morn—their father's last—make way for the fond
interchange of tender memories with the Queen :

> QUEEN : How thou hast suffered ! on thy dear worn cheek
> I see a history I dare not read.
> These poor grey hairs ! Oh ! Sweetheart, where was I
> As this hoar-frost of sorrow grew upon thee.
> KING : Mary, we both are changed ; and yet, and yet,
> It seems but yesterday, bright yesterday,
> Since first I met thee, a young fluttered stranger,
> Who came all trust, yet trembling, to my arms.

Methinks I see upon thy rippled hair
The olden sunshine and the woven shadows
Of moving leaves that floated o'er thy dress.

And then the bequests :

I have set by some little farewell tokens,
Dumb things that speak without the pain of words :
This emerald ring's for little Henriette—
Her tiny finger cannot fill it now :
In after years it will shine tenderly.

QUEEN : I'll keep it for her.

KING : Within yon ebon cabinet you'll find
A little book; some idle thoughts of mine,
Which to a loving ear may have some music :
Give it to my Elizabeth, from me.
Here is a locket, with our hairs in plait :
Send it to Mary—'tis a pretty emblem
Of our young married life begun so brightly.

QUEEN : What more? I would do something. I can't speak.

KING : Nay, nothing more.
This miniature that I have kissed so often,
Till, like the pilgrim's lips, love left its trace
On the worn velvet !
This I will carry with me to the grave !
Cursed be the hand which robs it from my bosom !

QUEEN : I am jealous of its place ; cursed be the hand
That strikes at thee and does not kill me too !

KING : Oh, my loved solace on my thorny road,
Sweet clue in all my labyrinth of sorrow,
What shall I leave to thee ?
To thee I do consign my memory !
Oh, banish not my name from off thy lips
Because it pains awhile in naming it.
Harsh grief doth pass in time into far music.
Red-eyed Regret, that waiteth on thy steps,
Will daily grow a gentle dear companion,
And hold sweet converse with thee of thy dead.
I fear me I may sometimes fade from thee,
That when thy heart expelleth grey-stoled grief
I live no longer in thy memory :
Oh, keep my place in it for ever green,
All hung with the immortelles of thy love ;

That sweet abiding in thy inner thought
I long for more than sculptured monument
Or proudest record 'mong the tombs of Kings.

As the guard draws up on either side, while the
bell tolls, the King, kneeling, kisses the Queen, who
seems to turn to stone in her speechless agony,
and at the door he looks back with the historic
word, ' Remember ! '

It is recorded that in this last scene the sympathetic sobs of the audience mingled with those
of the disconsolate wife. Women sobbed openly,
and even men showed an emotion which comported
ill with the habitual serenity of the stalls. There
was scarcely a dry eye in the house during the
parting of Charles and his Queen. But seldom
has there been beheld such a scene of enthusiasm
as followed the fall of the curtain. It was the
outburst of the pent-up emotion of a vast audience.
The night marked the advent of a great actor and
a great dramatist, and there was a consciousness
in that gathering of all the talents that it was not
merely the success of a play they were hailing,
but an event in literature and a landmark in
dramatic history. In that era of opera bouffe, a
play, written on the classical model, had taken the
town, and it seemed like the renaissance of the
poetic and historical drama.

As the lights went up tears were surprised on
the faces of the great assemblage, and every one
was glad that his neighbour's attention was distracted from his wet cheek to the pale actor who
appeared in relief against the curtain and thanked
the audience, and promised to convey to the author
their favourable verdict.

CHAPTER X.

NOTES ON THE PLAY AND ITS LIBERTIES WITH HISTORY.

THE play ran for one hundred and fifty nights, and whenever it has been revived has been received with the same enthusiasm as at first. In the published edition there were poetic redundancies omitted in representation which are marked by inverted commas, and in most cases justify their omission; but the author insisted on their appearing in print.

The original cast was as follows :—

CHARLES I.	MR. IRVING
OLIVER CROMWELL	MR. GEORGE BELMORE
MARQUIS OF HUNTLY. . . .	MR. ADDISON
LORD MORAY	MR. E. F. EDGAR
IRETON	MR. R. MARKBY
LADY ELEANOR	MISS G. PAUNCEFORT
AND	
QUEEN HENRIETTE MARIA . .	MISS ISABEL BATEMAN

This was somewhat varied in the representation in 1878, the principal change being the substitution of Miss Ellen Terry for Miss Isabel Bateman. Although it was said that it was almost too spiritual and refined for the footlights, it was a proof its popularity was not confined to the classes, that the pit and gallery were never more crowded than when ' Charles I.' was being played.

The fame it has maintained for twenty-five years stamps it as a century play. It is inevitable that myths should gather round such a work, and some curious stories are told of 'Charles I.,' which, to one who was much with the author at the time, have nothing in his recollections to support them. It has been stated that as the drama was first written it began with the second act and ended with the third; and that on some occasion Mr. Bateman exclaimed 'Bother politics,' and insisted on an opening and closing of domestic interest. But it was the invariable practice of the dramatist—and this was, most probably, the origin of the fable—to begin about the middle of his play, and when he saw distinctly its central idea to throw back a foreshadowing on the commencement. The first act was the key to the interest of the whole play, and it is in the highest degree unlikely that its material was a suggestion of the manager's.

From his earliest writing ('Life's Foreshadowings,' for instance,) Mr. Wills's method was to excite interest by some scene of havened happiness, through which tolls—like a far bell—a boding of ill to come. This system of vague suggestion, of tragedy in embryo lurking in a happy present, was productive of the first act, and it is a pure invention that the play was intended to come into the world without its extremities.

The tradition regarding the last act is probably equally mythical. The story runs that Mr. Bateman, one night, when he was supposed to be napping, suddenly opened his eyes and told the dramatist to go home and read the ending of 'Black-eyed

Susan.' But the germ of the incident, supposed to have been copied, is to be found in history, and it is the material Mr. Wills's imagination would most certainly have assimilated.

Of course, there were consultations at the theatre with the actor and manager; but, in my belief, this story is only the concrete form of somebody's theory.

Certain it is, however, that he wrote the act at one sitting, and a true story is told of his landlady coming into his room and finding him bathed in tears, and being with difficulty persuaded that he was not suffering from some personal bereavement. It may be mentioned that this sensibility was shared by both his parents; but, when in reading a book it caused him emotion, his father was so irritated by the weakness that he would fling the book to the other end of the room or into the fire. The son, in writing, was always moved to tears by pathetic passages, and when, at the end of more than one of the first-night performances, he was seen in a private box, the audience could plainly perceive the traces of his emotion. No writer ever caused so many tears in others; and, for the same reason, his own flowed—because the pathos of his plays came straight from his heart. He did not, like his father, resent being thus moved; for he has told me that it was the test of truth to nature when your composition drew tears.

The criticism that buzzes round the first production of a play has a tendency to fasten on small details, as if a microscope were applied to a picture. What care the public whether Charles called his

I

Queen 'Mary'; whether the guns were fired too
intermittently in the battle of Newark; whether
Cromwell hankered after an earldom ; whether
something that is made to take place between
Charles and his wife at the parting hour, in that
scene which has long been acknowledged to be the
most touching in English drama, should have taken
place between the King and an uninteresting
bishop, or whether the keepsakes should have been
sent by a 'third person'? In turning over old
notices of a play, which has long passed beyond its
probationary state, it is curious to note how such
small points as these, like the mote in the eye,
obscured from some writers' minds the merits of
the drama as a whole. There were those who told
the author the way in which he could have made a
play infinitely finer; how he and another writer
ought to have taken Charles and Cromwell
separately in hand—each doing his best for his own
hero. Others there were who asserted the play
was a mere wisp of unconnected scenes. This
criticism appeared in 'Punch,' and seemed especially to annoy the dramatist. But no history play
can have a closely woven plot ; and he followed the
correct usage of all the great historical dramas of
the French and English schools.

But it was as to its history that 'Charles I.'
provoked the severest criticism. The following
note appeared in the programme :—

The Author feels it unnecessary to confess or enumerate
certain historical inaccuracies, as to period and place, which have
arisen from sheer dramatic necessity, and are justified, he
believes, by the highest precedents.

He is not the first who has asserted the dramatist's irresponsibility as an historian, for Dumas claimed even a more absolute license. My brother has left a defence of his liberties with history in an article which appeared in the April number of the ' Theatre ' in 1880. He asserts that, owing to the want of dramatic art in history as it happens, it would be utterly unsuitable material for the dramatist—except as Sir Walter Scott used it, as a background for imaginary characters and events —unless it is lawful to mould it to his purpose. So long as the common apprehension is not offended by gross and palpable solecism, it is pleased to see likenesses of familiar characters, and not scandalised if they do not correspond with latter-day conceptions. The honest theatre-goer does not care whether it is the white-washed villain or the villain in his original dyes, provided the impersonation is sharp, distinct, and dramatic. The author has only to retain the flavour of fact; for him historical truth would be dramatic falsehood.

The historian is pardoned for his leanings ; is not a stronger bias to be excused in the dramatist, who is, by his trade, a writer of fiction ?

The dramatic canon, he claims, should be to keep within the bounds of popular knowledge, and not to destroy the *vraisemblance* by palpable anachronism or incongruity of facts ; and he cites, as precedents, the following instances of historical inaccuracies : Cardinal Wolsey's disgrace, which is made the pathetic end of a great career, was only temporary ; he lived to hear his King exclaim : ' I would not have you die for twenty

thousand pounds '; Richmond did not kill Richard ;
Macbeth was a good and virtuous king ; and, notwithstanding Schiller's play, Queen Elizabeth
never met the Queen of Scots.

He concludes by asking whether wisdom is not
justified of her children in the fact that a large
audience listens nightly for three hours, without a
stir or a cough, to a blank verse drama with but
little comic relief, and endorses it at the end of
each act with the heartiest applause.

My brother, as I mentioned, in his early
struggling days had an unconfessed attachment.
He was not then in a position to hope it would
be recognised by the family, and the object of
his secret affection died early of consumption.
Ophelia has her eyes and brow, in his picture
founded on the line : ' Here's rosemary—that's for
remembrance ; prithee, love, remember '; and the
following verses, which he wrote on the success of
' Charles I.' when he at last attained the literary
position towards which he had toiled so long, is
headed :

1872.

'Tis come at last, the golden year,
    The day that crowns my days ;
My foes no longer dare to sneer,
    My friends take heart to praise ;
And all is fair, and all is bright,
    As could be wished by me—
I would that one were here to-night,
    That one had lived to see.

And now I sit alone to think,
    Even on a night like this,
Like some parched man who stoops to drink
    Yet pauses in his bliss.

Now dreams of peace upon me break
And nothing troubles me,
Save for this wish, this ceaseless ache,
That she had lived to see.

The rancour of old envy dies,
Old cares I cast aside,
I gaze on men with kindlier eyes
Unwarped by want or pride—
I am aweary of the strife,
And now I will recline
In this sweet shadow of my life,
This blossomed life of mine.

And all is calm, and all is bright,
As could be wished by me ;
But none save I can feel to-night,
And none save I can see—
Oh ! for the smiles that might have been !
Oh ! for her lost delight:
Her love and pride, if she had seen
The glories of to-night !
How one soft word from her to me
This thronèd joy would crown !
The thought she did not live to see,
Strikes all my honours down.

CHAPTER XI.

IDIOSYNCRASIES AS A DRAMATIST.

THE great drama had borne its author to fame, and, for the time being, he stood foremost among contemporary dramatists. Thousands who saw 'Charles I.' carried away the printed edition sold at the theatre doors to study in private; passages from it were recited by high and low, in drawing-rooms and workmen's clubs: and hardly ever did a simple stage play do so much to make its author celebrated. The drawback, however, of such a leap to fame was that he was always expected to keep up to the height he had reached, due allowance not being made for the influence of subject, and the impossibility of systematically writing in crescendo. There was no other subject in history to inspire his pen as did the story of the martyr King, for although he was curiously out of touch with modern politics, he was very strongly imbued, as regards the past, with the old-fashioned Tory faith and the feelings of the Cavalier.

In connection with the sudden attainment of a great literary position, it was characteristic of him that when he became famous he remained un-known. He did not fill his fame with his person-ality; he left the niche he had won in Fame's temple empty. Beyond the Garrick Club he was

a name ; indeed, he elevated it to a principle that
an author should be the unknown quantity of his
works.   He greatly disliked personal publicity, and
one rule that he was inflexible in observing was,
never to appear before the curtain.   The curtain
call originated in France during the last century,
but was not adopted in England until an occasion
when Edmund Kean played Brutus.   Whether
it is dramatically desirable for the actor, who has
just made an heroic end, to relieve the feelings of
the audience by showing himself alive and well,
he at all events is a public character, and is in his
right in doing so.   It is otherwise with the author ;
that, at least, was my brother's strong opinion.
He thought it undignified for an author to bow
and smile at the footlights to gratify the imper-
tinent curiosity of those who want to see what
manner of man has written the play; the actors,
he considered, were the author's visible pre-
sentment.

In addition to believing it undignified to appear
in answer to the call, he thought that the verdict of
a first-night audience was not authoritative or
final.   The author of a play in this country is
much in the position of a culprit who has to
answer for a crime, and it is as absurd for him to
assume that he is acquitted by the clamour of the
theatre, as for a man on his trial, in response to the
applause which follows his advocate's speech, to
bow and simper in the dock.

It is the critics who pronounce the verdict ; and
although their judgment may sometimes be reversed by the public, it is the real verdict for the

time being. An author who accepted a triumph
over-night, and whose work was condemned by the
critics in the morning, would have put himself in a
humiliating position. Besides, the unhappy man
might simply have been decoyed before the curtain
to be hissed at or to encounter a very mixed reception. That the popular verdict is often reversed by
the critics was his own painful experience. There
were indeed times in his career when he became so
discouraged by the persistently adverse criticism
of the press that he made up his mind his next
play should be anonymous. He was very sensitive, and the smart of attacks at last made him
adopt the plan of not reading hostile criticism.
The disadvantage of this was that he deprived
himself of the wholesome lessons to be learned
from it.

It was the same temperament that kept him
away from first-night performances of his plays;
and, just as he never went to see his pictures hung
in exhibitions, so he was hardly ever present himself to share the honours. He usually learned the
result by telegraph or from the newspapers, subject
to a careful censorship, or the report of his friends
next morning. He felt a first night a terrible strain
upon his nerves, and has often told me that the
tension of anxiety was too great. In these days,
when the drama is taken so wickedly in earnest, the
reader who has never produced a play may hardly
be able to realise the ordeal to the man who has.
The author, if he lurks behind the curtains of a
private box, sees, in the stalls below him, the jury
about to sit on his play. All who envy him—

and who does not envy the man whose play is produced ?—are there present.

Their opportunity has come. The wrongs of
many an aspirant to dramatic honours, of men
of talent who have failed to climb the mountains of
inert obstacle to success, would make intolerable the
triumph of the author of the night. There seems to
the anxious mind of the man in the box a spiteful
conspiracy in the general acquaintanceship and
buzz of conversation among the literary people
below.   Here and there he sees a friend looking
grave and sad, as if to give significance to the pre-
vailing spirit of irreverent sprightliness.   The pit
has its wreckers, the gallery its jeering spirits, who
are quick to catch the unlucky line for an inop-
portune laugh.   Only in the dress and upper circles
are the good kind people.   Presently the strains of
the orchestra send a thrill through the unhappy
man ; they are his fate's prelude.   A hush falls on
the house as the curtain goes up at last.   The
charge is being rammed home in the first act.   At
its conclusion the door of the box opens, and a
friend enters to assure him that the piece is going
well and strongly.   The author is for a few minutes
released, but so is the jury.   The conspiracy
deepens.   Little knots collect at the bars, to whom
some person, haply the manager of a rival theatre,
holds forth.   It is tampering with the jury, a clear
case of undue influence ; there is silence as the
author and his friend approach ; he has a strong
feeling that the critical jury ought to be locked up
between the acts.   The critics settle down again for
the second act, which is the aim-taking of the play.

The visiting friend assures him all, so far, is as right as possible. Will the third act be equally strong ?— there is a tone of scepticism in the question. Up to this point the mind of the house is completely open. The third act speeds the bolt—it strikes the mark or miserably fails. When this is finished the author knows the verdict, for the fourth act is but the result of the impact. Nothing remains but the shouting—the dissentient voices are seldom absent; the author hears it announced that he has left the house, but that the good news will be conveyed to him by telegraph. The public give their verdict to-night, but the critics to-morrow; this may reverse the verdict of the audience. There is a night's suspense to be borne. Perhaps the author and his friends may sit up and wait for the papers. In the grey dawn the manager begins to receive slips; they are, of course, complimentary notices which are thus sent in advance. The ordeal of trial by the press lasts for days, from the dailies to the weeklies. No criminal has harder things said of him than the playwright. His position is worse than the pillory if he should have written a bad play. For all these reasons—the dignity of authorship, the incompleteness of a first-night verdict, and the tension of nerves involved—my brother, as a general rule, absented himself. But the manager's statement that Mr. Wills was not in the house was seldom accepted as literally true, and his non-appearance was sometimes resented. The calls would continue until his friends began to feel disconcerted, but it came to be understood at last that under no circumstances would he be tempted to step out of the author's rightful privacy.

His method of working when left to himself was as unmethodical as could be. Like Pope, he wrote on backs of envelopes or any scrap of paper handy. These, fastened together, would be flung into a wicker basket, and sorted out and arranged, like a puzzle, when a play was to be completed. Or he would write here and there in sketch-books, beginning at both ends, and then in the middle, and interspersing his notes among studies of limbs or leaves. As a result, he naturally suffered much from the disorder of his materials and mislaying of manuscripts. A friend of his tells how he unearthed once, from an old box that served the purpose of a dustbin, three acts and part of a fourth of a play called 'Merry and Wise,' since his death completed under another name. When shown to the author he was greatly delighted at the find, and exclaimed, ' My dear fellow, you have done me the greatest service in the world. This is one of the best plays I ever wrote, and I thought I had lost it years ago.' He went to work at five in the morning, like Victor Hugo, and he smoked all day, like Tennyson. After twelve in the day he would seldom do any writing, but would adjourn to his studio and paint till dusk. He never began at the beginning. He liked to get the most difficult scenes done first. He rarely corrected his work, and would never, if left to himself, rewrite any portion of it, as Mr. Herman, his collaborateur in ' Claudian,' insisted on his doing. His best work was done at the first intention, and with great rapidity ;

but his most slovenly work would also pass without revision. He had not that practical knowledge of the stage which Herman possessed in such a superlative degree, and his stage directions were few and far between. He imagined the action of his characters, and left it to the imagination of the actors. He disliked realism, and saw everything through the veil of poetry. He was impatient of being asked to make alterations, and he took no pains to see his work was properly interpreted. It was gall and wormwood to him to have to go over the same ground twice, and he washed his hands of his work as soon as he could. If he were much pressed to finish, when he did not feel the inclination, he laid a play aside or else wrote it badly. His good work was done by inspiration, not by mechanical labour and pen-polishing, although he brooded over his subject and realised his characters in his own mind until they surrounded him as creatures of flesh and blood; then they began to speak and act. He had a contempt for the help obtained by much reading, and all the materials he set to work with were a pencil and paper.

I think it was a result of the discomfort in which he lived that, from the time he had to work on his plays many hours in the day, he took to writing almost entirely in bed. This custom naturally spoiled his athletic powers, and helped to age him prematurely. But if he lost one kind of activity he gained the activity of thought which results from freedom from bodily tension. The relaxation of the muscular system takes the balance off and gives greater play to the mental; and in most people, not habituated to working under these conditions, it gives, as a subsequent result, an overwrought and strained feeling to the mind. This is quite distinct from the state when the mind is awake and the body asleep, in the short hour between waking and getting up in which happy inspirations come spontaneously. But writing in bed with muscles relaxed produces the feeling of exhausted nerve power. To him, however, it became a second nature. Indeed, except when he was making a clean copy of a play, I can hardly picture him to myself writing at a desk or table, and when he did it suggested an idea of discomfort, and was so unlike his habit that one felt distressed for him.

One consequence of the practice was that he soon found the convenience of having an amanuensis, to whom he dictated as fast as the pen in longhand could conveniently follow his thoughts. A man named Russell first acted in this capacity ; but afterwards a young dramatic aspirant became his secretary, and as my brother had learned from West-land Marston, so he learned from my brother the dramatic art and imbibed some of the characteristic feeling of his mind. The younger playwright was always ready to volunteer an opinion, and dispute the ground which he took up inch by inch. If my brother was made very savage by objections and aggravating criticisms, he has told me that it roused him to strong writing. A shade of mortification on his scribe's face when he was doing exceedingly well would make him secretly triumph, and dictate with increasing vigour and success. If the face of his amanuensis, on the contrary, cleared, he became depressed, and felt he was doing but in-differently well. This is too characteristic to omit; but I ought in fairness to say that this dramatic apprentice was my brother's very sincere friend; and that, except when he was beaten down and over-borne in argument—in which, when composing, my brother was intolerant and even violent—he would have been loyally delighted when his friend was in the vein. I can well understand, however, a certain mortification when, after being crushed, something very strong, delivered in vehement tones, seemed to add to his defeat. On the other hand, it was only human to feel complacency when his criticisms seemed justified by feebleness setting in.

One of my brother's idiosyncrasies as a dra-matist was the help which he received from music. It seemed to lend wings to his thought. He had a large musical-box which played a number of operatic airs, and he used to wind it up and write to its strains. In course of time, however, from being made the receptacle of hair-brushes and combs, and other odds and ends, it became disabled, and when it fell into my possession, all its teeth were gone ; but it now grinds out, as of old, ' Trovatore ' and ' Lucia.'

If the habit of writing in bed was the result, as I think, of the outside discomfort of the studio, it was, on the other hand, curious how he could abstract himself from a crowd, and actually found a flood of human beings about him helpful to composition. He would take a note-book to South Kensington Museum, or sit on the pier at Brighton, completely undisturbed by promenaders, or the public entertainers of the motley scene on the front, bodily present, but mentally caught up into a world of imagination. He was sub-consciously stimulated by the teeming life around him, but no more disturbed or distracted by it than by the sounds and sights of nature. When alone he grew restless, and could not settle down to his work. He wanted company, but such as would not disturb the surface of reflection, or break up its pictures into wavering fragments by trivial interruptions. He liked to be let alone—not left alone. If spoken to when thus enthralled by the scenes of his imagination, he would come out of his thoughts with a disagreeable effort, and answer at random, with evident preoccupation, but never-failing courtesy.

There was one other very congenial medium, not for writing, but for thinking out his plays, and that was a warm bath. He found this close to the studio in Fulham Road, and he was a constant patron of it; indeed it was there that he purchased his large musical-box, having experienced the pleasing effect of its accompaniment to his thoughts while luxuriously enjoying the plash of the water. From the fact that, in his absence of mind, he habitually smeared his face and bald head over with paint and charcoal, legends arose which might discredit this. Vezin once came in and begged him to allow him to illustrate the state he was in by washing the paint off half his face and head, whereupon he presented the semi-eclipsed appearance of the portrait in a picture-cleaner's window; but his habits were quite those of the present generation with regard to the tub.

CHAPTER XII.

OTHER LYCEUM PLAYS UNDER THE BATEMAN MANAGEMENT.

Mr. Irving's triumph in the character of Matthias, the Jew, suggested as a subject lending itself to a similar success the remorse of Eugene Aram.

In reciting Hood's ballad, the actor had always scored, and my brother's morbid genius was peculiarly fitted to forge a powerful drama from such a subject. Purists were forearmed with the objection that it would enlist sympathy for a criminal; but as a vivid picture of the tortures of remorse the drama was little open to objection on ethical grounds. From the first appearance of the haunted man in the old-fashioned vicarage garden it is obvious that his happiness is his misery and his misery is the only alleviation of his remorse. This, surely, is good morality.

Left to himself the author would have distributed the parts more equally, and the play would not have been so much of a monologue as it was. But he was rigidly kept to his theme—the remorse of Eugene Aram—and the gloomy figure of the schoolmaster dominates every scene. There are but four characters, exclusive of a servant and a child, and the action is compressed within the narrow compass of afternoon to dawn. Notwithstanding this, the play develops with inexorable sequence of plot and mental processes. There is not an imperfect or broken link or a weak line in the whole of it.

It was written for the most part at Brighton. Never was he so well fit for work as when away from London ; and in those days Brighton was his favourite resort. It took little to tempt him to its wide horizon and wholesome breezes ; and if a friend suddenly sprang upon him the suggestion (otherwise the *vis inertiæ* would prevail), he would take wing at an hour's notice, unimpeded by packing up and unencumbered by luggage. While engaged on ' Eugene Aram ' at Sydney Street, his friend Mr. W. L. Woodroffe called at his rooms and found he was not getting on with the play. He proposed Brighton, and my brother cheerfully welcomed the proposal ; but when the shirt, brush and comb, and manuscript were wrapt up in the morning's newspaper, a curious difficulty stood in the way. He found that he could not go because his landlady's spritish little daughter had mischievously hidden his wig. A short time before he explained to his friend, when he had mislaid an important manuscript, he offered for its recovery a reward of a guinea. The guinea was easily earned by the little girl ; but one thing after another began to disappear in turn, and to be thus held to ransom, and, at last, even his simplicity saw through the young brigand's plan, and he declined to offer any more rewards. Then, to compel him to offer another guinea, she hit upon the fiendish

K

stratagem of abstracting his wig, in which, like Samson's locks, resided his power to come or go. At times, however, he could be rather dogged, and, after two or three days' imprisonment in the house, his baldness covered by a skull cap, the girl was afraid her mother's intervention would be called in, and she restored the wig. Its owner immediately started for Brighton, where, as usual, he put up at the 'Old Ship Hotel,' the landlord of which always took the greatest care of him.

As was his wont, he made the story of Eugene Aram open with a scene of peaceful happiness. In the old-fashioned garden of the Vicarage the schoolmaster keeps tryst with Parson Meadows's daughter Ruth, to whom he is to be married the next day. She tries in vain to steal from him the secret of his melancholy; but a stranger has appeared upon the scene, who, on the plea of looking for stalactites in St. Robert's Cave, has borrowed a spade and pickaxe, and now in the evening returns at the Vicar's hospitable invitation, and suggests suspicion to Ruth that her lover's heart is not a virgin page, and that a love-secret is at the root of his melancholy. Aram confesses to her that he did love a woman long dead, but it was a boyish and unhappy passion. He then encounters the stranger, who turns out to be a man named Coleman, a witness of the unpremeditated blow with which Aram killed the man who had seduced and deserted his first love. Coleman has been digging in the cave where the murdered man was buried, in the hope of finding some loose guineas buried with the body, and the gardener who lent him the implements, suspecting a search for treasure, has followed. The skeleton is unearthed, giving dumb evidence of murder with its cleft skull. Eugene Aram has borne himself bravely up to this with Coleman and resisted the effort to blackmail him—the most dramatic scene in the whole play—but on the discovery being reported, and being called upon to view the body, his abject terror excites surprise and suspicion. He feels already as if a sort of day of judgment light were beating upon and revealing his guilt, and he cannot face that grisly witness. He is found in the churchyard in a dying condition by Ruth Meadows, lying among the tombstones, under the old yew-tree. In a pathetic scene he confesses to her his guilt, and her womanly pardon and pity at last seem to make a higher forgiveness credible. The palsied anguish is succeeded by a sigh of relief—

RUTH: Oh! with that sigh, the demon left your heart.
That moment from a legion lips of angels
Was murmured the word Pardon.

ARAM: Put my hair from my eyes; I cannot see you, love.

RUTH: There's nothing there; can you not see me?
You are worn and weary, but you are not ill.

ARAM (*trying to rise*): No, no, I am at peace.
Come in—together we will see your father.
Come in! the early cold strikes to my heart.   [*He falls back.*

RUTH (*watching him*): Your face seems altered! why do
    you smile?

ARAM: Oh Ruth! I shall not die a death of shame.

RUTH: No, you shall live.

ARAM (*shakes his head with a sad smile*): My hair—push it
    aside- I see you faintly.

RUTH: What change is this? Oh love, there steals a
    pallor
Across your cheek.

ARAM :   It is the dew.

RUTH : Why is your voice so hollow ? Still that phantom
      smile !
What is it, love ? Your fingers loose. Oh, you are dying !

    ARAM : No dying—no, my youth is back again.
Keep your eyes fixed on me, and do not fear.

    RUTH : What, what is this ? I see within your eyes
My mother's look -- the last farewell.

    ARAM : Oh love ! we will not breathe the word farewell.
Hush !   [*Faint music in the church.*

    RUTH : It is the morning choir—Oh ! try to rise—
I'll help you—we must think of your escape.

    ARAM : Oh Ruth, the gate is open—I am gone !

    RUTH : Oh God - his smile is fading !

    ARAM :   I would find
My burial in your arms—upon your lips
My only epitaph—and in your eyes
My first faint glimpse of heaven.

As Aram dies the music in the church peals
out, and morning, which has been breaking, strikes
with level beams under the great yew-tree, and
sheds a wan redness round the church, awaking
the matin song.

The play was again a triumph of tears. The
critic, preparing a savage attack upon the author,
dashed away the drops surprised by the morning
light diffused from the stage, and ladies openly
sobbed. Mr. Irving had more than fulfilled the
expectation of his being ideally great in the part of
the unhappy schoolmaster.

As usual to the loud calls for the author the
response was that he had left the house, but that
the manager would convey to him the favourable
verdict of the audience.

Of course my brother showed in this play his
wonted independence of fact. The murderer was

in reality hanged, and the crime was without the extenuating circumstances with which his pen invested it.

The Bateman management was now drawing to a close, but one more play my brother was to write in his capacity of dramatist of the Lyceum. It was called after the captain of the 'Phantom Ship,' Vanderdecken. The story of Vanderdecken originated about the time of the discovery of America. The name of the ship in which the mariner endeavoured to round the Cape of Good Hope, in the teeth of a tremendous hurricane, was 'The Flying Dutchman' of Amsterdam. His reply to a passing ship which inquired if he meant to shelter in the bay was, 'No, may I be eternally damned if I do, though I should beat about here until the day of judgment.' The impious mariner was taken at his word, and whenever a storm blows round the Cape, the blood-red sails of the 'Flying Dutchman' may still be seen striving to double the mist-wreathed headland. Heine invented the idea, when on a visit to London he saw FitzBall's drama founded on this legend, of the redemption of the obstinate Dutchman by a woman's love. Wagner says that the story, recalling the swamps and floods of his own life, was the first legendary poem that attracted him and impelled him to give it meaning and form in music. Vanderdecken is the embodiment of the universal yearning for rest in the troubled waters of life.

It was the opera that suggested Vanderdecken as a character suited to Mr. Irving, with his

wondrous gift of realising such weird and haunted
existences as the Jew in the 'Bells' or the
Schoolmaster in the 'Remorse of Eugene Aram.'
Mr. Percy Fitzgerald proposed and Mr. Irving was
irresistibly attracted to the subject. FitzBall's
hero was a devil's bond, a grim spectre who took
up ordinary humanity to make victims of his
wives. The Spectre returned to his master unre-
deemed, and the play has been described as 'a
thing of horror and blue fire,' produced in rivalry of
the fables of Frankenstein and 'Der Freischütz.'
Captain Marryat founded on the legend his novel
of the 'Phantom Ship,' and relieves the unhappy captain from his doom by the action of an
amulet.

The objection to the subject was inevitable to
a one-part play: it was the cheapening of the
supernatural element by bringing the mysterious
hero too much upon the stage. As to the merit of
the work, the beauty of the poetry was admitted by
all critics, but on its acting merits there were considerable differences of opinion.

Mr. Irving was as picturesque in the character
as the author expected he would be, and acted
with all his own intensity and gift of oratory; and
in the part of the old Norwegian pilot Nils—
whom Heine made a Scotchman—Mr. Fernandez
gave a most effective rendering. The fact that it
may one day be revised and revived makes it worth
while giving a brief outline of this strong and
admirably written play. There is a storm gathering up on the Christiania Fjord, but the neighbours
are met together in the snug cottage of the old

pilot Nils, to discuss the betrothal of his daughter
Thekla to the young sailor Olaf. We gather from
their conversation that she is a strange, dreaming
girl, and seems unconscious of her good fortune
in winning the heart of the bravest sailor on the
coast. Thekla has been brought up in the super-
stition and imaginativeness of a world-lonely shore,
where fancies linger among the sea-folk which have
long died out in the busy towns. An old picture
found in a ruin is connected with a legend of the
Fjord, and the face looking out from the canvas
has gained a strong hold over the girl's imagination. Her appearance, which was well realised by
Miss Isabel Bateman, has a wild haunted look,
and though she submits to the caresses of her
lover, it is evident that she is lost in some dreamy
maze. But when, in the rising storm, the conversation turns on the Flying Dutchman, and
her father asks her to recite the ballad, she obeys
with a strange excitement, and her figure sways
to the music like a willow in the wind ; and it is
evident that Vanderdecken, the hero of the ballad,
believed to be the original of the picture, is the
dream-lover to whom she has given her heart.
The ballad tells the story thus :—

> 'Tis a hundred years ago almost,
>   And never I ween since then
> Blew such a gale from the Norway coast,
>   To the peril of brave seamen.

> A ship stood boldly out to sea,
>   Her captain watched her sail ;
> 'I'll round the Jut to-night,' said he,
>   'Though the Devil be in the gale.'

He tacked and wore off the Norway shore,
　But never a knot made he ;
I'll round yon white headland to-night,
　Or curses fall on me.

The wind and the vessel did groan and wrestle,
　Her sails were took aback,
The seas o'erwhelm her sunken helm
　And blacken her frothy track.

'Oh ! turn again,' said the pale seamen,
　'And tempt the gale no more,'
But he clenched his hand at the dim headland,
　And an impious oath he swore.

'I'll tack and wear till my masts are bare,
　Nor hold a sheet or stay ;
Heaven hath no power to change my course,
　Though I sail to the Judgment Day.'

A crash was heard at the impious word—
　Heaven opened overhead ;
A gleam of blood shot through the scud,
　And dyed the sea blood-red.

'Thy doom is spoke,' a voice out-broke
　From the rift with a thunder note,
'Thou shalt sail for aye to the Judgment Day,
　A terror to all afloat.

'A wondrous curse in the universe
　For ages, till thou shalt win
That woman's love who shall steadfast prove,
　And give her life for your sin.'

The sky grew dark.　Lo ! a blood-red bark,
　Her sail the ghastly same,
Like a fiery scull her gleaming hull,
　And her spars like ribs of flame.

And her captain there, in the dismal glare,
    And paler than tongue can tell,
With clenchéd hand, as in mute command,
    And eyes like a soul's in hell,

A wonder and curse in the universe—
    Ah! where does that woman draw breath,
Who shall lift the ban from this hapless man
    And be faithful unto death.

This ballad, full of its author's simple power, was admirably recited by Miss Bateman. The meeting of neighbours is broken by a ship in distress being seen in the distance, and Nils is summoned to its assistance. Thekla, left with her nurse, sees out at sea the blood-red sails of the Phantom Ship, and the prologue ends with the return of the sailors and the excited discussion of the mysterious craft.

A ship lies besides the quay, and from behind its lifted sail Vanderdecken steps ashore and answers the curious questions of the fishermen. He accepts the invitation of old Nils to visit his cottage, and then we are made aware, in a passage of rare beauty, that the captain of the Phantom Ship, his time having come, as it does every seven years, to revisit the earth, is seeking the woman fated to cut the thread of doom and save him from an eternity of waiting. 'Where is this woman ordained for my release? What mien—what stature, of what form is she? Whence will she come? Comes she to-night? A hundred years' repentance for one brief moment's sin! How long, oh God, how long!' is the wail of the soul that haunts the sea; and the following lines conclude the rhapsody with which the released spirit

once more in one of those recurrent hours of hope
that ray eternity, revisits the mortal scene :—

> I go to meet her in a trance!
> My senses are so dulled with sorrow ;
> Sleeping without the rest, but with the dreams,
> A dead man with the consciousness of death !

The growth of Vanderdecken's influence over
Thekla, the while the human love, sustained by
the foresight of which he has lived a hundred
years, and the love born of dreams, are woven into
one another, is gradual but sure. Out of an infinite distance of space, drawn as it were by some
attraction which has been bringing them together,
they have met at last ; and all the world and its
duties and ties become the dream, as the dream to
Thekla becomes a reality. The luring promises
with which the being but half of earth tempts the
woman half-absorbed in the supernatural world to
follow him are written with weird fancy:—

> Dost thou see yonder where I point my finger—nor'ward ?
> A region lies untrod by foot of man,
> And nigh the Pole ; and mighty, vast, and bright
> As the Archangels guarding Heaven's portal,
> Float icebergs radiant with rainbow glories !
> And here and there above the sea, from point to point,
> Shine emerald caverns—diamond lustres, large as suns.
> At night all turns to opal, and the stars
> In frosty splendour seem to crown the bergs,
> Whilst the Aurora flits and dances up
> The silent ecstasy of Arctic night,
> That halo of the Pole !
>
> Wouldest thou go with me ! South'ard look—
> Yonder the tropics lie—the seas a realm
> Of heaving sapphire, and the skies a mimic heaven.
> And yonder are the lands, untracked by man,

But Nature's lavished hoard of all things beautiful
And reverend. The trees
Crypts of dim verdure of such shadowy growth,
That one alone could tent thy native village.
Bright birds be-jewel them by day ; beneath at night
The fire-flies spin their webs in starry circles ;
And for their flower the great Magnolia opes
Its alabaster portals shedding
A lake of perfume for a league around ;
And rivers silver-broad, inlaid with ivory lilies,
Glide silent 'neath the palms and tamarinds ;
But poison is in the beauty, death in loveliest guise.

The rivalry between the ghost-lover and the
flesh and blood one, Olaf, ends in a struggle in
which they fight on the wild cliff, first with swords
and then with daggers, and in a deadly grapple
on the brow, Vanderdecken is flung over into
the sea.

But death has no power over him, and he is
borne in the arms of the waves and laid upon the
shore unhurt; and then comes the last scene in
which Thekla carried to the Phantom Ship, and
awakened from her trance, has the secret of her
lover's existence disclosed to her, and the alternative of its prolongation to the Judgment, or its
being consigned to rest by the sacrifice of a woman's
love.

What is my doom ?
Worse than in Hell !   Eternal loneliness !
Eternal silence ! and in that awful silence
The worm of memory gnawing at my heart,
Anguish of thought within my brain, sleepless, intense,
Just hope enough to keep despair awake !
Around me forests of gigantic weeds
Weaving and writhing—
As if the skeletons which people them
But lie dead still, did move them.

Vast ribs of ships, and ribs of monstrous fish
Which look like wrecks ! Tall peaks of coral
Rising like pale cathedrals richly carved,
But where no bell is heard
Or murmuring of prayer to comfort me !
Ships I have seen go down—their crews,
Grasping the shrouds with bony hands,
Or, hanging o'er the bulwarks, nod at me
In their dead eyes silent upbraiding.
Strange things move by with noiseless crawl
And lift their goblin heads to look at me.
Around my phantom ship long shadows lie—
The sharks, ghouls of the sea,
Watch me with gloomy hungry eyes, knowing their caterer ;
For when the hurricane is loosed above,
Crushing the sea to angry white, and sails
Fly from their bolts and coward seamen quail,
Then do I move upon my phantom deck,
Tranced at the helm, fatal decoy to wreck
And to disaster.
Before me seems to stretch a dreary headland,
Beyond it a fixed dawn that never grows to day :
But 'neath the dappled cloud one spring of light
Shapes to thy angel face like a sweet veiled Madonna.
A fluttering hand then seems to beckon me ;
I strive to round the point, but beat about
In vain ! In vain !

Then the red frenzy rises in my brain,
Wild curses to my lips, and in the thunder
Sounds that do curse again shriek out—
'Sail on ! Sail on !' until the Judgment Day,
'Unless that woman come !'

Thekla, undaunted, makes her choice—she goes
on board the ship, built in the eclipse and rigged
with curses deep. Vanderdecken's shadowy company dissolve, and the lovers are left alone with
the stars on which they gaze in faith ; and on the
night-air comes the whisper, ' Pardon '—

>The wind a melody,
>Is laden with the murmur of God's pity.

Thus falls the curtain: and both the pictur-
esqueness of the drama and its literary merits
ought to have insured success; but the setting
was unworthy of the gem it enclosed, and the
play produced on July 8, 1878, did not run a long
course.   Its mere gloom, relieved by adequate
scenery and the splendid realism for which it
affords every opportunity, would not have pre-
vented the public from going to see it; but it
was poorly mounted, and the picture, unveiled
with the intention of great effect, proved to be
a daub, at which there arose irreverent titters.
'The ship was lost for a ha'porth of tar' was
the writer's comment. A sultry August emptied
the theatre, and 'Vanderdecken' was shortly withdrawn.

Of this play, Mr. Percy FitzGerald did the construction, but 'The Dramatist of the Lyceum' did
the bulk of the writing, including all Mr. Irving's
and Miss Bateman's parts.

It was the last play under the Bateman
management; and the agreement by which Mr.
Wills was connected with the Lyceum Theatre
came to an end. During the preparation of the
drama, Mr. Bateman, familiarly known as the
'Colonel,' had passed away, and Mrs. Bateman
became the manageress; but, on transferring the
theatre to Mr. Irving, she moved to a restored
Sadler's Wells.

It may be interesting to state that Mr. A. W.
Pinero played a small part in 'Vanderdecken.'

The following is his recollection of the play and its author :—

My share in the production of ' Vanderdecken' was a very unimportant one. I spoke a few lines and helped to swell the chorus of voices which chanted occasionally on the stage. I recall that the piece was acted in the course of a broiling summer, and that the character I played demanded that I should be heavily clad. My sufferings in this respect are my chief recollection of ' Vanderdecken.' Your brother, I think, attended no rehearsal, at any rate I did not see him in the theatre. It was at the Garrick Club that I used to meet W. G. Wills. He often asked me to go to his studio, but, to my regret now, I never visited him. I remember him as one who appeared to be full of kindness, and utterly without envy of other men's successes.

No man was more to be envied as a dramatist than Mr. Pinero himself, both for the excellence of his work, and for the large sums he received for it, and his testimony to my brother's freedom from the besetting sin of authorship is therefore valuable.

He was a warm admirer of ' Charles I.,' and used to recite some of its most eloquent and touching passages. Meeting the author one day at the Garrick, he said, ' My plays have been pretty successful, but I would barter them all to have written one of your masterpieces.' ' Very well,' said my brother, ' I'll call up old Nick and we'll sign the contract at once '; in telling the story he added pathetically, ' Pinero then left me.'

CHAPTER XIII.

OTHER HISTORY PLAYS AND LESSER DRAMATIC WORKS.

W. G. WILLS never carried on a regular correspondence with anyone but his mother. She,
however, had bundles of letters from him extending
over all his London life. They would have presented him in the most amiable light, and told
in his own words all that was of interest in his
literary, artistic, and dramatic career. But when
his mother died they were by his direction burned.
Their destruction was a great loss to his biographer,
as he probably intended it to be, for he disliked
publicity, especially of his feelings. In his letters
they were strongly expressed. It follows that in
the years succeeding his great dramatic success,
when he told her everything about himself that
would give her pleasure, there is little material left
for personal biography. All that his friends can
sift from their recollections relates to his plays,
commissions to write them, their production and
fortunes. They agree in one thing, that he was a
man of unbounded loveableness, overflowing with
the milk of human kindness, and not merely
incapable of making an enemy, but one nobody
that knew him could help loving. 'You are the
kindest-hearted, but dufferedest-hearted creature

alive,' wrote his cousin Major C——, who had
taken a fancy to the oval mirror, which I have
before mentioned, and was at once offered it as a
gift, but luckily found out that the owner had a
great regard for it, owing to certain associations,
although pretending it was valueless. But he
lived surrounded by persons who had no such com-
punctions, in a normal state of invasion and an
occasional state of siege. The big folding double
doors at the back of his studio admitted his
friendly visitors, and the gimlet holes in the front
reconnoitred his foes. He did a wonderful amount
of work in his time. Commissions for plays poured
in upon him at such a rate, and he accepted them
on such inadequate terms, that he was obliged
to take more than he could write with any credit
to himself. He never seemed to remember that
he was no longer the obscure literary man of
Clifford's Inn, and he would write a play for one
or two hundred pounds down, with prospective
royalties which were not always realised. Other
dramatic authors complained of his doing injury
to their craft by not exacting higher terms. There
were some of his friends too, who thought that he
ought to have realised enough by his best plays, to
put him above the need of overwriting himself and
undertaking adaptations and work of an unambitious order for the sake of a little ready money ;
but he did not think so himself. Indeed, his pen
was as little mercenary as could be the pen of any
man who had to live by it. He was full of gratitude
where his friends thought the sentiment misplaced.
He argued that there was but little demand for the

poetical drama, and the number of theatres where it was in request was limited ; but it was urged on the other side, there was an equally limited supply. He would answer with the strong emphasis he employed when his feelings were aroused : '. . . . . is a dear friend of mine—he is the most generous of men. Nothing would induce me to ask for more than he offers.'

He fully believed what he said, and allowed such bargains to be rather one-sided. I am sure, however, considering this, that he was very honourably dealt with, for the sums paid him were intrinsically large, and might, but for the sense of justice of those who were thus left to name their own terms, have been considerably less. But without the slightest reflection on anyone, I would say that he might have done better work if he had been better paid, for his work would not have become a drudgery. It was a congenial task to him to write poetical drama, but he could not afford to refuse distasteful commissions. In the course of twenty years he wrote thirty-two dramas, for which, according to his own computation, he received about 12,000l. As much has been realised by a single play in modern times. If he had been as fertile in inventing plots as he was facile in writing plays, so much was his pen in request, he would have surpassed all dramatists in the number he produced. But he had this limitation. He possessed the gift of imagination and the constructive faculty, but was less endowed with the power of inventing dramatic germs. His own germs generally grew into something cross-legged

L

or with a wry neck, or some congenital defect; he did better when he wrote, like the old dramatists, from a story or legend, or was indebted to the manager for a plot.

W. G. Wills, being now freed from his engagement as dramatist of the Lyceum Theatre, actors and actresses who had any respect for themselves wanted a play by the author of ' Charles I.' History plays had been for the time rehabilitated, and among others ' The Beautiful Mrs. Rousby,' as she was called, who had made a favourable impression in Taylor's ' Twixt Axe and Crown,' asked him to write one on the subject of ' The Queen o' Scots.' With Mary for Charles and John Knox for Cromwell, the dramatic material was evidently of inferior quality ; but still he contrived out of it a play full of his own charming and characteristic poetry and sentiment. The acting, however, ruined it.   Mrs. Rousby brought ·to it nothing but her good looks, and the delivery of her lines was for the most part inaudible. When audible, it was expressionless. Her husband made the drollest little character of the gaunt reformer, John Knox, and Mr. Harcourt was quite unsuited to represent Chastelard, the hero of the piece.   It was the illness of this actor that led to Mr. Forbes Robertson's introduction to the stage. The idea suddenly occurred to my brother on meeting him in the street that he was cast by nature for the poet-lover, and on the spot he proposed to him to step into the part.   With only two days' study he did so with striking success, and became the redeeming feature of the piece.

This play, like 'Charles I.,' was charged with libel. Admirers of John Knox were very wroth with its author for representing the stern reformer as brought under the glamour of Mary's beauty. Poor Mr. Rousby's personality and attempts to assume a Scotch accent, lapsing into the dialect of Yorkshire and other counties, aggravated the offence, and reduced the delineation to the broadest farce. The drama covered a more sympathetic period of Mary's life than Schiller's, and might well have raised its author's fame, if he had not made the mistake of intrusting his work to incompetent hands.

Mr. Henry Neville, for whom the next of his History plays was written, certainly could not come under this description, but yet in 'Buckingham,' produced at the Olympic in 1875, he failed entirely to realise the complex character of the madcap duke. The reckless cavalier, who could jest on a powder magazine, became in his hands the dignified counterpart of 'Charles I.,' and the outrageous daring, the mountebank buffoonery, the zest for intrigues and the unquenchable wit, sat as unnaturally on Mr. Neville's 'Duke,' as they would have done on Mr. Irving's 'Martyr-king.' Without bringing to a focus the two Buckinghams that possessed the one man, the character in the play seemed incredible; and in addition to Mr. Neville's failure to accomplish the feat of combining them naturally, the rest of the cast was of the weakest kind, and the play with all its power and intensity, with its skilful characterisation and its fine historical picture of the times, was never given a fair chance. Yet it was no unworthy sequel to 'Charles I.,' and was thought by the best judges to be in some respects superior to that play.

'Jane Shore' followed 'Buckingham' in the series of History plays. Like 'Ninon,' it was written without a commission, and lay on the shelf for years, as such plays generally do. Later on, the dramatist never wrote on speculation; but when he first took up the project of writing a historical series, the story of Edward IV.'s mistress presented a fresh subject. Rowe's play, in which, at the beginning of the century, Mrs. Siddons had shown her marvellous powers, possessed little (if any) literary merit, and my brother made no use whatever of it. Shakespeare passed by the episode, not introducing Jane, though naming her in the charge of witchcraft Richard brings against Queen Elizabeth. Her chequered career, her praise and blame, made Edward's favourite a subject after the dramatist's own heart. Sir Thomas More wrote of her, 'Many the king had, but her he loved, whose favour (for sin it were to belie the devil) she never abused to any man's hurt, but to many men's comfort and relief; and now she beggeth of many a man this day living, that at this day had begged if she had not been.'

After the dust had lain upon it for many a long year a tentative offer came. Miss Wallis proposed to produce it for her benefit. My brother mentioned this circumstance to Mr. Wilson Barrett, who called at the studio in Fulham Road, and he asked to be allowed to show it to his wife, professionally known as Miss Heath. She was a person of the greatest intelligence and discrimination, and held the honorary office at Court of the Queen's reader. She discerned at once the great qualities of the drama, and an agreement was entered into which resulted in its production at the Amphitheatre, Leeds, in March 1875, under Mr. Wilson Barrett's management. It was enthusiastically received, and ran a course of great success in the provinces ; and it was produced in London on September 30, 1876, at the Princess's Theatre, then under the management of Mr. F. B. Chatterton. The audience gave it a great reception, but the critics a cold one. They had reason, however, as time went on, to modify their first impressions. These are often influenced by transient causes, and when at a later date Mr. Wilson Barrett put the play on at the Princess's, intending it as a stop gap for a month, it had such a phenomenal success that it ran for an entire year. Its run was a record for a historical and poetic drama. A leading critic (' Times,' October 4, 1876) said, on its first production, ' A play in five acts, and in blank verse, on so gloomy, albeit if Mr. Wills pleases, dramatic a subject, must be a very good play indeed to please an audience of our day.'

It stood this test triumphantly, and vindicated itself as a ' very good play indeed.' In recognition of its success Mr. Wilson Barrett, although he had bought it out, always paid royalties to my brother whenever it was played in London. The success of the author was due to the fact that he was

really affected by the sorrows of his luckless
heroine. He used to say the secret of playwriting
was to get inside the ribs of your character, and he
knew that what was coined from his own heart
would reach the heart of others. The great scene of
the play was that at Old Charing Cross, where the
falling snow is spreading a white sheet of penance
over London, and the unhappy woman is driven
starving through the streets by Richard's agents.
Here the situation is so heartrending, and the sympathy of the audience is so powerfully excited, it
often occurred that individuals in the audience,
especially women, uttered cries of indignation,
such as 'Oh, you villains!' and could they have
reached the stage it would have fared ill with
Gloster's 'minions.'

A year divided the London production of these
two plays—'Buckingham' and 'Jane Shore'—and
in another, there followed ' England in the Days of
Charles II.,' an adaptation for Drury Lane of Scott's
' Peveril of the Peak.' As a framework for
pageantry rather than a literary drama was needed
at Drury Lane, my brother was not so well fitted
for its construction as a practical playwright of
Mr. Andrew Halliday's ability had been ; and
although it was received with acclamation by the
first night audience, the critics would not accept
such a work from the author of ' Charles I.'

As an illustration of the merry monarch's
reign ' Nell Gwynne ' did more justice to the
author's talents. The dialogue was sparkling, and
the madcap heroine is invested with the sympathy
to which, in spite of her failings, her goodness of

heart entitled her.   The piece was produced at the
Royalty Theatre by Miss Fowler, who thoroughly
grasped the character of Nell, and played it with
archness and artistic feeling.

The last of the History plays with which my
brother's name was associated was 'Sedgmoor,'
a drama written for Miss Marriott, formerly
manageress of Sadler's Wells Theatre.   Owing to
his engagements at the time, the play was en-
trusted to the writer of this memoir, but the
historical outline suggested contained material for
more than one drama ; and my brother, owing to his
absence from England, did not give the piece the
revision he intended should be his share of the
work.   If he had, his experience would have seen
the necessity for the re-construction to which the
play was afterwards subjected, when the action
was brought within the compass of Monmouth's
Rebellion.

I may, passing from his History plays, briefly
touch on some lesser plays of various merit,
detailed account of which would not be interesting
to the reader.   A table will be found in an
Appendix with the dates of production of all his
plays.   And first I am tantalised by one called
' Sappho,' written for Miss Geneviève Ward.
She speaks of it highly, and says the title rôle is a
fine part.   It was produced in the United Kingdom,
but there is no trace of it in the Lord Chamber-
lain's Office, and no copy extant but that in Miss
Ward's possession.   I mention the play because a
story characteristic of my brother is told about it
by Mr. Bram Stoker.   It was to be produced on a

Monday, but at Saturday's rehearsal the last act
was not forthcoming. The management tried to
assume an air of confidence, but the company
shrewdly suspected it was not written. On
Monday morning the missing act came forth, and
the play was successfully produced in the evening.
This reminds one of the story of the last act of
'Charles I.,' and shows how, from overwork, he
often flung his plays upon the stage.

One of Willie Wills's great fortes was adaptation. He could rapidly extract the pith from a
novel, grasping the main facts and all that was
essential, arranging the perspective and preserving
the characteristics. Cora and Camille were examples of his skill. Both were from the French ;
the former from M. Belot's 'L'Article 47' was
afterwards subjected to treatment by Mr. Frank
Marshall to purge it of a lingering taint of the
original sin of its French progenitor.

It was said that my brother had no humour,
but a play called 'Ellen,' produced at the Haymarket with a strong cast, though defective in
other respects, had in it a good deal of true
comedy. The earlier scenes contained much of
his best writing, and were admitted to be 'admirable in conception and dainty in execution.'
But the dazzling success of 'Olivia' in the year
before eclipsed its merits, and a heroine with
flaws in her conduct, if not in her character,
was then so unusual on the English stage
that the critics were scandalised and the public
disapproved. The period of the play was that
of the defeat of the Pretender at Culloden, and

the heroine is a Highland lass, who, to save her
lover, betrays his cause, and to gain his hand
deceives him into believing she is dying.   This
is a sample of what I have said, that his original
germs often took eccentric forms, like the stories
with most unexpected endings which he used to
tell children.   It was perilous and unwonted fare
to place before a British audience, and an unfortunate line gave an opportunity to an actor, dissatisfied with his part, somewhat disloyally to help
to wreck the piece.   There occurred in his lines
some such sentence as 'Enough of this rubbish,' to
which he gave such malicious emphasis that the
gallery, all at sea about the play, catching the
actors' meaning greeted it with a roar.   The play
was condemned and withdrawn in April, but it
contained so much good material that it was
recast, and, under the unfortunate title of ' Brag,'
re-appeared at the same theatre in July.   But the
rule ' nulla vestigia retrorsum ' is inexorable with
respect to plays, and there was no reversing the
doom pronounced or rehabilitating the erring young
woman, who in the new play was simply under a
cloud.   The piece is one the literary merit of
which will entitle it to be published with the dramatist's other works.   Thomas Pye is distinctly
a creation, and Madge Gowan a beautiful type of
womanly character.   Another play, in which my
brother had a collaborator, was written for the
provincial actor, Mr. Dillon, round the South
American hero ' Bolivar,' who gives its title to the
play.
     My brother was never partial to one act

dramas. He wrote several, however. One, for Miss Ellen Terry, was an adaptation of King René's daughter, and called ' Iolanthe '—a name borrowed by permission by Messrs. Gilbert and Sullivan—and represented the breaking of the visible world on one born blind. Another, ' Elizabeth,' written for the same actress, was never played. Its object was to give Miss Terry, as the apparently dying Queen, an opportunity of confounding the ambassadors and the emissaries of James, who, vulture-like, hover round her sick bed, by rising and executing a gavotte.

A third was the adaptation of Theodore de Banville's ' Gringoire.' The simple verses extemporised at the king's desire by the ragged bard are a divergence from the original ending of the play, but catch its feeling, and make an effective finish.

' The Little Pilgrim ' is an unambitious piece, founded on Ouida's story, telling pleasantly how a little maid in her guileless innocence sought her artist lover, making a pilgrimage of two hundred miles to his studio, and how she was rewarded by the bestowal upon her of her hero's hand and brush. She was played by Miss Annie Hughes, and the innocence and the artlessness of the maid were of the finest water, and the piece a complete success. Mrs. Langtry was perhaps less fitted with the similar part of ' A Young Tramp '; but, of course, looked very charming disguised as a boy. This latter play was produced at the ' Prince's Theatre,' Bristol (September 12, 1885), and had considerable success in the provinces and

America—where, however, another actress played
Jessie Daw, the girl who has the pleasure so few
are permitted of witnessing — her own funeral.
Another play, the last I will mention in this chapter,
illustrated the author's curious propensity to try
his hand upon things entirely strange to him.   To
write, for instance, on a subject about which he
knew absolutely nothing had the allurement for
him of a virgin wilderness for an adventurous ex-
plorer.   Challenged by the pictures that break out
on the bookstall at Christmas of a little girl and a
broom, he would try whether he could not produce
a similar picture advertisement.   At one time he
did the cartoons for a London paper, sometimes
writing the verses illustrated by his own engravings.   He took up photography, and would have
succeeded very well, but was so abstracted that he
at times forgot to remove the slide—thus taking
two pictures on one plate, and producing a *lusus
naturæ* with two heads and a plurality of legs and
arms.   Like his prototype in the eighteenth century, he was ready to trespass on any field, the
more aloof from his own the better.   In this spirit
he viewed the enormous posters representing
scenes such as the boat-race, familiar to the
London crowd, that illustrated the ' New Babylon,'
and his ambition was immediately fired to write a
similar play.   'Forced from Home,' first called
' The Stepmother,' was the result.   This piece,
intended for the Adelphi, was produced at the
Duke's, and afterwards at the Pavilion.   Mr. A. C.
Calmour played the villain of the piece, a German
tailor.   Its sensations were an attempted suicide

on a wintry night from Waterloo Bridge, and a real hansom cab drawn across the stage. Messrs. Holt and Willmott sent this play round the provinces, and it ran for years with great success, producing more in royalties than any play the author ever wrote. Of course the critics took a very lofty tone towards it, although it would be well for many a play treated with the respect due to its scenery and dressing if it were as free from exaggeration, as interesting in its story, and as well written in its dialogue.

A curious fact, however, came to light about this after my brother's death. Sensationalism had made such strides that it was considered necessary to write in scenes of an outrageous character in the worst taste and English. The new scenes were obtrusively patches on the old garment, and of the most shoddy material.

But in the middle of these plays, of which I have touched the salient points, there came in 1878, six years after ' Charles I.,' the second great success of his life, to which I must devote a separate chapter. The commission this time came from Mr. John Hare, great both as an actor and as a judge of a play, who was then the lessee of the Court Theatre. It so happened, another fortunate circumstance, that my brother was then in a serener atmosphere than that of the studio, having taken lodgings in Clairville Grove, close to his friends the Corkrans.

CHAPTER XIV.

WRITES 'OLIVIA.'

FOR once there was no discordant note in the chorus of praise with which a play by Mr. Wills was greeted in the press. 'Olivia' was pronounced one of the most tender and charming plays that ever graced the English stage. The dramatist used to say that he never wrote with the same ease and buoyancy. He enjoyed a great advantage in writing it in a pleasant house, in an atmosphere very different from that of the studio, and having for his voluntary secretaries two ladies who were admiring disciples, and delighted in taking down from his lips scene after scene as each came fresh into existence, and the pathetic story gradually unfolded itself. Although, as elsewhere noticed, he had the power of abstracting his mind from the most uncongenial surroundings, and even sought a crowd, and wrote more easily when he was freed from the restlessness of being alone, and individualism was lost in the concrete multitude, nothing could be so favourable as the cultured appreciation which drew out his best powers. I have heard him for an hour at a time dictate, as fast as one could comfortably take them down in longhand, scenes in which the language and sentiment were perfect. Goldsmith, himself, might have written ' Olivia,' and it is curious that the commission to write a play on an episode in the ' Vicar of Wakefield' should have been given to one who was not only a fellow countryman of his, but so like him in every characteristic. Probably, if Goldsmith had developed his germ into a play, there would have been a good deal more comedy and less pathos and sentiment.

The characters of Mrs. Primrose and Olivia are altered for the better in Mr. Wills's play. The one fact that in the original Olivia did not believe marriage was in question, and in the drama such belief is the mainspring, involves an essential difference in character. In the play, she is the most perfect study of woman's character conceivable, not tiresomely good, but yet divinely lovable. Her womanly waywardness, her spoiled child's petulance, her little penitent ways, her huffs and her relentings, her feminine want of logic and illogical loyalty, her playful wit and tenderness, her womanly heroic impulses of self-sacrifice, and her change to stone under the last deadly affront, all these fibres of character make up one of the creations of flesh and blood which the author of ' Olivia ' put upon the stage.[1] But it is not only in its characterisation, in atmosphere, and inci- dent the play differs widely from the novel. In the play there is more refinement of language and sentiment, and the broad drollery is toned down to quaintness. The ruin of the family is but an incident. The Vicar learns he need not leave Wakefield even while preparing his treasures for

[1] See Miss Bateman's letter about Clarissa Harlowe, page 265.

the sale—there are no fine ladies from London,
and no prison scenes.

The language is not borrowed except in one
passage, but it is exactly such as would have been
used by the characters of the time to which the
play belongs. The author's reading in early days
was so much in books of that period (for our
vicarage library—or, as Moses would call it—' Our
little Pantheon,' with the exception of reviews and
magazines, contained not much else), that he was
imbued with the language and spirit of Johnson's
and Goldsmith's day, and wrote for this reason the
real and not the Wardour Street imitation of eighteenth century English ; and the retired vicarage
in Ireland of his youthful associations was not
so remote in its *genius loci* from Dr. Primrose's
vicarage, that it would not have helped him to
enter into the spirit of the latter. Studiously
simple is the language employed; only a single
sentence has been pointed out in which one of
those recondite metaphors occurs, for which the
author had sometimes a curious fancy. He displayed in composition—if not always, certainly in
this play—the art of which he was devoid in
painting, of using the exact amount of colour
required, and no more. He wrote with skilful
reticence. There is in ' Olivia ' hardly an unnecessary word. No one knew better what would
tell on the stage ; and the reader of his plays who
does not observe the simple touches true to nature
that go home with conviction to gallery and stalls
alike, and are worth, as he used to say, a king's
ransom to the dramatist, may be disappointed at

not discovering the fine writing he expected in
' Olivia,' not knowing how well the lines lighted
up on the stage and produced exactly the effect
intended.

It is said that the ' Vicar of Wakefield' was
suggested to Goldsmith by ' The Diary of a Poor
Vicar.' The original vicar was a thoughtful,
tender-hearted gentleman whose chief fear was
being imprisoned for debt. The dramatist does
not owe much more to Goldsmith than Goldsmith
to the original vicar.[1]

It was in April 1878, that ' Olivia ' was produced at the Court Theatre under the perfect
management of Mr. Hare, and with Miss Ellen
Terry in the title rôle. Who can forget the scenes
and impressions of that first night ? The vicarage
orchard in apple harvest; the vicarage parlour
with its ancient spinnet and cuckoo clock; the
delightful children, and the vicar and his wife, just
stepped out of the olden time, quaint and beautiful ; the simple zest of country life ; the touching
sadness of troubles at home besetting this peaceful
household.

Mr. Hare could not sleep for anxiety ; the
cares of management were so great that he felt
it impossible to undertake Dr. Primrose. The
character was at first allotted to Mr. Kelly, but on

---

[1] ' Olivia ' is unlike any stage version of ' The Vicar of Wakefield '
before attempted. Dibdin's was of a musical nature. Tom Taylor's,
first produced in 1850, afforded no suggestion ; but it was the version
produced at the Aquarium Theatre as a sort of bid against Mr. Hare's,
as ' Cromwell ' at the same theatre was a feeble counterblast to
' Charles I.' In the Aquarium version, Mr. William Farren was the
vicar, Mr. H. B. Conway, Squire Thornhill, and Miss Litton the
heroine of the play.

his throwing it up, Hermann Vezin was happily asked to sustain the character of the vicar. Even in his dreams the play haunted the manager. He said : ' If this is a failure, I know nothing of management, and will retire from the stage.'

The author did not read the play to the company, as had been the custom, and he seldom came to rehearsals. He was unpractical, and had difficulty, when he did attend, in conveying his ideas, for he was too conscious of himself to be able to act, but nevertheless his ideas were generally essentially right. Sometimes, however, he would propose something utterly impossible. For instance, at an early rehearsal he suggested that when Olivia got off her couch, her dress should catch on a nail. He thought it would make a pretty picture. But what the author had in a high degree was the power of fitting an actress with a part, and never did he succeed so well as in writing that of Olivia for Miss Terry.

The charm which the play exercised upon society, high and low, we can all remember. It touched the fashions. It left its record in ' The Queen,' and all the modes were influenced by the sweet parson's daughter. Olivia's cap was everywhere, and many a young face looked charming under its sweet simplicity. The actress was made for the part, and the inexpressible charm she gave it will never be forgot. The playgoers of to-day, as of twenty years ago, know how it has affected them, for time has in no degree lessened the charm which Miss Terry gave to the part of the vicar's daughter. Olivia is still the same as we knew her

M

long ago. 'I wish I were younger for her sake,'
she says in a letter to the author. But time has
stood still for this incomparable actress. How the
part affects herself is the other side which the
playgoer might be curious to learn. 'Does Punch
feel?' was a question on which Mr. Irving once
wrote in a periodical—actors may be mechanical
in their art, but Miss Terry is not—she feels intensely, and in her voice the tears are real, for it is
her emotional nature that has made her great.

She thus writes to the author of the play:—

> I want to tell you that I'm at rehearsal all day long—for
> our readings for next week in the provinces—and in 'Olivia'
> every night, nearly die of emotion.

The following were the casts of the original production at the Court Theatre and, nine years after,
at the Lyceum:—

	COURT	LYCEUM
DR. PRIMROSE .	Mr. Hermann Vezin.	Mr. Henry Irving.
MOSES	Mr. Norman Forbes.	Mr. Norman Forbes.
DICK (His sons) .	Miss L. Neville.	
BILL	Miss N. Neville.	
MR. BURCHELL . .	Mr. F. Archer.	Mr. T. Wenham.
SQUIRE THORNHILL .	Mr. W. Terriss.	Mr. W. Terriss.
LEIGH (A Vagabond) .	Mr. Denison.	Mr. F. Izals.
FARMER FLAMBOROUGH .	Mr. R. Cathcart.	Mr. H. Howe.
SCHOOLMASTER . .	Mr. Franks.	
MRS. PRIMROSE . .	Mrs. C. Murray.	Miss L. Payne.
OLIVIA	Miss Ellen Terry.	Miss Ellen Terry.
SOPHIA	Miss K. Aubrey.	Miss Winifred Emery.
POLLY FLAMBOROUGH .	Miss M. Cathcart.	Miss Coleridge.
PHŒBE	Miss K. Nicholls.	
SARAH	Miss Turtle.	
GYPSY WOMAN . .	Miss Neville.	

Owing to the exigencies of copyright 'Olivia'
is still in manuscript, but I will endeavour, so far
as I may, to convey some idea of the play to those

who have not seen it performed. Those who have will be able to fill in the outline from their own recollections.

What playgoer does not remember the delightful pictures of the vicarage orchard, from the designs of Marcus Stone—the sunglow in the west, kindling orange flames in the windows of Squire Thornhill's mansion; the children's quaint games and disputes, the apple-gathering of the tough-rinded Burchell and homely Sophy, the dudgeon of sturdy Farmer Flamborough, and the rustic pride of the vicar's lady? or the scenes between Moses and Polly of old-fashioned humour, and the delightful battle of Burchell and Mrs. Primrose, waged in the stately mode of other days? Or, again, the beautiful mixture of the old English gentleman and humble-minded clergyman in the immortal vicar, who, in the shadow that falls across the happy day of their silver wedding, with such manly self-control and Christian fortitude draws to himself our sympathies—in the scenes touching to tears—in which he reveals to his wife their altered and fallen fortunes? Who can forget when Sister Livy is threatened with exile to York, as companion to an old lady, and is about to be torn from the young squire—who has sealed her lips with a vow not to reveal his proposals of marriage—the inimitably written scene in which the seducer at last persuades her to fly with him, followed by that in which 'Livy,' with the open secret, that instead of going to her humble place at York, she is about to elope with her false lover, bids them all that veiled good-bye, distributing her little

parting presents—a scene which left not a dry
eye wherever the play has been acted ? I cannot
refrain from quoting from this scene a few lines,
though of course they lose much from being taken
out of their setting.

Olivia has found the evening party gathered
in the parlour, and fancies she sees on each loved
face a forecast of her flight from home. Moses,
in his sententious fashion, has admonished her in
dealing with the old lady to remember she is a
Primrose, and that 'the humility of duty is
stronger than the tyranny of feebleness'; and then
Olivia distributes her keepsakes, and the phono-
graph of memory brings back each pathetic into-
nation of her voice.

OLIVIA: I want to make you all remember me. Mother,
come here (*to the children*), never mind us, talk and laugh
away, and look at your pretty picture-books. Mother, I want
to give you all little keepsakes as love tokens.

MRS. PRIMROSE: Oh! my dear, that will do to-morrow
morning.

OLIVIA: No; father and I go before you will be up.

MRS. PRIMROSE: Oh! I'll be up. To-night you'll make us
all cry.

OLIVIA: My eyes will be dry before bedtime, and I've got
such a headache.

MRS. PRIMROSE: How hot your head is, and how it trembles.

OLIVIA: This is the little gold and cornelian locket father
gave me; father's and my hair twisted in it, grey and gold.
You'll wear it, mother, for my sake ?

MRS. PRIMROSE: Dear, dear, have you kept it all this
time ?

OLIVIA: Wear it with the cornelian outside, but promise to
turn it every Sunday before the church bells.

MRS. PRIMROSE: Why then, child ?

OLIVIA: Because it's the time we are bound to forgive.

MRS. PRIMROSE: Why, one would think you were going to

die. You've been a good girl, and you're only going to York.

OLIVIA: If you want me to go away happy, you'll promise.

MRS. PRIMROSE: I'll promise thee, my poor pretty fool.

OLIVIA: And now, mother, call the children over, one by one. I don't want Mr. Burchell to hear—but first, good-night, mother, give me a kiss.

(*Mrs. Primrose kisses Olivia; goes to the children and whispers to them. Olivia sits in arm-chair, Sophy goes to her.*)

SOPHY: Dear Olivia, don't take it so much to heart. In sooth you need not go away. [*Sits on hassock.*

OLIVIA: I must, I must. I'm not well, and a word would make me cry.

SOPHY: How pale you are, and your hand trembles.

OLIVIA: There's a little present for you.

SOPHY: What! your pearl earrings? No, no, I cannot take them.

OLIVIA: Wear them on your wedding-day, and promise me one thing.

SOPHY: Anything.

OLIVIA: Anything—that's too much; but you know how the people talk. Take my part, Sophy, and when they say hard things of me, say it's not true.

SOPHY: What's not true?

OLIVIA: They might say I was thoughtless; perhaps they might say I was bad. To the end be true to me, and re-member this, Sophy, whatever betide you'll not be ashamed of your sister at the last. There, good-bye. We've played together, haven't we, and quarrelled often, and often made friends (*breaking down*). But you always loved me. Good-bye, dear, and God bless you (*kisses her*). And now, pets, what have I got for you (*dropping on her knees, children go to her*)? Dick, the pretty picture-book I used to read to you, 'The Pilgrim's Progress.' Here's Livy's own prayer book for you, Bill—you can read it now. And now, my little pets, you must promise me something. You always said your prayers at Livy's knee. Now you must say them at mother's. Every night before you go to bed you must say, 'Pray God, bless and forgive poor sister Livy'; you must say it always—if mother chides you for it, you must say it.

DICK: I'll say it.

BILL: I promise.

OLIVIA: Ah! my pets (*embraces them fondly. Burchell, who has been playing chess with the vicar, joins Sophy and Moses at the spinet*). Good-bye, Mr. Burchell, I've a headache and must be up betimes (*shakes hands with Burchell*). Good-bye, Moses (*kisses him*). You are going to sing. You won't disturb me (*turns to vicar*). Father, I need not say good-bye to you.

(*Church clock strikes eight, Olivia turns and darts over to vicar. Embracing him.*)

VICAR: Good-bye, my dearest, good-bye.   [*Exit hastily.*

The vicar says he has the advantage of them all, as he is going with her and will be absent two Sundays. No, not good-bye to him. And, as he goes to the fire and sits down, he repeats his gentle self-reproach of giving too much of his heart to his daughter away from God. 'Wrong, wrong. I shall be punished for it yet.' Mrs. Primrose places candles, and asks Sophy to sing her father's favourite song, and perhaps Mr. Burchell will have the condescension to join. The request is accompanied by a stately curtsey, to which he bows an equally stately consent, on the condition that she will lend the harmony of her voice. Sophy plays the spinet, and Moses the flute accompaniment.

SONG

Morn, happy morn, the time for lovers thou,
When hope-buds burst their sheath,
And gladness hangs its wreath
Of roses on the merry maiden's brow.
The shepherd's driven his flock afield,
His shoon with dew the grasses sprinkle.
And hark! Oh! hark, the collie's bark,
And how the sheep-bells go a-tinkle.

During this verse, Olivia is seen to pass the window, and look in.

Eve! gentle eve! it is the hour for love,
When love's despites and woes,
Their tearful petals close,
And through the mead the whispering lovers rove.
The rookery bids a hoarse good night:
In the low breeze the cornfields wrinkle:
And list! oh list! beyond the mist
How the sheep-bells go a-tinkle.

During the last verse, the vicar has taken down a letter, which he had supposed was a notice to quit, and opened it, and as they cease, he exclaims—

Beloved home! where my children were born, mine again.
The sweet garden, the meadows, the orchard with their sweet music and perfume, mine.

An unknown benefactor—supposed to be the young squire—has made over to him the freehold of his home, and he need not after all leave the place endeared by so many memories. And then comes the discovery of Olivia's flight, and the vicar's curse and his wife's gentle reproof, the only words in the play taken from the 'Vicar of Wakefield.' He tears up the deed of gift, which he believes now was the bait for the precious soul of his child, and he vows he will wander through the world till he finds her; but, calmed by his wife and Sophy, who assure him that Burchell has already gone in pursuit, he acknowledges ' She came between me and my love for God. I am punished for it at last. I am punished for it at last.'

Once more, we see in memory, Olivia at the Dragon Inn, full of home yearnings as Christmas draws near, and sick of concealment; the Squire, tired of the tame life he is leading, too willing to agree to her returning to the parental roof; Olivia's feverish preparations and resolve no longer to hide the secret that will reconcile her family; and then the terrible disclosure that they are not married.

OLIVIA : Not married! you answered to the service—so did I—You put this ring on my finger—what do you mean? We are married.

THORNHILL : A ring does not make a marriage. The ceremony was idle in law, as a children's game. 'Tis past crying for now ; I promise you, Olivia, if you are patient and good, we shall have a real marriage.

[He goes to her ; she shrinks from him.

OLIVIA : Is this the truth or some wicked mockery to wean my love from you and rid yourself of an incumbrance? What need is there of tricks? Say I am your wife, and then bid me go.

THORNHILL : We have had enough of falsehood, dear. Before I could atone to you I was compelled to tell you the truth.

OLIVIA : The truth- Ah! I must have time to understand —to think. No—no—'tis falsehood—I am your wife? what a horrible silence! I am your wife (*pulls his arm*)? Speak. Ah! the light of day breaks in upon me—where shall I hide my shame?

THORNHILL : Be calm a moment and listen.

OLIVIA : He ruined another—I didn't pity her—vain, blind fool.

THORNHILL : I wish to Heaven I'd not confessed.

OLIVIA : So all around me has been a hideous lie, my name upon that trunk that stands in the public hall—this ring upon my finger—his words—his smiles—all forgeries— his caresses, insults.

THORNHILL : I will not ask you to pardon me, I can only—

OLIVIA : What have I done to you? You're not fiend enough to ruin a young life for idle pleasure! You had some grudge against my poor father and me, and so worked out this bitter revenge.

THORNHILL : Nay, I have loved you, and will ever love you.

OLIVIA : Where is my home? Give me back my home.

If I have no husband, give me back father, mother, sister; you have robbed me of them. You have robbed me of my very soul. Your love, keep it, keep it for that other poor wretch you have ruined. You found me happy and innocent; you have left me what honest folks refuse to name.

THORNHILL : Be calm ; be calm ; I will provide for you.

OLIVIA : Devil ! (*She strikes him.*) Lost even my womanliness. (*Sinks on the ground, crying.*) [*Enter Burchell.*

THORNHILL : This room is engaged, sir, you intrude upon my privacy.

BURCHELL : The privacy of guilt claims no regard from me. My business with you is brief and immediate. Your victim.

OLIVIA : (*Rising*) Don't notice me, sir, my sorrow and my shame are my own. [*Exit sobbing.*

And then follows in our recollection the scene of righteous retribution, in which Burchell discloses himself as Sir William Thornhill and disinherits his nephew, the moving meeting of the old clergyman and his recovered treasure, the return home on Christmas morning, the hardness of the mother, the vicar's stern rebuke.

Woman, is it thus you follow the Bible example ? Is it thus you cast away the lost piece of silver you had found? She is penitent, and Heaven is rejoicing. Will you blaspheme against that joy by upbraiding ?

How well conceived is the ending of the play, and the reserve with which it concludes. After it has been discovered that the marriage after all was good in law, the repentant squire is brought on by his uncle, and rejecting the latter's promise of means befitting his position, craves his wife's pardon, but finds that the heart of flesh has been turned to one of stone, and is met by the relentless answer, ' Never.' It is then that her father pleads—

Child, remember yourself ; you are honestly married to the squire. Do not lead the neighbours to doubt it, and scandalise the whole family by your obstinacy. Appear in church with him to-day, countenanced by me and your sister, and my future son-in-law, Sir William Thornhill.

Sophy whispers to Sir William what perhaps is the key to that which lies beyond the curtain : ' I warrant she loved him through all.' But to her father, Olivia answers he had always told her that there was a deadly sin God will not forgive Is there no outrage which an insulted woman can't forgive ? She gave him all her heart. He wore it as a fop wears a button-hole for vanity, then tosses it in the mire. She had some joy, but shudders at it now can she forgive him ? Then Thornhill acknowledges he has been so false that when he speaks sad truth he is only receiving his deserts if she will not believe him. He will sit by her in church, tacitly acknowledging her as his wife, so that scandal ceases. Then he will begin his task of trying to win her back, if it take long years. Only to give some little hope that he may reclaim the love he has forfeited, let her not speak, but hold out her hand to him. The vicar takes it and gives it to Thornhill, who kneels and kisses it, and the old clergyman says—

Sir, she gives you hope. 'Tis Christmas ; 'tis merry, gentle Christmas. On every little cloud around the sun, methinks I see a herald angel singing peace and goodwill to men. We are all gathered happily together as on the evening of my silver wedding. What sorrow lay in ambush for us, that evening of deceitful peace ! On this sad day-break, joy lay in ambush for us—sorrow like a night fog has all melted into blessed day.

It is impossible to doubt that this play will live (perhaps in such strange company as Olivia at Ranelagh), long beyond the closing century, and take its permanent place as a classic. Stage copyright will, one day, no longer present an obstacle to its being printed and published along with the writer's other plays. So great was the stir it made at the time, when everyone in London went Olivia mad, that offers came from France, Germany, Italy, Holland, and Denmark, for its production abroad.

The American rights were sold to Miss Fanny Davenport, subject to the payment of a royalty, for 600*l*., but all rights now belong to Sir Henry Irving. Strange to say when produced at Berlin 'Olivia' was not a success. Its purely pastoral and English sentiment failed to be understood, and in America it did not gain the immense popularity it has since attained until the manager of the Lyceum appeared as Dr. Primrose, and Miss Ellen Terry as 'Olivia.' Mr. Hermann Vezin, who first played the vicar's part at the Court Theatre, has all the qualities of dignified and simple pathos the part demanded, but to eye as well as ear, Mr. Irving gave the most touching representation that can well be conceived of the old clergyman, and there is to this generation but one 'Olivia.' It was to her success in this play at the Court, that Miss Terry owed her permanent engagement at the Lyceum.

In the Lyceum production some of the business at the Court was missed. It may be the size of the theatre to some degree swamped it, and its pastoral character was more suited to a smaller house. There was a scene or tableau added of the vicar and his daughter on the steps of the vicarage going to the early service, the interior having changed to an exterior.

Dr. Primrose alone speaks and greets the happy morn, and then the play ends.

Hermann Vezin wrote to Irving for a seat on the first night. The reply was : 'Dear Vezin, delighted. Come round and see your daughter ; I am only her step-father.'

I may note by the way, that on the first night at the Court Theatre, when the weary vicar sleeps on the couch on Christmas morning, and, his mind charged with his sermon, mutters ' Dearly beloved brethren,' there was a little suppressed suggestion of a pathetic laugh. After the play, Frank Marshall said, ' Of course you'll leave that out.' Vezin replied he would do nothing of the kind, for he felt it was a laugh that had tears in it ; and he was perfectly right.

With all the change and development which the author found necessary in evolving a play out of this one episode of the story, he has preserved the gentle humours and pathos of Goldsmith's Dr. Primrose, the dry bluntness of his Mr. Burchell, the airs and graces of his Mrs. Primrose, and the incomparable charm of Olivia. An admirable inspiration of the dramatist was the stage direction in the scene at the Dragon Inn, when Thornhill promises money compensation, that Olivia should strike the seducer. It was a point in the play which had an electrical effect on the audience.

The song in the second act, set to music by Sir Arthur Sullivan, was at the Court accompanied on an old spinet of the date of 1768. I have the paper in my brother's handwriting, on which those exquisite verses are coming into existence.

CHAPTER XV.

CONTRADICTIONS.

'OLIVIA' showed in its writer a nature full of sentiment; partly that of the artist and poet, but partly that also of a man of great loyalty. With the contradictoriness of an Irishman's character, he combined a sort of faithlessness in his relations toward women with the greatest fidelity in his relations towards men, especially the unfortunate and friendless. I have spoken of him as a student of women. He studied the heart, and sometimes in playing on its strings drew forth feelings towards himself, which he felt when he discovered them, involved him in a difficulty. His manner of life was not of a kind which predisposes to marriage; nor did he, though he sometimes perhaps persuaded himself that he did, fall a genuine victim to love. Such a complication taught him a good deal, and he behaved in a becoming way through it all, but he soon cloyed of its endearments, and would even have to fortify himself to endure them. The problem, however, always solved itself. Although he had great influence over women, from his immense knowledge of their character, it would soon become apparent that he was not to be taken seriously. These little affairs were comedies woven round himself. They never had any depth.

One real attachment he formed in his ' daisy picking days.' The rest were rootless. How irresponsible was the way he regarded them, and how slight the hold on both sides the following story will serve to illustrate. After one of these little romances he met a friend travelling on the underground railway, and the following colloquy took place :—

'I suppose you know I have broken off with—— ? '

His friend expressed due astonishment.

' I had a long talk with her father and he quite agrees. It is all right.'

' And what does she think of it ? '

' Oh ! she is engaged to such a charming fellow. I go there on Sundays.'

' Really ; and what is his name ? '

' 'Pon my soul I forget.'

Those who had been attracted to him, so simple and so famous, by his quaint and loveable character and magnetic influence, generally became when the first feeling wore off his warm friends. If, however, they dropped out of sight, he could be amusingly oblivious of such bygones.

One day at the Louvre he got into conversation with a student who was copying a picture. She was very affable and turned out to be English. She seemed pleased to talk to him, and after a little asked him if he did not remember her. He had been engaged to be married to her once, but had quite forgotten her name. She turned out to be a Miss F——, whose family lived at Brighton. He happened to be there a few months afterwards, writing a play, seated in one of the shelters, as usual not the least disturbed by the nigger melodists and a fire-eater on the sands, directly below him. A lady came up and stood in front of him. He looked up like a man awaking from a dream, and said :

'Oh, Miss Hawthorne, I am just at work on your play.'

'Play,' she said, bitterly, 'are you still at that game? Do you not know me?'

'Oh, yes,' he said, 'I do now.'

'Well, what is my name?'

By the happiest chance he fetched it up out of his memory. She was the lady he had met in Paris that summer, and he mentioned her name.

'No,' she said, 'again you are wrong. I've been married since I last saw you.'

It must be understood that I do not mean to imply by faithlessness anything more than such stories illustrate, but the faithfulness of his friendship might be illustrated by numberless examples, and his cheque books are continual evidence of his generosity to needy men of letters and old friends who wanted his assistance. You might indeed have searched far for a man to whom his own words so truly applied, describing the heart as a mine of pity which the hand as a mint coined into deeds of kindness.

One of the literary failures he picked up and honoured as much as the world neglected him was an old war correspondent, of whom he used to say admiringly that he was always first in the field and first on the loot. His curious cross-grained portrait is drawn in 'Melchior' under the name of Wolfgang. He was a whimsical man with a good deal of rough independence, but he fell into ill-health and was living quite alone, without friends and separated from his wife. My brother used to take him presents of good wine and delicacies; and one of his friends tells a story of meeting him one evening on such an errand with a champagne bottle and pheasant done up in paper and a dessert of oranges in the hood of his ulster. He confessed in a shamefaced way on being questioned that he was taking them to poor S——n, who needed cheering up. Some days after, to inquiries as to the success of the feast, he confessed with a blank expression that his hood had been emptied on the way of all but one orange. S——n was not popular among his friends, being soured and cynical, but my brother used to stand up for him stoutly (I never knew him to run anyone down), and boast of his intellect and learning. In the last illness of his friend, who was dying painlessly, in absolute solitude, he used to say, 'If even he had a little pain it might be a companion to him.' He troubled himself to find out the sick man's wife, and succeeded in reconciling the pair, and he propitiated the landlady, who was, he thought, impatient with the querulous invalid, with a present of a gaudy handkerchief for her neck, and a pair of green gloves, which, as he said, would make her look like a barbarian queen. When the old war correspondent was very near his death, and his slender means were exhausted, he told the woman that she might count on him for all the expenses to which she had been put. He was with his friend when he died, and stooping over him asked, ' Do you know me, old friend ? I am Wills.' ' Wills, Wills,' murmured the dying man, ' Kindness, Friendship, Pity—that is Wills.' My brother paid all the expenses of the funeral, to which he went, a solitary mourner, although he had the greatest aversion to attending such functions. He forgot social engagements and disliked all the pomp and circumstance of life, but he would go out of his way, and think nothing a trouble for some poor waif or broken down scholar like this.

I have explained the decline of his popularity as a painter in pastels by the extraordinary hugger-mugger of his studio, and the company which used to assemble in it, generally including a model, who posed for the figure in the intervals of sitters' engagements. But all this, which seemed to his eyes but the normal aspect of things, grew confusion worse confounded when the necessity had passed away for even an attempt at order. The walls of the gaunt barnlike structure, with its great coach-house doors, opening out on the mews behind, were covered with white-washed match-lining. This was decorated with studies of human limbs and decapitated heads, like the butcher's shop of a cannibal tribe. The wooden lay figure I have spoken of, with contorted hands, still presided over the chaos, grown more chaotic. His plays and note-books were littered everywhere, the only place in which they were more or less gathered together

N

being the wicker clothes-basket. In this scene of
disorder one might meet with a company congenial
to it, and yet deeply would the master be hurt if
a word were said against any of those queer
characters whom he allowed to overrun his studio,
drink his wine, smoke his tobacco, and wear his
clothes. One of these retainers, stalking in with
a wolf-like air, he would allow to sit down and
eat the dinner that had been cooked for himself, while he, dinnerless, would go on with his
painting

The fame and success which would have caused
many men to turn their backs upon the friends of
their obscurity, never made the slightest alteration
in him. He was incapable of giving a man the
go-bye because he looked ragged and disreputable.
There was not in his whole composition a single
grain of that which is scripturally called ' respect
of persons.' He was rather devoid perhaps of the
bump of veneration ; but the poor he would treat
with chivalrous courtesy. He might well indeed
have been puffed up by the reputation attained by
the unparalleled success of ' Olivia.' It was then at
its zenith. Reviews and newspapers sought his
opinion on the drama. In the competitions which
were then in vogue the readers of journals voted
him the best dramatist of the day ; he was invited
to respond for the drama at Lord Mayors' banquets,
and if he had not disliked that kind of exploitation
might have been one of the lions of London
society. He even attained the crowning honour
of being called as an expert to pronounce on the
decency or indecency of Mr. W. S. Gilbert's

Pygmalion and Galatea in a public trial. The counsel was Mr. Karslake, I think, and he asked each witness for a definition of indecency. The friend who was sitting beside my brother whispered in his ear that he had better be prepared for the question to which all had failed to give a satisfactory answer; and when his turn came he gave a definition which was accepted as the only apt one, ' that which would bring the blush of shame to the cheek of modesty, or excite strong passion in a man.' This has passed into a light saying, but probably few remember the original authorship of it. It must not be supposed that his chivalry was limited to men. He had a great pity for the disconsolate and forlorn. One day he came across a starving Welsh girl and took her to his studio and fed her, though he could not understand a word she said. He found her lodgings, and allowed her to sit in the studio in the daytime, doing some needlework for him, or pretending to do it, for she generally sat doing nothing. The moment his step was heard she would be very industrious; but he never saw through it. He would say, ' Ah, Edith, there you are, always at work! '

A story is told which implies that with all his open-handedness to poor friends, he was not prone to give to beggars. But, as an Irishman, he liked to hear as well as to say pleasant things, and might be wheedled by flattery as well as touched by pity. One day, when he was pacing slowly along the street reading a newspaper, Mr. Beerbohm Tree came up behind him, and addressed him in the professional whine of a beggar, ' Please, sir, will you give me a copper?' 'Go away, go away,' replied the abstracted dramatist. 'Ah! Mr. Wills,' continued Mr. Tree in a wheedling voice; 'many is the time I have applauded your beautiful plays from the gallery.' The gratified dramatist immediately put his hand into his pocket, and was dropping a shilling into the beggar's hand, when he recognised the actor in a new character.

One of his contradictions was that this dramatist disliked the drama. It was difficult to induce him to go to a theatre, perhaps because he associated it with toil, not pleasure. The story is told, how he was persuaded by a friend to go to one much against his will, and the young man at the box-office showed no alacrity in getting them seats. The manager being referred to, they got the best in the house. My brother was greatly bored by the play, and, when leaving, paused and said, quite meaning it, 'I am looking for that kind-hearted young man who was for not letting us in; I would like to give him a shilling.' While, however, he was bored by sitting out a play, he had a keen dramatic discrimination. It is related that, on seeing a piece called 'Bygones,' written by Pinero, who was then quite an unknown man, he said to a friend that the writer of that play would make his mark as a dramatist.

Among lesser contradictions, it may be noticed that, while he had a liking for exploring all sorts of companies, and was at home with all kinds of queer people, nor overcome by rank and circumstance, he was of a singularly retiring disposition.

At the opening of the Kensington Free Library

by Princess Louise, he, as usual, kept in the back
ground, but the Princess sent for him, and invited
him to take a seat beside her on the platform. This
was, however, too much for his natural modesty,
and he respectfully declined the honour, although
he appreciated Her Royal Highness's great kindness and her sympathy with art.

One of the things he always impressed on tyros
in the dramatic art was the necessity of dotting
the ' i's ' and crossing the ' t's,' but he was himself
exceedingly inaccurate. I find among his papers
a letter from Mr. Burnand commencing : ' Dear
Wells,—I call you Wells because you call me
Bernand,' and it was constitutional to him to make
such blunders. ' One of Willie's blunders ' is an
echo from old home-days. They sometimes led
him into unpleasant positions. At a dinner which
was given to the Prince of Wales by the members
of the Garrick Club, he said to the gentleman
sitting next to him, ' Well, I think we have given
the Prince a good dinner.' His neighbour was the
Prince's Equerry.

CHAPTER XVI.

CHEQUERED SUCCESSES.

It happened to him, as it has to others, that when he acquired a name his early work came into requisition. 'Ninon,' originally called 'St. Cyr,' which, under the powerful auspices of Mr. Knight, had been shown to a number of managers and formed its author's introduction to the Lyceum management, at last found its mark. Miss Wallis produced and played the part of the Seamstress of Paris with great effect. Ninon, to revenge the supposed seduction of her sister by the Deputy St. Cyr, works herself into his affections, and in doing so falls into the toils of love herself. In the moment of betrayal to the Revolutionary Committee she discovers he is innocent. Alternative endings, a happy and a tragic one, were tried; and, as in the case of 'Jane Shore,' the happy ending meant success and the tragic a great falling off in the receipts.

There is a similarity in the main incident of 'Ninon' to 'Plot and Passion,' in which the female agent hired by Fouché is entangled in her own net; the likeness, however, was quite accidental. The Little Dauphin, whose famous picture my brother had seen at an exhibition in Dublin, was introduced as a motive in the play, being stolen from his cobbler jailer, 'Simon the Incorruptible,' by the secretly royalist Deputy. He formed a very pathetic element; and there was an admirable picture of a secretary, a sort of Boswell, who is the recording angel of the eloquent Deputy. It is rather perplexing to reconcile the excellent construction of this play with statements as to the author's want of playcraft at the period when he had already written it. 'Ninon' shows the artist's pencil as well as the poet's pen in the picture it presents of the time of the French Revolution. For this play my brother received royalties; and, under a similar arrangement, the play called 'William and Susan' was produced. It was under Mr. Hare's management that this version of Douglas Jerrold's nautical drama, 'Black-eyed Susan,' appeared at the St. James's Theatre, with Mr. and Mrs. Kendal in the parts of William and Susan. Mr. Blanchard Jerrold gave his consent to the last act of his father's play being fitted with two new acts by my brother. There were not wanting those who regarded the scenes and character of the original play as too sacred to be tinkered by a later dramatist, and the cry of 'bowdlerism' was of course raised. As my brother used to say, however, the manager of a society theatre like the St. James's, who put 'Black-eyed Susan' on the stage at the present day as it was written by Jerrold, would be entitled to be sent to a lunatic asylum. It is strange that the work of men whose lives met should mark lines of public taste so far apart. The affectation of nautical phraseology in the original is carried to the point of burlesque, and the sentimental speeches are of

the sort that survive only in transpontine melodrama. Turgidity and affectation were at high-
water mark when Jerrold wrote, and the admirably
touching third act of the play was simply restored
to the stage by being provided with preparatory acts
worthy to lead up to it. It was more respectful
to the author to fit it with an entirely new and original body, as was done, than to reconstruct the
old material. As it stands, two-thirds of ' William
and Susan ' are entirely W. G. Wills's, and one-
third entirely Douglas Jerrold's—surely preferable
to a hybrid work. The happy picture of Susan's
home, forming a sunny foreground to the pathetic
scenes which followed, made them far more touching than the misery which filled the original from
the beginning ; and this led to the curious charge
that the new author had deepened the gloom. If
he did it was simply by introducing sunshine. The
poetical and tenderly idyllic scenes were charged
with tears to come, and the consequence was that
the play was called ' The Cry,' for it made every one
in the audience shed tears. It is needless to say
that it was acted to perfection : that Mrs. Kendal
was an incomparable Susan ; that Mr. Kendal was
a manly and natural William, and that the *mise en
scène*, for which Mr. Hare was responsible, with the
fleet in the downs, the man-o'-war's cabin and deck
of a battleship, was of a level which stage art had
rarely reached before. I am glad to hear from Mr.
Kendal that it is intended to reproduce ' William
and Susan.'

My brother's next dramatic work was poetical.
Madame Modjeska commissioned him to write her

a play, and the plot of 'Juana' was submitted to her and accepted. This romantic drama in blank verse has for its central idea a man accepting death for a woman he loves, but who has never known his passion for her. Mr. Wilson Barrett played the self-sacrificing friar John. Mr. Forbes Robertson was Don Carlos, killed by his jealous wife under the influence of hereditary madness, the blood taint of her house. In the scenes of hysteria and madness Madame Modjeska held the audience spellbound; but in spite of its power and beauty and the freshness of the dialogue, the grim features of the play—the test of blood and the punishment of building a man up alive in the monastery wall—were too morbid for the public. The stalls and dress circle soon began to thin, and it was obvious the play was not destined to have a long life. I do not think that my brother, in all his dramatic career, felt any disappointment so keenly as this. He wrote 'Juana' with his heart in his work, as a poem as much as a play; and he manifested his anxiety for its success by doing what he hardly ever did—attending rehearsals and making suggestions to the actress.

In 1890 the tragedy was revived for a short time at the Opera Comique, and it was taken out on tour in a summer season by some members of the Lyceum company. It is a drama which, with a little skilful remodelling, contains the materials of a great and successful play, and, as it stands, is a fine literary work.

The adaptation of 'Jane Eyre' was undertaken for Mrs. Bernard Beere in 1882, and produced at

the Globe Theatre in the December of that year.
The plot is compressed into those scenes which
pass in or near Thornfield Hall. Mrs. Bernard
Beere was too tall and *débonnaire* for the thin, plain,
pale little person of the novel; but this on the
stage, where the eye has its dominion, was undoubtedly far from a disadvantage. The play
strikes—necessarily, perhaps—a very different key-
note from the novel; so much that could not be
compressed goes to making the latter. One cannot
compress a whole atmosphere on the stage. The
play is the love story of Jane and Rochester, with
the ghost of his mad wife standing between them.
The lunatic shriek is heard but once, and the sight
that appals the heroine's eyes only once appears;
the more sensational features of the novel are also
left in the background—the attempt to destroy
Rochester, the burning of the Hall, in which the
mad woman loses her life and he his sight. It is
the sentiment of the story that is woven into the
play, and this is done with success and good taste.
The public might have liked stronger fare, but the
piece held its ground well, and gained the sympathy
of the best judges by its pure and lofty tone, and
entire freedom from vulgar sensationalism. A
dramatist with less good taste would have crowded
his narrow stage canvas with all the incidents of
the novel, and entirely failed by doing so to give
its dramatic equivalent.

The last act was at first very carelessly written,
and Hermann Vezin, to whom it was read, re-
monstrated : ' Surely that is not to be the finished
act.' As usual, my brother's feathers were put up,

and he was extremely angry with his mentor; but when he had cooled down he entirely re-wrote it, and made it a very fine scene. More or less every dramatist has to submit to this process, of which W. G. Wills was so impatient, for when he had finished it, as he conceived, he liked to have done with a piece. I remember Mr. Henry Hermann one day showing me the piles of rejected editions of scenes in the 'Silver King' written over and over again. People little know how much hard work has been put into the narrow compass of successful drama.

The adaptation of 'Jane Eyre,' however, was written with great rapidity, for it was intended to take the place at the Globe of a play which was not paying its expenses, and the work occupied only a fortnight. Mr. Charles Wyndham attended a matinée of the piece, and was so delighted with Mrs. Bernard Beere that he asked her to join his Company. My brother's play was thus the making of her name, as his 'Olivia' gave to Miss Ellen Terry her opening to fame.

CHAPTER XVII.

ROME AND RIENZI.

I HAVE noticed the effect which historic scenes had upon my brother's mind; and, as may be supposed, a prolonged visit to Italy was the great event of his life. Rome was to him a city of visions; it rose again about him from the past. When he returned to England and wrote 'Rienzi' it so impregnated his imagination that Mr. Irving thus congratulated him on the play: 'It is simply magnificent. You have roused old Rome as you will dull London.' Where other travellers see only antiquities and interesting ruins, he looked at everything with the eye of a poet, and his mind grew ghostly-conversant with the past. 'Icenia,' as well as 'Rienzi,' drew its inspiration from this visit; and a strange grotesque poem, called 'John o' Dreams,' of great descriptive power, rose like a fantastic vapour out of his dreamings and imaginings at Rome.

Like most things he did, this journey South came about quite accidentally. One day his friend, Mr. W. L. Woodroffe, looked in at his lodgings in Sydney Street, and asked him to start with him for Rome the day but one following. The suddenness of the proposal made him go. If more time had been allowed a hundred difficulties and objections would have sprung up. But, as it happened, he had no work on hand at the moment except the words of a cantata for Mr. Fred Clay, the musical composer, for whom he had written ' Lalla Rookh,' and Mr. Clay had given him nonsense verses in different metres to turn into songs and choruses, along with the general outline of the plot of the cantata. The subject was ' Semiramis,' and this work he took with him to Italy, intending to do it at his leisure ; but he hardly touched it, and, at last, Mr. Clay losing patience, asked him not to trouble about it further, promising to pay him on his return for any work already done. It amounted to so little, however, that he never made any claim upon the composer.

As the travellers passed, *via* Rheims, through Basle and Lucerne, the novelty of the scenes keenly excited my brother's interest ; even the taking down of the shutters in the Platz, and the awaking of a foreign town from its night's repose, were eventful. He always had a great contempt for Swiss scenery, knowing it only from pictures. He used to say it was sensational, vulgar, and obvious ; but he was quite overcome by enthusiasm and delight as he looked up at the Righi and Pilatus. As they crossed the Alps from Lucerne a couplet from Tennyson was constantly on his lips —

> And I shall see before I die
> The palms and temples of the South.

He was, from his intense appreciation, a delightful companion to whom to act as guide. At Milan, when he was lured by surprise to see the ' Last Supper,' by Leonardo da Vinci, his enthusiasm

and the stimulation of his intellect by the picture
and its associations were delightfully fresh. When
a lad he had bought a plaster of paris plaque in
Waterford, and tinted in the figures and the background, the result being a curious coincidence with
the colouring of the original picture.

It was midnight when they reached Rome, in
frost and moonlight, and as they got out of the
station the first sight that greeted them was a
sentry lying asleep against his box, and my brother
chuckled over it, and said they only wanted the
Capitoline geese to fill up the classical legend.
With his usual indifference to everything material
when surrounded by such inspiring scenes, he has-
tened off in the morning without waiting for breakfast, and made his way to the Capitol. He returned
to the hotel greatly dissatisfied with the two statues
of Castor and Pollux by Praxiteles. He said the
Greek sculptor had glorified his hero by dwarfing
the horse—quite a true criticism, for the horse is
smaller than a cab horse, and the rider of heroic
proportions. But if he looked at art as an artist
only, his imagination carried him away among the
ruins of temples and amphitheatres, and the reminiscent ways of the Eternal City. He would sit
for an hour in the Colosseum, on the topmost storey
of the ruin, till he peopled the tiers of seats below
with the eager Roman crowd gazing on the Chris-
tians in the arena at their feet. Once he was
roused from his dream by what he thought was
the growl of a wild beast. It was a shaved French
poodle barking at a small child. One day Mr.
Woodroffe and he went together to the Catacombs.

There was a party of eight, and the guide supplied
them with torches, and took them along the intri-
cate underground windings, their candles like little
glimmering specks of light, showing for a moment
and then lost in the turnings of the passage. In
some places the points of interest, such as tombs
and sarcophagi, were so placed that they could not
all get round the guide to hear what he said. He,
a mere hireling, volleyed off his description, and
went on to the next point of interest, the passage
always diverging and twisting about. Suddenly
they missed Willie Wills. The guide got very
excited, and they cowered all close round him,
much frightened themselves; and he, abandoning
his learned-off lesson of description, ceased to be a
talking automaton, and seemed greatly concerned.
Ultimately, they came on the truant in a brown
study, unconscious of his risk or the excitement he
had occasioned, standing opposite the tomb of an
early Christian. The Italian flashed angry, snap-
ping reproofs, but my brother remained perfectly
stolid, and at last there came a quiet, amused smile
on his face. He told his friend Woodroffe that he
knew he was not in the slightest danger, because
he remembered, when a boy, being told by a priest
in Kilkenny that if you tore up little pieces of paper
and dropped them as you went along, you could
recover your path safely all through the Catacombs.
He had accordingly torn up a letter and laid a
trail, and he said he would have liked to put their
Cicero again into a fury just to see a particular
curve of his upper lip, when he displayed all his
beautifully-formed upper teeth at him with a snarl

like a hyæna, only he did not wish to hurt his feelings. The whimsical bent of his character could not be better illustrated.

His admiration at Rome was most awakened by an artist whom he irreverently alluded to as 'Old Mike.' He drifted with the ordinary crowd to the Medici Chapel, but lingered long after the crowd had ebbed away, penetrated by the vastness of the imagination of the sculptor.

At Venice he delighted in the gondolás. He was always trying to master a phrase—which he said he remembered by the Curse of Kehama— 'Come si chiama?' (What's the name?) He used to lie back in the gondolá, and say over and over again, to the delight of the gondolier, 'piano,' conscious that it was Italian, but not knowing that it meant, when addressed to a gondolier, 'slowly,' an invitation which exactly suited his indolent inclinations. Once he went in a barca, or sailing gondolá, to Torcello, with a party of eight, consisting of three men and five girls. T. C. Farrer, the painter, had hired the barca for the day, and Agostino, the gondolier, was rowing on the poop; the ladies were in the seats in the stern, and Willie Wills on one of the cross-seats, facing them and the gondolier. Diving into the pockets of his ulster, he came upon a second pipe of his, and, with a customary impulse of good nature, handed it over to the gondolier. Agostino, greatly delighted, bowed to him, and, holding up the pipe in his hands, said, 'Ricordo del vecchio!' (a memento of the old man) and then, after a pause, smiling at all the young girls, who were laughing, he added,

' Padre di tutti.'   These were, unfortunately, about
the only words in Italian that the subject of them
understood. ' Vecchio ' he would naturally have
recognised from Palma Vecchio in picture galleries,
and the name Vecchio clung to him.   He never
afterwards alluded to that voyage to Torcello with
any happiness, and I remember his telling me, with
a good deal of mortification, that he had been called
by the gondolier ' the father of them all.'

The pension where they put up in Florence was
a rambling kind of building, in which it was easy
to lose your way, and the lights were put out at
ten o'clock.   Willie Wills used, after dinner, to
adjourn to the famous Café Doney opposite.   One
night, returning late, he went in the dark into the
wrong room, where a lady was in bed, and, being
greeted by a little scream, he beat a precipitate
retreat.   The next morning, being convinced that
his apologies for the intrusion were due to a certain
lady, he insisted, notwithstanding Woodroffe's repeated remonstrances, that it was his duty to offer
them to her at the first opportunity.   Accordingly,
coming up behind her chair at the breakfast-table,
he said, in his resonant voice, that he had to apolo-
gise for going into her bedroom the previous night.
The gabble of the table was hushed in an instant,
while the lady, covered with blushes, indignantly
denied that he had done anything of the kind.
He was still, however, not satisfied—he made inquiries of the servants—and the following day he
saw, sitting in the reading-room, a lady who he
assured Woodroffe was undoubtedly the very person
he had intruded on, and he immediately crossed

o

the room to her, and in the same words and the same impressive voice apologised. It turned out that it was the same lady he had publicly apologised to at the breakfast-table, and she was so angry that she said if he did not cease annoying her she would leave the hotel. There was nothing unusual in his losing his way in a strange house. His friends were used to find him ascending to the bedrooms in search of the drawing-room ; and, at Windsor, a private postern so perversely impressed itself on his mind, that the sentries got quite accustomed to challenging him when attempting, by that way, to effect an entrance to the castle.

This adventure at Florence was not the only one of the kind. He was groping about one night in the dark, and a lady whom he knew had pity on him and lent him her candle. When the chambermaid came into his room in the morning, she volubly commented on the suspicious circumstance that there were two candlesticks. The only explanation he could give, owing to his want of Italian, was to repeat several times 'La Donna,' pointing in the direction of the lady's room, and this, coupled with the fact that there was no candlestick in her room, gave rise to some scandal. Another circumstance brought him into bad odour with the landlady. Off his bedroom there was a little paved dressing-room, which contained a basin and tap instead of the usual basin and ewer. He went down to breakfast leaving the tap on, and, some hour or two after, going into his room he found the carpet floating. There could not have been a worse arrangement for an absent-minded man, and ten days after he caused another flood in the same manner, to the great fury of the proprietress. Wherever he went his ulster coat caused consternation among hotel-keepers. His want of luggage, as well as his actual dress, excited suspicion, for he had with him only a small canvas-covered Gladstone bag, which he had borrowed from his landlady. It contained a scanty change of raiment, but a full equipment of tobacco, which was invariably seized at every frontier. But, although received with consternation, my brother had not been twenty-four hours in the hotel before he made himself extremely popular. When he got back to London he found in the pocket of his ulster, mixed up with a sheaf of visiting-cards of friends he had met on his journey, a museum of keys belonging to the bedrooms he had occupied at successive hotels. His usage had been always to leave his door open, and always to carry the key about in his pocket, for fear his property should be stolen.

One of the pleasures of his visit to Florence was a meeting with 'Ouida,' whose eye for character enabled her to appreciate his simplicity, gentleness, and sincerity. The companion of his travels says :—' The beautiful country, the associations of classic history, the wonderful sculptures, the frescoes at Orvieto and Siena, stimulated his mind, and brought out the power of it and the poetry of it, so that he seemed quite a different person from the absent-minded, dreamy London man of letters.' The day they left Florence he wrote on the flyleaf of Woodroffe's copy of ' Romola ' his adieu to the city :

o 2

Florence, thou garden of the dreamiest spell ;
Florence, thou sybil of the bigot age ;
Florence, thou scroll of art's own rainbow page ;
Florence, thou tomb of mighty dead, farewell !

It was towards the close of 1887, after his
return from Italy, and while his mind was charged
with its pictures and impressions, that he was
commissioned by Mr. Irving to write a play for
the Lyceum Theatre upon the subject of ' Rienzi.'
For writing it he received 800*l*. ; but, in reference
to what was said in another chapter, it ought to
be remembered that, although this would not be
considered a dazzling recompense by other dramatic
authors of the first rank, the manager of the
Lyceum bought and paid for plays which he did
not always produce. This is a fair answer from a
managerial point of view, although not very con-
soling from the author's. Willie Wills, although
he always considered his remuneration ample and
generous, naturally felt disappointed at his best
work during his lifetime being buried in oblivion.
This, however, is a grief shared by many dramatists
without the compensation of a good round sum of
money. Many years have come and gone since
' Rienzi ' was written, and the probability of its
production has reached near the vanishing point.
It is sad that the protection of dramatic copyright should prevent its being printed and published, for this drama contains more of the author
himself than any other play he ever wrote. The
expression of the actor-manager in the same letter
from which I have already quoted, ' You have surpassed yourself,' confirms me in the opinion that

it is the most powerful, as to me the most affecting, of all his plays. During its composition Mr. Irving writes, ' Go on while the spell is on you,' and the play was indeed written under the spell of his journey to Italy, and the great actor's comprehensive description of it is, ' simply magnificent.'

And yet it was written in circumstances which would have broken the spell for most men, but rather seemed to be a help to the author. I well remember the scene of hugger-mugger in which he used to dictate passages standing back from his easel painting his picture of ' Ophelia and Laertes.' After some fine flight of blank verse, full of poetry and tenderness, he would pause to caution Ophelia, who sat by the stove cooking her dinner, but distracted from her occupation by a flirtation with one of his visitors, that her chop was burning. While this was proceeding one of his pensioners, a man named Russell, employed out of charity to do copying, whose grey coat had lost its skirts, armed with the sword of Laertes, was stealthily pursuing round the studio another pensioner, Dunne, who, as I have said, usurped an easel in a front position. Russell, having been for some time in a much alcoholised condition, was decidedly dangerous, and was following Dunne with the strides of a panther. The dramatist, sublimely unconscious of pursuer and pursued, and of the by-play which had caused the chop to give forth an odour of burning, continued his dictation of the new play, while his secretary, taking it down, tried to smother his laughter.

Although it was very familiar to me, and many

passages of great beauty rest in my memory, I must not attempt to give any extracts from an unpublished and unproduced play. The author would have been faithless to his principles if he had slavishly adhered to history; still, the departures from fact are slight, for the Tribune's life was too dramatic to need much embellishment. The principal delinquencies, as historical purists would regard them, are representing Rienzi as attached to a daughter of the house of Orsini; making the enemy that threatens Rome the Emperor instead of a noble named Pepin; and the abdication following a victory, whereas it was really consequent on the refusal of the people to answer the call to arms.

Bulwer Lytton's novel has made the story of Rienzi familiar. I can remember what a charming scene the author of the play made of the meeting of the brothers. The elder, describing the mild and meditative commonwealth of the monastery in which he would induce the lad to seek a refuge; the life austere, but not without some grace and art. Then the brawl in which the boy is slain by one of the ruffianly barons who preyed upon Rome, the inward bleeding of Cola's grief, and the recasting, in the furnace of his passion, of the dreamy student into the man of action and revolutionary leader. There follows a scene of extraordinary power in the palace of the Baron Orsini, into which, like Brutus feigning madness, he has worked his way in the character of a jester. Without creating suspicion he has mined the ground under the nobles, and made all the preparation for a revolu-

tionary outbreak ; at the same time he has plotted
to engage the rival lords of Rome in a struggle
leading to their mutual destruction. The sort of
Belshazzar's feast, in which the crisis is worked up
while the enemy are at the gates, and the manner
in which this vitriol-tongued jester rules the storm
his wand has raised, the Mephistophelian irony
with which he sports with the situation, when he
has brought the Colonnas, disguised, into the tipsy
revel of the Orsini, make a powerful and exciting
act. The love interest woven in forms a tragic
element, for it is one of the house he has devoted
himself to destroy who entangles his heart. Her
worship of him has brought with it no sympathy
for the people's cause, and is in admirable contrast
with the unselfish love of the Roman mother, who
has devoted her son to the liberties of the people.
What I remember to have been the strongest
scene in the play was that in the church of St.
John Lateran, where Rienzi, preparatory to being
knighted and going forth to lead the citizen army
against the Emperor, watches his arms by night.
He falls asleep, and dreams of the final scene of
the play, in which the palace he has built becomes
his funeral pyre, and, whilst asleep, an assassin
employed by Orsini stalks him from pillar to pillar,
and is just raising his arm to strike the fatal blow
when Francesca Orsini rushes forward and awakes
him from his troubled dream. His stern ven-
geance on her kindred, naturally resented by her,
and for the time alienating the lovers ; the ingrati-
tude of the people when the victory is won ; Rienzi's
excommunication by the papal legate, and an affect-

ing scene, touching even to tears, with his dead
mother, which I remember thinking equal in pathos
to the last scene of ' Charles I. '; and, finally, the
historical fate of the Tribune, burned in his marble
palace, but united in death to his betrothed Orsini
wife, form a drama of extraordinary power and
poetic beauty.

CHAPTER XVIII.

THE LYCEUM 'FAUST.'[1]

IT was at the time when it remained doubtful whether in the shuffle of projects ' Rienzi ' would not come to the top, that Mr. Irving gave its author another commission to write a play for the Lyceum Theatre. It was to be on a subject which, like ' Vanderdecken,' had already been turned into a popular opera, and was familiar enough to all the world to interest every educated person. The impending production of the Roman play had been announced in many paragraphs; but, as the rumours died out, it was thought by some that its final scene being the destruction by fire of Rienzi's palace, the sensational burning of a theatre just about that time had made managers shy of mimic fires. The play which came in its place was ' Faust,' or, as it was at first intended it should be called, ' Mephisto.'

Great was the expectation of ' Faust.' Mr. Irving travelled to Nurnberg with Hawes Craven, the scene painter, and the author of the adaptation got descriptions of the scenery and interior life from his friend Carl Ambruster, descriptions on which, as he said, he used to go home to his

---

[1] This play is noticed in order of production, not of composition.

studio to simmer. His mind held in solution Goethe's great poem—the poem Germans venerate and which it took thirty years to create—for in close intercourse with Dr. Anster, the unapproachable translator of the great master, his work had become very familiar. The play was completed two or three years before its production. I was with my brother in Paris when it was commenced, in the summer of 1880. He had only the original German with him and a German dictionary. The play was produced in 1885. Never —was there such a first night. Royalty was represented by the Prince of Wales, and even the top gallery was occupied by persons of distinction. Many thousands of applications for seats came from Germany, and people gathered at the pit doors from nine o'clock in the morning. The scenery did not work quite smoothly on the first night, and the vision of Margaret at her spinning-wheel refused to illuminate the doctor's darkened study, but the success was, notwithstanding, overwhelming. More of what was called pantomime was afterwards introduced, as Mr. Irving, on the first night, foreshadowed to be his intention—Auerbach's cellar and the witches' kitchen were thrown in, but that the dramatist had brought the story within the three hours' traffic of the stage with a masterly hand, and that the play would be seen for hundreds of nights, was unquestionable. The actor predicted three hundred, four hundred, or five hundred nights; and its first run lasted for seven months, Miss Ellen Terry, before the time came for its withdrawal, quite breaking down and being obliged to relinquish the part of Margaret to Miss Winifred Emery.

It was a somewhat thankless task to be the adaptor of a great poem like Goethe's 'Faust.' It is not everyone who could cope with the difficulties of the task successfully. There are portions of the poem so dramatic that they need but a vigorous translation; others where the poetic element must be toned down and the dramatic heightened; but there are others where there must be a bold flight from crag to crag, and for this, at Goethe's elevation, no common pinions were needed. It is no little praise to W. G. Wills if it can be said—as I think it may—that he did not fall below the level of his task, and that his work was worthy of the great original into which it was interwoven. It was not his duty to found a drama upon the poem, but out of the poem to make a connected drama. This condition made it impossible to create a complete organism—a single muscular system—such as a drama ought to be; the result of his labours could only be a succession of tableaux. But in presenting this, the difference between a good and a bad performance needs an artist's eye to appreciate. The merit of the adaptation is that it is in excellent perspective. The eye that planned saw it as a whole; it blends artistically, and leaves a single—not a disjointed—impression.

The Lyceum 'Faust' has been the subject of so much praise and blame, it has been so enormously successful, and there is so much beauty in the text of the adaptation, that I may be forgiven

for linking some extracts with an outline of the
play as I saw it upon the first night.

' Faust,' as we all know, is the fable of a man
who, by his philosophy, has got behind Nature, as
it were, and seen its processes, until of his faith in
its outward effects, and the impressions derived
to the senses, is left no vestige ; he lives on from
' nothingness to nothingness,' and in his old age
discovers himself to be but a charlatan. He
resents the folly of having sacrificed his youth to
this vain pursuit :

> Curst be all knowledge ! blasted, root and branch,
> That rotten tree whose fruit crumbles to dust !
> Curst the illusions that dance by our side,
> While youth is on the hills, and singing nature,
> To leave us in our age, bare, blank, aghast,
> A fear unto ourselves !
> Curst be Hope's balsam and its leprous lees,
> Which rest like fire on the shrivell'd lip !
> Curst be ambition, lying, murderous sphinx !
> That burns the light of life in monuments,
> And flings away youth's crystal cup untasted !
> Curst be the slavish nature that I own
> Unbidden gift from my Creator's hand !
> And upon Patience be my deepest curse !

Cribbed in his wintry prison, he cries out :

> But for one year of youth, one large bland year,
> And let this leaden death drop from my limbs,
> This ache pass from my heart ;
> I reck not of the price I pay for it.

The fable makes a man permitted to relieve his
life, bound not to the quest of philosophy, but to
the cynical fiend of self-centred pleasure, come
again to a more terrible despair, in which, however, one feels there is at least a possibility that

he as well as his victim is redeemed by love. The
study scene, in which we see this barren despair—
the resolve to drink the poisoned goblet, the act
arrested by the Easter hymn, the invocation and
apparition of the fiend from vapour clouds, the
wondrous pictures of a life of joy with which, as by
an anodyne, Mephisto lulls the old philosopher
from his frenzy, the cynical element which then,
as in other dramas the vein of comedy, begins to
relieve the tragedy and so keeps on to the end—
all this, brought to a perfect focus, leaves one
impression on the mind, and when it fades away
we are in the old-world town of Nurnberg, and
Faust is young and gallant again, and steered by
this cynic pleasure-fiend ; and there is the mixture
of mediæval reality in the topers here drinking
outside the inn, the penitents going to confession,
the procession of monks issuing from one of the
offices of the church, convulsed by some joke which
is the reaction of the solemnity. Here Faust first
sees Margaret shrived, pure and white, pass like a
sunbeam from the church :

A regency of most unearthly beauty !

She chides his compliment, and leaves him
tranced :

By Heaven, the air is chiming with her words!
With what delicious petulance she answered!
And yet I saw the azure beam of pardon
In the quick glance beneath her damask lids.

The next act opens with Margaret's chamber.
Faust and Mephisto deposit the casket of jewels in
her box, and they are discovered by the maiden,

who is childishly delighted with her glittering toys,
and the distinction they lend to her appearance,
but, womanly, guesses the giver. A front scene
then carries us away to a hill overlooking the red-
tiled city, and for this view of Nurnberg alone it
was worth visiting the Lyceum. Mephisto is in a
fiendish rage because the jewels have been devoted
to holy church :

A morsel for her most insatiate maw !

Margaret's mother,

Who sniffs at every piece of furniture
To find if it smell holy or profane,

has scented something accursed in the trinkets.
Another casket must be found. With this other
casket of gems, more costly than the first, Margaret
visits her gossip Martha. As Margaret is encouraged illicitly to deck herself in her jewels, and
the old gossip fans the flame of growing fancy,
Mephisto visits the dame, on the excuse of bringing her tidings of her husband's death. This
amusing scene, in which nothing could be more
inimitable than Mr. Irving's acting, follows Goethe
closely. In the delightful and quaint garden
scene, outside Martha's cottage, the real and the
mock lovers—Faust and Margaret, Mephisto and
Martha alternately hold the stage. This scene
the dramatist has made full of tenderness, and
clothed in great beauty of language, while following the original in outline. He preserves the
beautiful love test of the flower, introducing it by
the lines :

MARGARET : My heart is full—tears come—I know not why.
To-night is like the first day spent in Heaven—
All peace, all trust, and yet all wonderment.
I had no warning of this happiness ;
The blessed Virgin sent no dream to me ;
And now I am so joyed—Dost love me so ?

Act III. begins with Faust's repentance of the task he has set himself. The scene is a wild gap in the hills, where he wanders, communing with Nature. His evil genius follows him. Mephisto taunts him with his inconsistency, and then draws a picture of poor deserted Margaret, and tempts him to return to her. He gives him the phial, a few drops of which will throw her mother into a deep sleep ; and, after a struggle with his conscience, Faust is persuaded to renew his pursuit. The fiend following, remarks contemptuously, that when cowards find themselves caught in a mesh and cannot clear away the gluey toils, they think it is the very crack of doom.

> Give me the man who will go straightly on
> With a strong will—pig-headed, damnable.
> The poorest, tamest devil of us all
> Is he who doubts and weighs, yet, in the end,
> Completes the crime with a weak, botching hand.

In Margaret's garden, where she sits spinning, Mephisto is a visitor, and, warning Margaret of one weakness of her lover, that if she talks of the Redemption, his love will wither, Margaret starts, crucifix in hand, and cries, holding it aloft—

> If you are evil, and God's enemy,
> Then let this holy symbol drive thee hence !

The fiend slinks away. Faust comes : the love-making is once more full of tenderness and beauty.

Margaret will not let him leave her again. She receives the phial, and retires into her mother's cottage. Mephisto mocks at her lover, still trying to compromise with his conscience, as a 'super-sensual sensualist,' who moralises even while he betrays, and exultantly exclaims—

Ay, but, to-night—to-night!

And, when Faust still shows some tendency to cheat the Devil by remaining constant to his love, instead of sating his passion and destroying its object, the fiend subdues the wavering intent in a speech superbly delivered—

Thou answerest me
As if I were some credulous mate.
I am a spirit, and I know thy thought;
You hope to wriggle out of our strait bond—
You think you might be fenced round by and by
With sprinkled holy water, lifted cross,
While you and your pale saint might hold a siege
Against the Devil! Ere that thing should be,
I'd tear thee limb from limb—thy mangled flesh
I'd scatter piecemeal, so that none could say
This carrion once was Faust! Thy blood I'd dash
Upon the wind, like rain!
Yon cottage would I snatch up in a whirlwind,
At midnight, like a pebble in a sling,
And whirl it leagues away—a crumbled mass—
With its crushed, quivering tenant under it!
This bond I'd tear to ribbons, and wipe out
This score between us in your body's blood.
While Hell's awake in me, speak! dost thou dare me?

This outburst of fiendish fury, in contrast to the hollow cynicism in which he is clothed as an ordinary garb, has a fine effect, and is artistically conceived.

The fourth act is three months after. Margaret

begins to be suspected and taunted by her companions. Her mother is dead—killed by the decoction in the phial. The unhappy girl's prayer before the image of the Virgin is deeply pathetic. As her shame is beginning to be known, her brother Valentine returns from the wars; and, as Faust and Mephisto serenade Margaret, the soldier steps forward and smashes the instrument on which the fiend, in his Grimalkin mood, strums.

In the duel that ensues, Mephisto foils the thrusts of the avenger, and each time the three swords cross, a blue electric flame flashes. The most touching scene in the play is that where Valentine lies dying, and, as he is surrounded by a crowd of neighbours, his sister rushes in; he forbids her to touch him, and gives cruel counsels how to ply her new trade of infamy, and reminds her of the days when she was his pet and pride—

No more, in snowy dress, before the altar
You'll take your stand. No more, with maiden pride,
In neat lace collar, lead the village dance,
But 'neath some shameless roof hide from your kind!

Then follows that tremendous scene in the church, while the music in the 'Dies Iræ' peals and wails away, in which the girl attempts to pray, but each prayer is strangled by the fell fiend behind her, who whispers counsels of despair. This agony of temptation, in which the tempter is visible, mingling in her prayers, brings the act to a powerful conclusion.

The fifth opens with the wonderful tableau of the Brocken. The scene is in the Hartz Mountains, among which the zigzag lightning flashes. To the left, old dwarfed trees; to the right, practicable

P

rocks, from which, in this region of cloudland, a huge white owl soars away on noiseless wing. Mephisto and Faust come toiling up the mountain, the former, in his red dress, the lurid centre of the picture. Lichened rocks seem to separate from themselves forms in grey, cobwebby robes, of sorcerers and witches and ape-like creatures, whose eldritch screeches greet the master Faust, spellbound, looking on at the diabolical revel. The plaints of the old bent sorcerer, who, for three hundred years, has been climbing up the mountain, and never reached the top, are chorused by wild shrieks of witches' laughter. Here—as the apes fawn upon him, the electric flames burst from the rocks on which he seats himself among his familiars, or as he stands, like a lightning blasted tree in malignant majesty, upon the Brocken's summit— Mr. Irving's Mephisto rises to real grandeur.

This weird scene, which may appear to the vulgar, perhaps, to be forced into the play for its own sake alone, and to have no connection with the action, save that which is derived from making Faust see a vision of Margaret with a red circle round her throat—a warning, as in a dream, of the fact that she is in the dungeon, under sentence of death—is necessary to make the fiend grow, in our conception, to the tragic requirements of the play. He must take off the mask for us, and we must see the Devil and his bond, to charge the last scene with its full measure of tragedy. With Faust's hurried recognition of the vision—

'Tis she! 'Tis she! I now remember all :
It is my Margaret's spirit. She is dead !

and the fiend's angry adjuration—-

> The curse of hell on it ! Vanish ! all vanish !

the weird crowd seems to blend into the lichened
rocks of the Brocken, and, while the mountain
beyond veils itself in an unearthly glare, the scene
changes to Margaret's dungeon. Margaret sits on
her pallet counting—

> One, two, three ! I have yet five hours to live !
> Let me divide them. There is one for prayer,
> And one to nurse my babe—its little breathings
> Are on my ruffled pillow. I can't see it,
> But it is there. I thank God it is there.
> Two hours for sleep. In dreams I meet my love.
> And then an hour to watch the rising sun,
> Whose setting I shall never, never see !

Faust enters to bear her away. She pleads
with him, as the supposed headsman ; he comes
too soon. In vain her lover tries to fix her wandering thoughts. She talks of her dead mother, and
the little child she drowned in her madness. Then
the half-daft recognition ; and, even in his embrace,
the unsettled mind wanders away :—

> Mother doth sleep ! The sweetbriar, wet with dew,
> Gives all its heavy sweetness to the night.
> Oh, welcome ! but speak low ; she might awake.

There follows the harrowing struggle between
the lover, desperate to save her, and the poor girl's
inability to understand his pleadings, and in this
crisis of fate, while grey dawn is breaking, showing
him how to range their graves, or seeing the drowning child, and crying for help, or whispering she
cannot pass the hill where her mother sits on a
stone—

> Her eyes are set—her hand lies
> Dead, and pale, and heavy.

P 2

Then she sees, in her daft fancy, the crowd and scaffold, and beseeches her lover, who passionately entreats her to seize the moment for escape—

O, Heinrich, let me see thee in that crowd ;
Stretch up thy hands that I may see thy face
When I am bound for death.   Oh, promise me
That thou wilt never take thine eyes from mine
Till——
    FAUST : I promise, Margaret, but thou shalt not die.
Upon my knees I beg of thee to come :
Thy prison doors are open : let us fly.
    MARG. : Ah ! I feel death, like a delivering angel
Sent straight from God, descending on my heart ;
Perchance, in mercy, I might die to-night.
Nay, let us kneel and pray that God may strike
The chains of sin from our despairing souls.
Because of our great love and all my sorrow,
He may have pity, and may save us both.

Mephisto, furious, enters—

> What is this mad delay ?   My horses stand
> In the chill morning air ; force her away !

Margaret flies to the foot of the cross, and clings to it for shelter ; the fiend plucks Faust away with the cry, ' Hither to me ! ' and the curtain falls on Margaret lying dead, and a flight of shining angels come to her succour.

Of course there were those who resented the adaptation of Goethe's poem, and thought that, if put on the stage, it ought to have been in the language of the original.   But had such counsels been followed, the play would not have been acted a greater number of times than any modern drama.

Three copies were printed for individuals whose names were on the title-page, so stringently has dramatic copyright to be guarded.

CHAPTER XIX.

PARIS never lost its spell upon my brother. For part of the year he made it his headquarters, living at his studio in the Impasse Hélène, Rue de Clichy. It is not a savoury part of the town, and the studio looked out on a dreary piece of waste ground where skeletons of old omnibuses took their last repose. When I stayed with him, our meals were prepared by the Concierge. My brother gave the dishes the finishing touch by his happy gift of imagination, investing them with all the appetising attributes of French cookery. If the sun were shining the little table would be laid on a sort of terrace on which all the studios opened, and he would point with pride and enjoyment to the dreamy loveliness of the stone walls and decrepid omnibuses, ' sainted,' as he expressed it, with the evening sunshine. Sometimes, instead of dining at home on the garlic-smelling preparations of the Concierge, we sallied forth to a restaurant outside, where one, ungifted by the imagination which seasoned all the dishes, not without qualms partook of unwonted food, while he vigorously practised French dialogue with the nearest bourgeois customer.

Among his neighbours in the studios were Van Beers and Falero. He was an ardent admirer of

French art, and Van Beers gave him many useful
hints, one of which I remember, as it was probably
called out by his carelessness in little matters, that
every detail in a picture should be amusing—by
which the artist meant interesting, and worth
examining. To this studio my brother consigned
some oak furniture, purchased in Normandy ; and
long after he had given up painting in Paris, he
went on paying the rent, and left the oak armoire
and chairs in possession, someone else, without his
knowledge, occupying and using the premises.

It was from this studio that he made excursions
into Normandy, and found out the delightful sea-
village of Etretat. He was one of those who, by
spreading its fame, helped to make the place, and
for several years he spent there a part of every
summer. In passing through the country he used
to delight in pointing out its un-English characteristics—the unfenced fields, the peasant in the tilled
ground with a huge blue umbrella, the discretion
in colour shown even in the farming implements.
The railway stopped within twelve miles of Etretat,
and the journey was completed by diligence.

The hotel-keeper was a great friend, and could
not make enough of my brother. Those were
halcyon days, the happiest, I think, of all his life.
In good health, a favourite alike with English and
Americans, he luxuriated in plunging into the sea,
clad in the sort of Spanish costume and straw hat
worn by all bathers, and swimming out long distances to float in the limpid sunshine, and he entered
into life as he never did at home, and was the
old Willie Wills of younger days. He immensely

enjoyed the French mode of living—the early bowl
of fragrant coffee, and the rolls and butter brought
to his bedside by the bonne in her white Norman
cap: the *déjeuner*, which finished the morning
section of the day, and then the long walks and
late dinner. Afterwards there was the pleasure of
looking across the sea where England lay, sipping
his black coffee and *petit ver* of cognac. This life,
free from the parasites of his London existence,
quite transformed him. It was at Etretat that one
of his plays, in which there is some of his best
work, was written. Two young ladies took turns
to act as his amanuenses, and he dictated to them
in the little wood adjoining the town. He would get
so wrapped up in the scenes as to forget his scribes,
and shed tears when his theme was sorrowful, and
speak in wrathful accents in scenes of anger; but
he never hesitated for a word—only at times he
would pause while the inspiration gathered, and
then move freely on again. The freedom with
which he moved in the dramatic medium was very
unlike the difficulty described by Vezin when he
first dictated a play to him.

His friends tell how, when the work was finished,
they had a feast in which he toasted the happy
days of work in ' his extraordinarily eloquent
British-French,' and made the waiters glad with
unwonted *largesse*. The next morning, however, joy
was turned to sorrow: he appeared on the scene with
looks of despair. His manuscript was lost. There
was a general commotion. Every one had been
interested in watching *l'auteur dramatique* at work,
and the whole community joined in the hunt. The

crier beat his drum through the streets, and announced the reward of a louis d'or for the lost
manuscript, but all in vain. The work of weeks had
vanished like the empty foam. But just when the
hour of departure had arrived, a poor woman came
in sight. waving the lost manuscript in her hand.
Her child had found it on the beach, where it had
dropped out of the author's pocket. As he had
not kept a single note of the play to help him to
re-write it, he confessed how much he had mentally
suffered at its loss. The play was 'Icenia,' written
for Miss Mary Anderson, the plot being by Mr.
Wilson Barrett. Miss Anderson paid three hundred
pounds in advance of royalties, but it was finished
only shortly before her marriage, and, on that event,
the agreement fell through, and it is still unproduced.
The heroine, who gives her name to the play, is a
young barbarian princess of Boadicea's blood ; and
it is not merely the poetry, full as it is of the flashes
of fancy which meet one in all the author's work,
nor the skill in construction due to Mr. Barrett,
nor yet the picturesque contrasts of wild Britain
and super-civilised Rome ripening to decay, or of
the virtues of the barbarian and the cruelty and
sensualism of the conqueror ; but in 'Icenia' there
is a study of nature in the inmost windings of a
woman's heart, which, with all his unrivalled skill
in making his characters flesh and blood realities,
he had hardly ever surpassed. The actress who
could realise the character he conceived in this
young Boadicea, would add to the repertory of the
stage a beautiful creation.

The Roman general, Julian, who has subdued

the heart of this wild nymph, and shelters her
from the sensualist Clotus by making her wear the
badge of his slave, and Fulvia, a type of the cruel
patrician lady, to whom he is betrothed, are
admirably drawn characters. Out of these rela-
tionships it can easily be seen how an interesting play was evolved : Julian's love of his slave,
Fulvia's jealousy and domestic tyranny, the wild
spirit of the captive, tamed to submission by love.
Scenes of Rome in its decline, such as Couture
painted, or the solemn oak groves starred with
mistletoe of the Druids, lend chances to the scenic
artist to give the dramatic poetry a worthy setting.
' Icenia ' is a great play waiting for a great actress.
There could not have been a more delightful scene
for play writing than Etretat, and under such
pleasurable conditions my brother did his best
work. I spent but one summer with him in Normandy, and not that which he devoted to dramatic
work—but one was like the other. Several of his
friends, the Miss Corkrans among others, shared
the discovery of this delightful out of the world
nook, and went there summer after summer ; so
that much of what was wholesome and pleasant in
his world accompanied him when he left behind
for a while the locust tribe that never endingly
was settled upon his studio. He did not, however,
leave behind the delightful blundering, abstracted
ways which went with him everywhere. A characteristic instance of his absence of mind is told of
one of these Etretat days. He set off on horseback to keep an appointment at Havre. Midway
he paused to light his pipe and turned his horse to

avoid the wind; when the pipe was lit he resumed his ride. 'Unfortunately,' the narrator says, 'he had omitted to turn his horse's head back towards Havre, and only became conscious of the fact when the horse stopped in the courtyard of the hotel from the stable of which he had started.'

The quaint fishing-village, the procession of fishermen with their offerings of sea-shells and little models of fishing-boats, the service which was a sort of harvest home of the seas, the lovely old Norman church (in which, however, he thought the Gregorian chants sepulchral), the apple-farms and peasant farmers in the country round, all charmed and interested my brother beyond measure; and here, summer after summer, he came and threw off his London slough and the unhealthy mode of life in the studio, and became altogether his delightful genial self. I do not know why he gave up his annual visit to the Norman village, but I think there was something he took umbrage at, one of those little insolences which brought out the quiet dignity of his character, and to which he would not expose himself a second time. Whatever it may have been he never visited Etretat again after that summer when I left him there, just as an invasion took place of the French coast by swarms of mosquitoes.

CHAPTER XX.

' CLAUDIAN.'

IF ' Icenia ' is associated with Etretat, ' Claudian ' had a homelier birthplace.

In the summer of 1882 my brother was captured by Henry Herman, then Mr. Wilson Barrett's manager in the heyday of the Princess's, and carried off to Margate to write a play, Herman providing the plot. The house in which ' Claudian ' was brought forth was in Harold Road, then the end of Cliftonville; and the window of the room where my brother wrote, as usual in bed, looked out on yellowing cornfields and blue seas in the direction of the North Foreland. After the morning's work he would get up and issue forth with the rest of the party to bathe. The Hermans were extremely hospitable, and the work of playwriting was done under the pleasantest conditions. In six weeks the drama was finished, and the writer of it returned to London, as usual with his parcel, containing a comb and brush and odd articles of clothing. Shirts he bought from day to day, and invariably left the accumulation behind him. I never remember his having a portmanteau, but he owned at one time a Gladstone bag, which had a trick of opening on the road when packed to the full, and relieving itself of the whole of its contents. It used to be a mystery what became of his clothes, of which little traces were ever to be found excepting in tailor's bills. It may have been the mystery of a Gladstone bag.

During the progress of the work, consultations and readings took place after breakfast in his bedroom, which was the workshop, and sometimes a fierce clash of disputation could be heard within. The writer of the play complained that he was not always supplied with bricks to build, meaning details of plot, and Herman, that the parts intended to afford comic relief would not get a laugh in ten years. In the end, I think, Mr. George Barrett had to supply two or three jokes for his own consumption, one of which was a homely reference to rates and taxes. Herman, as witness his comic opera, had not a trace of humour himself, but he was fertile in invention and teemed with melodrama, and had besides an excellent and refined judgment. In knowledge of stage effects and all it was possible to do with scenery he was a past master. He had in his study a miniature earthquake, showing how temples and classic palaces would topple down, as the effect was actually to be produced upon the Princess's stage. In the days of his prosperity he generally occupied the royal box, or the nearest approach to it available, at all first night performances; and his judgment was received with much deference, but his unfortunate comic opera broke the spell. His manner was that of the irritable foreigner, but he was thoroughly kind-hearted and chivalrous in his domestic life, and well maintained the dignity of a literary man.

The plot of 'Claudian,' a man cursed with immortality, and bringing ruin on all he loved, was suggested probably by the Wandering Jew. The development of the idea involved much morbid thinking out, and my brother told me that writing the play was a great strain on his nerves. When it was finished, Mr. Wilson Barrett was so pleased with it and thankful for the rapidity with which the work was done, that he added 100*l*. to the agreed price, of which my brother's share was thus made up to 700*l*., or at the rate of a hundred a week and a hundred over, as it took only six weeks to write. I do not know what Herman received, but probably as much more. Two adjournments of the production took place, owing to insufficient rehearsal, and the mechanical effects not being in perfect working order. When at last it was presented to an audience of the Princess's Theatre, accustomed to plays like the 'Silver King,' the sudden change of fare did not prevent it from having the most favourable reception. Mr. Ruskin has stated he admired the play so much that he went three times to see it, and he thought all its teaching entirely right. In these days, however, the higher criticism is applied to plays, as well as to the Scriptures. 'Claudian' gave rise to some curious questions in theology, and an opinion at variance with Professor Ruskin's was expressed by one of our most distinguished critics. He complains that 'Claudian's' punishment is inflicted on every-one but himself; and contrasts the story with that of Ahasuerus the Jew, 'who insults the Saviour, and is cursed with a restless everlasting life.' There is in his case only one interposition of supernatural power, and the punishment falls on the guilty, and on him alone. So it is with Vanderdecken. It appears from this, that the Wandering Jew is no one's enemy but his own, while 'Claudian' brings a century of disaster on the planet to punish his own crime—the punishment is vicarious—not one for all, but all for one. This is putting the case against the play strongly, but, on the other hand, taking as our authority Eugene Sue's version of the 'Wandering Jew,' so far from his being a harmless sufferer, a hideous plague accompanies his footsteps, causing more disaster than the armies of conquerors; the world is decimated by the pestilence the Almighty attaches to his presence wherever he is driven in his penance of everlasting insomnia.

Again, Vanderdecken's connection with disaster is not to be explained, as a way he had of being in at the death. Where his lurid sail is seen, he is the unwilling agent of divinely appointed calamities. It is in this office lies his punishment. But, leaving legend, the higher critic must turn his artillery on the Bible. He must apply his criticism to the message of the prophet, who offers David the choice of sword or famine or pestilence. It was the people, not David, who suffered, though they were in no wise responsible for his sin. 'Let Thy hand be upon me and upon my house; but these sheep, what have they done?' David's complaint is Mr. Archer's. But the dramatist ought only, I would submit, to be judged by the success with which he works out his problem, and the interest he manages to impart to its

development. Theatre-goers to such nice questions
would exclaim, like a well-known cleric, 'Hang
theology!' The critic has admitted indeed that he
had against him the general sense of the public, by
whom the play was enthusiastically received.

In the controversies upon it, another criticism
may be noticed. Like the ' Silver King,' who falls
on his knees to thank God for his escape, owing
to a trainful of passengers having been carbonised,
Claudian extracts a blessed thought of comfort
from the fleeting masses of poor fugitives clutching
the flaming lips of the abyss, and dropping writhing
down with stifled shrieks, that it is the omen of his
own release. Yet, surely, when the horror has
been wrought up to the full, what more natural than
such a transition? It is a true touch of nature,
that out of the unutterable horror steals this still
small voice of comfort and hope. Amid hecatombs
of dead, the exultation of victory is not deemed
unnatural, nor when hundreds are swept from the
wreck is it thought inhuman on the part of those
who are saved to be impulsively thankful for their
own deliverance. Singly, or in masses, men die
and must die, and a 'cheerful pessimism,' of
which the author of ' Claudian ' is accused, is, after
all, the most sensible frame of mind. But Claudian's cry of despair was: 'I alone cannot die.'
His joy is, not that he has escaped the common lot,
but that at last life's prison gate is open to him
and he can rid the world of his blighting presence.
He chooses death out of love and pity; and at the
moment, when after a hundred years of misery,
life seems worth possessing, he sacrifices it for the

sake of the woman he loves. That human existence
for a hundred years has been made a hot hell to
others that it may be a tepid purgatory to him is
a complete misstatement of the case, for those
material misfortunes he caused to others do not
make hell ; they make earth as it is. It is that little
chamber of the heart which may be the torture-
room of hell.

CHAPTER XXI.

WHIMS AND HOLIDAY COLLABORATIONS.

IT was while 'Claudian' was being written, that
a fierce attack upon one of the author's plays
appeared in the 'World.' Dutton Cooke's review
in this paper was what he most dreaded on the
production of a new play. The party assembled at
Harold Road took up the cudgels against the
unkind critic, and witchcraft was resorted to as a
means of revenge. The jest was forgotten, but a
curious coincidence gave it a serious turn two or
three days after, and was subsequently made use
of by the dramatist in a way which, without dis-
playing remarkable wit, was very illustrative of the
grave whimsicality of his character, in which so
much of the boy was left uneliminated.

In another publication which treats of the
events and foibles of London life from a humorous
standpoint, his plays were as a rule turned into
keen ridicule, by a writer who was always exceedingly friendly when they met at the club. The
dramatist did not probably realise that to emphasise
the humorous side of things was the *métier* of the
publication in question, and thought that serious
work deserved serious criticism. Much that was
written of in a light vein to raise a laugh, he
judged the writer thought really ridiculous. This

Q

persistent attitude of the critic, great friendliness
when they met, and of ridicule in his journal,
gradually disconcerted Willie Wills. One day,
fresh from the sting of what he thought a cruel
review, he told the perfidious critic of a singular
coincidence. He had amused his friends in Harold
Road by modelling with a lump of wax a little
image of the figure and face of Dutton Cooke.
When it was finished he stood it up in a saucer,
some distance from a roaring fire, and watched the
heat of the fire gradually assert itself on the traits
and features of the critic, until ultimately the
simulacrum tottered in the saucer, and sank into a
molten mass. The day but one afterwards, he
read in the first column of the 'Times' of the
death of Dutton Cooke. Now, he said, turning
sharply round to his friend, 'I can easily make a
little bust in wax of your head. Shall I do it?'

And after that he thought the criticisms were
more genial.

The summer following the production of 'Claudian,' while 'Faust,' which was written in 1880-1,
still lay on the shelf, there came a break in his
dramatic commissions. Henry Herman had taken
the Maisonette at Broadstairs, and my brother
spent a good part of the summer there. He and
Herman, combining holiday and work, were
engaged on a play which it was at first intended to
call 'A King's Ransom.' As that name, however,
had been appropriated, 'Honi Soit' was adopted, but
it was finally named 'A Royal Ransom.' It was a
curious illustration of Herman's talent for business
that, although never produced, this play realised

600*l.*, and yet the rights in it remain to the present unalienated. It came about on this wise. The American rights were purchased by a syndicate for 400*l.* Before the piece could be produced, the syndicate went into liquidation, and Herman refused to allow the assignees to have the rights. Mr. S. French then paid 100*l.* in advance of royalties, but failing to produce the play within the stipulated time, the agreement fell through. Then Miss Hawthorne bought the assignee's rights, but, in 1890 the contract expired. Messrs. Williamson and Garner paid an advance of 100*l.* for the Australian rights, and this contract also fell through by lapse of time. If Herman had not suffered reverses of fortune which injured his position in the dramatic world, so fine a play would hardly have been shelved ever since. The plot is laid in the reign of Charles II., and the merry monarch is introduced as one of the characters. The way in which the *dénouement* is brought about is effective, and, if not original, will certainly be new to most playgoers. Herman was very exacting as a collaborateur. Although not a master of English style, owing to his foreign extraction, he was an unerring judge of the work of others. My brother was not submissive to criticism, and the distant growl of storms on the horizon of his bedroom, might be heard at the Maisonette, as before, in Harold Road, when 'Claudian' was in process of incubation. Herman refused to accept carelessly done work, and after a stout resistance, scenes were refashioned to his satisfaction. The stormy weather of the morning left not a wrack

behind in the afternoon, which was devoted to
amicable strolls, and the porcupine of the morning,
whose every quill bristled to defend himself against
the terrier-like attack of Herman, was the most
genial of men and pleasantest of companions when
the nerve tension of composition was over. During
part of his long visit to the Maisonette, Mr.
E. W. Godwin, who was for several years one of
his closest friends, was also Herman's guest. He
was architect of the Northampton Town Hall,
which is considered a masterpiece of architectural
design, and he divided with Mr. Lewis Wingfield
the reputation of being the great authority on the
mounting and dressing of plays. I believe that it
was in the production of ' Juana ' the intimacy first
arose. In company with him and Lady Archibald
Campbell, my brother made that trip I have spoken
of, provided with a glass pickle jar, to the Goodwins,
to get a bottle of the yellow sands. He saw all
things through the medium of his imagination, and
conjured from this bottle of sand, with his power of
poetical imagery, the treasures and the drowned
sailors, and the gaunt wrecks buried in the Goodwins. Godwin claimed the sands as a sort of
patrimony, for they were, he asserted, named after
Godwin, Earl of Kent, his alleged Saxon ancestor.
Lady Archibald had come to the Maisonette to
consult the three wise men foregathered there
about the ' Pastoral Shepherd,' of which she
intended to give an open air representation, and
some little work of adaptation was done upon it by
my brother. A very pleasant association of his
friendship with Godwin was the pilgrimages they

made together to the dead cities of Holland, traces
of which are to be found in 'Melchior.'   The great
regard he had for Godwin found expression in the
following lines, written upon his friend's death—

'Tis hard to feel that he is passed from sight,
  The temple empty, lifeless beauty's priest ;
The Prospero who conjured up the light
  Of antique Grecian days, with them deceased.
We hardly deem those soft brown eyes are dim
  With deep observance, pensive kindness filled ;
The joyous laugh, the flash of playful whim,
  All silent ; and the fingers lithe and skilled
Forgetful of their cunning ; genius flown,
  Starved by a tasteless age and unfulfilled,
Finds its fond record on this honoured stone,
  Traced by a loving hand.   We left him here alone.

Looking back over those days of collaboration with
Herman one thinks what a pity it was that he
did not spend more of his life under such friendly
tutelage, and in such pleasant holiday tasks as this
play-writing at the Maisonette.   For some reason
the two drifted apart, though Herman retained a
great regard for his collaborateur.   Perhaps the
one was a little tyrannical, and the other impatient
of being obliged to take his work regularly.   A
collaborateur of a more peaceful kind was the Hon.
Mrs. Greene, in the last novel he wrote, or had a
share in writing, called 'Whose Hand.'   It was
the day when the 'Mystery of a Hansom Cab'
and 'Mr. Barnes of New York' created a demand
for that class of literature, and he suggested to his
cousin that they should weave together one of
those puzzles of crime.   Of course such a new
enterprise was congenial to him, and an interesting
book was the result.   This work, too, was combined

with a pleasant holiday at New Building, Horsham, where Mrs. Greene then lived.

I remember there was a battle royal over the book with his friend, Major Loftus Fox, who was particularly great in finding out likenesses and insinuating plagiarisms. He was a man who read everything that was worth reading, whereas my brother, although he was fond of Dickens in his latter days, did not read English novels. Nothing made him more angry than the injustice of charging him with copying from books he had never read or even heard of. Fox insisted that in 'Whose Hand' there was a scene practically identical with one in a book by Miss Rhoda Broughton. A man receives a telegram at night that his friend is dying; he has to wait a considerable time for a train, and when he arrives at a country station finds there is no conveyance. He sets out to walk, and the description of the wakening morning is the same; first a cock crows, then a peasant comes down the road rubbing his eyes, then the whole country blossoms into life. He arrives at the house to find the blinds down; the hush of death has fallen upon it; he has come too late. My brother insisted that he had not read Miss Broughton's book; Fox, that it was criminal negligence not to have done so, and thus avoided glaring parallelism. The two —the author, bursting with rage, furious and emphatic, throwing unwonted strength into his language; Fox, with a voice of brazen resonance, which nothing could drown or silence—wrangled and harangued; while a select party in the studio, huddled about the door of the bedroom where

Willie Wills lay in state, with difficulty suppressed their titters.

It was some time after one of those encounters before the angry bristles of the usually genial and placable author subsided.

On the death of Sir Charles Young, two of the manuscripts of his unfinished plays were sent to the studio to be completed. I can only put this among his holiday collaborations on the ground he made holiday instead of doing his work. It was with great difficulty, and when chance after chance of placing it had been lost, that he could be brought to finish even one. As a result of this tardiness, the play which is called 'The Sunset of Life' is still on the shelf, I believe, in the possession of Mr. Chapman, who was Sir Charles Young's agent. An inertness was now beginning to creep over his life, his mother and his home being still the one incentive to any sort of exertion. The long sedentary times in the studio began to tell their tale. If he could have been taken out of that rut into which his days had fallen he might still have done much good work, and lived many honoured years. But yet one other drama of the first importance lay before him, and one the history of which tinged with sadness and deepened the gloom of his latter days. Tennyson had been asked to write a drama upon 'The Idylls of the King,' but very wisely declined to do so. It was not for their author to use those exquisite poems as building materials. The task was then committed to my brother by Mr. Irving. He preserved the spirit, while using none of the actual material of Tennyson's 'Idylls.' I venture

to think that his treatment of this subject is of
some literary importance, and in the next chapter
will give as good an account as I can of Wills's
' King Arthur.' It was the last leap of the flame
of his dramatic genius, and, in the opinion of many
of his friends, one of the brightest.

CHAPTER XXII.

WRITES ' KING ARTHUR ' FOR SIR HENRY IRVING.

How delighted my brother would have been had he
lived to see ' King Arthur' on the Lyceum play-
bills, for he thought it one of the best of the plays
he was commissioned to write for Sir Henry Irving.
There is some documentary evidence that the latter
shared this view; he was certainly well satisfied,
and paid the author 800*l.* for his work. The production, however, is no slight part of the dramatist's
guerdon, and for this he waited seven years, as for
a still longer time he vainly waited in the hope of
seeing ' Rienzi' put upon the stage. ' Rienzi' may
one day be produced, but ' King Arthur' never. I
have been given permission to publish it, and I
hope to do so hereafter, when the rest of his plays
can appear. I propose here giving only a short
outline. Had the dramatist lived he would doubt-
less have been called in to make the many changes
necessary before a play is put upon the stage.
That being impossible, Sir Henry invited a dramatic writer of the first rank, Mr. Comyns Carr, to
make the alterations required. The play was sent
to him, and, after some consideration, he naturally
preferred to write an original play on the Arthu-
rian legend, and, having received permission to do
so, accomplished the task entirely to Sir Henry

Irving's satisfaction. I fortunately succeeded in
winnowing the loose pages of my brother's drama
from masses of old papers, and was rewarded by
successfully putting together the whole play, written
in his minute pencilling.

The drama opens in a stately hall at Camelot,
where Arthur's knights foreshadow the plot, won-
dering why Launcelot, the fourth ambassador for
the hand of Guenever, dallies a month at Camelliard—

> Such scurvy treatment touches all of us,
> A King whose fame, even as the bristling sun,
> Gilds half the world, that he should sue in vain.

Mordred's disloyalty to his uncle shows itself in
vaunting of the regal honours heaped upon himself
at Camelliard, and the acknowledgment of his
undoubtedly royal birth, while Arthur was spoken
of by the old King as

> A stream without a source,
> An infant found and foisted on the nation
> By an old trickster, Merlin.

The gem, as Tristram says, is witness to its own
worth, and tells its lustrous tale. And here the
first suggestion of Launcelot's bosom treason is
woven in by Dagonet, while Tristram defends him
as a prince of chivalry.

Arthur makes his entrance in the midst of a
comic combat between the court fool, who comes
capering in on a hobby-horse with a distaff for a
spear, and the surly knight, Sir Kay, who ever jeers
at chivalry.

> ARTHUR : Ye are merry. What is the jest?
> SIR TRISTRAM : Sir Kay is railing, sire.

ARTHUR : Well, 'tis as likely, Tristram,
As wind in winter.   At what raileth he ?
SIR TRISTRAM : At chivalry, my liege.
ARTHUR : Railing from heaven's bow its belt of rose.
SIR KAY : Your gracious pardon, sire—still at my jests.
ARTHUR : Aye, bay the moon, Sir Kay,
That takes no tarnish sailing over thee.
There's not a noble sentiment on earth—
Self-sacrifice, endurance, pardon, pity—
But still is dogged by pointing ridicule ;
Its pursuivant and herald is a sneer.
Sir Knights, I have good hopes a Queen is coming,
The fair apostle of our gentle creed ;
The music of her presence will subdue
The discord which the circling wine-cup breeds,
The strife that lurks in rugged strength of men.

Arthur at once stands forth as the central figure,
filling the eye and satisfying an heroic expectation.
In his restless, chafing mood he dismisses his
knights, and asks—

Why tarries Guenever ?
Comes she or comes she not ?   Is there no angel voice
To answer me ?   In all the smiling sky
Is there no tongue to answer yea or nay ?

To bring back the glamour of his courtship at
Camelliard he strikes upon a harp the chords of an
air that used to draw her to his side : but

The old fervours languish on the strings,
There's nought but melancholy left in it.

Arthur's craving for Merlin's counsel is answered
by the sudden appearance of the bard, who thus
accounts for his absence :—

Thy sly sister, Morgan,
Has played upon me, glued the ancient spider
In his own cobweb.

Of an old oak I was the living pith
As close as toad in rock, tombed in its trunk
By a most potent spell she learned of me.
I heard the blind mole stirring neath its roots,
The owl hoot by, the everlasting song
Of minstrel birds that sometimes paused to listen
Scared by my groans.   I had no night nor day.
The wind unkempt in tresses of the rain
Would rush upon my gnarled and leafy prison
And wrestle with big branches breast to breast,
To free me from my coil, but all in vain.
At length the Spirit of the Lake released me.

To the King's inquiry if Guenever comes, he is
warned that she brings ruin in her train—

The ravening sea to levy tax and truage
Of golden harvests.   Desolation comes.
War comes and ruin.   So comes Guenever.

He brings two gifts, the cup, the contents of which
the hand of the unchaste will spill—and which
Arthur receives with the words:

Thou tell-tale cup, ne'er shall I need thy gift—

and the magic sword Excalibur.

To Merlin's warning against Guenever and his
overtures to bar her way by magic spells, the King
replies:

Old man, to-day I know thee not— How oft
With quip and smile and counsel hast thou cheered me
Until I loved thy tones and sought thy smile,
Like rainy sunshine on a rugged elm.
Now hath thy voice the harshness of a screech owl
And all thy counsel is an axe's edge
Laid to the roots of all my happiness.
Hadst thou not led me first to Camelliard
These eyes, so witched with her, had never seen
Nor known what beauty is—I am undone
By having seen her.
Parched by hot longing when I stoop to drink
Thou criest—drink not for the draught is poison.

Merlin's argument, however, at last prevails that it is the penalty of royalty to sacrifice self for the people's weal. The King agrees to send a messenger to stay her coming. But, even while his old counsellor summons a messenger, he is transported back to Camelliard, and remembers how his kingship's worth seemed but to be to aspire to her love. On Merlin's return, he asks him whether this woe through Guenever is not fore-doomed. When the sage replies it is so written, he answers the end is then the same whether he make this sacrifice or not.

ARTHUR: (*rising*) Must I with surly boding thrust from me
The fleeting perfume of the chaliced rose
Because to-morrow it must taint with death?
Or close my eyes to golden snooded Eve
Because she is the herald of the night?
Age cometh! shall he fright me from the revel
Of buoyant youth whose blood is lusty red
Because the clanking staff is on the stair?
I tell thee, Merlin, Guenever comes first!
Let hobbling fate and ruin follow after.
Behold my lonely throne—I see beside it
A kindly radiance where shall sit my queen.

Merlin's effort frustrated, Mordred enters hastily, claiming a boon from the King, who, overlooking the request, questions him abstractedly 'How Guenever spoke of him at Camelliard.' Mordred tries to drop the poison of jealousy into his mind by telling him that while she echoed all his praise of Arthur, she listened while he talked of Launce-lot; and again, when the King asks if he told her how their meetings in the tempest of his life had been like summer isles:

She heard it all with a sweet gratitude—
Then in a lowered voice she asked of Launcelot.
    ARTHUR : Why dost thou jar with this false note?
Well knew she Launcelot was dear to me.
No more of her.
    MORDRED : My royal cousin I have asked a boon.
    ARTHUR : Mordred, not now thou art too double-tongued.
My heart is heavy and my hand is empty.
Ask when the trumpets of her welcome sound
And when the cry goes forth She comes! she comes!
Out of my joy I'll give you all you ask.

Mordred persists that, as his sister's son, he claims the mission to spur forth to meet the Queen, and lead her to his presence.

    ARTHUR : What dost thou ask me, man? She cometh not.
    MORDRED : Upon the hill there was a drift of dust,
No bigger than my hand. I watched it still,
The glitter of the sun on lance and helm,
And then a train of courtly knights and ladies.
At Launcelot's side rideth a lady fair,
In radiant vesture and of royal bearing.
    ARTHUR : Would'st torture me, Sir Mordred, with a tale?
Are all my watchmen blind, that none have warned me?
    MORDRED : I hindered them that I might ask a boon.
    ARTHUR : Oh! thou hast oped the dungeon of my heart
And let the summer in. I go to meet her!
    MORDRED : And so my boon is granted. I spur forth.
    ARTHUR : Nay, that were insult to Sir Launcelot
Who hath so well prevailed. Come thou with me.

This slight, as Mordred deems it, he seizes on as a justification for his secret hatred, and to give pretext to deeds at which he faltered. Morgan, his mother, discloses to him her plot to discredit Arthur with his people by fanning the loves of Launcelot and Guenever, and by the league of their kinsmen, King Mark and King Ryons, to

bring about the King's overthrow.   She overcomes
her son's last scruples, and sets him to his task,
biding at home to sow the tares of discontent while
Arthur goes to meet his enemies.

Then enters the procession, in which Arthur
leads in Guenever.   There is here a fine acting
scene for the Queen as she is introduced to the
famous Knights of the Round Table.   The arrival
of the hostile emissaries of King Ryons interrupts
the scene of welcome.   Sir Launcelot advises cold
waiting as a cure for haughtiness, but Guenever
chides him for his ill advice, and urges the King
not to let war thus tread upon her welcome, but to
receive them graciously.

The King consents to give them audience and
returns to consult with his Knights.   Launcelot
reproaches the Queen :

> What sudden winter, Guenever, hath fallen
> Between us.

With Arthur's danger her womanly loyalty prevails :

> Dost choose a moment such as this ?   Oh quit my side.

There follows then the scene with the Ambassadors,
in which, with lighted tapers, they declare war,
and, as they extinguish the tapers' flames, so doom
his glory to be extinguished.

Thus the act ends with the rude interruption
of the rejoicings, by clash of swords for wedding
bells, and the commencement of the fulfilment
of Merlin's prophecy.   Arthur hastens their
marriage—

> My stormy petrel,
> Thou art the unwilling herald of the tempest ;
> Yet do I hail thee 'neath its thunderous brow

More, Guenever, than any halcyon bird.
To-day the holy rites shall be performed
Uniting us whatever may befal.
I lead thee to thy throne, thou Queen of Britain.

All the elements of interest and suspense are thus
awakened in this first act, which is the overture
that prepares the mind for scenes to follow, and
makes the King, in his hour of happiness, ruffled
by forebodings of strife and danger, master of all
our sympathies.

In Act II. Guenever is at work with her
maidens on a banner for Arthur, returning from
his victory over Kings Mark and Ryons, and here
Mr. Wills shows his subtle mastery of a woman's
heart. She is trying to convince herself she
loves the King, and goes in quest of his praises.
Launcelot, whom, wounded on the battlefield, she
has nursed to health again, she makes herself believe
is reduced to the rank of a friend, and she is exag-
gerated in expressions of devotion to her husband.
Believing that she has shaken off the chain of a
misplaced love, she is feverishly light-hearted, and
bids her maids prepare a merry punishment for old
Sir Kay, who, by his gibes and railing has brought
the ladies of the Court like angry bees about his
head. On Launcelot's entrance they are dismissed
to find their weapons, the willow wands with
which they are to chastise the craven knight who
despises woman's favours ; and Guenever bids
Launcelot recount his rescue by the King.

If thou wilt pleasure me, I will begin,
For thou so hot in fight art cold in speech
When prayed by any to recount thy deeds.
Foremost alone as is thy reckless wont,

Into the thickest turmoil of the strife
Thou spurredst on, one knight, a hundred foes—
Now you are started fair come to the King.
LAUNCELOT: Spare me, Guenever.
GUENEVER: Launcelot! I prithee—
LAUNCELOT: The rest was shame to me.
Beset and overwhelmed fell horse and man.
I challenged Death, and in his grip I lay
Helpless and bleeding : many mailéd hands
Clutched down upon me to unlace my helm,
And swords too eager foiled each other's stroke,
When, sudden as a cloud glides o'er the sun,
A shield o'er-spread me and I thought I saw
St. Michael's self tower o'er me and bestride.
Unhelmeted he was, his golden hair
Was like a nimbus in that hustling hell—
King Arthur's life for mine !   Lady, no more—
I swooned—he rescued me.
      GUENEVER: Oh, noble king! saidst thou a St. Michael?
I will remember that.
And would it not be base and foul of thee
To wrong that glorious and surpassing friend?
No infamy so black or so unfathomed.
      LAUNCELOT : Lady, if I would cast a burden from me,
And one restored it to my galléd shoulders,
He purposed well, but I could scarcely thank him.
Arthur gave back to me my worthless life.
      GUENEVER : Oh ! there is something loveless in thy nature.
      LAUNCELOT : Love, lady, which hath broke the pale of honour,
Tramples on gratitude. I am thy servant.
      GUENEVER : Launcelot, I love thee not.   Breathe not again
A word of love to me, for I am changed.
I, too, did strive to drop a burden from me,
And I can gaze on thee indifferently.
Tarry thou at the court, it will content me ;
And if thou wert to go to-morrow morn
For ever and for aye, it will content me.
      LAUNCELOT : I hear, Guenever.
      GUENEVER : I am in love with him, my grand St. Michael,
Long for his coming as a festival—
As children long for Yule-tide, I for him.
Involuntary reverie seizes upon me :

R

I catch his name, low murmuring on my lip.
Is not this true wife love—dost thou believe me?
    LAUNCELOT: I hear thee, Guenever.
    GUENEVER: Aye, with a cold and sceptical regard :
I would I could persuade thee that I love him.
    LAUNCELOT: I see that thou would'st fain persuade thyself.
    GUENEVER: It angers me thy cold insensate tone.
I'll tell thee how this happy freedom came.
Last night I kept a vigil in the chapel,
Before the altar where the hurried rites
Of marriage were performed, whilst thou didst arm
And at the gates the embattled kings approached.
Even as a knight doth consecrate his sword
I watched and prayed to Mary, Queen of Heaven,
To lift from me the aching evil heart,
And in its stead to plant a holy love
Of the true wife. A peace and sunny gladness
Came to me at the singing of the birds ;
Since then I feel as I could dance and sing.
Since merry childhood when the lilies white
Were taller than my head, I have not felt
So happy, Launcelot. This thou shalt believe.
If thou talk love to me, I'll mock at thee.
Our past henceforth is buried in oblivion—
This I demand—this thou shalt promise me.
    LAUNCELOT: The past, dear lady, is a sunken wreck :
The bright salt tide doth swell and cover it
With diamonded expanse, but at the ebb
Rise the gaunt ribs again.
    GUENEVER: The wreck breaks up and drifts away from sight.
Thou canst not justly say I sinned so deeply
That I am lost to penitence and pardon.
    LAUNCELOT: Nor thou nor I shall see the Holy Grail.

The entrance of Arthur interrupts the scene.
Some feeling that he cannot analyse makes him
gaze an instant, but when Guenever asks him why
he stood so solemn—

    A sadness fell on me, I know not wherefore ;
    But when I saw thee waiting for me here,
    As in the falling bosom of a wave,

> Flashes the sudden dazzle of the sun,
> A joy shot through me.

Launcelot replies to Arthur's wonder that his wounds are healed so soon, 'It was by the magic of this lady's touch,' and pleads inability by deeds to thank him where words are wanting. Arthur says, taking each by the hand :

> Didst thou not win her for me? was this nothing?
> If my Creator who ordained my birth
> Upon life's threshold said, choose thou two gifts,
> I should have asked a friend as true as thou,
> And a pure woman's love, my Queen, like thine.

Guenever, to hide her agitation, busies herself unloosing his armour. When the prisoners, King Ryons and King Mark, are announced, Arthur bids them kneel to his Queen, to whom they offer their fealty, and she gives them life and liberty.

After a merry scene between the jester and the churlish Sir Kay—and Mr. Wills' sport, if unfertile of laughter and somewhat reasoned, was less stiff and far-fetched than the Shakespearian clowning usually employed in like plays—the Queen sets her maids to chase the unchivalrous Sir Kay round the ancient garden, to which the scene changes. And as, followed by Guenever, the merry chase disappears, Arthur, beset by the hateful suggestions of his sister Morgan and her son Mordred, comes down the broad walk fighting against their slanders. Morgan urges that in the long month he wooed by proxy—the comeliest knight and the fairest princess—what was Love about? She has watched 'a blush, a quick-pitched breath, a broken word,' the alphabet of love, the merest trifles; the sum

of all proves Guenever untrue.   All eyes could see
but his.   To which he returns:

> Mine is the vision of a simple faith,
> And she I wholly love, I wholly trust.

Mordred recounts how he has watched her services
to Launcelot:

> Sleepless she kept her gaze upon his face.
> Doubtless it was reflected love to thee,
> Because Sir Launcelot was thy bosom friend.
> Her lids were red with watching and with weeping,
> But consecrated doubtless were her tears to thee.
> She talked of Camelliard with faltering tongue
> When she and he sat whispering 'neath the vines:
> Doubtless it was the sweet association
> Of thy remembered courtship long ago.
> She held his hand in hers, and stroked his brow,
> It was to feel the pulsings of his blood
> With a physician's soft solicitude.
>   ARTHUR: Peace, sir.
> Thou either art a spy, or spawned these falsehoods.
> In either office thou dost forfeit credence.

As Morgan thrusts home her charges Arthur
pathetically prays his sister to forbear this poison-
ing of his new found happiness:

> Now you have whispered doubt,
> I know 'tis but the phantom of your hate,
> And yet have pity on me, good my sister.
> Hast thou the cruelty upon this day,
> The first few hours when my havened life
> Dimmed with the storm of battle asks for peace—
> The first, the cloudless time so oft I promised
> My longing heart, to shake me with a dream.
>   MORDRED: 'Twere worse to waken and to find it truth.
>   ARTHUR: (*Seizing him*) Thou specious liar, I will choke that
> sneer.

Morgan steps between and offers a test, Elaine,

whom Launcelot loved—let Guenever but see them brought together, and jealousy will tell its tale.

Guenever returns, and some brief tongue-thrusts pass between the women. Morgan and Mordred seek Launcelot; and Arthur questions Guenever how she had spent the time while he was absent.

> First thing at morning and the last at even,
> I ran up to the battlements and listened.
> A poor lone coney, upright anxious ears,
> To hear the distant murmurs of the battle;
> And still I thought of thee, and wondered sadly
> What cheer was thine, if scatheless in the strife.

The King does not unbend to the half playful, half pathetic little story, but asks:

> Now I must prompt thee—Launcelot was wounded—
> Borne in a litter back to Camelot.
>   Well?
> GUENEVER: Well! Arthur, I am skilled in lady's leech craft
> And tended him.   He needed all my care.
> ARTHUR: And had he died?
> GUENEVER: Oh, say not such a word—I feared—I felt—
> ARTHUR: And now I look at you, methinks you're pale
> And thinner than your wont.   You say you felt—
> GUENEVER: Arthur, it is the saddest sight I know
> To see the strong man helpless as a babe,
> And hear the well-graced tongue in piteous babble—
> To feel that with a slender woman's hand
> I could hold down the arm—the mighty arm
> All piteous feeble—that goes to the heart;
> Then pity loses sleep and vigil keeps:
> And zeal is weariless—invention eager
> To find new services to minister—
> And every morn you scan the hollow cheek
> And beaded brow to look for any change,
> But never heed the change upon yourself.

Arthur, whose probe has touched the mischief, concludes the interview with stern abruptness:

And so the change—Go to thy ladies.

As the startled Queen goes up, Launcelot and Mordred meet him. Arthur, with a subtle touch, takes note how peaceful is this garden after the battlefield. Then turning suddenly on the group, he bids them read a parable: 'A king went forth to war and left a bright escutcheon, but returning, found it foully smirched, whether by treachery or wicked slander he must resolve.'

Guenever, who has crept near, steps forward to reply. She recalls the hour she came a stranger to the Court beset by enemies; how slander's seeds were sown and rankly grew—the escutcheon was the honour of a Queen—and that foul smirch on it the blot of slander. Here she almost triumphs, but Morgan leads on Elaine, who, transported by the sight of Launcelot, approaches him with simple terms of endearment. The jealous Queen is overcome with sudden faintness. Arthur pours wine into the magic horn which hangs from his belt. Her hand trembles, for she knows the test, and pretends to fear that Morgan has poisoned the 'tell-tale cup.' Arthur releases her from the test:

I see you fear to drink——

and turning fiercely on Mordred banishes him the kingdom; Launcelot he sends to Normandy on service of high honour. He has smothered if not crushed his suspicion that he may shield Guenever. And thus ends a strong scene.

'The Queen's Maying' is the title of the third
act.   The scene is laid in a wood.   The hawthorn
is in bloom.   Guenever enters with a train of
knights and ladies whom she sends on quests of
love to 'nooks and banks and tented branches.'
Even the repentant Sir Kay finds a dame ; and
Dagonet discourses with a rustic maid, and warns
her as a country mouse, come to visit her town
relations, there is a great cat called Scandal, waiting to eat her up.   'Notice nothing, say nothing,
look at nothing.'   She is warned to discretion, for
each lady she asks about coupled with her knight,
is some other knight's wife ; and Sir Launcelot,
whom she sees apart in company with the Queen, is
supposed to be away in Normandy.   Some solvent
is acting on the morals of the Court, where all were
blameless once.   To stop the treason of her rustic
tongue the jester sings his song, 'The Seven
Champions of Christendom,' but, after St. George,
bids her number them on her plump fingers, and
cry a fig for each :

> St. Denis of France with his oriflamme flag,
>   Oh ! he was a knight of high degree :
> But he wagged his tail when changed to a stag,
>   And none knew it was he but his wonderful nag ;
> While St. Denis rubbed horns against a tree
>   For seven long years and more.
>
> Sir Hubert a princess had for his schatz—
>   He was great at his cups, at the trencher prime.
> He lay in a dungeon seven years with the rats,
>   And the stags they bellowed at rutting time
> To think how St. Hubert had lost his time
>   For seven long years and more.

Oh ! St. George was a knight no knight beneath
When he slogged an army or sacked a town ;
He picked the rampant dragon's teeth
And twenty giants cleft he down
In his morning ride when he wore his crown
For seven long years and more.

Between each verse a bird chorus of nightin-
gales and thrushes bursts from the pink and white
blossom-laden thickets. Knights and ladies stroll
by making love speeches they do not mean, in this
masque of love. Thus Tristram to Isonde :

We do not always marry those we love.
Come, there's a sweet conspiracy around
Among the flowers that you and I be friends.
I saw a coaxing wild rose touch your cheek
With damp pink lips and thoughtless you swept by—
I envied it, and said, ' Thou cunning blossom '
I too have stolen one in happier times—

suiting the action to the word.

Guenever and Launcelot come upon the scene
exchanging experiences of their separation. Mordred, trading on her blushes, has been whispering
overtures of love. The King she dare not ask for
pardon, placing between her heart and lips endless
divorce. But in his eyes there sits a speechless
suspicion that cuts her to the heart. His banish-
ment of Launcelot was mad, for lawless fancy
plied his cause too well. Of Elaine, Launcelot
assures her :

I love but once. Children make mimic gardens
Of rootless flowers—so Elaine and I.

The Queen, her jealousy at rest, asks, then bids
him not to tell her, lest it might spoil her happi-

ness, where he has been, what he has done in
exile:

> My life and I keep colder company
> Each day. But now for once I break from school
> Wild with the spirit for the maddest things.
> Just as the jewelled dragon fly doth rise
> Through dusky pool to quiver and to poise
> O'er sunny sedge, so I am on the beam!

Launcelot claims the confession that he has all
her heart, and when she says:

> Why wilt thou question? more than words have told
> thee—

with the vehemence of passion he declares how
vainly he has struggled to pray down his love,
but still her image rose and seemed to claim the
prayer. The King enters, led by Morgan and
Mordred, during this speech:

> I have done all a leaf or straw could do:
> Tost twirling in the torrent tide of passion.
> Headlong I'm swept, my puny struggles o'er,
> With thee my Queen—I reck not whither.
> Prayer, penance, solitude, were bonds of grass.
> Conscience and gratitude and duty—all
> A fence of wattles 'gainst a foaming flood.
> You see me a devoted vanquished wretch,
> Whose only law of life is love of thee,
> Whose heaven or whose grave is in thine arms.

As they embrace the King mutters to Morgan,
'Why hast thou led me here to this espial?'
'That you might *see*,' his sister hisses in his ear.
Mordred, in jealous fury, slinks away. The guilty
lovers rise, and in words sharper than strokes of
steel the King reproaches his recreant friend who
bids him strike:

> I offer my unshielded breast.

He refuses Arthur's challenge of combat *à outrance*; he will not raise his hand against the King.

And dost thou make thy loyalty a shield?

Launcelot bids him bare his sword and pierce his heart; even though he strike he will not draw on him. Arthur replies with an effort:

> Sir Knight, thou knowest well
> I could not strike an unresisting foe.
> I will not call thee craven—grief and wrath
> Shall never breed a falsehood on my tongue.
> 'Twas well thou art as brave as thou art false;
> And I am so outworn with my despair
> I'd liefer die upon thy sword than slay thee.
> Depart and tell not to the thoughtless world
> That thou hast seen thy King in such a plight,
> Or boys will laugh at me. Hence from my sight.

The King's heart-broken reproaches to Guenever, melting from bitter anguish to tender grief, thus conclude:

> No more for me shall love of ladye fair
> Rouse to the battle and the flash of swords.
> The songs of minstrels, uninformed by love,
> Which are the history of chivalry,
> All dead to me! and thou hast left me only
> A sickening at the flushing of the morn,
> Despair to see the loveless shut of day.
> Oh! to bring back the hour of thy first welcome!
> But since I cannot, since there is no pardon,
> Would I could lay upon my riven heart
> The pain that is laid up in store for thee.
> Never in hall or bower, in weal or woe,
> On any pleasant path beneath the sun
> Queen Guenever can I e'er meet thee more.

I can imagine the dramatist's face as he wrote those lines, streaming with tears. The act finishes

with a meeting between Arthur and his faithful
knights Tristram and Tor, to whom he declares his
intention to go upon a lonely pilgrimage, and bids
them take his signet and govern in his absence.
He refuses their company, but bids them guard
the Queen—if any point or shake their heads at
her they'll smite the slanderer on the mouth—
silence the whisper ere it come to life.   They do
not, however, respond to his appeal but receive it
coldly.   Left alone by his unwilling knights, he
holds there is no truth in anything, honour and
faith and love and chivalry but names.   Those
who wrought his wretchedness and looked upon
him, he should have scattered with white-hot words,
or cleft them to the earth :

> My weakness hath been Mercy—that pale angel
> Who ever pleadeth in a rotten cause.

In sparing Launcelot he has condemned himself
and borne what none should bear.   He can never
return :

> I might go mad with wrong, and in blind vengeance
> Make reparation with my mailed heel
> Upon the human vermin who will smile
> And whisper of me a vile epithet
> That shrivels on my lip.

He will go hide him in the woods, but even
there the beasts will fight in jealous fury for their
mate—he rises in a frenzy and cries that he will
after the traitor, and strike him dead.   ' Oh have I
sunk so low as to have spared him ? ' but he is gone
—it is too late—and as he moans ' Oh to forget,'
Merlin appears and tries to rouse him from his
despair, but Arthur only asks oblivion.

> Snatch from memory her lash of snakes.
> That false and fatal image branded on
> My heart, oh let it vanish like a mirror vision.
>   Hast thou such blessed spell?

The scene closes as the mighty wizard grants his boon.

> Lull him—lull him—softly close
> Haggard eyes in long repose.
> Numb the nerve of grief that rages,
> And as in a sleep of ages
> Be his slumbers senseless deep.
> As from death, when breaks his sleep,
> All the glory of his lot
> And its anguish be forgot!
> Let false friend and faithless Queen
> Be as though they ne'er had been.
> As the stars do drown away
> At the jubilee of day,
> So let all his sorrows pass
> As an image in the glass.

Arthur under Merlin's spell becomes a man without a past, a stranger to himself, a wanderer in the land. Launcelot has disappeared. Mordred by the help of King Mark takes possession of the vacant throne. Guenever refuses to share it with him, and his passion baulked he condemns her to be burned at the stake for her unfaithfulness to Arthur. She demands a champion to defend her cause in the lists, and King Mark, if one should appear, is chosen to meet him; but Arthur's knights hold back. Guenever's sin has broken up their order, and even Tristram and Tor leave her to her fate. Only old Sir Kay and Dagonet, the Jester, pity and befriend her. Her only hope is in a dream in which she has seen the King clad as a beggar, but pity melting on his brow, and

she believes her peril will convey itself to him
by subtle power of sympathy wherever he may
wander. Mordred has made his last attempt to
gain his villainous ends, but Tristram has inter-
fered when he would have resorted to violence.
The preparations for her execution, however, are
complete, when Arthur comes wandering in, a
minstrel in rags, a stranger to Camelot, to
Guenever, to Dagonet ; perfectly sane, but absolutely dissevered from his former self. Will he
recover his consciousness of his old self in time
to save the Queen ? The few moments left are
running out. He treats Dagonet's homage to him
as his lord and king, his welcome, his warnings, as
but a sorry jest. Bewildered he describes how
strangers stared and soldiers at the portal fled ;
and still some shadowy gleams of recognition stir
in him. The tapestries of knightly deeds bring
to his eyes a tearful cloud. The trees as he came
by seemed trees in dreams.

> I heard a trumpet sound—my heart upleaped
> And at the gleam of lance my fingers gripped—
> My sinews seemed to curve to supple steel,
> And, by the Mass, I had to bridle back
> My mounting voice lest it should lift itself
> In mad command. There is enchantment here.

Guenever prostrated in her anguish is roused
by the familiar voice, and sees the Arthur of her
dream. The King courteously, and with the calm
smile of strangerhood, asks pardon for intruding an
unbidden guest, but claims the minstrel's privilege
of food and shelter. Guenever's distraught appeal
to him as her King seems to him as if he were

among people mad or enchanted, or as an echo of
the jester's fooling. Kneeling at his feet she entreats his pardon, but he knows no wrong, and
seems to her to smile in scorn. Lifting her up he
bids her not to kneel to him.

> Trust me, I do not smile in any scorn,
> But who can hear that hath an empty heart
> Of pains it ne'er hath felt, of love unknown,
> Of treasons ne'er endured, without a smile?
> All here seem dreaming, I alone awake.

To Guenever in her extremity of need it is
Arthur who seems distraught, and she desperately
tries to convince him of his identity with the King.

> If thou couldst persuade me, gentle lady,
> I should indeed be mad, a straw-crowned King;
> And I might strut and frown, mouth forth commands,
> Startle with sudden laugh and point at air:
> But with a healthy though astonied mind
> I see these dragons, giants, warlocks, knights,
> And do not watch to see them gape or lunge:
> I know fair ladies' fingers limned them all:
> I hearken to thy fearful phantasy
> Of guilt and doom, and of a wrongéd King,
> As a spectator gazing on a pageant.
> Acted to life, doth half believe the while.

Arthur wandering to the throne seats himself
upon it with unconscious custom, and asks Guenever if she is not Mordred's Queen. He startles
himself by the trick of authority when he orders
out Sir Kay, who interrupts them.

> Give place, sir, we are private—dost thou hear? give place.

He hears the name of Launcelot with indifference, and asks what is her gentle name? The
passion of the Queen breaks out:

Dost thou forget it ?   Ask it not of me !
For what is it to thee ?
Thy throne usurped, thy land more plagued and poisoned
Than by the pest or monster of the hills,
Thy Queen disgraced, deserted, left for death—
What is it all to thee ?
Better thine anger than that flitting smile :
Hast thou no pity or no memory, Arthur.
ARTHUR : Thou callest me aright—my name is Arthur.

He unslings his harp, and to soothe her distraction, plays a melody.   Guenever flings herself in passionate grief on the steps of the throne, sobbing wildly.   A vague pity fills him.   He bids her weep no more :

Aching compassion fills me at thy tears.
Let sorrow sleep ; and if to tell that tale
Which quivers on thy lips would give a pang
Then I will take thy sorrow upon trust.
But up and down the world I'll quest
To do thee worship and to solace thee !

Through her tears she asks but one word— 'pardon '—to which he answers he almost wishes she had wronged him, for the pure delight of pardoning.   Yet, if there's virtue in the word

I'll speak it though my heart be blindfolded.
If thou hast done me wrong, I pardon thee.

But there is no balm in the unmeaning word.   If she cannot carry his real pardon to her death, a watchword in the darkness, let her, since he is powerless to save, in the flames see him, meet his gaze of pity, and she will choke her cries,

Trembling and silent in my agony.

But he would liefer die with her—

> This shall not be :
> Command me what to do—give me a sword.
> These hands are empty.

New hope awakened, she bids him summon his royalty—show himself to his people. To this Arthur replies he will find knightly arms to do battle for her—but when he is gone, her heart sinks. What can he do, all crazy? and she is powerless to rescue him. The guard comes to lead her out to the flames :

> Oh, Mary, Mother, save me,
> And guard my King.

We are now taken to the lists where Guenever is bound to the stake, and King Mark on horseback waits for any champion that may answer to the summons to do battle for the Queen.

Mordred is on the throne with Morgan Le Fay on his right. The third and last trumpet call challenges, when it is answered by a bugle without, and Arthur enters on foot, a king in rags, with battle-mace and shield. Mordred in terror asks,

> Who art thou? Dost thou live,
> Or are those rags thy cerements? Speak.

Arthur, still disclaiming kingship, says he will do battle in the lady's cause if the King but grant him knightly arms. Tristram and Tor close up to protect him. There is a wavering cry, 'The King!' Mordred asks him to declare before the knights assembled if he be King Arthur.

> My name is Arthur, but thou seest no king.

Morgan whispers that he is distraught; she

sees a magic spell within his eyelids, and bids her
son humour his madness. Mordred would have
King Mark dismount and circle him with his knights
and slay him, but Morgan checks him. The
moment is supreme—two thunderclouds are drawing nigh. Mark's knights and Arthur's paladins
gather upon opposing sides. Morgan asks him if
he is a knight, to which he replies a stroke of the
king's sword will make him one. Mordred cries,
he confesses himself a vagabond and bids them cast
him out of the lists. The soldiers advance upon
him, but they retreat from a burst of overlording
anger; Arthur, pointing to his golden spurs, bids
King Mark dismount and fight afoot :

> And I will prove upon thy body here
> This injured lady's slandered innocence.

King Mark treats the challenge contemptuously,
and Tristram dissuades Arthur from fighting.
Morgan, with design to avert the present peril and
work by treachery, bids them release Guenever,
and tells her to humour his illusion—

> 'Tis death to him to know himself as king :
> 'Twill save a massacre.

Here Merlin enters disguised, and draws Arthur's
eyes upon him—the other knights see him not,
as he lifts his wand, dropping his disguise. While
Guenever, as directed by Morgan, thanks the King
for her safety, the more that they are strangers,
for a chance resemblance had deceived her, and
he had never seen her face before. But he must
hasten to depart—death is in delay. As she thus
denies him, the spell is giving way, and slowly

s

his old self is coming back. 'Have we not met
before,' he says, 'in other days?' Guenever tells
him they conspire against his life—their swords
will smite his helmless head; let them fly together
to other lands, where in some holy convent she will
hide her head, and his protection hover round her.
But the light is growing. 'I'm sure I knew thee
once.' 'Oh! we have never met,' she cries in terror.
Mordred looks on them with eyes of deadly fire. The
guards close on the portals; still the light is growing.

An ancient garden and a mossy dial—
Cedars that spread abroad their level gloom.
    GUENEVER: I know it not.
    ARTHUR: Did you not—nay, it was so—soft you now?
The fragments of a past come back to me;
I fear they'll vanish e'er I seize on them.
Did you not tell me once you loved me, lady?
    GUENEVER: Oh! let be, sir, placidly you dream
Amid the tempest that is heaving round you.
    ARTHUR: But if you said so, *I* must first have wooed.
The filmy ghosts of memory return,
Take their old places in the empty mansion
As long familiar things and stare at me.
Now, now—the pictured images take shape!
And step down living from their frames to greet me.
Did I not *worship* thee? Thy words this morn
Then seeming children's tales, take meaning now.
How my love slept within me when you spoke—
As an unquarried gem, rayless it lay
Mayhap for years—but it was tranced within.
It lives, it sparkles into clustered stars
Illuming every chamber of my heart.
Didst thou say, come?
I'll follow thee as shadows follow light!
    GUENEVER: Oh! haste thou!
    ARTHUR: Dost thou remember a bright tuneful forest
In the full joyous revel of the spring,
The air embalmed with May—a knightly throng
And ladies fair—a bank whereon you sat.

GUENEVER: No more ; you conjure serpents up to sting you.
ARTHUR: Serpents? A knight—a *friend*—whose face—soft
  now—
And I was standing in the shade of trees.
My lady love and friend close—pressing closer
Ye whispered with your fingers twined in his,
Hot words, and—by hell's quenchless fire !
Thou art Guenever !

She totters as he pauses, and then turning he
says, ' Sir Tristram, lead this lady from my sight.'
' Look to your King,' she cries, as she rushes wildly
through the throng and disappears. Morgan then
beseeches her brother not to drown the land in
blood ; he deserted his people, and revolution has
swept away old landmarks, and set the crown upon
his nephew's head. But at Arthur's stern command
Mordred descends from the throne. He offers his
uncle the compromise of dwelling at peace in
Camelot or leaving Britain under honourable
convoy. The King contemptuously rejects Mordred's offers, but, as he would not turn the knightly
lists into a slaughter-house, challenges him to
mortal combat. They are both unharnessed, and
Arthur will lay aside the magic sword with which
Merlin had re-armed him, and fight with equal
weapons. King Mark, aside, bids Mordred accept
the challenge ; he will watch the moment to succour and to deal the King a treacherous blow.
Giving charge to his page, Guy, concerning Excalibur, he engages Mordred. Mordred falls, and
King Mark and his knights rush on Arthur, who is
wounded, but rescued by his knights. The stage
darkens, and in a crash of thunder the curtain falls.

The last scenes are by the mere. Guenever,

seeking for Arthur, has revisited the field where the combat of the kings had ended in a pitched battle between their followers.

> On each dead face that lay upturned and chill,
> With clenchéd teeth or open-mouthed mute shout
> I thought I saw a grim and settled curse.
>
> .   .   .   .
>
> There's a denouncing spirit following me.
> Thou, Guenever, thou art the cause of all.
> Why doth thy presence mar this taintless scene.
> Thou lingering flake of night, forgotten, left
> Behind her on the innocent smile of morn?

Merlin comes to heap hot coals of reproach on her. Is it to blight his closing hour she comes, the canker of his life, to see the King? She prays him to lead her to him if he lives, that she may win a full forgiveness. Merlin, however, who has rescued Arthur from the desperate havoc, has no pity, and, when she will not leave the King's path, sends her Launcelot. The knight openly makes the King's mortal wounds the portals of their happiness. He has come to rescue her, surrounded as she is by enemies. His horses are in the wood close by.

> The past is dead. We hide away the dead.
> Another future shall we build together
> Out of its wreck.

His arm encircles her; but, as a strain of dirge-like music swells on the air, she starts from his side, exclaiming,

> Wilt play the tempter's part at such an hour?

At her entreaty in bitter submission he leaves her, and, as she watches Arthur from the distance, not

even a single glance she spares him from that
famished gaze. When the wounded King comes,
borne on a litter and is laid beside the mere, she
conceals herself until Arthur's retinue having retired, he sends his page to restore Excalibur to the
Lake spirit. Then, when the youth is gone, there
follows a pathetic scene in which she pleads for
pardon. He bids her go in peace ; his jealous anger,
even his grief itself, he left on yonder mangled
battlefield, where all that is noble, all that is knightly
perished, and chivalry's last splendour set in blood.
But still she pleads—

> If night shall find this mercy unfulfilled
> Then it can never be—I am quite friendless
> And refugeless. I cannot bear the burden
> Of thy displeasure. Art thou sorry for me?

He hears the glamour in her voice, her beauty is
unwithered, the tempest that has laid him low has
lightly passed on her. His sternness melts.

> Gaze not on me so. Oh, did I tell thee
> That I could look on thee unmoved in heart?
> That piteous little phrase 'Art sorry for me?'
> So reasonless and womanly, it moveth
> More than all cunning eloquence. Aye, sorry!
> I could as soon bid back my ruthful tears
> As the warm blood drops oozing from my wounds.
> I pardon thee, full and unstinted pardon—
> Wide as the sky above us—boundless pardon.
> Take it and fill thy famished heart withal.
> If any point at thee or taunt thy past,
> Say Arthur loved thee so that he forgave thee,
> And took thee to his inmost heart again,
> Ere it grew cold.

Meanwhile Guy has been faithless in his mission,
and is sternly warned not again to fail. Guenever

supports the King, and while they wait for Guy's
return, he bids her seek the holy roof of Aylmesbury.

> There in the convent shade
> Thou shalt another, higher pardon find.
> There in lone eves God walketh in the Garden
> To commune with the spirit that is bruised.

The page has now at last fulfilled his trust, and
flung into the lake the magic sword and seen the
mystic hand receive it. He tells of the barge with
the draped figures that approaches over the still
waters of the lake to bear the wounded King to
Avalon, vale of perfect rest. Arthur thus bids
farewell to Guenever—

> If sometimes a soft memory of me
> As once I was may wander back to thee
> From a bright past before the shadows came,
> I do not bid thee chase that guest away,
> For we can meet no more except in thought.

The barge glides by, and the mystic Queens lead
the King to his couch; and then it passes slowly,
Guenever kneeling with outstretched hands.

CHAPTER XXIII.

MANY playgoers will recall the beautiful pictures of eighteenth century life which charmed society in 'The Pompadour' when produced at the Haymarket. In this play W. G. Wills and Mr. Sydney Grundy collaborated, and the terms of the agreement with Mr. Tree may interest the many who dream some time or other they may write a play. Mr. Tree acquired the exclusive rights for ten years in the United Kingdom, the United States and Canada. Each part author was to receive 2½ per cent. on the gross takings if they did not exceed 700*l.* a week. If they did exceed, 5 per cent. For morning performances, the percentage was the same. For Canada and the United States as in London. If the rights were sold the authors divided half of the sum received. On provincial productions the royalty was 2½ per cent. on the gross receipts. The agreement was signed in November 1887, and the play was produced in March 1888, on the withdrawal of 'The Red Lamp.'

'The Pompadour' was founded on Brachvögel's 'Narcisse,' which was produced by Herr Bandmann at the Lyceum twenty years before. The play was splendidly mounted, and drew crowded houses, notwithstanding the bad send-off the critics gave it. Mr. Tree's 'Narcisse Rameau,' who seeks his wife through France, and finds her the mistress of the King, was a fine representation. As he pours his reproaches on his false wife she learns that a young man she has sent to execution for insolence is her own son, and as she hears the rattle of the volley, the scourge of France, as she is represented, falls down and expires. It was the right thing to do—but not history.

In the same year (1887) in which this play was commenced, Sir Henry Irving asked my brother to undertake a dramatic version of 'Don Quixote,' and for the accomplishment of this difficult task he received 600l. That he felt the impossibility of making a good play out of such grotesque material and without female interest, is suggested by an entry in one of his note books—'Publish "Don Quixote" with my poems.' However, so imminent did its production at one time appear, that his cousin, Mr. Robert Martin (the author of 'Ballyhooly') waived his intention of writing a burlesque of 'Don Quixote' for the Gaiety Theatre, as it was thought it might be injurious to the drama at the Lyceum. But the sketch form in which it was ultimately produced, in 1891, was probably all that was possible outside burlesque. Don Quixote is as ineffective on the stage as Malvolio would be cut out of 'Twelfth Night,' or Shylock severed from 'The Merchant of Venice.'

It was in December 1888, that Miss Isabel Bateman commissioned him to write a play on a subject her mother had suggested ten years previously—namely, 'Clarissa Harlowe.' The play

was for the Compton Company, then commencing its career. Miss Bateman says in her letter
that they thought a fine play might be made
from the novel, ' Putting that master touch of
yours that turns your characters into real flesh and
blood creatures, not at all like the wooden
individuals we poor actors have sometimes to try
to make the public think are alive.'

The play was to be ready by the following
September, which allowed ample time ; but the
author required a good deal of persuasion to make
him work, and from Miss Bateman's letters of
entreaty it may be gathered that it was still more
difficult to coax him to carry out alterations, or to
go over the same ground a second time. At last,
however, the piece was got into shape (like ' Ninon '
and ' Jane Shore,' with alternative endings) and
produced with great success.

Miss Isabel Bateman says : ' The play went off
without a hitch, and was received with great enthusiasm. I never saw a smoother first performance. Why did you not come ? There were
shouts for the author after the 2nd, 3rd, 4th, and
5th acts, especially the 4th. I could have cried
that you were not with us.'

She was exceedingly emphatic during the
preparation in begging of him not to allow it to
leak out that he was writing this drama. ' Some
inferior play on the same topic, produced before
ours, would seriously injure us.' Curiously, another
' Clarissa ' did appear at the Vaudeville ; and
Mr. Compton was annoyed at some remarks in
the papers which seemed, as he said, to imply that

Mr. Thorne's theatre had a 'monopoly of old novel dramatisation.'

Circumstances with regard to another play of my brother's, which occurred four or five years after his death, would, if posthumous matters were worth referring to, form a curious commentary on this coincidence.

An adaptation of ' Esmond ' made by permission of Thackeray's representatives was originally intended for the Kendals, and Mr. Kendal admitted that, as it was finally amended, it was the best he could conceive. He came to the conclusion, however, that they could not undertake the production of ' Esmond ' in any form; yet, when played by a party of amateurs at St. George's Hall, it received very high praise from the leading critics, and was even said to possess some of the sterling merits of ' Olivia.' All the world that loves the book would have gone to see it in its dramatic garb, and played to the perfection to which the first class theatres have accustomed us. A conventional standard is hardly to be applied to such a play, overlooking the profound interest which would be lent to it by the world famous novel.

' A Royal Divorce ' was the last piece to which my brother's name was appended. The basis was a very poor American play, and the adaptation, if such it can be called, was unworthy of his fame. Still the character of Napoleon caught on with the people and made the play strangely popular. The reputed author was in bad health when he undertook the commission, and much of the work that he did upon it was discarded and the original substituted; so that it retained little of Wills, and much of the American author and Miss Grace Hawthorne.

In this concluding chapter on his dramatic work, I may mention some other plays of his, which, like 'Esmond,' are still unproduced. One of these, called 'My Lady Bountiful,' was written in collaboration with Mr. W. Dubourg, and before Mr. Pinero's play appropriated its title. Lady Monckton, I gather, thought of producing it. She says: 'If she ("My Lady Bountiful") does not find a home, I may yet put a roof over her head.' Another stillborn play is 'A Mute Witness,' a dramatisation of his own novel, 'A Wife's Evidence.' With his cousin, Sir Joscelyn Coghill, he wrote a drama on the beautiful French poisoner, the Marchioness de Brinvilliers. Abigail Hill was the heroine of a half-written piece, and 'The Young Cleopatra' (for Mary Anderson) of another. A drama on Claud Duval remains a fragment; but 'The Scarlet Letter,' with a prologue antedating the novel, has been completed since the dramatist's death. The play he called 'Merry and Wise,' which a friend disinterred from the clothes basket, and the author said was the best he had ever written, has also been finished since, under the title of 'The Rosiere.' Its ultimate adventure was being lent to Mr. Comyns Carr, and again lost! It is hardly to be hoped that another dustbin will give up its dead.

To this brief catalogue of his unproduced or fragmentary plays, is to be added one founded on the story of Æsop. It bears the peculiar stamp of his mind in every line, and the hunchback with his beautiful soul in a deformed body, his love, philosophy, and self-sacrifice, is a very touchingly and tenderly drawn picture.

CHAPTER XXIV.

POETRY.

I HAVE always felt how much of himself my brother put into his novels, plays and poems, but most of all into his poems. A hundred touches recall the man. Instances of this will be found in ' Noon ' and ' Pride,' but most of all in ' John o' Dreams,' a name he used to apply to himself.

His principal poem was ' Melchior,' published by Macmillan in 1884. It was in the year preceding, during a long visit to his mother, that this poem was written. The earlier ambition had returned to leave a long poem as to the great work of his life. Its basis was his own drama ' Herman, the Fatalist,' written for Herr Bandmann. I can find no record of the play having been produced. It was literary and unsuited to the stage. The old housekeeper at Wellington Road, Norah Burke, the most faithful of old servants, used to get breakfast for him at five o'clock. He would then write in bed for several hours, painting in the daytime, and spending the evening with his mother. He told me, when he returned to London, that he had never before known the freshness of her mind and the extent of its resources. When he was away from her she used to feel uneasiness about his religious welfare; and he made her very happy during this visit by going to church with her, and receiving the sacrament by her side.

'Melchior' was dedicated to Robert Browning, whom he called 'as a poet, the deepest thinker and most individualistic of the century.' The following is Mr. Browning's acknowledgment of the dedication :

19 Warwick Crescent, W.: October 19, 1884.

MY DEAR MR. WILLS,—Neither your most generous gift, nor the signal honour done myself by its dedication, were to be acknowledged in a hasty fashion, much less was the poem to be glanced over and appreciated of a sudden. Let me say *provisionally* that I am deeply indebted to you for the gift and the dedication—and that having carefully read more than half the poem with the greatest interest I have so far been as gratified, I believe, as you would desire. When I have finished the poem I will attempt to give you (as briefly as possible) my impression of it. Meantime and always—Believe me, dear Mr. Wills,

Yours cordially and gratefully,
ROBERT BROWNING.

On completing the perusal of the book, he thus wrote :

19 Warwick Crescent, W.: November 5, 1884.

MY DEAR MR. WILLS,—I must not delay any more the little I have to say, concerning the much I feel on the subject of 'Melchior.' I think it very original both in design and conception, filled—perhaps to overflowing—with bright thoughts and fancy. The felicitous expressions are profuse indeed, and altogether it is a work you may well be proud of—accustomed to successes as you are. I am greatly honoured by the dedication of such a work, and shall ever be—Gratefully yours,

ROBERT BROWNING.

The feeling with which he set to work upon the poem is suggested by the following lines at its commencement when describing the old world city:

> When toil and care grim traceries imprint
> On brow and cheek, and time with thriftless score
> Doth haste his grizzled reckoning of my days,
> It lists me well to give my world the slip
> And, dropping from the clouds within the sound
> Of its old fluttering chimes, to hide me there.

He stole out of his world into this dropped-from-the-clouds seclusion to hide in his imagined town of Ort, where Time, standing still, seems to have fallen asleep.

Melchior is a dreamy musician who forms a spiritual love for his patron, Saint Cecilia; but there comes into his life in flesh and blood a woman Blanca, whom he rescues from drowning. He has an omen of his death in a vision of his doppelganger, and believes that, in a year from the time he has seen it, he is fated to die. But this beautiful woman's love awakens him from his dreams and fancies. When, however, he asks her to be his wife some secret in her past comes between them, and he is then advised to send her away. His crazy fancies return in her absence. He imagines she is drowned. His friends plot to cheat him of his madness, and bring her back to impersonate St. Cecilia. On the disclosure that the vision is Blanca, a fancy seizes him that the apparition of the drowned girl is a demon, and in his frenzy he shoots her. The fatal day comes, on which he believes he will die at noon. His friends again try to cheat his fancy by putting on the clock, and telling him that noon is passed; but twelve booms from the Dom Kirche, and his spirit passes away:

> All held their breath—a little gleam—a chill.

This, in brief, is the story stripped of the complications of character and incident which somewhat overcumber it. The group that surrounds Melchior is drawn with a master hand; Wolfgang, the bitter and blighted, arrogant and brutal; his very antithesis, the painter Hans; the well-intentioned but generally mistaken Hirschvogel.

In 'Melchior' my brother showed his complete mastery of blank verse, the secret of which it was the stock phrase of his critics to say he did not possess, because in his dramas he merely aimed at a certain dignity of expression and rhythm of form. Here he employs it without becoming stilted, and with perfect ease and naturalness. From the long habit of writing stage poetry the verse is perhaps more accessible than is the fashion of the present age; the meaning is seldom veiled; but the originality of expression and individualism of thought make the poem notwithstanding essentially modern.

He shows himself a profound psychologist in his studies of character, and there is much of the brilliant epigram, essentially Irish, which appeared in his novels. The reception of this poem by the press was, however, disappointing, and the book had but a small circulation.

The visit home, in which Melchior was written, was of some months' duration. When he left her, his mother had another pleasure in her old age in the visit to Dublin, especially on her account, of her cousin, Sir Francis Doyle, author of 'The Return of the Guards,' and sometime Professor of Poetry at Oxford. They had long carried on a correspondence, but Sir Francis was desirous to hear from her own lips the family lore of which she was the only living repository. His poem 'The Spanish Mother' was a great favourite with my brother, who when a lad painted a picture of the woman in her passionate triumph announcing to the French soldiers who had killed her husband that the wine she has given them was poisoned.

As 'Melchior' was a poem founded on a drama, so two shorter poems, called 'Noon' and 'Pride,' contain dramatic germs in poetic form. Both of these poems, though in print, are still unpublished. My brother used to get his friends to read them to him, and would with the back of his hand wipe away his tears.

He wrote many shorter poems, but perhaps the best known is his famous song in the libretto of 'Lalla Rookh,' 'I'll Sing Thee Songs of Araby.' The first verse sings itself :

I'll sing thee songs of Araby
And tales of fair Cashmere—
Wild tales to cheat thee of a sigh,
Or charm thee with a tear.
Dreams of delight shall on thee break
And rainbow visions rise,
And all my soul shall strive to wake
Sweet wonder in thine eyes.

It was in the direction of poetry or of painting that his mind turned if left to itself. His ambition lay where there was no gain of money. A mercenary object took away the pleasure and freedom of his work. To write poems which no publisher would buy, and to paint pictures which nothing would induce him to sell, were to him un-

T

alloyed pleasures. He loved, without the sense of
work upon him, to dream whole days away lost in
bright imaginings. The last months of his life were
spent in writing the poem I have spoken of, ' John o'
Dreams '—as he called it, a ' grotesque.' His fancy
runs riot in this strange poem. John astonishes old
Rome with modern inventions. Nero is a vividly
depicted monster, and there are wonderful descriptive flashes which seem momentarily to light up
the ancient city; but the poem ends like some of
Beethoven's sonatas with a sort of mockery of itself.

By nature he was a poet as by circumstance
a dramatist; but his busy and anxious life did not
allow him to indulge his natural bent. For this
last year only, as in his youth, he used to sit apart,
seldom joining in his friends' conversation, but
with his face turned upward in deep abstraction,
dreaming and weaving his fancies into verse. The
following is an example of the grim kind of verses
for which he had a special turn:

BALLAD OF GRAF BRÖM.

OLD Graf Bröm is dying at last,
He's alone in his bed, and sinking fast;
And his shutter is pushed by the bluff night blast
Howling oh, wul-lul-lul-lul-lul-lo —
Ho! ho!
Howling oh, wul-lul-lul-lul-lul-lo!

His lips are gluey, extremities cold,
His nose is pinched, and the life blood rolled
With a slow, dull beat, like a bell that is tolled,
With a dead wul-lul-lul-lul-lo!

'Tis dismal to finish a life of sin
With the night without, and the night within;
To buckle alone the last struggle and grin
With a sick wul-lul-lul-lul-lo!

Old Graf Bröm was a scandalous rake,
Women have done queer things for his sake;
'Tis well that the dead can never awake,
Shrieking oh, wul-lul-lul-lul-lul-lo—
Ho! ho!
Shrieking oh, wul-lul-lul-lul-lul-lo!

Oh, woman, poor woman, by dozens undone,
And the young love, the true love, the heart-broken one,
Long dead, long sped, and pitied by none,
Sobbing oh, wul-lul-lul-lul-lul-lo—
Woe! Woe!
Sobbing oh, wul-lul-lul-lul-lul-lo!

Oh, hush! oh, hark! his ears can catch
A fumble of hands on his hall door latch;
His hair stood up in a grisly thatch;
Who comes with this wul-lul-lul-lo?

A smothered din, a stirring of feet,
That stumble upstairs with irregular beat,
And murmurs resembling a gibber or bleat,
Or a creepy wul-lul-lul-lo!

Up they come with a step that lags,
Hollow-eyed maidens and rickety hags;
The moss on their bones can be seen through the rags,
Creaking oh, wul-lul-lul-lul-lul-lo!

The skeleton wantons come tottering in,
All dead, all sped—his pupils in sin,
To witness their master's last struggle and grin
With a shivering wul-lul-lul-lo!

They chattered and wagged their chins like the dumb;
Skeleton babies were suckled by some,
Or horribly dandled at old Dad Bröm,
With the lullaby—wul-lul-lul-lul-lo—
Ho! ho!
With the lullaby wul-lul-lul-lul-lo!

Oh, woman, poor woman, by dozens beguiled,
And the young love, the true love, the poor, poor child,
Her yellow hair sullied, her hazel eye wild,
Who died long ago, deserted, defiled,
Crooning oh, wul-lul-lul-lul-lul-lo—
Woe! Woe!
Crooning oh, wul-lul-lul-lul-lul-lo!

Rattle the shutters, and rattles his throat,
His white beard heaves in gasps like a goat,
While his tatterdemalions peer and gloat
With a clamour of wul-lul-lul-lo!

Old Graf Bröm is dead at last,
Alone in his bed, all stark and aghast;
And his shutter is bursten in by the blast,
Roaring oh, wul-lul-lul-lul-lul-lo—
Ho! ho!
Roaring oh, wul-lul-lul-lul-lul-lo!

CHAPTER XXV.

THE DEATH OF HIS MOTHER—THE END.

It was in September or October 1887 that his mother became seriously ill. The successive deaths of Lady Plunket and Mrs. Fox, both of whom in her later years she, so wonderfully active for her age, used to visit almost daily, came upon her as great shocks, and the loss of her eldest son, his wife and one of her grandsons, all three of whom died in succession at her house, weighed her down with accumulated sorrows. It was only, however, in a physical sense, for she was very happy in her religion, and she saw in her son all that was noble and devoted, and had lived to rejoice in his garnered fame. If ever there was a woman who deserved to be repaid for a long life of duty and service it was she. The best of daughters, wives, and mothers, she relieved the sufferings and sickness of thousands of the poor. To her talents, which enabled her to give her husband so much help in his writings, she united simplicity and goodness and tenderness of heart, and she found in her old age that she had laid up for herself the treasure of a son's devotion and loyalty—which never failed her to the last hour of her life.

At the end of 1886 and the beginning of 1887,

my brother was himself in bad health, and could not go over to Dublin to see her. Indeed, he could not bear to see her sufferings; but as he said in one of his letters, he would have coined his heart's blood to relieve them if he could. The sadness of life had been growing upon him for some years, and though physically brave, the ghostly footfall of death had followed him from childhood. His mother gave him a curious-looking dark ring to remind him of her, and counteract the tendencies induced by low spirits and morbid thoughts. It had that effect upon him while he wore it, and he used to speak of it as an amulet, and did at last ascribe to it some occult virtue. I did not tell him that when a schoolboy I had carved it from a cocoanut shell by boring a round hole with a red-hot poker, and then filing out the ring, but I knew there was no magic in it but a mother's love.

On April 3, 1887, Mrs. Wills's illness ended fatally.

The following letter from Mrs. Greene, sister of the late Archbishop of Dublin, shows her son was unprepared for the end—

DEAREST WILLIE,—Your news has not surprised me. I have known for some time that Philip [1] expected the end was not far off. I could not bring myself to tell you so, as you seemed as if it would overset you. Why did you never come to see me or answer my letter asking for a telegram? Come now, whenever you like—please don't wait for any invitation—or are you going over to the funeral?

You have lost, I believe, the very best woman who ever breathed, and the most devoted mother. I am so thankful to think how she rejoiced over your life, such as it has been for a

---

[1] Sir Philip Smyly, who attended her in her illness.

long time now. The expression of perfect rejoicing and happiness I shall never forget. She and I were *more* than friends.

Ever your most loving friend and cousin,

LOUISA GREENE.

Mrs. Wills had, herself, been fully aware that the end was coming. She divided many little presents which she wished to give to my brother and to me, recalling to my mind the scene in which ' Livy ' is dividing her keepsakes. Among other things she gave me the Lytton wedding ring.[1] It was her custom all through life in sleepless nights to draw on her store of poetry, and on the night of her death she repeated the whole of one of Chaucer's ' Canterbury Tales.' My brother did not attend the funeral ; he had done everything possible for her in life, and he felt unequal to facing the ordeal. Mrs. Wills's godson, the Archbishop of Dublin, accompanied the funeral to Kingsbridge Station ; and the funeral service at Attanagh, where she is buried beside Dr. Wills, was read by her nephew, Archdeacon Gorman. Three years after her faithful servant, Norah Burke, who was with her for thirty years, and whom my brother supported in her old age, was taken back to Attanagh also, and laid beside her old mistress.

With the death of his mother there came a great change. The motive for exertion seemed to have entirely gone—in fact, the mainspring was taken out of his life. All dramatic work that came to him he put only a languid hand to.

I have already mentioned how he kept Sir Charles Young's plays, ' Glenarch ' and ' The Sunset

---

[1] It was sent to her after Lady Lytton's death.

of Life,' for months, without having the energy
to set to work on them. He dabbled a little in
photography, but without success. He had moved
to a new studio at Walham Green, where he was
further removed from his more desirable friends;
and the one companion who flapped about him was
the least calculated to drive away melancholy. His
appearances at the Garrick Club were few, and
the change in him shocked his old friends. The
gloom and bleakness of life still grew upon him.
In 1891 his earnings were only 200*l.*, and as he
felt the failing of his powers, and that his strength
was tottering, he became uneasy about the future.
He had never put by money, but in the last year
of his life he replenished his banking account
by selling rights that he still had retained in his
plays. At his death, however, he left little more
than paid his debts and funeral expenses, and
sufficed to keep up until her death the pension of
his mother's old servant—about 500*l.* in all. He
had lodgings near, but sometimes slept in his
studio; and when his last illness, an attack of
jaundice, set in, he lay there for days among
persons whose remedies only aggravated the
complaint. At last, at his own desire, he was
taken as a private patient to Guy's Hospital,
where his friend Dr. Steele, the head physician, a
member of the Garrick Club, had before pulled him
through a similar illness; but his constitution had
now given way, and he had not strength to bear up
against the disease. When I asked if he wanted
money, he said he had sufficient in the bank, but
then in an unwonted tone he added, 'But it is the

future!' I suggested that we should live together again, and he seemed to like the idea; he had often proposed this arrangement himself, but our work had lain far apart—as far as the east is from the west. He was perfectly cheerful in his illness, and, when Mr. David Plunket (Lord Rathmore) came to see him, and he woke from a doze, he greeted his friend in his old hearty way, and then he took out a newspaper and said, 'Have you seen this? Here are fresh honours. Why, we shall be as grand as ever!' and he showed him an appreciative notice of his work in a Manchester paper, *à propos* of the reproduction of one of his plays. He was boyishly pleased, and when his cousin recalled some amusing story of old times, added, as he used to do, a humorous touch of his own, and laughed heartily over the reminiscence. He spoke of being made very comfortable in the hospital, and noticed in his old way the ladders of wintry sunshine let down from each window across the long ward. Then in a few minutes his mind began to wander a little, and seeing that his strength was exhausted, Mr. Plunket bid him good-bye.

Almost the last thing he said to me in full consciousness was, 'Well, at all events, mother never wanted'—and a tear trickled down his furrowed cheek. He did not seem to have any uneasiness as to the result of his illness. In the last few days his mind lost its way in the mists of unconsciousness that rose about him. His boyhood's friend, Lord Plunket, came to visit him in those last hours. Other old friends stole reverently up the long hospital ward, and stood by

U

his bedside, but he knew no one. He muttered a little, and the last words I caught were, 'There is nothing more.' In the early morning of December 13, 1891, he passed away peacefully—*multis ille bonis flebilis occidit.*

Like Goldsmith, he will certainly be remembered—and the more as time clears his memory from the surrounding things given to oblivion—as one of the best-loved men of letters of his age.

The following appreciation of him by a very old and faithful friend, Mr. W. L. Woodroffe, brings back his image distinctly in a few words:

I think of him now with that full sonorous voice, and frank, genial, hearty manner. There was a chivalry about the man, a simplicity, a sincerity, a gentleness, a genuineness. These were what made him so popular with women, what gave him a charm above all those gifts of intellect about which he was himself so modest. How kind he was to struggling men of letters, how little the one hand knew what the other so prodigally gave, how charitable he was in his judgments, and with what nobility of nature he could forgive an injury, there will be many of those who gather round his grave to-day to testify.

At the funeral service in the Savoy Chapel were Sir Henry Irving and Miss Terry, as well as many of his old friends among authors and actors. It was as beautiful as a poet's funeral should be, the violet-scarved choir carrying in procession through the churchyard he had so often passed on his way to the Savage Club the wreaths which bore many a last message of affection. He was buried in a spot in Brompton Cemetery, where he had once said to a friend he would like to rest. There was a wish at the time to place over him some public memorial, and for this reason not even a head-stone marks his last resting-place. While his memory lives among his friends he needs no other, and would ask no better.   In his own words :

> That sweet abiding in thy inner thought,
> I long for more than sculptured monument.

CHRONOLOGICAL TABLE OF W. G. WILLS'S ACTED PLAYS.

TITLE.	WHERE PRODUCED.	DATE.
' The Man o' Airlie '	Princess's .	July, 1867
' Hinko ' .	Queen's .	September, 1871
' Broken Spells ' (With Dr. Westland Marston)	Court	April, 1872
' Medea in Corinth '.	Lyceum .	July, 1872
' Charles I.' .	Lyceum .	September, 1872
' Eugene Aram '	Lyceum .	April, 1873
' Mary Queen of Scots '	Princess's .	February, 1874
' Sappho '	Theatre Royal, Dublin	1875
' Buckingham '.	Olympic .	November, 1875
' Jane Shore ' .	Princess's	September, 1876
' Cora '	.	March, 1877
' Camille '.	Theatre Royal, Cambridge	August, 1877
' England in the Days of Charles II.' .	Drury Lane	September, 1877
' Olivia ' .	Court	March, 1878
' Nell Gwynne'	Royalty	May, 1878.
' Vanderdecken '	Lyceum .	June, 1878
' Ellen,' afterwards ' Brag '	Haymarket	April, 1879
' Bolivar '	Theatre Royal, Dublin	November, 1879
' Ninon ' .	Adelphi	February, 1880
' Forced from Home '	Duke's	February, 1880
' Iolanthe '	Lyceum .	May, 1880
' William and Susan '	St. James's	October, 1880
' Juana ' .	Court	May, 1881
' Sedgmoor ' (with Freeman Wills) .	Sadler's Wells. .	August, 1881
' Jane Eyre ' .	Globe	December, 1882
' Claudian ' (with Henry Herman)	Princess's .	December, 1883
' Gringoire '	Prince's .	June, 1885
' A Young Tramp ' .	Prince's Theatre, Bristol	September, 1885
' Faust ' .	Lyceum .	December, 1885
' The Little Pilgrim '	Criterion	July, 1886
' Pompadour ' (with Sydney Grundy) .	Haymarket	March, 1888
' Clarissa '	Theatre Royal, Birmingham	December, 1889
' A Royal Divorce ' .	Olympic .	1891

Spottiswoode & Co. Printers, New-street Square, London.

A Classified Catalogue

OF WORKS IN

GENERAL LITERATURE

PUBLISHED BY

LONGMANS, GREEN, & CO.

39 PATERNOSTER ROW, LONDON, E.C.

91 AND 93 FIFTH AVENUE NEW YORK, AND 32 HORNBY ROAD, BOMBAY.

CONTENTS.

INDEX OF AUTHORS AND EDITORS.

History, Politics, Polity, Political Memoirs, &c.

Abbott.—*A HISTORY OF GREECE.* By EVELYN ABBOTT, M.A., LL.D.
Part I.—From the Earliest Times to the Ionian Revolt. Crown 8vo., 10s. 6d.
Part II.—500-445 B.C. Crown 8vo., 10s. 6d.

Acland and Ransome.—*A HANDBOOK IN OUTLINE OF THE POLITICAL HISTORY OF ENGLAND TO* 1896. Chronologically Arranged. By the Right Hon. A. H. DYKE ACLAND, M.P., and CYRIL RANSOME, M.A. Crown 8vo., 6s.

ANNUAL REGISTER (THE). A Review of Public Events at Home and Abroad, for the year 1896. 8vo., 18s.
Volumes of the *ANNUAL REGISTER* for the years 1863-1895 can still be had. 18s. each.

Arnold.—*INTRODUCTORY LECTURES ON MODERN HISTORY.* By THOMAS ARNOLD, D.D., formerly Head Master of Rugby School. 8vo., 7s. 6d.

Baden-Powell. — *THE INDIAN VILLAGE COMMUNITY.* Examined with Reference to the Physical, Ethnographic, and Historical Conditions of the Provinces; chiefly on the Basis of the Revenue-Settlement Records and District Manuals. By B. H. BADEN-POWELL, M.A., C.I.E. With Map. 8vo., 16s.

Bagwell.—*IRELAND UNDER THE TUDORS.* By RICHARD BAGWELL, LL.D. (3 vols.) Vols. I. and II. From the first invasion of the Northmen to the year 1578. 8vo., 32s. Vol. III. 1578-1603. 8vo., 18s.

Ball.—*HISTORICAL REVIEW OF THE LEGISLATIVE SYSTEMS OPERATIVE IN IRELAND,* from the Invasion of Henry the Second to the Union (1172-1800). By the Rt. Hon. J. T. BALL. 8vo., 6s.

Besant.—*THE HISTORY OF LONDON.* By Sir WALTER BESANT. With 74 Illustrations. Crown 8vo., 1s. 9d. Or bound as a School Prize Book, 2s. 6d.

Brassey (LORD).—PAPERS AND ADDRESSES.

NAVAL AND MARITIME. 1872-1893. 2 vols. Crown 8vo., 10s.

MERCANTILE MARINE AND NAVIGATION, from 1871-1894. Crown 8vo., 5s.

IMPERIAL FEDERATION AND COLONISATION FROM 1880-1894. Cr. 8vo., 5s.

Brassey (LORD) PAPERS AND ADDRESSES—*continued.*

POLITICAL AND MISCELLANEOUS. 1861-1894. Crown 8vo., 5s.

Bright.—*A HISTORY OF ENGLAND.* By the Rev. J. FRANCK BRIGHT, D.D.
Period I. *MEDIÆVAL MONARCHY*: A.D. 449-1485. Crown 8vo., 4s. 6d.
Period II. *PERSONAL MONARCHY.* 1485-1688. Crown 8vo., 5s.
Period III. *CONSTITUTIONAL MONARCHY.* 1689-1837. Crown 8vo., 7s. 6d.
Period IV. *THE GROWTH OF DEMOCRACY.* 1837-1880. Crown 8vo., 6s.

Buckle.—*HISTORY OF CIVILISATION IN ENGLAND AND FRANCE, SPAIN AND SCOTLAND.* By HENRY THOMAS BUCKLE. 3 vols. Crown 8vo., 24s.

Burke.—*A HISTORY OF SPAIN* from the Earliest Times to the Death of Ferdinand the Catholic. By ULICK RALPH BURKE, M.A. 2 vols. 8vo., 32s.

Chesney.—*INDIAN POLITY:* a View of the System of Administration in India. By General Sir GEORGE CHESNEY, K.C.B. With Map showing all the Administrative Divisions of British India. 8vo., 21s.

Corbett.—*DRAKE AND THE TUDOR NAVY,* with a History of the Rise of England as a Maritime Power. By JULIAN S. CORBETT. With Portraits. Illustrations and Maps. 2 vols. 8vo., 36s.

Creighton. — *A HISTORY OF THE PAPACY FROM THE GREAT SCHISM TO THE SACK OF ROME, 1378-1527.* By M. CREIGHTON, D.D., Lord Bishop of London. 6 vols. Crown 8vo., 6s. each.

Cuningham. — *A SCHEME FOR IMPERIAL FEDERATION:* a Senate for the Empire. By GRANVILLE C. CUNINGHAM, of Montreal, Canada. With an Introduction by Sir FREDERICK YOUNG, K.C.M.G. Crown 8vo., 3s. 6d.

Curzon.—*PERSIA AND THE PERSIAN QUESTION.* By the Right Hon. GEORGE N. CURZON, M.P. With 9 Maps, 96 Illustrations, Appendices, and an Index. 2 vols. 8vo., 42s.

De Tocqueville.—*DEMOCRACY IN AMERICA.* By ALEXIS DE TOCQUEVILLE. 2 vols. Crown 8vo., 16s.

History, Politics, Polity, Political Memoirs, &c.—*continued.*

Dickinson.—*THE DEVELOPMENT OF PARLIAMENT DURING THE NINETEENTH CENTURY.* By G. LOWES DICKINSON, M.A. 8vo., 7s. 6d.

Eggleston. *THE BEGINNERS OF A NATION:* a History of the Source and Rise of the Earliest English Settlements in America, with Special Reference to the Life and Character of the People. By EDWARD EGGLESTON. With 8 Maps. Cr. 8vo.,7s. 6d.

Froude (JAMES A.).

THE HISTORY OF ENGLAND, from the Fall of Wolsey to the Defeat of the Spanish Armada.
   Popular Edition. 12 vols. Crown 8vo., 3s. 6d. each.
   'Silver Library' Edition. 12 vols. Crown 8vo., 3s. 6d. each.

THE DIVORCE OF CATHERINE OF ARAGON. Crown 8vo., 3s. 6d.

THE SPANISH STORY OF THE ARMADA, and other Essays. Cr. 8vo., 3s. 6d.

THE ENGLISH IN IRELAND IN THE EIGHTEENTH CENTURY. 3 vols. Cr. 8vo., 10s. 6d.

ENGLISH SEAMEN IN THE SIXTEENTH CENTURY. Cr. 8vo., 6s.

THE COUNCIL OF TRENT. Crown 8vo., 3s. 6d.

SHORT STUDIES ON GREAT SUBJECTS. 4 vols. Cr. 8vo., 3s. 6d. each.

CÆSAR: a Sketch. Cr. 8vo., 3s. 6d.

Gardiner (SAMUEL RAWSON, D.C.L., LL.D.).

HISTORY OF ENGLAND, from the Accession of James I. to the Outbreak of the Civil War, 1603-1642. 10 vols. Crown 8vo., 6s. each.

A HISTORY OF THE GREAT CIVIL WAR, 1642-1649. 4 vols. Cr. 8vo., 6s. each.

A HISTORY OF THE COMMONWEALTH AND THE PROTECTORATE. 1649-1660. Vol. I. 1649-1651. With 14 Maps. 8vo., 21s. Vol. II. 1651-1654. With 7 Maps. 8vo., 21s.

WHAT GUNPOWDER PLOT WAS. With 8 Illustrations. Crown 8vo., 5s.

Gardiner (SAMUEL RAWSON, D.C.L., LL.D.) *continued.*

CROMWELL'S PLACE IN HISTORY. Founded on Six Lectures delivered in the University of Oxford. Cr. 8vo., 3s. 6d.

THE STUDENT'S HISTORY OF ENGLAND. With 378 Illustrations. Crown 8vo., 12s.

   Also in Three Volumes, price 4s. each.
   Vol. I. B.C. 55—A.D. 1509. 173 Illustrations.
   Vol. II. 1509-1689. 96 Illustrations.
   Vol. III. 1689-1885. 109 Illustrations.

Greville. *A JOURNAL OF THE REIGNS OF KING GEORGE IV., KING WILLIAM IV., AND QUEEN VICTORIA.* By CHARLES C. F. GREVILLE, formerly Clerk of the Council. 8 vols. Crown 8vo., 3s. 6d. each.

HARVARD HISTORICAL STUDIES.

THE SUPPRESSION OF THE AFRICAN SLAVE TRADE TO THE UNITED STATES OF AMERICA, 1638-1870. By W. E. B. DU BOIS, Ph.D. 8vo., 7s. 6d.

THE CONTEST OVER THE RATIFICATON OF THE FEDERAL CONSTITUTION IN MASSACHUSETTS. By S. B. HARDING, A.M. 8vo., 6s.

A CRITICAL STUDY OF NULLIFICATION IN SOUTH CAROLINA. By D. F. HOUSTON, A.M. 8vo., 6s.

NOMINATIONS FOR ELECTIVE OFFICE IN THE UNITED STATES. By FREDERICK W. DALLINGER, A.M. 8vo., 7s. 6d.

A BIBLIOGRAPHY OF BRITISH MUNICIPAL HISTORY, INCLUDING GILDS AND PARLIAMENTARY REPRESENTATION. By CHARLES GROSS, Ph.D. 8vo., 12s.

THE LIBERTY AND FREE SOIL PARTIES IN THE NORTHWEST. By THEODORE C. SMITH, Ph.D. 8vo.

   ** Other Volumes are in preparation.

Hammond. *A WOMAN'S PART IN A REVOLUTION.* By Mrs. JOHN HAYS HAMMOND. Crown 8vo., 2s. 6d.

Historic Towns. Edited by E. A. FREEMAN, D.C.L., and Rev. WILLIAM HUNT, M.A. With Maps and Plans. Crown 8vo., 3s. 6d. each.

Bristol. By Rev. W. Hunt.	Oxford. By Rev. C. W. Boase.
Carlisle. By Mandell Creighton, D.D.	Winchester. By G. W. Kitchin, D.D.
Cinque Ports. By Montague Burrows.	York. By Rev. James Raine.
Colchester. By Rev. E. L. Cutts.	New York. By Theodore Roosevelt.
Exeter. By E. A. Freeman.	Boston (U.S.) By Henry Cabot Lodge.
London. By Rev. W. J. Loftie.	

History, Politics, Polity, Political Memoirs, &c.—*continued.*

Joyce (P. W., LL.D.).

A SHORT HISTORY OF IRELAND, from the Earliest Times to 1603. Crown 8vo., 10s. 6d.

A CHILD'S HISTORY OF IRELAND. From the Earliest Times to the Death of O'Connell. With specially constructed Map and 160 Illustrations, including Facsimile in full colours of an illuminated page of the Gospel Book of Mac-Durnan, A.D. 850. Fcp. 8vo., 3s. 6d.

Kaye and Malleson.—*HISTORY OF THE INDIAN MUTINY,* 1857-1858. By Sir JOHN W. KAYE and Colonel G. B. MALLESON. With Analytical Index and Maps and Plans. 6 vols. Crown 8vo., 3s. 6d. each.

Knight.—*MADAGASCAR IN WAR TIME: THE EXPERIENCES OF 'THE TIMES' SPECIAL CORRESPONDENT WITH THE HOVAS DURING THE FRENCH INVASION OF 1895.* By E. F. KNIGHT. With 16 Illustrations and a Map. 8vo., 12s. 6d.

Lang (ANDREW).

PICKLE THE SPY: or, The Incognito of Prince Charles. With 6 Portraits. 8vo., 18s.

ST. ANDREWS. With 8 Plates and 24 Illustrations in the Text by T. HODGE. 8vo., 15s. net.

Laurie. — *HISTORICAL SURVEY OF PRE-CHRISTIAN EDUCATION.* By S. S. LAURIE, A.M., LL.D. 8vo., 12s.

Lecky (The Rt. Hon. WILLIAM E. H.) *HISTORY OF ENGLAND IN THE EIGHTEENTH CENTURY.*

Library Edition. 8 vols. 8vo., £7 4s.

Cabinet Edition. ENGLAND. 7 vols. Crown 8vo., 6s. each. IRELAND. 5 vols. Crown 8vo., 6s. each.

HISTORY OF EUROPEAN MORALS FROM AUGUSTUS TO CHARLEMAGNE. 2 vols. Crown 8vo., 16s.

HISTORY OF THE RISE AND INFLUENCE OF THE SPIRIT OF RATIONALISM IN EUROPE. 2 vols. Crown 8vo., 16s.

DEMOCRACY AND LIBERTY. 2 vols. 8vo., 36s.

THE EMPIRE: its value and its Growth. An Inaugural Address delivered at the Imperial Institute, 20th November, 1893. Cr. 8vo., 1s. 6d.

Lowell. — *GOVERNMENTS AND PARTIES IN CONTINENTAL EUROPE.* By A. LAWRENCE LOWELL. 2 vols. 8vo., 21s.

Macaulay (LORD).

THE LIFE AND WORKS OF LORD MACAULAY. 'Edinburgh' Edition. 10 vols. 8vo., 6s. each.

Vols. I.-IV. *HISTORY OF ENGLAND.*
Vols. V.-VII. *ESSAYS; BIOGRAPHIES; INDIAN PENAL CODE; CONTRIBUTIONS TO KNIGHT'S 'QUARTERLY MAGAZINE'.*
Vol. VIII. *SPEECHES; LAYS OF ANCIENT ROME: MISCELLANEOUS POEMS.*
Vols. IX. and X. *THE LIFE AND LETTERS OF LORD MACAULAY.* By the Right Hon. Sir G. O. TREVELYAN, Bart.

This Edition is a cheaper reprint of the Library Edition of LORD MACAULAY'S *Life and Works.*

COMPLETE WORKS.

Cabinet Edition. 16 vols. Post 8vo., £4 16s.
Library Edition. 8 vols. 8vo., £5 5s.
'Edinburgh' Edition. 8 vols. 8vo., 6s. each.

HISTORY OF ENGLAND FROM THE ACCESSION OF JAMES THE SECOND.

Popular Edition. 2 vols. Cr. 8vo., 5s.
Student's Edition. 2 vols. Cr. 8vo., 12s.
People's Edition. 4 vols. Cr. 8vo., 16s.
Cabinet Edition. 8 vols. Post 8vo., 48s.
'Edinburgh' Edition. 4 vols. 8vo., 6s. each.
Library Edition. 5 vols. 8vo., £4.

CRITICAL AND HISTORICAL ESSAYS, WITH LAYS OF ANCIENT ROME, etc., in 1 volume.

Popular Edition. Crown 8vo., 2s. 6d.
Authorised Edition. Crown 8vo., 2s. 6d., or gilt edges, 3s. 6d.
'Silver Library' Edition. With Portrait and 4 Illustrations to the 'Lays'. Cr. 8vo., 3s. 6d.

CRITICAL AND HISTORICAL ESSAYS.

Student's Edition. 1 vol. Cr. 8vo., 6s.
People's Edition. 2 vols. Cr. 8vo., 8s.
'Trevelyan' Edition. 2 vols. Cr. 8vo., 9s.
Cabinet Edition. 4 vols. Post 8vo., 24s.
'Edinburgh' Edition. 3 vols. 8vo., 6s. each.
Library Edition. 3 vols. 8vo., 36s.

ESSAYS, which may be had separately, sewed, 6d. each; cloth, 1s. each.

Addison and Walpole.	Ranke and Gladstone.
Croker's Boswell's Johnson.	Milton and Machiavelli.
Hallam's Constitutional History.	Lord Byron.
Warren Hastings.	Lord Clive.
The Earl of Chatham (Two Essays).	Lord Byron, and The Comic Dramatists of the Restoration.
Frederick the Great.	

MISCELLANEOUS WRITINGS

People's Edition. 1 vol. Cr. 8vo., 4s. 6d.
Library Edition. 2 vols. 8vo., 21s.

History, Politics, Polity, Political Memoirs, &c.—*continued.*

Macaulay (LORD)- *continued.*
MISCELLANEOUS WRITINGS, SPEECHES AND POEMS.
Popular Edition. Crown 8vo., 2s. 6d.
Cabinet Edition. 4 vols. Post 8vo., 24s.
SELECTIONS FROM THE WRITINGS OF LORD MACAULAY. Edited, with Occasional Notes, by the Right Hon. Sir G. O. Trevelyan, Bart. Crown 8vo., 6s.

MacColl. THE SULTAN AND THE POWERS. By the Rev. MALCOLM MACCOLL, M.A., Canon of Ripon. 8vo., 10s. 6d.

Mackinnon. THE UNION OF ENGLAND AND SCOTLAND: A STUDY OF INTERNATIONAL HISTORY. By JAMES MACKINNON Ph.D. Examiner in History to the University of Edinburgh. 8vo., 16s.

May.—THE CONSTITUTIONAL HISTORY OF ENGLAND since the Accession of George III. 1760-1870. By Sir THOMAS ERSKINE MAY, K.C.B. (Lord Farnborough). 3 vols. Cr. 8vo., 18s.

Merivale (CHARLES, D.D.), sometime Dean of Ely.
HISTORY OF THE ROMANS UNDER THE EMPIRE. 8 vols. Crown 8vo., 3s. 6d. each.
THE FALL OF THE ROMAN REPUBLIC: a Short History of the Last Century of the Commonwealth. 12mo., 7s. 6d.
GENERAL HISTORY OF ROME, from the Foundation of the City to the Fall of Augustulus, B.C. 753-A.D. 476. With 5 Maps. Crown 8vo, 7s. 6d.

Montague. — THE ELEMENTS OF ENGLISH CONSTITUTIONAL HISTORY. By F. C. MONTAGUE, M.A. Crown 8vo., 3s. 6d.

Richman. APPENZELL: PURE DEMOCRACY AND PASTORAL LIFE IN INNER-RHODEN. A Swiss Study. By IRVING B. RICHMAN, Consul-General of the United States to Switzerland. With Maps. Crown 8vo., 5s.

Seebohm (FREDERIC).
THE ENGLISH VILLAGE COMMUNITY Examined in its Relations to the Manorial and Tribal Systems, etc. With 13 Maps and Plates. 8vo., 16s.
THE TRIBAL SYSTEM IN WALES: Being Part of an Inquiry into the Structure and Methods of Tribal Society. With 3 Maps. 8vo., 12s.

Sharpe.—LONDON AND THE KINGDOM: a History derived mainly from the Archives at Guildhall in the custody of the Corporation of the City of London. By REGINALD R. SHARPE, D.C.L., Records Clerk in the Office of the Town Clerk of the City of London. 3 vols. 8vo. 10s. 6d. each.

Smith. —CARTHAGE AND THE CARTHAGINIANS. By R. BOSWORTH SMITH, M.A., With Maps, Plans, etc. Cr. 8vo., 3s. 6d.

Stephens. A HISTORY OF THE FRENCH REVOLUTION. By H. MORSE STEPHENS. 3 vols. 8vo. Vols. I. and II. 18s. each.

Stubbs.- HISTORY OF THE UNIVERSITY OF DUBLIN, from its Foundation to the End of the Eighteenth Century. By J. W. STUBBS. 8vo., 12s. 6d.

Sutherland.--THE HISTORY OF AUSTRALIA AND NEW ZEALAND, from 1606-1890. By ALEXANDER SUTHERLAND, M.A., and GEORGE SUTHERLAND, M.A. Crown 8vo., 2s. 6d.

Taylor.—A STUDENT'S MANUAL OF THE HISTORY OF INDIA. By Colonel MEADOWS TAYLOR, C.S.I., etc. Cr. 8vo., 7s. 6d.

Todd. — PARLIAMENTARY GOVERNMENT IN THE BRITISH COLONIES. By ALPHEUS TODD, LL.D. 8vo., 30s. net.

Wakeman and Hassall.—ESSAYS INTRODUCTORY TO THE STUDY OF ENGLISH CONSTITUTIONAL HISTORY. By Resident Members of the University of Oxford. Edited by HENRY OFFLEY WAKEMAN, M.A., and ARTHUR HASSALL, M.A. Crown 8vo., 6s.

Walpole.—HISTORY OF ENGLAND FROM THE CONCLUSION OF THE GREAT WAR IN 1815 TO 1858. By Sir SPENCER WALPOLE, K.C.B. 6 vols. Crown 8vo., 6s. each.

Wood-Martin.—PAGAN IRELAND: AN ARCHÆOLOGICAL SKETCH. A Handbook of Irish Pre-Christian Antiquities. By W. G. WOOD-MARTIN, M.R.I.A. With 512 Illustrations. Crown 8vo., 15s.

Wylie. — HISTORY OF ENGLAND UNDER HENRY IV. By JAMES HAMILTON WYLIE, M.A., one of H.M. Inspectors of Schools. 3 vols. Crown 8vo. Vol. I., 1399-1404, 10s. 6d. Vol. II., 1405-1406, 15s. Vol. III., 1407-1411, 15s. [Vol. IV. *In the press.*]

Biography, Personal Memoirs, &c.

Armstrong.—*THE LIFE AND LETTERS OF EDMUND J. ARMSTRONG.* Edited by G. F. SAVAGE ARMSTRONG. Fcp. 8vo., 7s. 6d.

Bacon.—*THE LETTERS AND LIFE OF FRANCIS BACON, INCLUDING ALL HIS OCCASIONAL WORKS.* Edited by JAMES SPEDDING. 7 vols. 8vo., £4 4s.

Bagehot.—*BIOGRAPHICAL STUDIES.* By WALTER BAGEHOT. Crown 8vo., 3s. 6d.

Blackwell. — *PIONEER WORK IN OPENING THE MEDICAL PROFESSION TO WOMEN:* Autobiographical Sketches. By Dr. ELIZABETH BLACKWELL. Cr. 8vo., 6s.

Boyd (A. K. H.) ('A.K.H.B.').
TWENTY-FIVE YEARS OF ST. ANDREWS. 1865-1890. 2 vols. 8vo. Vol. I. 12s. Vol. II. 15s.

ST. ANDREWS AND ELSEWHERE: Glimpses of Some Gone and of Things Left. 8vo., 15s.

THE LAST YEARS OF ST. ANDREWS: SEPTEMBER 1890 TO SEPTEMBER 1895. 8vo., 15s.

Brown.—*FORD MADOX BROWN:* A Record of his Life and Works. By FORD M. HUEFFER. With 45 Full-page Plates (22 Autotypes) and 7 Illustrations in the Text. 8vo., 42s.

Buss.—*FRANCES MARY BUSS AND HER WORK FOR EDUCATION.* By ANNIE E. RIDLEY. With 5 Portraits and 4 Illustrations. Crown 8vo, 7s. 6d.

Carlyle.—*THOMAS CARLYLE:* A History of his Life. By JAMES ANTHONY FROUDE.
1795-1835. 2 vols. Crown 8vo., 7s.
1834-1881. 2 vols. Crown 8vo., 7s.

Digby.—*THE LIFE OF SIR KENELM DIGBY, by one of his Descendants,* the Author of 'Falklands.' etc. With 7 Illustrations. 8vo., 16s.

Duncan.—*ADMIRAL DUNCAN.* By THE EARL OF CAMPERDOWN. With 3 Portraits. 8vo.

Erasmus.—*LIFE AND LETTERS OF ERASMUS.* By JAMES ANTHONY FROUDE. Crown 8vo., 6s.

FALKLANDS. By the Author of 'The Life of Sir Kenelm Digby,' etc. With 6 Portraits and 2 other Illustrations. 8vo., 10s. 6d.

Faraday.—*FARADAY AS A DISCOVERER.* By JOHN TYNDALL. Crown 8vo, 4s. 6d.

Fox. — *THE EARLY HISTORY OF CHARLES JAMES FOX.* By the Right Hon. Sir G. O. TREVELYAN, Bart.
Library Edition. 8vo., 18s.
Cabinet Edition. Crown 8vo., 6s.

Halifax.—*THE LIFE AND LETTERS OF SIR GEORGE SAVILE, BARONET, FIRST MARQUIS OF HALIFAX.* With a New Edition of his Works, now for the first time collected and revised. By H. C. FOXCROFT. 2 vols. 8vo., 32s.

Halford.—*THE LIFE OF SIR HENRY HALFORD, BART., G.C.H., M.D., F.R.S.* By WILLIAM MUNK, M.D., F.S.A. 8vo., 12s. 6d.

Hamilton.—*LIFE OF SIR WILLIAM HAMILTON.* By R. P. GRAVES. 8vo. 3 vols. 15s. each. ADDENDUM. 8vo., 6d. sewed.

Harper. — *A MEMOIR OF HUGO DANIEL HARPER, D.D.,* late Principal of Jesus College, Oxford, and for many years Head Master of Sherborne School. By L. V. LESTER, M.A. Crown 8vo., 5s.

Havelock.—*MEMOIRS OF SIR HENRY HAVELOCK, K.C.B.* By JOHN CLARK MARSHMAN. Crown 8vo., 3s. 6d.

Haweis.—*MY MUSICAL LIFE.* By the Rev. H. R. HAWEIS. With Portrait of Richard Wagner and 3 Illustrations. Crown 8vo., 7s. 6d.

Holroyd.—*THE GIRLHOOD OF MARIA JOSEPHA HOLROYD (Lady Stanley of Alderley).* Recorded in Letters of a Hundred Years Ago, from 1776-1796. Edited by J. H. ADEANE. With 6 Portraits. 8vo., 18s.

Jackson. — *STONEWALL JACKSON.* By Lieut.-Col. G. F. HENDERSON, York and Lancaster Regiment. With Portrait, Maps and Plans. 2 vols. 8vo., 42s.

Lejeune.—*MEMOIRS OF BARON LEJEUNE,* Aide-de-Camp to Marshals Berthier, Davout, and Oudinot. Translated and Edited from the Original French by Mrs. ARTHUR BELL (N. D'ANVERS). With a Preface by Major-General MAURICE, C.B. 2 vols. 8vo., 24s.

Luther. — *LIFE OF LUTHER.* By JULIUS KÖSTLIN. With 62 Illustrations and 4 Facsimilies of MSS. Translated from the German. Crown 8vo., 3s. 6d.

Macaulay.—*THE LIFE AND LETTERS OF LORD MACAULAY.* By the Right Hon. Sir G. O. TREVELYAN, Bart.
Popular Edition. 1 vol. Cr. 8vo., 2s. 6d.
Student's Edition. 1 vol. Cr. 8vo., 6s.
Cabinet Edition. 2 vols. Post 8vo., 12s.
'Edinburgh' Edition. 2 vols. 8vo., 6s. each.
Library Edition. 2 vols. 8vo., 36s.

Biography, Personal Memoirs, &c.—*continued.*

Marbot. — *THE MEMOIRS OF THE BARON DE MARBOT.* Translated from the French. 2 vols. Crown 8vo., 7s.

Max Müller. *AULD LANG SYNE.* By the Right Hon. F. MAX MÜLLER. With Portrait. 8vo., 10s. 6d.
CONTENTS Musical Recollections Literary Recollections Recollections of Royalties Beggars.

Nansen. *FRIDTIOF NANSEN,* 1861-1893. By W. C. BRÖGGER and NORDAHL ROLFSEN. Translated by WILLIAM ARCHER. With 8 Plates, 48 Illustrations in the Text, and 3 Maps. 8vo., 12s. 6d.

Place. *THE LIFE OF FRANCIS PLACE,* 1771-1854. By GRAHAM WALLAS, M.A. With 2 Portraits. 8vo., 12s.

Rawlinson. — *A MEMOIR OF MAJOR-GENERAL SIR HENRY CRESWICKE RAWLINSON, BART., K.C.B., F.R.S., D.C.L., F.R.G.S., ETC.* By GEORGE RAWLINSON, M.A., F.R.G.S., Canon of Canterbury. With Portraits and a Map, and a Preface by Field-Marshal Lord ROBERTS of Kandahar, V.C. 8vo.

Reeve. *THE LIFE AND LETTERS OF HENRY REEVE, C.B.,* late Editor of the 'Edinburgh Review,' and Registrar of the Privy Council. By J. K. LAUGHTON, M.A.

Romanes. — *THE LIFE AND LETTERS OF GEORGE JOHN ROMANES, M.A., LL.D., F.R.S.* Written and Edited by his WIFE. With Portrait and 2 Illustrations. Crown 8vo., 6s.

Seebohm. — *THE OXFORD REFORMERS —JOHN COLET, ERASMUS AND THOMAS MORE:* a History of their Fellow-Work. By FREDERIC SEEBOHM. 8vo., 14s.

Shakespeare. — *OUTLINES OF THE LIFE OF SHAKESPEARE.* By J. O. HALLIWELL-PHILLIPPS. With Illustrations and Fac-similes. 2 vols. Royal 8vo., £1 1s.

Shakespeare's *TRUE LIFE.* By JAMES WALTER. With 500 Illustrations by GERALD E. MOIRA. Imp. 8vo., 21s.

Verney. — *MEMOIRS OF THE VERNEY FAMILY.*

Vols. I. & II., *DURING THE CIVIL WAR.* By FRANCES PARTHENOPE VERNEY. With 38 Portraits, Woodcuts and Fac-simile. Royal 8vo., 42s.

Vol. III. *DURING THE COMMONWEALTH.* 1650-1660. By MARGARET M. VERNEY. With 10 Portraits, etc. Royal 8vo., 21s.

Wakley. *THE LIFE AND TIMES OF THOMAS WAKLEY,* Founder and First Editor of the 'Lancet,' Member of Parliament for Finsbury, and Coroner for West Middlesex. By S. SQUIRE SPRIGGE, M.B. Cantab. With 2 Portraits. 8vo., 18s.

Wellington. — *LIFE OF THE DUKE OF WELLINGTON.* By the Rev. G. R. GLEIG, M.A. Crown 8vo., 3s. 6d.

Travel and Adventure, the Colonies, &c.

Arnold. — *SEAS AND LANDS.* By Sir EDWIN ARNOLD. With 71 Illustrations. Crown 8vo., 3s. 6d.

Baker (SIR S. W.).

EIGHT YEARS IN CEYLON. With 6 Illustrations. Crown 8vo., 3s. 6d.

THE RIFLE AND THE HOUND IN CEYLON. With 6 Illustrations. Crown 8vo., 3s. 6d.

Bent. — *THE RUINED CITIES OF MASHONALAND:* being a Record of Excavation and Exploration in 1891. By J. THEODORE BENT. With 117 Illustrations. Crown 8vo., 3s. 6d.

Bicknell. — *TRAVEL AND ADVENTURE IN NORTHERN QUEENSLAND.* By ARTHUR C. BICKNELL. With 24 Plates and 22 Illustrations in the Text. 8vo., 15s.

Brassey. — *VOYAGES AND TRAVELS OF LORD BRASSEY, K.C.B., D.C.L.,* 1862-1894. Arranged and Edited by Captain S. EARDLEY-WILMOT. 2 vols. Cr. 8vo., 10s.

Brassey (THE LATE LADY).

A VOYAGE IN THE 'SUNBEAM'; OUR HOME ON THE OCEAN FOR ELEVEN MONTHS.

Cabinet Edition. With Map and 66 Illustrations. Crown 8vo., 7s. 6d.

'*Silver Library' Edition.* With 66 Illustrations. Crown 8vo., 3s. 6d.

Popular Edition. With 60 Illustrations. 4to., 6d. sewed, 1s. cloth.

School Edition. With 37 Illustrations. Fcp., 2s. cloth, or 3s. white parchment.

Travel and Adventure, the Colonies, &c.—*continued.*

Brassey(THE LATE LADY)—*continued.*

SUNSHINE AND STORM IN THE EAST.
Cabinet Edition. With 2 Maps and 114
Illustrations. Crown 8vo., 7s. 6d.
Popular Edition. With 103 Illustrations.
4to., 6d. sewed, 1s. cloth.
*IN THE TRADES, THE TROPICS, AND
THE 'ROARING FORTIES'.*
Cabinet Edition. With Map and 220
Illustrations. Crown 8vo., 7s. 6d.
Popular Edition. With 183 Illustrations,
4to., 6d. sewed, 1s. cloth.
THREE VOYAGES IN THE 'SUNBEAM'.
Popular Ed. With 346 Illust. 4to., 2s. 6d.

Browning.—*A GIRL'S WANDERINGS
IN HUNGARY.* By H. ELLEN BROWNING.
With Map and 20 Illustrations. Crown 8vo.,
3s. 6d.

Churchill.—*THE STORY OF THE
MALAKAND FIELD FORCE,* 1897. By
WINSTON SPENCER CHURCHILL, Lieut., 4th
Queen's Own Hussars. With Maps and
Plans. Crown 8vo.

Froude (JAMES A.).

OCEANA: or England and her Colonies. With 9 Illustrations. Crown 8vo.,
2s. boards, 2s. 6d. cloth.
THE ENGLISH IN THE WEST INDIES:
or, the Bow of Ulysses. With 9 Illustrations. Crown 8vo., 2s. boards. 2s. 6d. cloth.

Howitt.—*VISITS TO REMARKABLE
PLACES.* Old Halls, Battle-Fields, Scenes,
illustrative of Striking Passages in English
History and Poetry. By WILLIAM HOWITT.
With 80 Illustrations. Crown 8vo., 3s. 6d.

Jones.—*ROCK CLIMBING IN THE
ENGLISH LAKE DISTRICT.* By OWEN
GLYNNE JONES, B.Sc. (Lond.), Member of
the Alpine Club. With 30 Full-page Illustrations in Collotype and 9 Lithograph
Plate Diagrams of the Chief Routes. 8vo.,
15s. net.

Knight (E. F.).

THE CRUISE OF THE 'ALERTE': the
Narrative of a Search for Treasure on the
Desert Island of Trinidad. With 2 Maps
and 23 Illustrations. Crown 8vo., 3s. 6d.
WHERE THREE EMPIRES MEET: a
Narrative of Recent Travel in Kashmir,
Western Tibet, Baltistan, Ladak, Gilgit,
and the adjoining Countries. With a
Map and 54 Illustrations. Cr. 8vo., 3s. 6d.
THE 'FALCON' ON THE BALTIC: a
Voyage from London to Copenhagen in
a Three-Tonner. With 10 Full-page
Illustrations. Crown 8vo., 3s. 6d.

Lees and Clutterbuck. B.C. 1887:
A RAMBLE IN BRITISH COLUMBIA. By J. A.
LEES and W. J. CLUTTERBUCK. With Map
and 75 Illustrations. Crown 8vo., 3s. 6d.

Macdonald.—*THE GOLD COAST: PAST
AND PRESENT.* By GEORGE MACDONALD,
Director of Education and H.M. Inspector
of Schools for the Gold Coast Colony and
the Protectorate. With Illustrations.

Max Müller.—*LETTERS FROM CON-
STANTINOPLE.* By Mrs. MAX MÜLLER.
With 12 Views of Constantinople and the
neighbourhood. Crown 8vo., 6s.

Nansen (FRIDTJOF).

*THE FIRST CROSSING OF GREEN-
LAND.* With 143 Illustrations and a Map,
Crown 8vo., 3s. 6d.
ESKIMO LIFE. With 31 Illustrations.
8vo., 16s.

Oliver.—*CRAGS AND CRATERS:*
Rambles in the Island of Réunion. By
WILLIAM DUDLEY OLIVER, M.A. With
27 Illustrations and a Map. Cr. 8vo., 6s.

Quillinan.—*JOURNAL OF A FEW
MONTHS' RESIDENCE IN PORTUGAL,* and
Glimpses of the South of Spain. By Mrs.
QUILLINAN (Dora Wordsworth). With
Memoir by EDMUND LEE. Crown 8vo., 6s.

Smith.—*CLIMBING IN THE BRITISH
ISLES.* By W. P. HASKETT SMITH. With
Illustrations by ELLIS CARR, and Numerous
Plans.
Part I. *ENGLAND.* 16mo., 3s. 6d.
Part II. *WALES AND IRELAND.* 16mo.,
3s. 6d.
Part III. *SCOTLAND.* [*In preparation.*

Stephen.—*THE PLAY-GROUND OF
EUROPE* (The Alps). By LESLIE STE-
PHEN. With 4 Illustrations. Crown 8vo.,
6s. net.

THREE IN NORWAY. By Two
of Them. With a Map and 59 Illustrations.
Crown 8vo., 2s. boards, 2s. 6d. cloth.

Tyndall.—*THE GLACIERS OF THE
ALPS:* being a Narrative of Excursions
and Ascents. An Account of the Origin
and Phenomena of Glaciers, and an Exposition of the Physical Principles to which
they are related. By JOHN TYNDALL,
F.R.S. With 6 Illustrations. Crown 8vo.,
6s. 6d. net.

Vivian.—*SERVIA:* the Poor Man's
Paradise. By HERBERT VIVIAN, M.A.,
Officer of the Royal Order of Takovo.
With Map and Portrait of King Alex-
ander. 8vo., 15s.

Veterinary Medicine, &c.

Steel (JOHN HENRY, F.R.C.V.S., F.Z.S., A.V.D.), late Professor of Veterinary Science and Principal of Bombay Veterinary College.

A TREATISE ON THE DISEASES OF THE DOG; being a Manual of Canine Pathology. Especially adapted for the use of Veterinary Practitioners and Students. With 88 Illustrations. 8vo., 10s. 6d.

A TREATISE ON THE DISEASES OF THE OX; being a Manual of Bovine Pathology. Especially adapted for the use of Veterinary Practitioners and Students. With 2 Plates and 117 Woodcuts. 8vo., 15s.

A TREATISE ON THE DISEASES OF THE SHEEP; being a Manual of Ovine Pathology for the use of Veterinary Practitioners and Students. With Coloured Plate and 99 Woodcuts. 8vo., 12s.

OUTLINES OF EQUINE ANATOMY: a Manual for the use of Veterinary Students in the Dissecting Room. Cr. 8vo., 7s. 6d.

Fitzwygram. *HORSES AND STABLES.* By Major-General Sir F. Fitzwygram, Bart. With 56 pages of Illustrations. 8vo., 2s. 6d. net.

Schreiner. - *THE ANGORA GOAT* (published under the auspices of the South African Angora Goat Breeders' Association), and a Paper on the Ostrich (reprinted from the *Zoologist* for March, 1897). By S. C. CRONWRIGHT SCHREINER. 8vo.

'Stonehenge.' - *THE DOG IN HEALTH AND DISEASE.* By 'STONEHENGE'. With 78 Wood Engravings. 8vo., 7s. 6d.

Youatt (WILLIAM).

THE HORSE. Revised and Enlarged by W. WATSON, M.R.C.V.S. With 52 Wood Engravings. 8vo., 7s. 6d.

THE DOG. Revised and Enlarged. With 33 Wood Engravings. 8vo., 6s.

Sport and Pastime.

THE BADMINTON LIBRARY.

Edited by HIS GRACE THE DUKE OF BEAUFORT, K.G., and A. E. T. WATSON.

Complete in 28 Volumes.   Crown 8vo., Price 10s. 6d. each Volume, Cloth.

** The Volumes are also issued half-bound in Leather, with gilt top. The price can be had from all Booksellers.

ARCHERY. By C. J. LONGMAN and Col. H. WALROND. With Contributions by Miss LEGH. Viscount DILLON, etc. With 2 Maps, 23 Plates and 172 Illustrations in the Text. Crown 8vo., 10s. 6d.

ATHLETICS AND FOOTBALL. By MONTAGUE SHEARMAN. With 6 Plates and 52 Illust. in the Text. Cr. 8vo., 10s. 6d.

BIG GAME SHOOTING. By CLIVE PHILLIPPS-WOLLEY.

Vol. I. AFRICA AND AMERICA. With Contributions by Sir SAMUEL W. BAKER, W. C. OSWELL, F. C. SELOUS, etc. With 20 Plates and 57 Illustrations in the Text. Crown 8vo., 10s. 6d.

Vol. II. EUROPE, ASIA, AND THE ARCTIC REGIONS. With Contributions by Lieut.-Colonel R. HEBER PERCY, Major ALGERNON C. HEBER PERCY, etc. With 17 Plates and 56 Illustrations in the Text. Cr. 8vo., 10s. 6d.

BILLIARDS. By Major W. BROADFOOT, R.E. With Contributions by A. H. BOYD, SYDENHAM DIXON, W. J. FORD, etc. With 11 Plates, 19 Illustrations in the Text, and numerous Diagrams. Cr. 8vo., 10s. 6d.

BOATING. By W. B. WOODGATE. With 10 Plates, 39 Illustrations in the Text, and 4 Maps of Rowing Courses. Cr. 8vo., 10s. 6d.

COURSING AND FALCONRY. By HARDING Cox and the Hon. GERALD LASCELLES. With 20 Plates and 56 Illustrations in the Text. Crown 8vo., 10s. 6d.

CRICKET. By A. G. STEEL and the Hon. R. H. LYTTELTON. With Contributions by ANDREW LANG, W. G. GRACE, F. GALE, etc. With 12 Plates and 52 Illustrations in the Text. Crown 8vo., 10s. 6d.

CYCLING. By the EARL OF ALBEMARLE and G. LACY HILLIER. With 19 Plates and 44 Illustrations in the Text. Crown 8vo., 10s. 6d.

DANCING. By Mrs. LILLY GROVE, F.R.G.S. With Contributions by Miss MIDDLETON, The Hon. Mrs. ARMYTAGE, etc. With Musical Examples, and 38 Full-page Plates and 93 Illustrations in the Text. Crown 8vo., 10s. 6d.

DRIVING. By His Grace the DUKE of BEAUFORT, K.G. With Contributions by A. E. T. WATSON the EARL OF ONSLOW, etc. With 12 Plates and 54 Illustrations in the Text. Crown 8vo., 10s. 6d.

Sport and Pastime—*continued.*

THE BADMINTON LIBRARY—*continued.*

FENCING, BOXING, AND WRESTLING. By WALTER H. POLLOCK, F. C. GROVE, C. PRÉVOST, E. B. MITCHELL, and WALTER ARMSTRONG. With 18 Plates and 24 Illust. in the Text. Cr. 8vo., 10s. 6d.

FISHING. By H. CHOLMONDELEY-PENNELL.

Vol. I. SALMON AND TROUT. With Contributions by H. R. FRANCIS, Major JOHN P. TRAHERNE, etc. With 9 Plates and numerous Illustrations of Tackle, etc. Crown 8vo., 10s. 6d.

Vol. II. PIKE AND OTHER COARSE FISH. With Contributions by the MARQUIS OF EXETER, WILLIAM SENIOR, G. CHRISTOPHER DAVIS, etc. With 7 Plates and numerous Illustrations of Tackle, etc. Crown 8vo., 10s. 6d.

GOLF. By HORACE G. HUTCHINSON. With Contributions by the Rt. Hon. A. J. BALFOUR, M.P., Sir WALTER SIMPSON, Bart., ANDREW LANG, etc. With 25 Plates and 65 Illustrations in the Text. Cr. 8vo., 10s. 6d.

HUNTING. By His Grace the DUKE OF BEAUFORT, K.G., and MOWBRAY MORRIS. With Contributions by the EARL OF SUFFOLK AND BERKSHIRE, Rev. E. W. L. DAVIES, G. H. LONGMAN, etc. With 5 Plates and 54 Illustrations in the Text. Cr. 8vo., 10s. 6d.

MOUNTAINEERING. By C. T. DENT. With Contributions by Sir W. M. CONWAY, D. W. FRESHFIELD, C. E. MATTHEWS, etc. With 13 Plates and 95 Illustrations in the Text. Cr. 8vo., 10s. 6d.

POETRY OF SPORT (THE).—Selected by HEDLEY PEEK. With a Chapter on Classical Allusions to Sport by ANDREW LANG, and a Special Preface to the BADMINTON LIBRARY by A. E. T. WATSON. With 32 Plates and 74 Illustrations in the Text. Crown 8vo., 10s. 6d.

RACING AND STEEPLE-CHASING. By the EARL OF SUFFOLK AND BERKSHIRE, W. G. CRAVEN, the Hon. F. LAWLEY, ARTHUR COVENTRY, and A. E. T. WATSON. With Frontispiece and 56 Illustrations in the Text. Crown 8vo., 10s. 6d.

RIDING AND POLO. By Captain ROBERT WEIR, THE DUKE OF BEAUFORT, THE EARL OF SUFFOLK AND BERKSHIRE, THE EARL OF ONSLOW, etc. With 18 Plates and 41 Illustrations in the Text. Crown 8vo., 10s. 6d.

SEA FISHING. By JOHN BICKERDYKE, Sir H. W. GORE-BOOTH, ALFRED C. HARMSWORTH, and W. SENIOR. With 22 Full-page Plates and 175 Illustrations in the Text. Crown 8vo., 10s. 6d.

SHOOTING.

Vol. I. FIELD AND COVERT. By LORD WALSINGHAM and Sir RALPH PAYNE-GALLWEY, Bart. With Contributions by the Hon. GERALD LASCELLES and A. J. STUART-WORTLEY. With 11 Plates and 94 Illusts. in the Text. Cr. 8vo., 10s. 6d.

Vol. II. MOOR AND MARSH. By LORD WALSINGHAM and Sir RALPH PAYNE-GALLWEY, Bart. With Contributions by LORD LOVAT and Lord CHARLES LENNOX KERR. With 8 Plates and 57 Illustrations in the Text. Crown 8vo., 10s. 6d.

SKATING, CURLING, TOBOGGANING. By J. M. HEATHCOTE, C. G. TEBBUTT, T. MAXWELL WITHAM, Rev. JOHN KERR, ORMOND HAKE, HENRY A. BUCK, etc. With 12 Plates and 272 Illustrations in the Text. Crown 8vo., 10s. 6d.

SWIMMING. By ARCHIBALD SINCLAIR and WILLIAM HENRY, Hon. Secs. of the Life-Saving Society. With 13 Plates and 106 Illustrations in the Text. Crown 8vo., 10s. 6d.

TENNIS, LAWN TENNIS, RACKETS AND FIVES. By J. M. and C. G. HEATHCOTE, E. O. PLEYDELL-BOUVERIE, and A.C. AINGER. With Contributions by the Hon. A. LYTTELTON, W. C. MARSHALL, Miss L. DOD, etc. With 12 Plates and 67 Illustrations in the Text. Crown 8vo., 10s. 6d.

YACHTING.

Vol. I. CRUISING, CONSTRUCTION OF YACHTS, YACHT RACING RULES, FITTING-OUT, etc. By Sir EDWARD SULLIVAN, Bart., THE EARL OF PEMBROKE, LORD BRASSEY, K.C.B., C. E. SETH-SMITH, C.B., G. L. WATSON, R. T. PRITCHETT, E. F. KNIGHT, etc. With 21 Plates and 93 Illustrations in the Text. Crown 8vo., 10s. 6d.

Vol. II. YACHT CLUBS, YACHTING IN AMERICA AND THE COLONIES, YACHT RACING, etc. By R. T. PRITCHETT, THE MARQUIS OF DUFFERIN AND AVA, K.P., THE EARL OF ONSLOW, JAMES MCFERRAN, etc. With 35 Plates and 160 Illustrations in the Text. Crown 8vo., 10s. 6d.

Sport and Pastime—*continued.*

FUR, FEATHER. AND FIN SERIES.

Edited by A. E. T. Watson.

Crown 8vo., price 5s. each Volume, cloth.

* *The Volumes are also issued half-bound in Leather, with gilt top. The price can be had from all Booksellers.*

THE PARTRIDGE. Natural History, by the Rev. H. A. Macpherson; Shooting, by A. J. Stuart-Wortley; Cookery, by George Saintsbury. With 11 Illustrations and various Diagrams in the Text. Crown 8vo., 5s.

THE GROUSE. Natural History, by the Rev. H. A. Macpherson; Shooting, by A. J. Stuart-Wortley; Cookery, by George Saintsbury. With 13 Illustrations and various Diagrams in the Text. Crown 8vo., 5s.

THE PHEASANT. Natural History, by the Rev. H. A. Macpherson; Shooting, by A. J. Stuart-Wortley; Cookery, by Alexander Innes Shand. With 10 Illustrations and various Diagrams. Crown 8vo., 5s.

THE HARE. Natural History, by the Rev. H. A. Macpherson; Shooting, by the Hon. Gerald Lascelles; Coursing, by Charles Richardson; Hunting, by J. S. Gibbons and G. H. Longman; Cookery, by Col. Kenney Herbert. With 9 Illustrations. Crown 8vo, 5s.

RED DEER.— Natural History, by the Rev. H. A. Macpherson; Deer Stalking, by Cameron of Lochiel; Stag Hunting, by Viscount Ebrington; Cookery, by Alexander Innes Shand. With 10 Illustrations by J. Charlton and A. Thorburn. Crown 8vo., 5s.

THE SALMON. By the Hon. A. E. Gathorne-Hardy, etc. With Illustrations, etc.   [*In the press.*

THE TROUT. By the Marquis of Granby, etc. With Illustrations, etc.   [*In preparation.*

THE RABBIT. By J. E. Harting, etc. With Illustrations.   [*In preparation.*

WILDFOWL. By the Hon. John Scott Montagu, etc. With Illustrations, etc.   [*In preparation.*

André.—*Colonel Bogey's Sketch-Book.* Comprising an Eccentric Collection of Scribbles and Scratches found in disused Lockers and swept up in the Pavilion, together with sundry After-Dinner Savings of the Colonel. By R. André, West Herts Golf Club. Oblong 4to., 2s. 6d.

BADMINTON MAGAZINE (The) of Sports and Pastimes. Edited by Alfred E. T. Watson ("Rapier"). With numerous Illustrations. Price 1s. monthly.

Vols. I.-V. 6s. each.

DEAD SHOT (The): or, Sportsman's Complete Guide. Being a Treatise on the Use of the Gun, with Rudimentary and Finishing Lessons in the Art of Shooting Game of all kinds. Also Game-driving, Wildfowl and Pigeon-shooting, Dog-breaking, etc. By Marksman. With numerous Illustrations. Crown 8vo., 10s. 6d.

Ellis.—*Chess Sparks;* or, Short and Bright Games of Chess. Collected and Arranged by J. H. Ellis, M.A. 8vo., 4s. 6d.

Folkard.—*The Wild-Fowler:* A Treatise on Fowling, Ancient and Modern, descriptive also of Decoys and Flight-ponds, Wild-fowl Shooting, Gunning-punts, Shooting-yachts, etc. Also Fowling in the Fens and in Foreign Countries, Rock-fowling, etc., etc., by H. C. Folkard. With 13 Engravings on Steel, and several Woodcuts. 8vo., 12s. 6d.

Ford.—*The Theory and Practice of Archery.* By Horace Ford. New Edition, thoroughly Revised and Re-written by W. Butt, M.A. With a Preface by C. J. Longman, M.A. 8vo., 14s.

Francis.—*A Book on Angling:* or, Treatise on the Art of Fishing in every Branch; including full Illustrated List of Salmon Flies. By Francis Francis. With Portrait and Coloured Plates. Crown 8vo., 15s.

Sport and Pastime—*continued.*

Gibson.—*TOBOGGANING ON CROOKED RUNS.* By the Hon. HARRY GIBSON. With Contributions by F. DE B. STRICKLAND and 'LADY-TOBOGANNER'. With 40 Illustrations. Crown 8vo., 6s.

Graham.—*COUNTRY PASTIMES FOR BOYS.* By P. ANDERSON GRAHAM. With 252 Illustrations from Drawings and Photographs. Crown 8vo., 3s. 6d.

Lang.—*ANGLING SKETCHES.* By ANDREW LANG. With 20 Illustrations. Crown 8vo., 3s. 6d.

Lillie.—*CROQUET:* its History, Rules and Secrets. By ARTHUR LILLIE, Champion, Grand National Croquet Club, 1872; Winner of the 'All-Comers' Championship,' Maidstone, 1896. With 4 Full-page Illustrations by LUCIEN DAVIS, 15 Illustrations in the Text, and 27 Diagrams. Crown 8vo., 6s.

Longman.—*CHESS OPENINGS.* By FREDERICK W. LONGMAN. Fcp. 8vo., 2s. 6d.

Madden.—*THE DIARY OF MASTER WILLIAM SILENCE:* a Study of Shakespeare and of Elizabethan Sport. By the Right Hon. D. H. MADDEN, Vice-Chancellor of the University of Dublin. 8vo., 16s.

Maskelyne.—*SHARPS AND FLATS:* a Complete Revelation of the Secrets of Cheating at Games of Chance and Skill. By JOHN NEVIL MASKELYNE, of the Egyptian Hall. With 62 Illustrations. Crown 8vo., 6s.

Moffat.—*CRICKETY-CRICKET:* Rhymes and Parodies. By DOUGLAS MOFFAT, with Frontispiece by Sir FRANK LOCKWOOD, Q.C., M.P., and 53 Illustrations by the Author. Crown 8vo, 2s. 6d.

Park.—*THE GAME OF GOLF.* By WILLIAM PARK, Jun., Champion Golfer, 1887-89. With 17 Plates and 26 Illustrations in the Text. Crown 8vo., 7s. 6d.

Payne-Gallwey (Sir RALPH, Bart.).

LETTERS TO YOUNG SHOOTERS (First Series). On the Choice and use of a Gun. With 41 Illustrations. Crown 8vo., 7s. 6d.

LETTERS TO YOUNG SHOOTERS (Second Series). On the Production, Preservation, and Killing of Game. With Directions in Shooting Wood-Pigeons and Breaking-in Retrievers. With Portrait and 103 Illustrations. Crown 8vo., 12s. 6d.

Payne-Gallwey (Sir RALPH, Bart.) —*continued.*

LETTERS TO YOUNG SHOOTERS. (Third Series.) Comprising a Short Natural History of the Wildfowl that are Rare or Common to the British Islands, with complete directions in Shooting Wildfowl on the Coast and Inland. With 200 Illustrations. Crown 8vo., 18s.

Pole (WILLIAM).

THE THEORY OF THE MODERN SCIENTIFIC GAME OF WHIST. Fcp. 8vo., 2s. 6d.

THE EVOLUTION OF WHIST: a Study of the Progressive Changes which the Game has undergone. Cr. 8vo., 2s. 6d.

Proctor.—*HOW TO PLAY WHIST: WITH THE LAWS AND ETIQUETTE OF WHIST.* By RICHARD A. PROCTOR. Crown 8vo., 3s. 6d.

Ribblesdale.—*THE QUEEN'S HOUNDS AND STAG-HUNTING RECOLLECTIONS.* By LORD RIBBLESDALE, Master of the Buckhounds, 1892-95. With Introductory Chapter on the Hereditary Mastership by E. BURROWS. With 24 Plates and 35 Illustrations in the Text. 8vo., 25s.

Ronalds.—*THE FLY-FISHER'S ENTOMOLOGY.* By ALFRED RONALDS. With 20 coloured Plates. 8vo., 14s.

Thompson and Cannan. *HAND-IN-HAND FIGURE SKATING.* By NORCLIFFE G. THOMPSON and F. LAURA CANNAN, Members of the Skating Club. With an Introduction by Captain J. H. THOMSON, R.A. With Illustrations and Diagrams. 16mo., 6s.

Watson.—*RACING AND 'CHASING:* a Collection of Sporting Stories. By ALFRED E. T. WATSON, Editor of the 'Badminton Magazine'. With 16 Plates and 36 Illustrations in the Text. Crown 8vo, 7s. 6d.

Wilcocks.—*THE SEA FISHERMAN:* Comprising the Chief Methods of Hook and Line Fishing in the British and other Seas, and Remarks on Nets, Boats, and Boating. By J. C. WILCOCKS. Illustrated. Cr. 8vo., 6s.

Mental, Moral, and Political Philosophy.

LOGIC, RHETORIC, PSYCHOLOGY, &c.

Abbott. *THE ELEMENTS OF LOGIC.* By T. K. ABBOTT, B.D. 12mo., 3s.

Aristotle.
THE ETHICS: Greek Text, Illustrated with Essay and Notes. By Sir ALEXANDER GRANT, Bart. 2 vols. 8vo., 32s.

AN INTRODUCTION TO ARISTOTLE'S ETHICS. Books I.-IV. (Book X. c. vi.-ix. in an Appendix). With a continuous Analysis and Notes. By the Rev. E. MOORE, D.D. Crown 8vo. 10s. 6d.

Bacon (FRANCIS).
COMPLETE WORKS. Edited by R. L. ELLIS, JAMES SPEDDING and D. D. HEATH. 7 vols. 8vo., £3 13s. 6d.

LETTERS AND LIFE, including all his occasional Works. Edited by JAMES SPEDDING. 7 vols. 8vo., £4 4s.

THE ESSAYS: with Annotations. By RICHARD WHATELY, D.D. 8vo. 10s. 6d.

THE ESSAYS: with Notes. By F. STORR and C. H. GIBSON. Cr. 8vo, 3s. 6d.

THE ESSAYS: with Introduction, Notes, and Index. By E. A. ABBOTT, D.D. 2 Vols. Fcp. 8vo., 6s. The Text and Index only, without Introduction and Notes, in One Volume. Fcp. 8vo., 2s. 6d.

Bain (ALEXANDER).
MENTAL SCIENCE. Cr. 8vo., 6s. 6d.
MORAL SCIENCE. Cr. 8vo., 4s. 6d.
The two works as above can be had in one volume, price 10s. 6d.

SENSES AND THE INTELLECT. 8vo., 15s.
EMOTIONS AND THE WILL. 8vo., 15s.
LOGIC, DEDUCTIVE AND INDUCTIVE. Part I. 4s. Part II. 6s. 6d.
PRACTICAL ESSAYS. Cr. 8vo., 2s.

Baldwin.—*THE ELEMENTS OF EXPOSITORY CONSTRUCTION.* By Dr. CHARLES SEARS BALDWIN, Instructor in Rhetoric in Yale University.

Bray.—*THE PHILOSOPHY OF NECESSITY:* or, Law in Mind as in Matter. By CHARLES BRAY. Crown 8vo., 5s.

Crozier (JOHN BEATTIE).
CIVILISATION AND PROGRESS: being the Outlines of a New System of Political, Religious and Social Philosophy. 8vo., 14s.
HISTORY OF INTELLECTUAL DEVELOPMENT: on the Lines of Modern Evolution.
Vol. I. Greek and Hindoo Thought; Græco-Roman Paganism; Judaism; and Christianity down to the Closing of the Schools of Athens by Justinian, 529 A.D. 8vo., 14s.

Davidson.—*THE LOGIC OF DEFINITION,* Explained and Applied. By WILLIAM L. DAVIDSON, M.A. Crown 8vo., 6s.

Green (THOMAS HILL).—*THE WORKS OF.* Edited by R. L. NETTLESHIP.
Vols. I. and II. Philosophical Works. 8vo., 16s. each.
Vol. III. Miscellanies. With Index to the three Volumes, and Memoir. 8vo., 21s.

LECTURES ON THE PRINCIPLES OF POLITICAL OBLIGATION. With Preface by BERNARD BOSANQUET. 8vo., 5s.

Hodgson (SHADWORTH H.).
TIME AND SPACE: A Metaphysical Essay. 8vo., 16s.

THE THEORY OF PRACTICE: an Ethical Inquiry. 2 vols. 8vo., 24s.

THE PHILOSOPHY OF REFLECTION. 2 vols. 8vo., 21s.

THE METAPHYSIC OF EXPERIENCE. Book I. General Analysis of Experience; Book II. Positive Science; Book III. Analysis of Conscious Action; Book IV. The Real Universe. 4 vols. 8vo.

Hume.—*THE PHILOSOPHICAL WORKS OF DAVID HUME.* Edited by T. H. GREEN and T. H. GROSE. 4 vols. 8vo., 56s. Or separately, Essays. 2 vols. 28s. Treatise of Human Nature. 2 vols. 28s.

James.—*THE WILL TO BELIEVE,* and Other Essays in Popular Philosophy. By WILLIAM JAMES, M.D., LL.D., etc. Crown 8vo., 7s. 6d.

Justinian.—*THE INSTITUTES OF JUSTINIAN:* Latin Text, chiefly that of Huschke, with English Introduction, Translation, Notes, and Summary. By THOMAS C. SANDARS, M.A. 8vo., 18s.

Kant (IMMANUEL).
CRITIQUE OF PRACTICAL REASON, AND OTHER WORKS ON THE THEORY OF ETHICS. Translated by T. K. ABBOTT, B.D. With Memoir. 8vo., 12s. 6d.

FUNDAMENTAL PRINCIPLES OF THE METAPHYSIC OF ETHICS. Translated by T. K. ABBOTT, B.D. Crown 8vo, 3s.

INTRODUCTION TO LOGIC, AND HIS ESSAY ON THE MISTAKEN SUBTILTY OF THE FOUR FIGURES. Translated by T. K. ABBOTT. 8vo., 6s.

Mental, Moral and Political Philosophy—*continued.*
LOGIC, RHETORIC, PSYCHOLOGY, &C.

Killick.—*HANDBOOK TO MILL'S SYSTEM OF LOGIC.* By Rev. A. H. KILLICK, M.A. Crown 8vo., 3s. 6d.

Ladd (GEORGE TRUMBULL).

PHILOSOPHY OF KNOWLEDGE: an Inquiry into the Nature, Limits and Validity of Human Cognitive Faculty. 8vo., 18s.

PHILOSOPHY OF MIND: An Essay on the Metaphysics of Psychology. 8vo., 16s.

ELEMENTS OF PHYSIOLOGICAL PSYCHOLOGY. 8vo., 21s.

OUTLINES OF PHYSIOLOGICAL PSYCHOLOGY. 8vo., 12s.

PSYCHOLOGY, DESCRIPTIVE AND EXPLANATORY. 8vo., 21s.

PRIMER OF PSYCHOLOGY. Cr. 8vo., 5s. 6d.

Lewes.—*THE HISTORY OF PHILOSOPHY,* from Thales to Comte. By GEORGE HENRY LEWES. 2 vols. 8vo., 32s.

Lutoslawski.—*THE ORIGIN AND GROWTH OF PLATO'S LOGIC.* With an Account of Plato's Style and of the Chronology of his Writings. By WINCENTY LUTOSLAWSKI. 8vo., 21s.

Max Müller (F.).

THE SCIENCE OF THOUGHT. 8vo., 21s.

THREE INTRODUCTORY LECTURES ON THE SCIENCE OF THOUGHT. 8vo., 2s. 6d. net.

Mill.—*ANALYSIS OF THE PHENOMENA OF THE HUMAN MIND.* By JAMES MILL. 2 vols. 8vo., 28s.

Mill (JOHN STUART).

A SYSTEM OF LOGIC. Cr. 8vo., 3s. 6d.

ON LIBERTY. Crown 8vo., 1s. 4d.

CONSIDERATIONS ON REPRESENTATIVE GOVERNMENT. Crown 8vo., 2s.

UTILITARIANISM. 8vo., 2s. 6d.

EXAMINATION OF SIR WILLIAM HAMILTON'S PHILOSOPHY. 8vo., 16s.

NATURE, THE UTILITY OF RELIGION, AND THEISM. Three Essays. 8vo., 5s.

Monck. — *AN INTRODUCTION TO LOGIC.* By WILLIAM HENRY S. MONCK, M.A. Crown 8vo., 5s.

Romanes.—*MIND AND MOTION AND MONISM.* By GEORGE JOHN ROMANES, LL.D., F.R.S. Cr. 8vo., 4s. 6d.

Stock (ST. GEORGE).

DEDUCTIVE LOGIC. Fcp. 8vo., 3s. 6d.

LECTURES IN THE LYCEUM; or, Aristotle's Ethics for English Readers. Edited by ST. GEORGE STOCK. Crown 8vo., 7s. 6d.

Sully (JAMES).

THE HUMAN MIND: a Text-book of Psychology. 2 vols. 8vo., 21s.

OUTLINES OF PSYCHOLOGY. 8vo., 9s.

THE TEACHER'S HANDBOOK OF PSYCHOLOGY. Crown 8vo., 6s. 6d.

STUDIES OF CHILDHOOD. 8vo., 10s. 6d.

CHILDREN'S WAYS: being Selections from the Author's 'Studies of Childhood'. With 25 Illustrations. Crown 8vo., 4s. 6d.

Sutherland. — *THE ORIGIN AND GROWTH OF THE MORAL INSTINCT.* By ALEXANDER SUTHERLAND, M.A.

Swinburne. — *PICTURE LOGIC:* an Attempt to Popularise the Science of Reasoning. By ALFRED JAMES SWINBURNE, M.A. With 23 Woodcuts. Crown 8vo., 5s.

Webb.—*THE VEIL OF ISIS:* a Series of Essays on Idealism. By THOMAS E. WEBB, LL.D., Q.C. 8vo., 10s. 6d.

Weber.—*HISTORY OF PHILOSOPHY.* By ALFRED WEBER, Professor in the University of Strasburg. Translated by FRANK THILLY, Ph.D. 8vo., 16s.

Whately (ARCHBISHOP).

BACON'S ESSAYS. With Annotations. 8vo., 10s. 6d.

ELEMENTS OF LOGIC. Cr. 8vo., 4s. 6d.

ELEMENTS OF RHETORIC. Cr. 8vo., 4s. 6d.

LESSONS ON REASONING. Fcp. 8vo., 1s. 6d.

Zeller (Dr. EDWARD).

THE STOICS, EPICUREANS, AND SCEPTICS. Translated by the Rev. O. J. REICHEL, M.A. Crown 8vo., 15s.

OUTLINES OF THE HISTORY OF GREEK PHILOSOPHY. Translated by SARAH F. ALLEYNE and EVELYN ABBOTT, M.A., LL.D. Crown 8vo., 10s. 6d.

PLATO AND THE OLDER ACADEMY. Translated by SARAH F. ALLEYNE and ALFRED GOODWIN, B.A. Crown 8vo., 18s.

SOCRATES AND THE SOCRATIC SCHOOLS. Translated by the Rev. O. J. REICHEL, M.A. Crown 8vo., 10s. 6d.

ARISTOTLE AND THE EARLIER PERIPATETICS. Translated by B. F. C. COSTELLOE, M.A., and J. H. MUIRHEAD, M.A. 2 vols. Crown 8vo., 24s.

Mental, Moral, and Political Philosophy—*continued.*

MANUALS OF CATHOLIC PHILOSOPHY.
(Stonyhurst Series.)

A MANUAL OF POLITICAL ECONOMY. By C. S. DEVAS, M.A. Crown 8vo., 6s. 6d.

FIRST PRINCIPLES OF KNOWLEDGE. By JOHN RICKABY, S.J. Crown 8vo., 5s.

GENERAL METAPHYSICS. By JOHN RICKABY, S.J. Crown 8vo., 5s.

LOGIC. By RICHARD F. CLARKE, S.J. Crown 8vo., 5s.

MORAL PHILOSOPHY (ETHICS AND NATURAL LAW). By JOSEPH RICKABY, S.J. Crown 8vo., 5s.

NATURAL THEOLOGY. By BERNARD BOEDDER, S.J. Crown 8vo., 6s. 6d.

PSYCHOLOGY. By MICHAEL MAHER, S.J. Crown 8vo., 6s. 6d.

History and Science of Language, &c.

Davidson.—*LEADING AND IMPORT-ANT ENGLISH WORDS:* Explained and Exemplified. By WILLIAM L. DAVIDSON, M.A. Fcp. 8vo., 3s. 6d.

Farrar.—*LANGUAGE AND LANGUAGES:* By F. W. FARRAR, D.D., Dean of Canterbury. Crown 8vo., 6s.

Graham. — *ENGLISH SYNONYMS,* Classified and Explained: with Practical Exercises. By G. F. GRAHAM. Fcp. 8vo., 6s.

Max Müller (F.).

THE SCIENCE OF LANGUAGE.—Founded on Lectures delivered at the Royal Institution in 1861 and 1863. 2 vols. Crown 8vo., 21s.

Max Müller (F.)—*continued.*

BIOGRAPHIES OF WORDS, AND THE HOME OF THE ARYAS. Crown 8vo., 7s. 6d.

THREE LECTURES ON THE SCIENCE OF LANGUAGE, AND ITS PLACE IN GENERAL EDUCATION, delivered at Oxford, 1889. Crown 8vo., 3s. net.

Roget. - *THESAURUS OF ENGLISH WORDS AND PHRASES.* Classified and Arranged so as to Facilitate the Expression of Ideas and assist in Literary Composition. By PETER MARK ROGET, M.D., F.R.S. With full Index. Crown 8vo., 10s. 6d.

Whately.—*ENGLISH SYNONYMS.* By E. JANE WHATELY. Fcp. 8vo., 3s.

Political Economy and Economics.

Ashley.—*ENGLISH ECONOMIC HISTORY AND THEORY.* By W. J. ASHLEY, M.A. Crown 8vo., Part I., 5s. Part II., 10s. 6d.

Bagehot.—*ECONOMIC STUDIES.* By WALTER BAGEHOT. Crown 8vo., 3s. 6d.

Barnett.—*PRACTICABLE SOCIALISM.* Essays on Social Reform. By the Rev. S. A. BARNETT, M.A., Canon of Bristol, and Mrs. BARNETT. Crown 8vo., 6s.

Brassey. *PAPERS AND ADDRESSES ON WORK AND WAGES.* By Lord BRASSEY. Edited by J. POTTER, and with Introduction by GEORGE HOWELL, M.P. Crown 8vo., 5s.

Channing.— *THE TRUTH ABOUT AGRICULTURAL DEPRESSION:* an Economic Study of the Evidence of the Royal Commission. By FRANCIS ALLSTON CHANNING. M.P., one of the Commission. Crown 8vo., 6s.

Devas.—*A MANUAL OF POLITICAL ECONOMY.* By C. S. DEVAS, M.A. Cr. 8vo., 6s. 6d. (*Manuals of Catholic Philosophy.*)

Dowell.—*A HISTORY OF TAXATION AND TAXES IN ENGLAND,* from the Earliest Times to the Year 1885. By STEPHEN DOWELL. (4 vols. 8vo). Vols. I. and II. The History of Taxation. 21s. Vols. III. and IV. The History of Taxes, 21s.

Jordan.—*THE STANDARD OF VALUE.* By WILLIAM LEIGHTON JORDAN. Cr.8vo.,6s.

Leslie. —*ESSAYS ON POLITICAL ECONOMY.* By T. E. CLIFFE LESLIE, Hon. LL.D., Dubl. 8vo, 10s. 6d.

Macleod (HENRY DUNNING).

BIMETALISM. 8vo., 5s. net.

THE ELEMENTS OF BANKING. Cr. 8vo., 3s. 6d.

THE THEORY AND PRACTICE OF BANKING. Vol. I. 8vo., 12s. Vol. II. 14s.

THE THEORY OF CREDIT. 8vo. In 1 Vol., 30s. net; or separately, Vol. I., 10s. net. Vol. II., Part I., 10s. net. Vol. II., Part II., 10s. net.

A DIGEST OF THE LAW OF BILLS OF EXCHANGE, BANK-NOTES, &c. 8vo., 5s. net.

THE BANKING SYSTEM OF ENGLAND. [In preparation.

Political Economy and Economics—*continued*.

Mill.—*POLITICAL ECONOMY.* By
JOHN STUART MILL.
Popular Edition. Crown 8vo., 3s. 6d.
Library Edition. 2 vols. 8vo., 30s.

Mulhall. —*INDUSTRIES AND WEALTH
OF NATIONS.* By MICHAEL G. MULHALL,
F.S.S. With 32 full-page Diagrams.
Crown 8vo., 8s. 6d.

Soderini.—*SOCIALISM AND CATHOLI-
CISM.* From the Italian of Count EDWARD
SODERINI. By RICHARD JENERY-SHEE.
With a Preface by Cardinal VAUGHAN.
Crown 8vo., 6s.

Symes.—*POLITICAL ECONOMY:* a
Short Text-book of Political Economy.
With Problems for Solution, and Hints for
Supplementary Reading; also a Supple-
mentary Chapter on Socialism. By Pro-
fessor J. E. SYMES, M.A., of University
College, Nottingham. Crown 8vo., 2s. 6d.

Toynbee.- *LECTURES ON THE IN-
DUSTRIAL REVOLUTION OF THE 18TH CEN-
TURY IN ENGLAND:* Popular Addresses,
Notes and other Fragments. By ARNOLD
TOYNBEE. With a Memoir of the Author
by BENJAMIN JOWETT, D.D. 8vo., 10s. 6d.

Vincent.—*THE LAND QUESTION IN
NORTH WALES:* being a Brief Survey of
the History, Origin, and Character of the
Agrarian Agitation, and of the Nature and
Effect of the Proceedings of the Welsh
Land Commission. By J. E. VINCENT.
8vo., 5s.

Webb (SIDNEY and BEATRICE).
THE HISTORY OF TRADE UNIONISM.
With Map and full Bibliography of the
Subject. 8vo., 18s.

INDUSTRIAL DEMOCRACY: a Study
in Trade Unionism. 2 vols. 8vo., 25s. net.

STUDIES IN ECONOMICS AND POLITICAL SCIENCE.
Issued under the auspices of the London School of Economics and Political Science.

*THE HISTORY OF LOCAL RATES IN
ENGLAND:* Five Lectures. By EDWIN
CANNAN, M.A. Crown 8vo., 2s. 6d.

GERMAN SOCIAL DEMOCRACY. By
BERTRAND RUSSELL, B.A. With an Ap-
pendix on Social Democracy and the
Woman Question in Germany by ALYS
RUSSELL, B.A. Crown 8vo., 3s. 6d.

*SELECT DOCUMENTS ILLUSTRATING
THE HISTORY OF TRADE UNIONISM.*
1. The Tailoring Trade. Edited by
W. F. GALTON. With a Preface by
SIDNEY WEBB, LL.B. Crown 8vo., 5s.

DEPLOIGE'S REFERENDUM EN SUISSE.
Translated, with Introduction and Notes,
by C. P. TREVELYAN, M.A. [*In preparation.*

*SELECT DOCUMENTS ILLUSTRATING
THE STATE REGULATION OF WAGES.*
Edited, with Introduction and Notes, by
W. A. S. HEWINS, M.A. [*In preparation.*

HUNGARIAN GILD RECORDS. Edited
by Dr. JULIUS MANDELLO, of Budapest.
[*In preparation.*

*THE RELATIONS BETWEEN ENGLAND
AND THE HANSEATIC LEAGUE.* By Miss
E. A. MACARTHUR. [*In preparation.*

Evolution, Anthropology, &c.

Clodd (EDWARD).

THE STORY OF CREATION: a Plain
Account of Evolution. With 77 Illustrations. Crown 8vo., 3s. 6d.

A PRIMER OF EVOLUTION: being a
Popular Abridged Edition of 'The Story
of Creation'. With Illustrations. Fcp.
8vo., 1s. 6d.

Lang.—*CUSTOM AND MYTH:* Studies
of Early Usage and Belief. By ANDREW
LANG. With 15 Illustrations. Crown 8vo.,
3s. 6d.

Lubbock.—*THE ORIGIN OF CIVILISA-
TION,* and the Primitive Condition of Man.
By Sir J. LUBBOCK, Bart., M.P. With 5
Plates and 20 Illustrations in the Text.
8vo., 18s.

Romanes (GEORGE JOHN).

DARWIN, AND AFTER DARWIN: an
Exposition of the Darwinian Theory, and a
Discussion on Post-Darwinian Questions.
Part I. THE DARWINIAN THEORY. With
Portrait of Darwin and 125 Illustrations.
Crown 8vo., 10s. 6d.
Part II. POST-DARWINIAN QUESTIONS:
Heredity and Utility. With Portrait of
the Author and 5 Illustrations. Cr. 8vo.,
10s. 6d.
Part III. Post-Darwinian Questions:
Isolation and Physiological Selection.
Crown 8vo., 5s.

*AN EXAMINATION OF WEISMANN-
ISM.* Crown 8vo., 6s.

ESSAYS. Edited by C. LLOYD
MORGAN, Principal of University College,
Bristol. Crown 8vo., 6s.

Classical Literature, Translations, &c.

Abbott. —*HELLENICA.* A Collection of Essays on Greek Poetry, Philosophy, History, and Religion. Edited by EVELYN ABBOTT, M.A., LL.D. 8vo., 16s.

Æschylus. *EUMENIDES OF ÆSCHY-LUS.* With Metrical English Translation. By J. F. DAVIES. 8vo., 7s.

Aristophanes. *THE ACHARNIANS OF ARISTOPHANES,* translated into English Verse. By R. Y. TYRRELL. Crown 8vo., 1s.

Aristotle. *YOUTH AND OLD AGE, LIFE AND DEATH, AND RESPIRATION.* Translated, with Introduction and Notes, by W. OGLE, M.A., M.D. 8vo., 7s. 6d.

Becker (W. A.). Translated by the Rev. F. METCALFE, B.D.

   GALLUS: or, Roman Scenes in the Time of Augustus. With Notes and Excursuses. With 26 Illustrations. Post 8vo., 3s. 6d.

   CHARICLES: or, Illustrations of the Private Life of the Ancient Greeks. With Notes and Excursuses. With 26 Illustrations. Post 8vo., 3s. 6d.

Butler. *THE AUTHORESS OF THE ODYSSEY, WHERE AND WHEN SHE WROTE, WHO SHE WAS, THE USE SHE MADE OF THE ILIAD, AND HOW THE POEM GREW UNDER HER HANDS.* By SAMUEL BUTLER, Author of 'Erewhon,' etc. With Illustrations and 4 Maps. 8vo., 10s. 6d.

Cicero. —*CICERO'S CORRESPONDENCE.* By R. Y. TYRRELL. Vols. I., II., III., 8vo., each 12s. Vol. IV., 15s. Vol. V., 14s.

Egbert. —*INTRODUCTION TO THE STUDY OF LATIN INSCRIPTIONS.* By JAMES C. EGBERT, Junr., Ph.D. With numerous Illustrations and Facsimiles. Square crown 8vo., 16s.

Horace. *THE WORKS OF HORACE, RENDERED INTO ENGLISH PROSE.* With Life, Introduction and Notes. By WILLIAM COUTTS, M.A. Crown 8vo., 5s. net.

Lang. *HOMER AND THE EPIC.* By ANDREW LANG. Crown 8vo., 9s. net.

Lucan. —*THE PHARSALIA OF LUCAN.* Translated into Blank Verse. By Sir EDWARD RIDLEY. 8vo., 14s.

Mackail. —*SELECT EPIGRAMS FROM THE GREEK ANTHOLOGY.* By J. W. MAC-KAIL. Edited with a Revised Text, Introduction, Translation, and Notes. 8vo., 16s.

Rich. —*A DICTIONARY OF ROMAN AND GREEK ANTIQUITIES.* By A. RICH, B.A. With 2000 Woodcuts. Crown 8vo., 7s. 6d.

Sophocles. --Translated into English Verse. By ROBERT WHITELAW, M.A., Assistant Master in Rugby School. Cr. 8vo., 8s. 6d.

Tacitus. --*THE HISTORY OF P. CORNELIUS TACITUS.* Translated into English, with an Introduction and Notes, Critical and Explanatory, by ALBERT WILLIAM QUILL, M.A., T.C.D. 2 vols. Vol. I. 8vo., 7s. 6d. Vol. II. 8vo., 12s. 6d.

Tyrrell. —*DUBLIN TRANSLATIONS INTO GREEK AND LATIN VERSE.* Edited by R. Y. TYRRELL. 8vo., 6s.

Virgil.

   THE ÆNEID OF VIRGIL. Translated into English Verse by JOHN CONINGTON. Crown 8vo., 6s.

   THE POEMS OF VIRGIL. Translated into English Prose by JOHN CONINGTON. Crown 8vo., 6s.

   THE ÆNEID OF VIRGIL, freely translated into English Blank Verse. By W. J. THORNHILL. Crown 8vo., 7s. 6d.

   THE ÆNEID OF VIRGIL. Translated into English Verse by JAMES RHOADES. Books I.-VI. Crown 8vo., 5s. Books VII.-XII. Crown 8vo., 5s.

Wilkins. —*THE GROWTH OF THE HOMERIC POEMS.* By G. WILKINS. 8vo., 6s.

Poetry and the Drama.

Allingham (WILLIAM).

   IRISH SONGS AND POEMS. With Frontispiece of the Waterfall of Asaroe. Fcp. 8vo., 6s.

   LAURENCE BLOOMFIELD. With Portrait of the Author. Fcp. 8vo., 3s. 6d.

   FLOWER PIECES; DAY AND NIGHT SONGS; BALLADS. With 2 Designs by D. G. ROSSETTI. Fcp. 8vo., 6s. large paper edition, 12s.

Allingham (WILLIAM)—*continued.*

   LIFE AND PHANTASY: with Frontispiece by Sir J. E. MILLAIS, Bart., and Design by ARTHUR HUGHES. Fcp. 8vo., 6s.; large paper edition, 12s.

   THOUGHT AND WORD, AND ASHBY MANOR: a Play. Fcp. 8vo., 6s.; large paper edition, 12s.

   BLACKBERRIES. Imperial 16mo., 6s.

   Sets of the above 6 vols. may be had in uniform Half-parchment binding, price 30s.

Poetry and the Drama—*continued.*

Armstrong (G. F. SAVAGE).

POEMS : Lyrical and Dramatic. Fcp. 8vo., 6s.

KING SAUL. (The Tragedy of Israel, Part I.) Fcp. 8vo., 5s.

KING DAVID. (The Tragedy of Israel, Part II.) Fcp. 8vo., 6s.

KING SOLOMON. (The Tragedy of Israel, Part III.) Fcp. 8vo., 6s.

UGONE : a Tragedy. Fcp. 8vo., 6s.

A GARLAND FROM GREECE : Poems. Fcp. 8vo., 7s. 6d.

STORIES OF WICKLOW : Poems. Fcp. 8vo., 7s. 6d.

MEPHISTOPHELES IN BROADCLOTH : a Satire. Fcp. 8vo., 4s.

ONE IN THE INFINITE : a Poem. Crown 8vo., 7s. 6d.

Armstrong.—*THE POETICAL WORKS OF EDMUND J. ARMSTRONG.* Fcp. 8vo., 5s.

Arnold.—*THE LIGHT OF THE WORLD :* or, The Great Consummation. By Sir EDWIN ARNOLD. With 14 Illustrations after HOLMAN HUNT. Crown 8vo., 6s.

Beesly (A. H.).

BALLADS AND OTHER VERSE. Fcp. 8vo., 5s.

DANTON, AND OTHER VERSE. Fcp. 8vo., 4s. 6d.

Bell (MRS. HUGH).

CHAMBER COMEDIES : a Collection of Plays and Monologues for the Drawing Room. Crown 8vo., 6s.

FAIRY TALE PLAYS, AND HOW TO ACT THEM. With 91 Diagrams and 52 Illustrations. Crown 8vo., 6s.

Cochrane (ALFRED).

THE KESTREL'S NEST, and other Verses. Fcp. 8vo., 3s. 6d.

LEVIORE PLECTRO : Occasional Verses. Fcap. 8vo., 3s. 6d.

Douglas.—*POEMS OF A COUNTRY GENTLEMAN.* By Sir GEORGE DOUGLAS, Bart., Author of 'The Fireside Tragedy'. Crown 8vo., 3s. 6d.

Goethe.

FAUST, Part I., the German Text, with Introduction and Notes. By ALBERT M. SELSS, Ph.D., M.A. Crown 8vo., 5s.

THE FIRST PART OF THE TRAGEDY OF FAUST IN ENGLISH. By THOS. E. WEBB, LL.D., sometime Fellow of Trinity College ; Professor of Moral Philosophy in the University of Dublin, etc. New and Cheaper Edition, with *THE DEATH OF FAUST,* from the Second Part. Crown 8vo., 6s.

Gurney (Rev. ALFRED, M.A.).

DAY-DREAMS : Poems. Crown 8vo., 3s. 6d.

LOVE'S FRUITION, and other Poems.

Ingelow (JEAN).

POETICAL WORKS. Complete in One Volume. Crown 8vo., 7s. 6d.

POETICAL WORKS. 2 vols. Fcp. 8vo., 12s.

LYRICAL AND OTHER POEMS. Selected from the Writings of JEAN INGELOW. Fcp. 8vo., 2s. 6d. cloth plain, 3s. cloth gilt.

Lang (ANDREW).

GRASS OF PARNASSUS. Fcp. 8vo., 2s. 6d. net.

THE BLUE POETRY BOOK. Edited by ANDREW LANG. With 100 Illustrations. Crown 8vo., 6s.

Layard and Corder.—*SONGS IN MANY MOODS.* By NINA F. LAYARD ; *THE WANDERING ALBATROSS,* etc. By ANNIE CORDER. In One Volume. Crown 8vo., 5s.

Lecky.—*POEMS.* By the Right Hon. W. E. H. LECKY. Fcp. 8vo., 5s.

Lytton (THE EARL OF), (OWEN MEREDITH).

MARAH. Fcp. 8vo., 6s. 6d.

KING POPPY : a Fantasia. With 1 Plate and Design on Title-Page by Sir EDWARD BURNE-JONES, Bart. Crown 8vo., 10s. 6d.

THE WANDERER. Cr. 8vo., 10s. 6d.

LUCILE. Crown 8vo., 10s. 6d.

SELECTED POEMS. Cr. 8vo., 10s. 6d.

Poetry and the Drama—*continued.*

Macaulay. *LAYS OF ANCIENT ROME,* *ETC.* By Lord MACAULAY.
Illustrated by G. SCHARF. Fcp. 4to., 10s. 6d.
————————— Bijou Edition.
18mo., 2s. 6d. gilt top.
————————— Popular Edition.
Fcp. 4to., 6d. sewed, 1s. cloth.
Illustrated by J. R. WEGUELIN. Crown 8vo., 3s. 6d.
Annotated Edition. Fcp. 8vo., 1s. sewed, 1s. 6d. cloth.

Macdonald (GEORGE, LL.D.).
A BOOK OF STRIFE, IN THE FORM OF THE DIARY OF AN OLD SOUL: Poems. 18mo., 6s.
RAMPOLLI: GROWTHS FROM A LONG-PLANTED ROOT: being Translations, New and Old (mainly in verse), chiefly from the German; along with 'A Year's Diary of an Old Soul'. Crown 8vo., 6s.

Moffat.—*CRICKETY CRICKET:* Rhymes and Parodies. By DOUGLAS MOFFAT. With Frontispiece by Sir FRANK LOCKWOOD, Q.C., M.P., and 53 Illustrations by the Author. Crown 8vo, 2s. 6d.

Morris (WILLIAM).
POETICAL WORKS—LIBRARY EDITION.
Complete in Ten Volumes. Crown 8vo., price 6s. each.
THE EARTHLY PARADISE. 4 vols. 6s. each.
THE LIFE AND DEATH OF JASON. 6s.
THE DEFENCE OF GUENEVERE, and other Poems. 6s.
THE STORY OF SIGURD THE VOLSUNG, AND THE FALL OF THE NIBLUNGS. 6s.
LOVE IS ENOUGH; or, the Freeing of Pharamond: A Morality; and *POEMS BY THE WAY.* 6s.
THE ODYSSEY OF HOMER. Done into English Verse. 6s.
THE ÆNEIDS OF VIRGIL. Done into English Verse. 6s.

Certain of the POETICAL WORKS may also be had in the following Editions:—
THE EARTHLY PARADISE.
Popular Edition. 5 vols. 12mo., 25s.; or 5s. each, sold separately.
The same in Ten Parts, 25s.; or 2s. 6d. each, sold separately.
Cheap Edition, in 1 vol. Crown 8vo., 7s. 6d.

Morris (WILLIAM)—*continued.*
POEMS BY THE WAY. Square crown 8vo., 6s.
°° For Mr. William Morris's Prose Works, see pp. 22 and 31.

Nesbit.—*LAYS AND LEGENDS.* By E. NESBIT (Mrs. HUBERT BLAND). First Series. Crown 8vo., 3s. 6d. Second Series. With Portrait. Crown 8vo., 5s.

Riley (JAMES WHITCOMB).
OLD FASHIONED ROSES: Poems. 12mo., 5s.
A CHILD-WORLD: POEMS. Fcp. 8vo., 5s.
POEMS: HERE AT HOME. 16mo, 6s. net.
RUBÁIYÁT OF DOC SIFERS. With 43 Illustrations by C. M RELYEA. Crown 8vo.

Romanes.—*A SELECTION FROM THE POEMS OF GEORGE JOHN ROMANES, M.A., LL.D., F.R.S.* With an Introduction by T. HERBERT WARREN, President of Magdalen College, Oxford. Crown 8vo., 4s. 6d.

Shakespeare.—*BOWDLER'S FAMILY SHAKESPEARE.* With 36 Woodcuts. 1 vol. 8vo., 14s. Or in 6 vols. Fcp. 8vo., 21s.
THE SHAKESPEARE BIRTHDAY BOOK. By MARY F. DUNBAR. 32mo., 1s. 6d.

Tupper.—*POEMS.* By JOHN LUCAS TUPPER. Selected and Edited by WILLIAM MICHAEL ROSSETTI. Crown 8vo., 5s.

Wordsworth. — *SELECTED POEMS.* By ANDREW LANG. With Photogravure Frontispiece of Rydal Mount. With 16 Illustrations and numerous Initial Letters. By ALFRED PARSONS, A.R.A. Crown 8vo., gilt edges, 6s.

Wordsworth and Coleridge.—*A DESCRIPTION OF THE WORDSWORTH AND COLERIDGE MANUSCRIPTS IN THE POSSESSION OF MR. T. NORTON LONGMAN.* Edited, with Notes, by W. HALE WHITE. With 3 Facsimile Reproductions. 4to., 10s. 6d.

Fiction, Humour, &c.

Allingham.—*CROOKED PATHS.* By FRANCIS ALLINGHAM. Crown 8vo., 6s.

Anstey (F., Author of 'Vice Versâ').

VOCES POPULI. Reprinted from 'Punch'. First Series. With 20 Illustrations by J. BERNARD PARTRIDGE. Crown 8vo., 3s. 6d.

THE MAN FROM BLANKLEY'S: a Story in Scenes, and other Sketches. With 24 Illustrations by J. BERNARD PARTRIDGE. Post 4to., 6s.

Astor.—*A JOURNEY IN OTHER WORLDS:* a Romance of the Future. By JOHN JACOB ASTOR. With 10 Illustrations. Cr. 8vo., 6s.

Beaconsfield (THE EARL OF).

NOVELS AND TALES. Complete in 11 vols. Crown 8vo., 1s. 6d. each.

Vivian Grey.	Sybil.
The Young Duke, etc.	Henrietta Temple.
Alroy, Ixion, etc.	Venetia.
Contarini Fleming, etc.	Coningsby.
	Lothair.
Tancred.	Endymion.

NOVELS AND TALES. The Hughenden Edition. With 2 Portraits and 11 Vignettes. 11 vols. Crown 8vo., 42s.

Black.—*THE PRINCESS DÉSIRÉE.* By CLEMENTINA BLACK. With 8 Illustrations by JOHN WILLIAMSON. Cr. 8vo., 6s.

Crump.—*WIDE ASUNDER AS THE POLES.* By ARTHUR CRUMP. Cr. 8vo., 6s.

Deland (MARGARET).

PHILIP AND HIS WIFE. Crown 8vo., 2s. 6d.

THE WISDOM OF FOOLS. Stories. Crown 8vo., 5s.

Diderot.—*RAMEAU'S NEPHEW:* a Translation from Diderot's Autographic Text. By SYLVIA MARGARET HILL. Crown 8vo., 3s. 6d.

Dougall.—*BEGGARS ALL.* By L. DOUGALL. Crown 8vo., 3s. 6d.

Doyle (A. CONAN).

MICAH CLARKE: A Tale of Monmouth's Rebellion. With 10 Illustrations. Cr. 8vo., 3s. 6d.

THE CAPTAIN OF THE POLESTAR, and other Tales. Cr. 8vo., 3s. 6d.

THE REFUGEES: A Tale of the Huguenots. With 25 Illustrations. Cr. 8vo., 3s. 6d.

THE STARK MUNRO LETTERS. Cr. 8vo., 3s. 6d.

Farrar (F. W., DEAN OF CANTERBURY).

DARKNESS AND DAWN: or, Scenes in the Days of Nero. An Historic Tale. Cr. 8vo., 7s. 6d.

GATHERING CLOUDS: a Tale of the Days of St. Chrysostom. Cr. 8vo., 7s. 6d.

Fowler (EDITH H.).

THE YOUNG PRETENDERS. A Story of Child Life. With 12 Illustrations by PHILIP BURNE-JONES. Crown 8vo., 6s.

THE PROFESSOR'S CHILDREN. With 24 Illustrations by ETHEL KATE BURGESS. Crown 8vo., 6s.

Froude.—*THE TWO CHIEFS OF DUNBOY:* an Irish Romance of the Last Century. By JAMES A. FROUDE. Cr. 8vo., 3s. 6d.

Gilkes.—*KALLISTRATUS:* an Autobiography. A Story of Hannibal and the Second Punic War. By A. H. GILKES, M.A., Master of Dulwich College. With 3 Illustrations by MAURICE GREIFFENHAGEN. Crown 8vo., 6s.

Graham.—*THE RED SCAUR:* A Story of the North Country. By P. ANDERSON GRAHAM. Crown 8vo., 6s.

Gurdon.—*MEMORIES AND FANCIES:* Suffolk Tales and other Stories; Fairy Legends; Poems; Miscellaneous Articles. By the late LADY CAMILLA GURDON, Author of 'Suffolk Folk-Lore'. Crown 8vo., 5s.

Haggard (H. RIDER).

HEART OF THE WORLD. With 15 Illustrations. Crown 8vo., 6s.

JOAN HASTE. With 20 Illustrations. Crown 8vo., 3s. 6d.

THE PEOPLE OF THE MIST. With 16 Illustrations. Crown 8vo., 3s. 6d.

MONTEZUMA'S DAUGHTER. With 24 Illustrations. Crown 8vo., 3s. 6d.

SHE. With 32 Illustrations. Crown 8vo., 3s. 6d.

ALLAN QUATERMAIN. With 31 Illustrations. Crown 8vo., 3s. 6d.

MAIWA'S REVENGE: Cr. 8vo., 1s. 6d.

COLONEL QUARITCH, V.C. With Frontispiece and Vignette. Cr. 8vo., 3s. 6d.

CLEOPATRA. With 29 Illustrations. Crown 8vo., 3s. 6d.

Fiction, Humour, &c.—*continued.*

Haggard (H. RIDER) *continued.*

BEATRICE. With Frontispiece and Vignette. Cr. 8vo., 3s. 6d.

ERIC BRIGHTEYES. With 51 Illustrations. Crown 8vo., 3s. 6d.

NADA THE LILY. With 23 Illustrations. Crown 8vo., 3s. 6d.

ALLAN'S WIFE. With 34 Illustrations. Crown 8vo., 3s. 6d.

THE WITCH'S HEAD. With 16 Illustrations. Crown 8vo., 3s. 6d.

MR. MEESON'S WILL. With 16 Illustrations. Crown 8vo., 3s. 6d.

DAWN. With 16 Illustrations. Cr. 8vo., 3s. 6d.

Haggard and Lang.—*THE WORLD'S DESIRE.* By H. RIDER HAGGARD and ANDREW LANG. With 27 Illustrations. Crown 8vo., 3s. 6d.

Harte.—*IN THE CARQUINEZ WOODS* and other stories. By BRET HARTE. Cr. 8vo., 3s. 6d.

Hope.—*THE HEART OF PRINCESS OSRA.* By ANTHONY HOPE. With 9 Illustrations by JOHN WILLIAMSON. Crown 8vo., 6s.

Hornung.—*THE UNBIDDEN GUEST.* By E. W. HORNUNG. Crown 8vo., 3s. 6d.

Jerome.—*SKETCHES IN LAVENDER: BLUE AND GREEN.* By JEROME K. JEROME. Author of 'Three Men in a Boat,' etc. Crown 8vo., 6s.

Lang.—*A MONK OF FIFE;* a Story of the Days of Joan of Arc. By ANDREW LANG. With 13 Illustrations by SELWYN IMAGE. Crown 8vo., 3s. 6d.

Levett-Yeats (S.).

THE CHEVALIER D'AURIAC. Crown 8vo., 6s.

A GALAHAD OF THE CREEKS, and other Stories. Crown 8vo., 6s.

Lyall (EDNA).

THE AUTOBIOGRAPHY OF A SLANDER. Fcp. 8vo., 1s., sewed.

Presentation Edition. With 20 Illustrations by LANCELOT SPEED. Crown 8vo., 2s. 6d. net.

THE AUTOBIOGRAPHY OF A TRUTH. Fcp. 8vo., 1s., sewed; 1s. 6d., cloth.

DOREEN. The Story of a Singer. Crown 8vo., 6s.

WAYFARING MEN. Crown 8vo., 6s.

Melville (G. J. WHYTE).

The Gladiators.	Holmby House.
The Interpreter.	Kate Coventry.
Good for Nothing.	Digby Grand.
The Queen's Maries.	General Bounce.

Crown 8vo., 1s. 6d. each.

Merriman. *FLOTSAM:* A Story of the Indian Mutiny. By HENRY SETON MERRIMAN. With Frontispiece and Vignette by H. G. MASSEY, A.R.E. Crown 8vo., 6s.

Morris (WILLIAM).

THE SUNDERING FLOOD. Cr. 8vo.

THE WATER OF THE WONDROUS ISLES. Crown 8vo., 7s. 6d.

THE WELL AT THE WORLD'S END. 2 vols. 8vo., 28s.

THE STORY OF THE GLITTERING PLAIN, which has been also called The Land of the Living Men, or The Acre of the Undying. Square post 8vo., 5s. net.

THE ROOTS OF THE MOUNTAINS, wherein is told somewhat of the Lives of the Men of Burgdale, their Friends, their Neighbours, their Foemen, and their Fellows-in-Arms. Written in Prose and Verse. · Square crown 8vo., 8s.

A TALE OF THE HOUSE OF THE WOLFINGS, and all the Kindreds of the Mark. Written in Prose and Verse. Square crown 8vo., 6s.

A DREAM OF JOHN BALL, AND A KING'S LESSON. 12mo., 1s. 6d.

NEWS FROM NOWHERE; or, An Epoch of Rest. Being some Chapters from an Utopian Romance. Post 8vo., 1s. 6d.

. For Mr. William Morris's Poetical Works, see p. 20.

Newman (CARDINAL).

LOSS AND GAIN: The Story of a Convert. Crown 8vo. Cabinet Edition, 6s.; Popular Edition, 3s. 6d.

CALLISTA: A Tale of the Third Century. Crown 8vo. Cabinet Edition, 6s.; Popular Edition, 3s. 6d.

Oliphant.—*OLD MR. TREDGOLD.* By Mrs. OLIPHANT. Crown 8vo., 2s. 6d.

Phillipps-Wolley.—*SNAP:* a Legend of the Lone Mountain. By C. PHILLIPPS-WOLLEY. With 13 Illustrations. Crown 8vo., 3s. 6d.

Quintana.—*THE CID CAMPEADOR:* an Historical Romance. By D. ANTONIO DE TRUEBA Y LA QUINTANA. Translated from the Spanish by HENRY J. GILL, M.A., T.C.D. Crown 8vo., 6s.

Fiction, Humour, &c.—*continued.*

Rhoscomyl (OWEN).

THE JEWEL OF YNYS GALON: being a hitherto unprinted Chapter in the History of the Sea Rovers. With 12 Illustrations by LANCELOT SPEED. Cr. 8vo., 3s. 6d.

BATTLEMENT AND TOWER: a Romance. With Frontispiece by R. CATON WOODVILLE. Crown 8vo., 6s.

FOR THE WHITE ROSE OF ARNO: a Story of the Jacobite Rising of 1745. Crown 8vo., 6s.

Sewell (ELIZABETH M.).

A Glimpse of the World.	Amy Herbert
Laneton Parsonage.	Cleve Hall.
Margaret Percival.	Gertrude.
Katharine Ashton.	Home Life.
The Earl's Daughter.	After Life.
The Experience of Life.	Ursula. Ivors.

Cr. 8vo., 1s. 6d. each cloth plain. 2s. 6d. each cloth extra, gilt edges.

Stevenson (ROBERT LOUIS).

THE STRANGE CASE OF DR. JEKYLL AND MR. HYDE. Fcp. 8vo., 1s. sewed. 1s. 6d. cloth.

THE STRANGE CASE OF DR. JEKYLL AND MR. HYDE; WITH OTHER FABLES. Crown 8vo., 3s. 6d.

MORE NEW ARABIAN NIGHTS—THE DYNAMITER. By ROBERT LOUIS STEVENSON and FANNY VAN DE GRIFT STEVENSON. Crown 8vo., 3s. 6d.

THE WRONG BOX. By ROBERT LOUIS STEVENSON and LLOYD OSBOURNE. Crown 8vo., 3s. 6d.

Suttner.—*LAY DOWN YOUR ARMS* (*Die Waffen Nieder*): The Autobiography of Martha von Tilling. By BERTHA VON SUTTNER. Translated by T. HOLMES. Cr. 8vo., 1s. 6d.

Taylor. — *EARLY ITALIAN LOVE-STORIES.* Edited and Retold by UNA TAYLOR. With 12 Illustrations by H. J. FORD.

Trollope (ANTHONY).

THE WARDEN. Cr. 8vo., 1s. 6d.

BARCHESTER TOWERS. Cr. 8vo., 1s. 6d.

Walford (L. B.).

IVA KILDARE: a Matrimonial Problem. Crown 8vo., 6s.

Walford (L. B.)—*continued.*

MR. SMITH: a Part of his Life. Crown 8vo., 2s. 6d.

THE BABY'S GRANDMOTHER. Cr. 8vo., 2s. 6d.

COUSINS. Crown 8vo., 2s. 6d.

TROUBLESOME DAUGHTERS. Cr. 8vo., 2s. 6d.

PAULINE. Crown 8vo., 2s. 6d.

DICK NETHERBY. Cr. 8vo., 2s. 6d.

THE HISTORY OF A WEEK. Cr. 8vo. 2s. 6d.

A STIFF-NECKED GENERATION. Cr. 8vo. 2s. 6d.

NAN, and other Stories. Cr. 8vo., 2s. 6d.

THE MISCHIEF OF MONICA. Cr. 8vo., 2s. 6d.

THE ONE GOOD GUEST. Cr. 8vo. 2s. 6d.

'PLOUGHED,' and other Stories. Crown 8vo., 2s. 6d.

THE MATCHMAKER. Cr. 8vo., 2s. 6d.

Watson.—*RACING AND 'CHASING:* a Collection of Sporting Stories. By ALFRED E. T. WATSON, Editor of the ' Badminton Magazine '. With 16 Plates and 36 Illustrations in the Text. Crown 8vo., 7s. 6d.

Weyman (STANLEY).

THE HOUSE OF THE WOLF. With Frontispiece and Vignette. Crown 8vo., 3s. 6d.

A GENTLEMAN OF FRANCE. With Frontispiece and Vignette. Cr. 8vo., 6s.

THE RED COCKADE. With Frontispiece and Vignette. Crown 8vo., 6s.

SHREWSBURY. With 24 Illustrations by CLAUDE A. SHEPPERSON. Cr. 8vo., 6s.

Whishaw (FRED.).

A BOYAR OF THE TERRIBLE: a Romance of the Court of Ivan the Cruel, First Tzar of Russia. With 12 Illustrations by H. G. MASSEY, A.R.E. Crown 8vo., 6s.

A TSAR'S GRATITUDE: A Story of Modern Russia. Crown 8vo., 6s.

Woods.—*WEEPING FERRY,* and other Stories. By MARGARET L. WOODS, Author of ' A Village Tragedy '. Crown 8vo., 6s.

Popular Science (Natural History, &c.).

Butler.—*OUR HOUSEHOLD INSECTS.*
An Account of the Insect-Pests found in
Dwelling-Houses. By EDWARD A. BUTLER,
B.A., B.Sc. Lond.). With 113 Illustra-
tions. Crown 8vo., 3s. 6d.

Furneaux (W.).

THE OUTDOOR WORLD: or The
Young Collector's Handbook. With 18
Plates (16 of which are coloured), and 549
Illustrations in the Text. Crown 8vo.,
7s. 6d.

BUTTERFLIES AND MOTHS (British).
With 12 coloured Plates and 241 Illustrations in the Text. Crown 8vo., 7s. 6d.

LIFE IN PONDS AND STREAMS.
With 8 coloured Plates and 331 Illustrations in the Text. Crown 8vo., 7s. 6d.

Hartwig (DR. GEORGE).

THE SEA AND ITS LIVING WONDERS.
With 12 Plates and 303 Woodcuts. 8vo.,
7s. net.

THE TROPICAL WORLD. With 8
Plates and 172 Woodcuts. 8vo., 7s. net.

THE POLAR WORLD. With 3 Maps,
8 Plates and 85 Woodcuts. 8vo., 7s. net.

THE SUBTERRANEAN WORLD. With
3 Maps and 80 Woodcuts. 8vo., 7s. net.

THE AERIAL WORLD. With Map, 8
Plates and 60 Woodcuts. 8vo., 7s. net.

HEROES OF THE POLAR WORLD. With
19 Illustrations. Cr. 8vo., 2s.

WONDERS OF THE TROPICAL FORESTS.
With 40 Illustrations. Cr. 8vo., 2s.

WORKERS UNDER THE GROUND. With
29 Illustrations. Cr. 8vo., 2s.

MARVELS OVER OUR HEADS. With
29 Illustrations. Cr. 8vo., 2s.

SEA MONSTERS AND SEA BIRDS.
With 75 Illustrations. Cr. 8vo., 2s. 6d.

DENIZENS OF THE DEEP. With 117
Illustrations. Cr. 8vo., 2s. 6d.

Hartwig (DR. GEORGE)—*continued.*

VOLCANOES AND EARTHQUAKES.
With 30 Illustrations. Cr. 8vo., 2s. 6d.

WILD ANIMALS OF THE TROPICS.
With 66 Illustrations. Cr. 8vo., 3s. 6d.

Helmholtz.—*POPULAR LECTURES ON
SCIENTIFIC SUBJECTS.* By HERMANN VON
HELMHOLTZ. With 68 Woodcuts. 2 vols.
Cr. 8vo., 3s. 6d. each.

Hudson (W. H.).

BRITISH BIRDS. With a Chapter
on Structure and Classification by FRANK
E. BEDDARD, F.R.S. With 16 Plates (8
of which are Coloured), and over 100 Illustrations in the Text. Cr. 8vo., 7s. 6d.

BIRDS IN LONDON. With numerous
Illustrations from Drawings and Photographs.

Proctor (RICHARD A.).

LIGHT SCIENCE FOR LEISURE HOURS.
Familiar Essays on Scientific Subjects. 3
vols. Cr. 8vo., 5s. each.

ROUGH WAYS MADE SMOOTH. Familiar Essays on Scientific Subjects. Crown
8vo., 3s. 6d.

PLEASANT WAYS IN SCIENCE. Crown
8vo., 3s. 6d.

NATURE STUDIES. By R. A. PROC-
TOR, GRANT ALLEN, A. WILSON, T.
FOSTER and E. CLODD. Crown 8vo.,
3s. 6d.

LEISURE READINGS. By R. A. PROC-
TOR, E. CLODD, A. WILSON, T. FOSTER
and A. C. RANYARD. Cr. 8vo., 3s. 6d.

***.* For Mr. Proctor's other books see pp. 13,
28 and 31, and Messrs. Longmans & Co.'s
Catalogue of Scientific Works.**

Stanley.—*A FAMILIAR HISTORY OF
BIRDS.* By E. STANLEY, D.D., formerly
Bishop of Norwich. With 160 Illustrations.
Cr. 8vo., 3s. 6d.

Popular Science (Natural History, &c.)—*continued.*

Wood (REV. J. G.).

HOMES WITHOUT HANDS: A Description of the Habitations of Animals, classed according to the Principle of Construction. With 140 Illustrations. 8vo., 7s. net.

INSECTS AT HOME : A Popular Account of British Insects, their Structure, Habits and Transformations. With 700 Illustrations. 8vo., 7s. net.

INSECTS ABROAD: a Popular Account of Foreign Insects, their Structure, Habits and Transformations. With 600 Illustrations. 8vo., 7s. net.

BIBLE ANIMALS: a Description of every Living Creature mentioned in the Scriptures. With 112 Illustrations. 8vo., 7s. net.

PETLAND REVISITED. With 33 Illustrations. Cr. 8vo., 3s. 6d.

OUT OF DOORS; a Selection of Original Articles on Practical Natural History. With 11 Illustrations. Cr. 8vo., 3s. 6d.

Wood (REV. J. G.)—*continued.*

STRANGE DWELLINGS: a Description of the Habitations of Animals, abridged from 'Homes without Hands'. With 60 Illustrations. Cr. 8vo., 3s. 6d.

BIRD LIFE OF THE BIBLE. With 32 Illustrations. Cr. 8vo., 3s. 6d.

WONDERFUL NESTS. With 30 Illustrations. Cr. 8vo., 3s. 6d.

HOMES UNDER THE GROUND. With 28 Illustrations. Cr. 8vo., 3s. 6d.

WILD ANIMALS OF THE BIBLE. With 29 Illustrations. Cr. 8vo., 3s. 6d.

DOMESTIC ANIMALS OF THE BIBLE. With 23 Illustrations. Cr. 8vo., 3s. 6d.

THE BRANCH BUILDERS. With 28 Illustrations. Cr. 8vo., 2s. 6d.

SOCIAL HABITATIONS AND PARASITIC NESTS. With 18 Illustrations. Crown 8vo., 2s.

Works of Reference.

Gwilt.—*AN ENCYCLOPÆDIA OF ARCHITECTURE.* By JOSEPH GWILT, F.S.A. Illustrated with more than 1100 Engravings on Wood. Revised (1888), with Alterations and Considerable Additions by WYATT PAPWORTH. 8vo, £2 12s. 6d.

Longmans' *GAZETTEER OF THE WORLD.* Edited by GEORGE G. CHISHOLM, M.A., B.Sc. Imp. 8vo., £2 2s. cloth, £2 12s. 6d. half-morocco.

Maunder (Samuel).

BIOGRAPHICAL TREASURY. With Supplement brought down to 1889. By Rev. JAMES WOOD. Fcp. 8vo., 6s.

TREASURY OF GEOGRAPHY, Physical, Historical, Descriptive, and Political. With 7 Maps and 16 Plates. Fcp. 8vo., 6s.

THE TREASURY OF BIBLE KNOWLEDGE. By the Rev. J. AYRE, M.A. With 5 Maps, 15 Plates, and 300 Woodcuts. Fcp. 8vo., 6s.

TREASURY OF KNOWLEDGE AND LIBRARY OF REFERENCE. Fcp. 8vo., 6s.

HISTORICAL TREASURY. Fcp. 8vo., 6s.

Maunder (Samuel)—*continued.*

SCIENTIFIC AND LITERARY TREASURY. Fcp. 8vo., 6s.

THE TREASURY OF BOTANY. Edited by J. LINDLEY, F.R.S., and T. MOORE, F.L.S. With 274 Woodcuts and 20 Steel Plates. 2 vols. Fcp. 8vo., 12s.

Roget. — *THESAURUS OF ENGLISH WORDS AND PHRASES.* Classified and Arranged so as to Facilitate the Expression of Ideas and assist in Literary Composition. By PETER MARK ROGET, M.D., F.R.S. Recomposed throughout, enlarged and improved, partly from the Author's Notes, and with a full Index, by the Author's Son, JOHN LEWIS ROGET. Crown 8vo., 10s. 6d.

Willich.--*POPULAR TABLES* for giving information for ascertaining the value of Lifehold, Leasehold, and Church Property, the Public Funds, etc. By CHARLES M. WILLICH. Edited by H. BENCE JONES. Crown 8vo., 10s. 6d.

Children's Books.

Crake (Rev. A. D.).

EDWY THE FAIR; or, The First Chronicle of Æscendune. Cr. 8vo., 2s. 6d.

ÆLFGAR THE DANE; or, The Second Chronicle of Æscendune. Cr. 8vo. 2s. 6d.

THE RIVAL HEIRS: being the Third and Last Chronicle of Æscendune. Cr. 8vo., 2s. 6d.

THE HOUSE OF WALDERNE. A Tale of the Cloister and the Forest in the Days of the Barons' Wars. Crown 8vo., 2s. 6d.

BRIAN FITZ-COUNT. A Story of Wallingford Castle and Dorchester Abbey. Cr. 8vo., 2s. 6d.

Lang (ANDREW). EDITED BY.

THE BLUE FAIRY BOOK. With 138 Illustrations. Crown 8vo., 6s.

THE RED FAIRY BOOK. With 100 Illustrations. Crown 8vo., 6s.

THE GREEN FAIRY BOOK. With 99 Illustrations. Crown 8vo., 6s.

THE YELLOW FAIRY BOOK. With 104 Illustrations. Crown 8vo., 6s.

THE PINK FAIRY BOOK. With 67 Illustrations. Crown 8vo., 6s.

THE BLUE POETRY BOOK. With 100 Illustrations. Crown 8vo., 6s.

THE BLUE POETRY BOOK. School Edition, without Illustrations. Fcp. 8vo., 2s. 6d.

THE TRUE STORY BOOK. With 66 Illustrations. Crown 8vo., 6s.

THE RED TRUE STORY BOOK. With 100 Illustrations. Crown 8vo., 6s.

THE ANIMAL STORY BOOK. With 67 Illustrations. Crown 8vo., 6s.

Molesworth —*SILVERTHORNS.* By Mrs. MOLESWORTH. With 4 Illustrations. Cr. 8vo., 5s.

Meade (L. T.).

DADDY'S BOY. With 8 Illustrations. Crown 8vo., 3s. 6d.

DEB AND THE DUCHESS. With 7 Illustrations. Crown 8vo., 3s. 6d.

THE BERESFORD PRIZE. With 7 Illustrations. Crown 8vo., 3s. 6d.

THE HOUSE OF SURPRISES. With 6 Illustrations. Crown 8vo. 3s. 6d.

Praeger. *THE ADVENTURES OF THE THREE BOLD BABES: HECTOR, HONORIA AND ALISANDER.* A Story in Pictures. By S. ROSAMOND PRAEGER. With 24 Coloured Plates and 24 Outline Pictures. Oblong 4to., 3s. 6d.

Stevenson.—*A CHILD'S GARDEN OF VERSES.* By ROBERT LOUIS STEVENSON. Fcp. 8vo., 5s.

Sullivan. –*HERE THEY ARE!* More Stories. Written and Illustrated by JAS. F. SULLIVAN. Crown 8vo., 6s.

Upton (FLORENCE K. AND BERTHA).

THE ADVENTURES OF TWO DUTCH DOLLS AND A 'GOLLIWOGG'. With 31 Coloured Plates and numerous Illustrations in the Text. Oblong 4to., 6s.

THE GOLLIWOGG'S BICYCLE CLUB. With 31 Coloured Plates and numerous Illustrations in the Text. Oblong 4to., 6s.

THE VEGE-MEN'S REVENGE. With 31 Coloured Plates and numerous Illustrations in the Text. Oblong 4to., 6s.

Wordsworth.—*THE SNOW GARDEN, AND OTHER FAIRY TALES FOR CHILDREN.* By ELIZABETH WORDSWORTH. With 10 Illustrations by TREVOR HADDON. Crown 8vo., 3s. 6d.

Longmans' Series of Books for Girls.
Price 2s. 6d. each.

ATELIER (THE) DU LYS: or, an Art Student in the Reign of Terror.

BY THE SAME AUTHOR.

MADEMOISELLE MORI: a Tale of Modern Rome.

IN THE OLDEN TIME: a Tale of the Peasant War in Germany.

A YOUNGER SISTER.

ATHERSTONE PRIORY. By L. N. COMYN.

THE STORY OF A SPRING MORNING, etc. By Mr. MOLESWORTH. Illustrated.

THE PALACE IN THE GARDEN. By Mrs. MOLESWORTH. Illustrated.

NEIGHBOURS. By Mrs. MOLESWORTH.

THAT CHILD.

UNDER A CLOUD.

HESTER'S VENTURE

THE FIDDLER OF LUGAU.

A CHILD OF THE REVOLUTION.

THE THIRD MISS ST. QUENTIN. By Mrs. MOLESWORTH.

VERY YOUNG; AND QUITE ANOTHER STORY. Two Stories. By JEAN INGELOW.

CAN THIS BE LOVE? By LOUISA PARR.

KEITH DERAMORE. By the Author of 'Miss Molly'.

SIDNEY. By MARGARET DELAND.

AN ARRANGED MARRIAGE. By DOROTHEA GERARD.

LAST WORDS TO GIRLS ON LIFE AT SCHOOL AND AFTER SCHOOL. By MARIA GREY.

_____

STRAY THOUGHTS FOR GIRLS. By LUCY H. M. SOULSBY. 16mo., 1s. 6d. net.

The Silver Library.

CROWN 8vo. 3s. 6d. EACH VOLUME.

Arnold's (Sir Edwin) Seas and Lands. With 71 Illustrations. 3s. 6d.

Bagehot's (W.) Biographical Studies. 3s. 6d.

Bagehot's (W.) Economic Studies. 3s. 6d.

Bagehot's (W.) Literary Studies. With Portrait. 3 vols. 3s. 6d. each.

Baker's (Sir S. W.) Eight Years in Ceylon. With 6 Illustrations. 3s. 6d.

Baker's (Sir S. W.) Rifle and Hound in Ceylon. With 6 Illustrations. 3s. 6d.

Baring-Gould's (Rev. S.) Curious Myths of the Middle Ages. 3s. 6d.

Baring-Gould's (Rev. S.) Origin and Development of Religious Belief. 2 vols. 3s. 6d. each.

Becker's (W. A.) Gallus: or, Roman Scenes in the Time of Augustus. With 26 Illus. 3s. 6d.

Becker's (W. A.) Charicles: or, Illustrations of the Private Life of the Ancient Greeks. With 26 Illustrations. 3s. 6d.

Bent's (J. T.) The Ruined Cities of Mashonaland. With 117 Illustrations. 3s. 6d.

Brassey's (Lady) A Voyage in the 'Sunbeam'. With 66 Illustrations. 3s. 6d.

Butler's (Edward A.) Our Household Insects. With 7 Plates and 113 Illustrations in the Text. 3s. 6d.

Clodd's (E.) Story of Creation: a Plain Account of Evolution. With 77 Illustrations. 3s. 6d.

Conybeare (Rev. W. J.) and Howson's (Very Rev. J. S.) Life and Epistles of St. Paul. With 46 Illustrations. 3s. 6d.

Dougall's (L.) Beggars All: a Novel. 3s. 6d.

Doyle's (A. Conan) Micah Clarke. A Tale of Monmouth's Rebellion. With 10 Illusts. 3s. 6d.

Doyle's (A. Conan) The Captain of the Polestar, and other Tales. 3s. 6d.

Doyle's (A. Conan) The Refugees: A Tale of the Huguenots. With 25 Illustrations. 3s. 6d.

Doyle's (A. Conan) The Stark Munro Letters. 3s. 6d.

Froude's (J. A.) The History of England, from the Fall of Wolsey to the Defeat of the Spanish Armada. 12 vols. 3s. 6d. each.

Froude's (J. A.) The English in Ireland. 3 vols. 10s. 6d.

Froude's (J. A.) The Divorce of Catherine of Aragon. 3s. 6d.

Froude's (J. A.) The Spanish Story of the Armada, and other Essays. 3s. 6d.

Froude's (J. A.) Short Studies on Great Subjects. 4 vols. 3s. 6d. each.

Froude's (J. A.) The Council of Trent. 3s. 6d.

Froude's (J. A.) Thomas Carlyle: a History of his Life.
1795-1835. 2 vols. 7s.
1834-1881. 2 vols. 7s.

Froude's (J. A.) Cæsar: a Sketch. 3s. 6d.

Froude's (J. A.) The Two Chiefs of Dunboy: an Irish Romance of the Last Century. 3s. 6d.

Gleig's (Rev. G. R.) Life of the Duke of Wellington. With Portrait. 3s. 6d.

Greville's (C. C. F.) Journal of the Reigns of King George IV., King William IV., and Queen Victoria. 8 vols. 3s. 6d. each.

Haggard's (H. R.) She: A History of Adventure. With 32 Illustrations. 3s. 6d.

Haggard's (H. R.) Allan Quatermain. With 20 Illustrations. 3s. 6d.

Haggard's (H. R.) Colonel Quaritch, V.C.: a Tale of Country Life. With Frontispiece and Vignette. 3s. 6d.

Haggard's (H. R.) Cleopatra. With 29 Illustrations. 3s. 6d.

Haggard's (H. R.) Eric Brighteyes. With 51 Illustrations. 3s. 6d.

Haggard's (H. R.) Beatrice. With Frontispiece and Vignette. 3s. 6d.

Haggard's (H. R.) Allan's Wife. With 34 Illustrations. 3s. 6d.

Haggard's (H. R.) Montezuma's Daughter. With 25 Illustrations. 3s. 6d.

Haggard's (H. R.) The Witch's Head. With 16 Illustrations. 3s. 6d.

Haggard's (H. R.) Mr. Meeson's Will. With 16 Illustrations. 3s. 6d.

Haggard's (H. R.) Nada the Lily. With 23 Illustrations. 3s. 6d.

Haggard's (H. R.) Dawn. With 16 Illusts. 3s. 6d.

Haggard's (H. R.) The People of the Mist. With 16 Illustrations. 3s. 6d.

Haggard's (H. R.) Joan Haste. With 20 Illustrations. 3s. 6d.

Haggard (H. R.) and Lang's (A.) The World's Desire. With 27 Illustrations. 3s. 6d.

Harte's (Bret) In the Carquinez Woods and other Stories. 3s. 6d.

Helmholtz's (Hermann von) Popular Lectures on Scientific Subjects. With 68 Illustrations. 2 vols. 3s. 6d. each.

Hornung's (E. W.) The Unbidden Guest. 3s. 6d.

Howitt's (W.) Visits to Remarkable Places. With 80 Illustrations. 3s. 6d.

Jefferies' (R.) The Story of My Heart: My Autobiography. With Portrait. 3s. 6d.

Jefferies' (R.) Field and Hedgerow. With Portrait. 3s. 6d.

Jefferies' (R.) Red Deer. With 17 Illusts. 3s. 6d.

Jefferies' (R.) Wood Magic: a Fable. With Frontispiece and Vignette by E. V. B. 3s. 6d.

Jefferies (R.) The Toilers of the Field. With Portrait from the Bust in Salisbury Cathedral. 3s. 6d.

Kaye (Sir J.) and Malleson's (Colonel) History of the Indian Mutiny of 1857-8. 6 vols. 3s. 6d. each.

Knight's (E. F.) The Cruise of the 'Alerte': the Narrative of a Search for Treasure on the Desert Island of Trinidad. With 2 Maps and 23 Illustrations. 3s. 6d.

Knight's (E. F.) Where Three Empires Meet: a Narrative of Recent Travel in Kashmir, Western Tibet, Baltistan, Gilgit. With a Map and 54 Illustrations. 3s. 6d.

Knight's (E. F.) The 'Falcon' on the Baltic: a Coasting Voyage from Hammersmith to Copenhagen in a Three-Ton Yacht. With Map and 11 Illustrations. 3s. 6d.

Köstlin's (J.) Life of Luther. With 62 Illustrations and 4 Facsimiles of MSS. 3s. 6d.

Lang's (A.) Angling Sketches. With 20 Illustrations. 3s. 6d.

Lang's (A.) Custom and Myth: Studies of Early Usage and Belief. 3s. 6d.

The Silver Library—*continued.*

Lang's (A.) Cock Lane and Common-Sense. 3s. 6d.

Lang's (A.) The Monk of Fife: a Story of the Days of Joan of Arc. With 13 Illusts. 3s. 6d.

Lees (J. A.) and Clutterbuck's (W. J.) B. C. 1887, A Ramble in British Columbia. With Maps and 75 Illustrations. 3s. 6d.

Macaulay's (Lord) Essays and Lays of Ancient Rome, etc. With Portrait and 4 Illustrations to the Lays. 3s. 6d.

Marbot's (Baron de) Memoirs. Translated. 2 vols. 7s.

Marshman's (J. C.) Memoirs of Sir Henry Havelock. 3s. 6d.

Max Müller's (F.) India, what can it teach us? 3s. 6d.

Max Müller's (F.) Introduction to the Science of Religion. 3s. 6d.

Merivale's (Dean) History of the Romans under the Empire. 8 vols. 3s. 6d. each.

Mill's (J. S.) Political Economy. 3s. 6d.

Mill's (J. S.) System of Logic. 3s. 6d.

Milner's (Geo.) Country Pleasures: the Chronicle of a Year chiefly in a Garden. 3s. 6d.

Nansen's (F.) The First Crossing of Greenland. With 142 Illustrations and a Map. 3s. 6d.

Phillipps-Wolley's (C.) Snap: a Legend of the Lone Mountain With 13 Illustrations. 3s. 6d.

Proctor's (R. A.) The Orbs Around Us. 3s. 6d.

Proctor's (R. A.) The Expanse of Heaven. 3s. 6d.

Proctor's (R. A.) The Moon. 3s. 6d.

Proctor's (R. A.) Other Worlds than Ours. 3s. 6d.

Proctor's (R. A.) Our Place among Infinities: a Series of Essays contrasting our Little Abode in Space and Time with the Infinities around us. 3s. 6d.

Proctor's (R. A.) Other Suns than Ours. 3s. 6d.

Proctor's (R. A.) Rough Ways made Smooth. 3s. 6d.

Proctor's (R. A.) Pleasant Ways in Science. 3s. 6d.

Proctor's (R. A.) Myths and Marvels of Astronomy. 3s. 6d.

Proctor's (R. A.) Nature Studies. 3s. 6d.

Proctor's (R. A.) Leisure Readings. By R. A. PROCTOR, EDWARD CLODD, ANDREW WILSON, THOMAS FOSTER, and A. C. RANYARD. With Illustrations. 3s. 6d.

Rhoscomyl's (Owen) The Jewel of Ynys Galon. With 12 Illustrations. 3s. 6d.

Rossetti's (Maria F.) A Shadow of Dante. 3s. 6d.

Smith's (R. Bosworth) Carthage and the Carthaginians. With Maps, Plans, etc. 3s. 6d.

Stanley's (Bishop) Familiar History of Birds. With 160 Illustrations. 3s. 6d.

Stevenson's (R. L.) The Strange Case of Dr. Jekyll and Mr. Hyde; with other Fables. 3s. 6d.

Stevenson (R. L.) and Osbourne's (Ll.) The Wrong Box. 3s. 6d.

Stevenson (Robert Louis) and Stevenson's (Fanny van de Grift) More New Arabian Nights.—The Dynamiter. 3s. 6d.

Weyman's (Stanley J.) The House of the Wolf: a Romance. 3s. 6d.

Wood's (Rev. J. G.) Petland Revisited. With 33 Illustrations. 3s. 6d.

Wood's (Rev. J. G.) Strange Dwellings. With 60 Illustrations. 3s. 6d.

Wood's (Rev. J. G.) Out of Doors. With 11 Illustrations. 3s. 6d.

Cookery, Domestic Management, &c.

Acton. *MODERN COOKERY.* By ELIZA ACTON. With 150 Woodcuts. Fcp. 8vo., 4s. 6d.

Bull (THOMAS, M.D.).

HINTS TO MOTHERS ON THE MANAGEMENT OF THEIR HEALTH DURING THE PERIOD OF PREGNANCY. Fcp. 8vo., 1s. 6d.

THE MATERNAL MANAGEMENT OF CHILDREN IN HEALTH AND DISEASE. Fcp. 8vo., 1s. 6d.

De Salis (MRS.).

CAKES AND CONFECTIONS À LA MODE. Fcp. 8vo., 1s. 6d.

DOGS: A Manual for Amateurs. Fcp. 8vo., 1s. 6d.

DRESSED GAME AND POULTRY À LA MODE. Fcp. 8vo., 1s. 6d.

DRESSED VEGETABLES À LA MODE. Fcp. 8vo., 1s 6d.

De Salis (MRS.).—*continued.*

DRINKS À LA MODE. Fcp. 8vo., 1s. 6d.

ENTRÉES À LA MODE. Fcp. 8vo., 1s. 6d.

FLORAL DECORATIONS. Fcp. 8vo., 1s. 6d.

GARDENING À LA MODE. Fcp. 8vo. Part I., Vegetables, 1s. 6d. Part II., Fruits, 1s. 6d.

NATIONAL VIANDS À LA MODE. Fcp. 8vo., 1s. 6d.

NEW-LAID EGGS. Fcp. 8vo., 1s. 6d.

OYSTERS À LA MODE. Fcp. 8vo., 1s. 6d.

PUDDINGS AND PASTRY À LA MODE. Fcp. 8vo., 1s. 6d.

SAVOURIES À LA MODE. Fcp. 8vo., 1s. 6d.

SOUPS AND DRESSED FISH À LA MODE. Fcp. 8vo., 1s. 6d.

Cookery, Domestic Management, &c.—*continued.*

De Salis (MRS.)—*continued.*
SWEETS AND SUPPER DISHES À LA
MODE. Fcp. 8vo., 1s. 6d.
TEMPTING DISHES FOR SMALL IN-
COMES. Fcp. 8vo., 1s. 6d.
WRINKLES AND NOTIONS FOR
EVERY HOUSEHOLD. Crown 8vo., 1s. 6d.

Lear.—MAIGRE COOKERY. By H. L.
SIDNEY LEAR. 16mo., 2s.

Poole.—COOKERY FOR THE DIABETIC.
By W. H. and Mrs. POOLE. With Preface
by Dr. PAVY. Fcp. 8vo., 2s. 6d.

Walker (JANE H.).
A BOOK FOR EVERY WOMAN.
Part I., The Management of Children
in Health and out of Health. Crown
8vo., 2s. 6d.
Part II. Woman in Health and out of
Health. Crown 8vo., 2s. 6d.

A HANDBOOK FOR MOTHERS :
being Simple Hints to Women on the
Management of their Health during
Pregnancy and Confinement, together
with Plain Directions as to the Care of
Infants. Crown 8vo., 2s. 6d.

Miscellaneous and Critical Works.

Allingham.—VARIETIES IN PROSE.
By WILLIAM ALLINGHAM. 3 vols. Cr. 8vo.,
18s. (Vols. 1 and 2, Rambles, by PATRICIUS
WALKER. Vol. 3, Irish Sketches, etc.)

Armstrong.—ESSAYS AND SKETCHES.
By EDMUND J. ARMSTRONG. Fcp. 8vo., 5s.

Bagehot.—LITERARY STUDIES. By
WALTER BAGEHOT. With Portrait. 3 vols.
Crown 8vo., 3s. 6d. each.

Baring-Gould.—CURIOUS MYTHS OF
THE MIDDLE AGES. By Rev. S. BARING-
GOULD. Crown 8vo., 3s. 6d.

Baynes. — SHAKESPEARE STUDIES,
and other Essays. By the late THOMAS
SPENCER BAYNES, LL.B., LL.D. With a
Biographical Preface by Professor LEWIS
CAMPBELL. Crown 8vo., 7s. 6d.

Boyd (A. K. H.) ('**A.K.H.B.**').
And see MISCELLANEOUS THEOLOGICAL
WORKS, p. 32.
AUTUMN HOLIDAYS OF A COUNTRY
PARSON. Crown 8vo., 3s. 6d.
COMMONPLACE PHILOSOPHER. Cr.
8vo., 3s. 6d.
CRITICAL ESSAYS OF A COUNTRY
PARSON. Crown 8vo., 3s. 6d.
EAST COAST DAYS AND MEMORIES.
Crown 8vo., 3s. 6d.
LANDSCAPES, CHURCHES, AND MORA-
LITIES. Crown 8vo., 3s. 6d.
LEISURE HOURS IN TOWN. Crown
8vo., 3s. 6d.
LESSONS OF MIDDLE AGE. Crown
8vo., 3s. 6d.
OUR LITTLE LIFE. Two Series.
Crown 8vo., 3s. 6d. each.
OUR HOMELY COMEDY: AND TRA-
GEDY. Crown 8vo., 3s. 6d.
RECREATIONS OF A COUNTRY PARSON.
Three Series. Crown 8vo., 3s. 6d. each.

Brookings and Ringwalt.—BRIEFS
AND DEBATE ON CURRENT, POLITICAL,
ECONOMIC AND SOCIAL TOPICS. Edited
by W. DU BOIS BROOKINGS, A.B. of the
Harvard Law School, and RALPH CURTIS
RINGWALT, A.B. Assistant in Rhetoric in
Columbia University, New York. With an
Introduction on 'The Art of Debate' by
ALBERT BUSHNELL HART, Ph.D. of Har-
vard University. With full Index. Crown
8vo., 6s.

Butler (SAMUEL).
EREWHON. Crown 8vo., 5s.

THE FAIR HAVEN. A Work in Defence of the Miraculous Element in our
Lord's Ministry. Cr. 8vo., 7s. 6d.

LIFE AND HABIT. An Essay after a
Completer View of Evolution. Cr. 8vo.,
7s. 6d.

EVOLUTION, OLD AND NEW. Cr.
8vo., 10s. 6d.

ALPS AND SANCTUARIES OF PIED-
MONT AND CANTON TICINO. Illustrated.
Pott 4to., 10s. 6d.

LUCK, OR CUNNING, AS THE MAIN
MEANS OF ORGANIC MODIFICATION ?
Cr. 8vo., 7s. 6d.

EX VOTO. An Account of the Sacro
Monte or New Jerusalem at Varallo-Sesia.
Crown 8vo., 10s. 6d.

SELECTIONS FROM WORKS, with Re-
marks on Mr. G. J. Romanes' 'Mental
Evolution in Animals,' and a Psalm of
Montreal. Crown 8vo., 7s. 6d.

THE AUTHORESS OF THE ODYSSEY,
WHERE AND WHEN SHE WROTE, WHO
SHE WAS, THE USE SHE MADE OF THE
ILIAD, AND HOW THE POEM GREW UNDER
HER HANDS. With 14 Illustrations.
8vo., 10s. 6d.

Miscellaneous and Critical Works—*continued.*

CHARITIES REGISTER, THE ANNUAL, AND DIGEST: being a Classified Register of Charities in or available in the Metropolis, together with a Digest of Information respecting the Legal, Voluntary, and other Means for the Prevention and Relief of Distress, and the Improvement of the Condition of the Poor, and an Elaborate Index. With an Introduction by C. S. LOCH, Secretary to the Council of the Charity Organisation Society. London. 8vo., 4s.

Dowell.—*THOUGHTS AND WORDS.* By STEPHEN DOWELL. 3 vols. Crown 8vo., 31s. 6d.

* This is a collection of passages in prose and verse of all ages, ancient and modern, arranged according to the subject.

Dreyfus. *LECTURES ON FRENCH LITERATURE.* Delivered in Melbourne by IRMA DREYFUS. With Portrait of the Author. Large crown 8vo., 12s. 6d.

Evans.—*THE ANCIENT STONE IMPLEMENTS, WEAPONS AND ORNAMENTS OF GREAT BRITAIN.* By Sir JOHN EVANS, K.C.B., D.C.L., LL.D., F.R.S., etc. With 537 Illustrations. Medium 8vo., 28s.

Hamlin.—*A TEXT-BOOK OF THE HISTORY OF ARCHITECTURE.* By A. D. F. HAMLIN, A.M. With 229 Illustrations. Crown 8vo., 7s. 6d.

Haweis.—*MUSIC AND MORALS.* By the Rev. H. R. HAWEIS. With Portrait of the Author, and numerous Illustrations, Facsimiles, and Diagrams. Cr. 8vo., 7s. 6d.

Hime.—*STRAY MILITARY PAPERS.* By Lieut.-Colonel H. W. L. HIME (late Royal Artillery). 8vo., 7s. 6d.

CONTENTS. Infantry Fire Formations — On Marking at Rifle Matches—The Progress of Field Artillery The Reconnoitering Duties of Cavalry.

Hullah (JOHN, LL.D.).
THE HISTORY OF MODERN MUSIC; a Course of Lectures. 8vo., 8s. 6d.
THE TRANSITION PERIOD OF MUSICAL HISTORY; a Course of Lectures. 8vo., 10s. 6d.

Jefferies (RICHARD).
FIELD AND HEDGEROW: With Portrait. Crown 8vo., 3s. 6d.
THE STORY OF MY HEART: my Autobiography. With Portrait and New Preface by C. J. LONGMAN. Cr. 8vo., 3s. 6d.
RED DEER. With 17 Illustrations by J. CHARLTON and H. TUNALY. Crown 8vo., 3s. 6d.

Jefferies (RICHARD) *continued.*
THE TOILERS OF THE FIELD. With Portrait from the Bust in Salisbury Cathedral. Crown 8vo., 3s. 6d.
WOOD MAGIC: a Fable. With Frontispiece and Vignette by E. V. B. Crown 8vo., 3s. 6d.
THOUGHTS FROM THE WRITINGS OF RICHARD JEFFERIES. Selected by H. S. HOOLE WAYLEN. 16mo., 3s. 6d.

Johnson.—*THE PATENTEE'S MANUAL:* a Treatise on the Law and Practice of Letters Patent. By J. & J. H. JOHNSON, Patent Agents, etc. 8vo., 10s. 6d.

Lang (ANDREW).
THE MAKING OF RELIGION. 8vo.
MODERN MYTHOLOGY: a Reply to Professor Max Müller. 8vo., 9s.
LETTERS TO DEAD AUTHORS. Fcp. 8vo., 2s. 6d. net.
BOOKS AND BOOKMEN. With 2 Coloured Plates and 17 Illustrations. Fcp. 8vo., 2s. 6d. net.
OLD FRIENDS. Fcp. 8vo., 2s. 6d. net.
LETTERS ON LITERATURE. Fcp. 8vo., 2s. 6d. net.
ESSAYS IN LITTLE. With Portrait of the Author. Crown 8vo., 2s. 6d.
COCK LANE AND COMMON-SENSE. Crown 8vo., 3s. 6d.
THE BOOK OF DREAMS AND GHOSTS. Crown 8vo., 6s.

Macfarren. — *LECTURES ON HARMONY.* By Sir GEORGE A. MACFARREN. 8vo., 12s.

Madden.—*THE DIARY OF MASTER WILLIAM SILENCE:* a Study of Shakespeare and Elizabethan Sport. By the Right Hon. D. H. MADDEN, Vice-Chancellor of the University of Dublin. 8vo., 16s.

Max Müller (The Right Hon. F.).
INDIA: WHAT CAN IT TEACH US? Crown 8vo., 3s. 6d.
CHIPS FROM A GERMAN WORKSHOP.
Vol. I. Recent Essays and Addresses. Crown 8vo., 6s. 6d. net.
Vol. II. Biographical Essays. Crown 8vo., 6s. 6d. net.
Vol. III. Essays on Language and Literature. Crown 8vo., 6s. 6d. net.
Vol. IV. Essays on Mythology and Folk Lore. Crown 8vo., 8s. 6d. net.
CONTRIBUTIONS TO THE SCIENCE OF MYTHOLOGY. 2 vols. 8vo., 32s.

Miscellaneous and Critical Works—*continued.*

Milner.—*COUNTRY PLEASURES:* the Chronicle of a Year chiefly in a Garden. By GEORGE MILNER. Crown 8vo., 3s. 6d.

Morris (WILLIAM).

SIGNS OF CHANGE. Seven Lectures delivered on various Occasions. Post 8vo., 4s. 6d.

HOPES AND FEARS FOR ART. Five Lectures delivered in Birmingham, London, etc., in 1878-1881. Crown 8vo., 4s. 6d.

Orchard.—*THE ASTRONOMY OF 'MILTON'S PARADISE LOST'.* By THOMAS N. ORCHARD, M.D., Member of the British Astronomical Association. With 13 Illustrations. 8vo., 15s.

Poore (GEORGE VIVIAN), M.D., F.R.C.P.

ESSAYS ON RURAL HYGIENE. With 13 Illustrations. Crown 8vo., 6s. 6d.

THE DWELLING HOUSE. With 36 Illustrations. Crown 8vo., 3s. 6d.

Proctor.—*STRENGTH:* How to get Strong and keep Strong, with Chapters on Rowing and Swimming, Fat, Age, and the Waist. By R. A. PROCTOR. With 9 Illustrations. Crown 8vo., 2s.

Rossetti.—*A SHADOW OF DANTE:* being an Essay towards studying Himself, his World and his Pilgrimage. By MARIA FRANCESCA ROSSETTI. With Frontispiece by DANTE GABRIEL ROSSETTI. Crown 8vo., 3s. 6d.

Solovyoff.—*A MODERN PRIESTESS OF ISIS* (*MADAME BLAVATSKY*). Abridged and Translated on Behalf of the Society for Psychical Research from the Russian of VSEVOLOD SERGYEEVICH SOLOVYOFF. By WALTER LEAF, Litt.D. With Appendices. Crown 8vo., 6s.

Soulsby (LUCY H. M.).

STRAY THOUGHTS ON READING. Small 8vo., 2s. 6d. net.

STRAY THOUGHTS FOR GIRLS. 16mo., 1s. 6d. net.

STRAY THOUGHTS FOR MOTHERS AND TEACHERS. Fcp. 8vo., 2s. 6d. net.

STRAY THOUGHTS FOR INVALIDS. 16mo., 2s. net.

Southey.—*THE CORRESPONDENCE OF ROBERT SOUTHEY WITH CAROLINE BOWLES.* Edited, with an Introduction, by EDWARD DOWDEN, LL.D. 8vo., 14s.

Stevens.—*ON THE STOWAGE OF SHIPS AND THEIR CARGOES.* With Information regarding Freights, Charter-Parties, etc. By ROBERT WHITE STEVENS, Associate-Member of the Institute of Naval Architects. 8vo., 21s.

Turner and Sutherland.—*THE DEVELOPMENT OF AUSTRALIAN LITERATURE.* By HENRY GYLES TURNER and ALEXANDER SUTHERLAND. With Portraits and Illustrations. Crown 8vo., 5s.

Warwick.—*PROGRESS IN WOMEN'S EDUCATION IN THE BRITISH EMPIRE:* being the Report of Conferences and a Congress held in connection with the Educational Section, Victorian Era Exhibition. Edited by the COUNTESS OF WARWICK. Crown 8vo., 6s.

White.—*AN EXAMINATION OF THE CHARGE OF APOSTACY AGAINST WORDSWORTH.* By W. HALE WHITE, Editor of the 'Description of the Wordsworth and Coleridge MSS. in the Possession of Mr. T. Norton Longman'.

Miscellaneous Theological Works.

⁎⁎⁎ For Church of England and Roman Catholic Works see MESSRS. LONGMANS & CO.'S *Special Catalogues.*

Balfour.—*THE FOUNDATIONS OF BELIEF:* being Notes Introductory to the Study of Theology. By the Right Hon. ARTHUR J. BALFOUR, M.P. 8vo., 12s. 6d.

Bird (ROBERT).

A CHILD'S RELIGION. Cr. 8vo., 2s.

JOSEPH, THE DREAMER. Crown 8vo., 5s.

Bird (ROBERT)—*continued.*

JESUS, THE CARPENTER OF NAZARETH. Crown 8vo., 5s.

To be had also in Two Parts, price 2s. 6d. each.

Part I. GALILEE AND THE LAKE OF GENNESARET.

Part II. JERUSALEM AND THE PERÆA.

Miscellaneous Theological Works—*continued.*

Boyd (A. K. H.) ('A.K.H.B.').

OCCASIONAL AND IMMEMORIAL DAYS: Discourses. Crown 8vo., 7s. 6d.

COUNSEL AND COMFORT FROM A CITY PULPIT. Crown 8vo., 3s. 6d.

SUNDAY AFTERNOONS IN THE PARISH CHURCH OF A SCOTTISH UNIVERSITY CITY. Crown 8vo., 3s. 6d.

CHANGED ASPECTS OF UNCHANGED TRUTHS. Crown 8vo., 3s. 6d.

GRAVER THOUGHTS OF A COUNTRY PARSON. Three Series. Crown 8vo., 3s. 6d. each.

PRESENT DAY THOUGHTS. Crown 8vo., 3s. 6d.

SEASIDE MUSINGS. Cr. 8vo., 3s. 6d.

'*TO MEET THE DAY*' through the Christian Year : being a Text of Scripture, with an Original Meditation and a Short Selection in Verse for Every Day. Crown 8vo., 4s. 6d.

Davidson. —*THE SOUL*, as Grounded in Human Nature, Historically and Critically Handled. Being the Burnett Lectures for 1892 and 1893, delivered at Aberdeen. By WILLIAM L. DAVIDSON, M.A., LL.D. 8vo., 15s.

Gibson. —*THE ABBÉ DE LAMENNAIS, AND THE LIBERAL CATHOLIC MOVEMENT IN FRANCE.* By the Hon. W. GIBSON. With Portrait. 8vo., 12s. 6d.

Kalisch (M. M., Ph.D.).

BIBLE STUDIES. Part I. Prophecies of Balaam. 8vo., 10s. 6d. Part II. The Book of Jonah. 8vo., 10s. 6d.

COMMENTARY ON THE OLD TESTAMENT; with a New Translation. Vol. I. Genesis. 8vo., 18s. Or adapted for the General Reader. 12s. Vol. II. Exodus. 15s. Or adapted for the General Reader. 12s. Vol. III. Leviticus, Part I. 15s. Or adapted for the General Reader. 8s. Vol. IV. Leviticus, Part II. 15s. Or adapted for the General Reader. 8s.

Macdonald (GEORGE).

UNSPOKEN SERMONS. Three Series. Crown 8vo., 3s. 6d. each.

THE MIRACLES OF OUR LORD. Crown 8vo., 3s. 6d.

10,000/2/98.

Martineau (JAMES).

HOURS OF THOUGHT ON SACRED THINGS: Sermons, 2 vols. Crown 8vo., 3s. 6d. each.

ENDEAVOURS AFTER THE CHRISTIAN LIFE. Discourses. Crown 8vo., 7s. 6d.

THE SEAT OF AUTHORITY IN RELIGION. 8vo., 14s.

ESSAYS, REVIEWS, AND ADDRESSES. 4 Vols. Crown 8vo., 7s. 6d. each.
I. Personal; Political. II. Ecclesiastical; Historical. III. Theological; Philosophical. IV. Academical; Religious.

HOME PRAYERS, with *TWO SERVICES* for Public Worship Crown 8vo., 3s. 6d.

Max Müller (F.).

HIBBERT LECTURES ON THE ORIGIN AND GROWTH OF RELIGION, as illustrated by the Religions of India. Cr. 8vo., 7s. 6d.

INTRODUCTION TO THE SCIENCE OF RELIGION : Four Lectures delivered at the Royal Institution. Crown 8vo., 3s. 6d.

NATURAL RELIGION. The Gifford Lectures, delivered before the University of Glasgow in 1888. Crown 8vo., 10s. 6d.

PHYSICAL RELIGION. The Gifford Lectures, delivered before the University of Glasgow in 1890. Crown 8vo., 10s. 6d.

ANTHROPOLOGICAL RELIGION. The Gifford Lectures, delivered before the University of Glasgow in 1891. Cr. 8vo., 10s. 6d.

THEOSOPHY, OR PSYCHOLOGICAL RELIGION. The Gifford Lectures, delivered before the University of Glasgow in 1892. Crown 8vo., 10s. 6d.

THREE LECTURES ON THE VEDÂNTA PHILOSOPHY, delivered at the Royal Institution in March, 1894. 8vo., 5s.

Romanes. —*THOUGHTS ON RELIGION.* By GEORGE J. ROMANES, LL.D., F.R.S. Crown 8vo., 4s. 6d.

Vivekananda.— *YOGA PHILOSOPHY :* Lectures delivered in New York, Winter of 1895-96, by the SWAMI VIVEKANANDA, on Raja Yoga ; or, Conquering the Internal Nature ; also Patanjali's Yoga Aphorisms, with Commentaries. Crown 8vo, 3s. 6d.

www.ingramcontent.com/pod-product-compliance
Lightning Source LLC
Chambersburg PA
CBHW060533030726
47498CB00004B/1181